# Worth Trying

## Chloe B. Young

RIPTIDE
PUBLISHING

Riptide Publishing
PO Box 1537
Burnsville, NC 28714
www.riptidepublishing.com

Worth Trying

Cover art: L.C. Chase, lcchase.com
Editor: Veronica Vega
Layout: L.C. Chase, lcchase.com

ISBN: 978-1-62649-955-3

First edition
September, 2021

Also available in ebook:
ISBN: 978-1-62649-956-0

# Worth Trying

## Chloe B. Young

# Table of
# Contents

# Chapter One

**C**harlie's mother had a habit of calling completely innocuous things *the devil's work*. Public transportation delays? *The devil's work*. Cable companies charging an arm and a leg for a basic package? They, too, did the devil's work. Diet soda? Satan had a hand in that. Charlie usually rolled his eyes and went back to whatever he was doing, but sometimes, he couldn't help but agree. Diet soda was definitely a product of a hell-like realm.

He didn't share too many characteristics with Ma, but as he approached the ancient age of a quarter century, he was starting to notice things coming out of his mouth or popping into his brain that sounded just like her.

Ornate brass door handles truly were *the devil's work*.

Charlie didn't mind cleaning, normally. It was a better job than a lot of things, and at least he got to be alone while he did it. He could take his cart, his assigned floor, and his comfortable shoes away by himself and polish and sweep and empty garbage cans in peace, without a radio or a coworker in his ear.

But his fingers were getting raw from digging into the decorative grooves of the handles of the fancy offices he was nearly finished cleaning. The lemon-scented disinfectant was burning his nostrils, and his back hurt from bending over for so long. And all because some germaphobe at the building recently added to their roster had decided that every door knob needed polishing to within an inch of its life.

"One more room, one more room," he muttered to himself as he straightened and cracked his back. "Christ."

He was too young for the kind of exhaustion he was feeling. Sighing, he tossed his rag back onto the cart, then swung it around so he could back it into the last room he had to clean. He was completely beat. He'd finished his shift at the restaurant and come straight to the office building without a break. He was still a little bitter about losing his single night off for the week, but it was entirely his fault. He could've said no to Norm, who was "sick" and couldn't make it to work, but the fact was, he needed the money more than he needed a few hours of relaxing and fighting sleep at eight o'clock on a Saturday like an old man.

After he'd wrestled the cart inside, he shook out his stiff hands and took a good look around the office, the biggest one on the floor.

"Whoa," he said to the room.

It looked like a museum. He imagined that it was very much like a diorama of a gentleman's study from some century-old home. But way tackier. There was gold everywhere. On the frames of college degrees and tastefully bland art, in a slim band around a gleaming pen in a stand on the desk, wrapping around the gleaming balls of a Newton's cradle, it seemed everything was gilded in some way, with enough precious metal to be worth more than Charlie's daily pay.

All the furniture—the desk, the chairs sitting in front of it, the couch off to the side of the room—was oversized and even more ornate than the doorknobs. On its own, the selection of furniture might have been nice, just on the right side of too much, but when combined with the jarringly modern—and massive—computer, it was pushed firmly over the edge into extravagance.

Charlie took his time looking at the room, resting his back and allowing himself a bit of mean-spirited judgment of whichever asshole lawyer worked here.

(*Innes Kent*, according to the nameplate Charlie had already polished, which was just so perfectly *douchey*.)

The huge executive's chair was a steampunk-esque amalgamation of old and new. The rich brown leather was beautiful, and the adjustable arms were intimidating, but it didn't look very comfortable. There was a heavy statue of Atlas on the edge of the wide desk. A set of encyclopedias with shiny lettering took up a ton of space on the bookshelf, but they looked like they'd never been opened. And was that a cigar box?

"Ugh." Charlie liked to think he knew a little something about design and composition, and this place made every tasteful part of him cringe.

Under the weight of all that privilege, Charlie's knees bent, but only so he could sit down in a straight-backed chair in front of the desk. No farther, and not for long.

If he let himself sit for too lengthy a time, it'd be harder to get back up, and even though this was the less lucrative of his two jobs, he couldn't afford to lose it, especially not this week.

Charlie didn't believe in fate. Usually. Except when rent was due, his mandatory nonslip work shoes needed replacing, and his dentist had informed him that he had a goddamn cavity to be filled, all in the same week. Then, he was sure fate was real and was laughing at him.

With a muttered curse, Charlie stood, picked up the cloth, and started again, putting his dwindling savings account away to worry about some other time.

He wiped all the surfaces in the methodical way he'd perfected since he'd started working for the company, scrubbing as hard as he would his own furniture. Harder, actually, since he didn't spend much time cleaning anything that didn't get in his way at home.

He cleaned the room well because that was what he was paid to do, and even though he was fuming at the opulence of it all, it wasn't worth getting fired, or getting called in from across town to have a chat with his boss.

It didn't stop him from getting pissed. He channeled his irritation into elbow grease while he was scrubbing at boot scuffs on the walls, fuming at the unfairness of the world. The fact that a single person could enjoy and display so much excessive wealth while Charlie fought to keep himself and his ma above the poverty line made his blood boil. There was so much *stuff* surrounding him—decorative shit that didn't even serve a purpose to justify how much money they must have cost to be in an office like this. Charlie could appreciate art in all its forms, even the useless ones, but how many tiny vases did someone need before they started to forget how many they had in the first place?

Charlie's hand froze mid-wipe of the dark wood coffee table. He could vaguely make out the shape of his face in the shiny, spotless surface. With its pale skin and blond hair, his fuzzy reflection looked a little like he imagined an angel would look to a person coding in an ambulance and fixating on a paramedic with fair coloring.

He was far from angelic, though.

He straightened up and flicked his dust cloth, his mind racing. Would someone who had so many things in their office realize that something was missing? And should it end up on eBay, would the owner find it? If someone— He shook his head. Might as well be honest, at least to himself: If *he* took something from the overstocked shelves, would he be able to sneak it out without anyone knowing?

His employers were pretty lax on monitoring their staff. Charlie reported to a shift manager at the end of the night or in the early morning, but they didn't check his bags before he left. They relied solely on the criminal record checks they requested—and didn't pay for, because they weren't that generous—and the idea that no one they hired would be stupid enough to steal from one of their clients.

He shook his head rapidly and pushed his too-long hair off his sweaty forehead. The room he was cleaning was a *lawyer's office*, for Christ's sake. He was probably delirious. He needed to finish quickly, get out of here, and crash hard before he started thinking other crazy things were perfectly reasonable. Like robbing a bank.

He tried, but the entire time he was vacuuming—the last thing he had to do before he could get off his aching feet—he couldn't get the idea out of his head. It was like a song he hated playing over and over in his brain, popping in whenever he turned a corner, before he shoved it away.

He was still thinking about it when he turned off the vacuum and hefted it up onto the cart. He leaned hard on the push bar, delaying leaving for good, even though his back was screaming and his eyes felt like they were permanently squinted.

Becoming a thief would be an incredibly stupid idea, but that didn't stop him from considering it. Hard. He had no idea what one of the nine or ten little glass vases on the shelves was worth, but the person who sat in this office didn't seem to be the kind of person to pinch pennies by grabbing something cheap from Bed Bath & Beyond to fill out his collection.

He lifted his head to peer blearily at his watch. It read 12:57, but it was consistently six minutes slow, so that put it past one in the morning. The only people around were his coworkers, who didn't give a shit about what he did or if his messenger bag was a little bit more full on the way out.

"Fucking fuck," Charlie muttered, his legs tensing against the easiest payday he'd ever make.

The reasons why and why not kept coming, too fast for him to push them away.

Jail time and a permanent record. *But a few nights off next month.*

Fired without notice, no paycheck until he found something else that worked with his schedule. *But a little wiggle room in the budget that might save him the next time he had an emergency expense.*

Stealing was a shitty thing to do. But this old-money jerkwad could handle it.

"Jesus." He slipped his sweaty hands off the bar of the cart and leaned on his exhausted arms. He muttered into his worn-out beige uniform shirt, "This is a new low. There's no way."

There *was* a way, though, and even trying to talk himself out of it wasn't doing any good. Cursing himself for a damned fool the whole time, Charlie straightened and wiped his hands on his clenched thighs. His skinny legs were trembling a little under his palms, so he dug his fingers in and breathed deeply until they stopped.

If he was going to do this, the last thing he needed was to look like a kid with his hand caught in the expensive, ornately decorated cookie jar.

No one was going to catch him, he reminded himself as he stepped up to the wall of built-in shelves. It was past one in the morning and he was probably the only one on the entire floor. All the things he'd told himself *could* happen simply *wouldn't*, because the only time someone had ever shown up to bother him, it was Norm, who walked like he cosplayed an AT-AT on weekends.

Reassured, but still jumpy, he squinted up at his options. There were plenty of books to choose from, but he figured they wouldn't be valuable enough, not to a sleazy pawnshop where he would want to get rid of his score. There were a couple of bowls and jars that looked like they'd fetch a good amount, but they were breakable, and might not make it out of the building if stuffed into the bottom of a messenger bag.

He scanned the neat and orderly shelves with the same eye for detail that made him great at choosing the right fabric for a project, until it fell on a chunky, dark piece of metal. A statue of some kind. Vaguely East Asian looking, in a fancy but still kind of racist way. Only about five inches tall, and half as wide. Placed in the upper third of the wall, higher than eye level, it wouldn't be missed in a hurry.

Perfect.

A taller guy might have been able to reach it, he noted with a pang of bitterness he usually only felt when strangers asked him what grade he was in. Charlie had to use the bottom shelf as a stepping stool to reach it, but once he was up there, he had a better view of the thing. It was even tackier up close, but promisingly heavy. It would make a hell of a noise if he dropped it, so he tucked it in close to his chest and prepared to hop down, but a glint of glass pulled his focus like the statue had. Charlie peered into the shadow of the deep shelf, and nearly dropped the statue.

Behind the wonky circle of un-dust sat a blob of amber. Big. Probably expensive. Pushed to the back of a shelf where no one, not even a seven-foot-tall giant, could see it.

"Are you kidding me?" Charlie asked the empty room.

This guy. This freaking guy who sat in his leather chair, with his feet up on a massive desk, surrounded by physical manifestations of his wealth. He actually had so much stuff that he had to shove some of it out of sight completely to avoid messing up the aesthetic.

"Goddamn capitalism," Charlie muttered, his thoughts racing with another decision. His feet were getting sore from standing on tiptoe on the shelf. The rest of the crew downstairs would be finishing up soon, and someone might come looking for him if he didn't hurry up and report in.

The decision to take two things instead of one was pretty easy to make compared to the first big dilemma. He didn't much go in for arguments that relied on a slippery slope, but if he was ever going to be convinced, now would be the time.

It still didn't stop him from taking the amber paperweight, balancing it against the statue already clutched to his chest as he carefully climbed down.

One for him, and one for his ma, he thought when he was back on solid ground. In a way, though, they were both for his ma. The way he lived his life, scrimping and saving, letting go of the things he wanted in favor of things that would make him the most money . . .

That was all for her.

Remembering his timeline, Charlie went back to the cart, yanking his canvas messenger bag off the bottom by the strap, grimacing at the thought of how bad his shoulder would ache by the time he got home. His heart pounded as he carefully nestled the items into either side of the center pocket, in between crumpled-up napkins and loose change.

And like a masterpiece of fine art in the middle of a McDonald's, it was the contrast that made him stop and actually think.

This was so stupid. If he was caught, he would lose his job, and then what? He wouldn't even have a couple pawnable trinkets to help him make rent until he found something else. That risk was definitely not worth the possible reward.

He couldn't. No way.

Knowing that didn't make it any easier to take the statue out of the bag.

Later, he'd blame the roaring in his ears for why he didn't hear the footsteps until they were right outside the open door.

"Well, what have we here?"

Charlie froze, but there was no way to change the fact that his hands were still caught in the act of untangling the statue from the strap of his ratty brown sack. Swallowing thickly, Charlie looked over and up at the owner of the voice. He saw a spotless tailored suit, a modern cut of dark hair styled to perfection, and a black watch with glinting gold buttons that screamed *expensive*. As expensive as the owner of this office must be per hour.

*Oh, shit.*

*Two Hours Earlier*

If someone had been at home enjoying a night in before getting a phone call and going out again, did it still count as the same day?

Innes didn't think so. His day had been over, his dinner long finished, and he'd just been getting into bed when his phone rang, and now, here he was, watching the clock inch toward the birth of Sunday. He was idling in front of a picturesque home in Malibu, which gave no indication it provided shelter for the Antichrist.

That kind of road trip surely counted as an entire day. Especially when the journey was only halfway completed.

The gleaming white front door opened, and a young woman emerged, yanking a wheeled suitcase across the threshold and slamming the door behind her. As she stalked down the curved, neatly edged walkway, the door opened again.

Innes only caught a glimpse of a fuzzy pink bathrobe before he was flipping his visor down to cover his face and obscure his vision. He knew he wasn't invisible. She could obviously see him. But he valued his soul too much to make eye contact.

Thankfully, the passenger-side door opened and the suitcase—and its owner—plopped heavily into the car. Innes put the car in gear and pulled hastily away from the curb before she even finished buckling her seat belt. In the rearview mirror, he caught a glimpse of the front door closing. Smug pleasure unfurled in his gut and made him punch the accelerator just a little bit harder in celebration.

*I win this time, bitch.*

His prize—although she'd probably hit him for calling her that—hadn't yet said anything, so he did the honors. "Hello, Mimi," he said as he turned the corner at the end of the street.

A short sigh gusted past Mimi's lips. "Hey," she said, staring out the windshield with an expression of polite disinterest.

As always, his brain got caught on the few seconds of dead air after her standard greeting. It wasn't as if he expected her to suddenly start calling him Dad. She hadn't since she was nine and realized what kind of co-parent he was—or wasn't. But she didn't call him by his first name either, putting that last little bit of distance between them. She typically avoided calling him anything, mostly by avoiding *him*. And that was fine. They got along better that way.

The brush-off still stung a little, though. Like a flu shot: a practical, acceptable burst of a pain that was more inconvenient than truly uncomfortable, but something he could do without.

They drove in tense silence for a while. Music wouldn't fill it adequately, so Innes didn't bother to turn on the state-of-the-art sound system. Mimi had a way of projecting her annoyance at every song he chose that he didn't care to experience again. It was better for her to hunch over her phone in the seat next to him, tapping away with her nail-bitten fingers.

The drive to LAX wasn't a short one, but they still managed to make it three-quarters of the way without speaking another word to each other, and it was only to check if she wanted anything from the Starbucks drive-thru.

"No, thanks," she said, flipping her long hair over her shoulder, revealing the pursed line of her lips as she fought—and failed—not to appear annoyed at the pit stop.

*God, she looks like me*, Innes thought as he pulled up to the window, one eye on her and the other on the change in his hand. Her hair, grown out, while he kept his trimmed short, was the exact shade of nondescript brown as his. The shape of her eyes and her high cheekbones were identical to his, and her irises were the same dark chocolate. He was vain enough to think she'd gotten all her best features from him. The rest—lips on the thin side, the prominent, squared chin a tad too masculine with her small features, and the ears that skewed on the large side—he could choose to blame on her other parent if he wanted.

It wasn't the first time he'd noticed their resemblance. He had pictures buried on a hard drive somewhere of them smiling for an elf in Santa's grotto when Mimi had been around three that had floored him the first time he'd looked at them, months after Christmas was over.

Mimi glanced up and Innes whipped his head around to the still-closed drive-thru window to avoid being caught staring. It probably hadn't worked, but the last thing he needed was for her to think he was getting sentimental for a bygone era. What he remembered most about that time in her life wasn't the pictures, or the red-and-green toddler-sized dresses. What came to mind more readily were the cold silences from Mimi's mother that had sent him scurrying long before the end of his allotted visit and the judgmental gazes from his parents when he slunk past the living room when he got back home.

The good old days.

The window finally opened, and he paid for his drink, pulling away as soon as the maniacally cheerful smile of the late-night coffee shop worker started to dim. The coffee was burnt, but it was better than nothing, and it would keep him awake more than the scintillating conversation.

As he steered out of the parking lot and back onto the road, he tried to think of when he'd turned into such an old man. Time was, he'd only just be leaving the house for a night on the town at midnight, and he'd stumble into his bed at dawn. When had that changed? After university, surely. Law school had taken a lot out of him, but he'd done his fair share of irresponsible drinking and attempting to convert to a nocturnal sleep schedule. But lately, he'd been disinclined to try to recapture that kind of communal inconvenience-shedding. Without even realizing it, he'd started to prefer the silence of his apartment.

How lately, though? When had it happened?

He considered *old* to be a state of mind rather than a numerical value. Going by his scale, his own parents had been old before he'd even been born and had aged metaphorically at a rate far quicker than they had physically.

Innes was thirty-six. Closer to forty than to twenty, but not over the hill just yet. He had plenty of energy to spend fighting off vertigo in a dance club or talking over the loud music in a bar or any of the things he used to do. What he lacked was the drive, and with a little thinking as he watched the streetlights pass by his car, he figured out when he'd lost it.

He'd spent the last holiday season and most of January sulking. He was man enough to admit it. After nearly two years of a mutually satisfying arrangement, the guy he'd paid to sleep with him at his beck and call had given him the boot. Or, well, he'd given himself the boot, letting himself out of Innes's place after laying down a dumping that was clear and concise, yet not without passion. It'd been rather like the rest of their relationship, in that way, except, for once, Innes hadn't had the upper hand. He had no interest in continuing an entanglement where the other party was anything less than willing, but it irked him that there was nothing he could have done to manipulate the situation to his benefit. Thus, the sulking.

He didn't miss Elliott as much as he missed the convenience of him, which was probably why they'd fizzled out in the end. He no longer wanted what they had, but he now found himself wanting the practical things the arrangement gave him: a weekly trip to somewhere fun that wasn't his apartment, a plus-one at boring charity dinners and work functions, and most poignantly of all, a warm body to get off with.

Innes shifted in his leather seat, suddenly aware of where his thoughts were straying and how strange it was to be following that path with his daughter in the car next to him. She wouldn't be able to tell anything from his professional poker face, but it still weirded him out.

He looked down at the clock on the brightly lit display. If his timing was right, they had less than ten minutes left of their touching father-daughter road trip to endure. If he was going to try to ask what had happened to make the whole thing necessary, he wasn't going to get a better opportunity. He staved off a sigh, then braced himself for a tough conversation neither of them wanted to have.

"So, back to school?" Stanford, to be exact.

"Yep," she said.

He waited, hopefully, for her to throw him a bone, but nothing seemed forthcoming.

"This was your break week, right?"

"Yeah."

"Nice."

Innes slapped on the turn signal, then rolled his shoulders when he finished rounding the corner. She sure wasn't making it easy for him, but, then again, when had she ever? And when had he ever earned that?

"Thanks for coming all the way out to get me," she said, surprising Innes into looking over. "I would have called Kristen, but she went to Cabo instead of coming home."

"It's fine, really." He might have bowed out of her childhood, but inconvenient timing and brief pre-midlife crisis aside, he didn't begrudge her a ride to the airport. Especially since, as far as he could guess, the whole reason why she needed him was that she was running away from her mother.

She hadn't mentioned her reasoning when she'd called him for the favor, but what else would make an 18-year-old girl—one responsible enough to decline a liquor-soaked vacation with her friends in favor of studying and visiting home—suddenly decide at ten o'clock on the second-to-last day of her break that she couldn't stay a minute longer?

"Everything okay at home?" Innes tried, bracing himself for a swift and merciless shutdown, the likes of which he'd never taught her but was nonetheless extremely proud of, in a tiny corner of his withered heart.

Silence this time. Not even a monosyllabic brush-off. That either meant she was even more annoyed at the necessity of his presence than he'd thought, or . . . she was actually considering a response.

"Not really," she said, her eyes still fixed out the window and her fingers fussing with the cuffs of her sweatshirt in the edge of Innes's vision.

"You want to talk about it?"

She stiffened a bit. "Why? Like you care?"

"Shocking as you might find it, yes. I do care about your well-being." He kept his eyes on the road, noting the sign for LAX up ahead. "And I know how your mother can be, so I thought you might appreciate a sympathetic ear."

"Why do you assume it's her?" Mimi asked, more amusement than accusation coming through in her tone. "It could be Jerry I have a problem with."

Innes scoffed. "Oh, please. The last person Jerry fought with was probably his accountant, and it was likely about who was the most boring. He doesn't have enough of an opinion on anything to fight with you."

Mimi laughed, and Innes felt a jolt of pride. *Don't get cocky*, he warned himself. Just because she could appreciate a good joke at her stepfather's expense didn't mean Innes was her friend.

"It is Mom, really," she said. "She's driving me crazy; I just couldn't stay there anymore."

"Ah. Anything specifically?"

Mimi sighed gustily and pulled her knees up to her chest, her heavy boots digging into the soft Italian leather of the seat. "She wants me to transfer to Pepperdine for my second year. It's closer to her, and I could live at home and save money on housing." She paused, holding her breath for a few tense seconds, then letting it go in a rush of words. "But I like Stanford. The political science program is better, the profs are better, it isn't a religious conservative wasteland, and most importantly, it's far away from her."

Innes nearly missed his exit, snapping his turn signal on mid-lane change. He snuck a glance at Mimi when he reached a straight course, looking for any hint that she was joking or exaggerating.

He should probably have expected some friction between Mimi and her mother, now that she was no longer a child. Mimi was headstrong, and so was her mother. There was bound to be a bit of tension between them occasionally. That level of vehemence, however, was surprising, but it seemed he'd overestimated Mimi's willingness to be micromanaged.

Back when Mimi was in high school, and he'd still taken her out for her birthday instead of just sending an expensive present by mail, she'd spent half of each awkward coffee date telling him what her mother thought about everything he cared to bring up. In the last year, as Mimi had attempted to get to know her aunts, uncles, and cousins on Innes's side—while still avoiding him as much as possible—no one had cared to inform him that Theresa was no longer Mimi's yardstick for the concepts of right and wrong.

"Ah," he said, fighting to hide his shock. "That sucks."

She snorted. "Yeah, it does. We fought about it all week. I was supposed to be charging up for the rest of the year, not spending my time avoiding her or arguing until she cries or I want to kill her."

*Oh, boy, wouldn't that be a nice early birthday present*, he thought, then he reflected for a moment. He had just made a casual joke—in his head, but still—about the death of the mother of his first and only child. He waited for the guilt to set in, taking a sip of his coffee.

He waited.

Nope. Not a pang. He wondered if he should be worried about how passionately he still hated Theresa after so long. They hadn't even spoken for a good—tremendously good—five years.

He only wondered about it for a minute. Thoughts like those led to appointments with shrinks, and he didn't have the time for that crap.

"Well, I'm glad you called me, then," he said. "Though I'm sorry you had to cut your break short. Do you have a flight already? Oh, and which terminal?"

"Four. Yeah, I booked a redeye; it'll get me there in a shorter time than the one I originally bought."

"Can you afford that?" His hand inched along the soft material of his tailored suit pants toward his pocket.

Mimi smiled so widely that Innes could see the reflection of her straight, white teeth in the windshield. "I made Jerry pay for it."

A short snicker bubbled up in Innes's throat. "That's my girl," he said, grinning.

Mimi's smile disappeared, and she turned her face back to the window, clearing her throat in the sudden silence.

*"That's my girl"?*

Where the hell had that come from? Aside from the creepy purity ring implications, it wasn't accurate. Mimi was a good kid and would become an even better young woman, but that had happened largely without his influence and in spite of her mother's.

He coughed, gripping the steering wheel tighter. "Well. For what it's worth, I think you made the right choice."

Mimi frowned. "What right choice?"

"By leaving, I mean. It would probably do more harm than good to stay and try to work out your issues now, while you're pissed at each other. Discretion being the better part of valor, and all that."

"Hmm. Is that what you tell yourself?"

His stomach swooped at the coldness in her tone. "Pardon?"

"When you sleep at night. Is that how you convince yourself that you didn't need to be around, like, ever?"

Heat started to prickle at the back of his neck as he gaped and tried to pay attention to navigating lanes to the nearing airport. "I was under the impression that you were perfectly happy with the way things were."

Mimi tossed her hair over her shoulder, sitting straighter in her seat. "Oh, really? Are you sure about that? Or is that what you choose to believe because it's easier than just admitting you're selfish."

"That's absolutely not true." He already knew he was selfish, and he wasn't in the habit of lying to himself. Only to other people. "I have never—"

"No, you haven't. That's the problem."

He worked his jaw back and forth, attempting to stop the clenching of his back molars. "I'm here, aren't I? You said jump, I said how high."

"God, what a hardship." Mimi started yanking on the strap of her small suitcase, pulling it from the footwell to her lap as they slowed into the departures parking area. "I ask you for a single favor in, what, four years? And that suddenly means you're father of the year? Give me a break."

"I'm not pretending that I was any kind of father to you, Mimi," he ground out, slamming the gear stick into park and thumbing the growing headache behind his eyebrows. "I'm not an idiot, and neither are you."

"Fine. So, why are you arguing with me?"

"I don't know!" A woman dragging luggage out of the car in front of him jumped and glared at him for yelling, but he was beyond caring. "I never fucking know with you, whether you want me to tell you that I'm an asshole and walk away, or if you want me to beat my head against a brick wall trying to convince you that I give a shit."

"Do whatever you want," Mimi spat, wrestling with her seat belt and the lock on the car door at the same time. "I already know what I need to."

"And what's that? Tell me, I'm dying to hear."

The metal of her seat belt clunked harshly on the window, and Mimi whipped around to face him, an all-too-familiar mixture of hurt and anger shining in her dry eyes. "That you *are* an asshole, and there's nothing you could do to make me believe that you give a shit, because you obviously don't."

"Mimi, wait a minute—"

She was already out of the car, slamming the door on her final word. "Thanks for the fucking ride."

He watched her stalk away, then stared at the ceiling to avoid the curious gazes of the other midnight flyers until his knuckles weren't quite so white on the wheel. Pulling out of his space and gathering speed, he left Mimi behind but didn't leave a single word of their argument in the dust.

*Argument.* More of a single-sided character flaying. Humiliating, but not undeserved.

Innes sighed, fogging up the windshield just a bit in the cold night. He flicked on the heater with too much force, the button clicking loudly in protest.

How did it always happen just that way? He saw Mimi twice a year these days if he was lucky, and every time, it ended with her hurt or angry or both, walking away with an even worse opinion of him than before, if that was possible. He no longer remembered what the arguments had been about, but it never seemed to matter what he said, since the outcome was always the same.

Once had been about Stanford, he was pretty sure. He'd been asking about the stats, the classes, what she planned to do with her degree, and Mimi had taken his customary skepticism to be a critique. As if he'd been anything other than damned proud of her for getting into such a well-respected school.

He recalled a dozen other conversations-turned-yelling-matches without being able to conjure any detail or explanation for where it went wrong, but none of them mattered. They all boiled down to the same thing, a themed question made crystal clear today:

*Where the hell were you, huh?*

Innes squinted against the bright lights of the city getting thicker as he drove farther into the jungle of LA. The headache that had been brewing the entire drive from Malibu was full-blown now, pounding in time with his pulse in his temples and reminding him with every beat of the warning his doctor had given him about watching his blood pressure. Like an old man, fragile and declining toward bran flakes and frequent peeing. Over the hill at thirty-six.

"Well, fuck it," he told his rearview mirror as he took an exit that wouldn't lead immediately home but rather to his office, where he'd left a particularly good bottle of whiskey, given to him by a client a few weeks before. He was in the mood for an expensive sort of drunk, the kind that he couldn't achieve from the wine he kept at home, or the mostly empty bottle of rotgut Jim Beam he kept in the back of a cabinet for emergencies.

It was 1 a.m. on Sunday. He already felt like shit. Why shouldn't he spend one evening—or very early morning—making decisions that were bad for his liver?

He pulled into a space in front of his building, vacant, for once because of the late hour. Only a white van with a cleaning service's logo had a closer spot. He pocketed his keys and pulled out his phone, one hand on the door latch and the other gripping the reflective screen.

He wondered if he should say something to Mimi. A follow-up to the argument to smooth things over and set them back on the right track to distant politeness rather than outright hostility.

But how was he supposed to reach out to her? He had her phone number, but only because he'd begged it out of his brother and sister-in-law. It would probably be weird to call out of the blue. He followed her on Twitter, would that work? No. It would too easily become apparent that the only reason he had Twitter was to check up on her. So far, he'd learned: she liked fruit for breakfast, her political views skewed toward socialism, and she thought John Lennon was overrated.

A text, then. More personal than an email, less invasive than cluttering up her voice mail. But what in god's name was he supposed to say? *I'm sorry, don't hate me, but don't expect anything more from me, for reasons that were too complicated to explain when you were eight, that still apply even now.* Perfect, that would clear everything up.

He went with simplicity. The more detail or defense of his character he included, the more she'd doubt his honesty, according to articles in magazines trying to help people calling in sick to work.

*I'm sorry. It was nice to see you, and I hope you enjoy the rest of your break. Good luck with the end of the school year.*

Short. Sincere. Not an attempt to deny any of the things she'd accused him of. His thumb hovered over the Send button, then, after some debate, added his first name to the end. It was unlikely she would be receiving many apology texts from unknown numbers, but he wanted her to know one hundred percent that it was him. A deliberate peace offering she could reject or deny.

He waited for her response but gave up after a few minutes. He had whiskey to drink, and he still needed to drive home before he started. He tossed his phone into the passenger seat, and then locked the car behind him with the click of a button and a chirp. Maybe the locked doors would be enough to discourage thieves, maybe not. He was living on the edge tonight, an absolute rebel.

The lobby was unlocked, presumably for the owners of the cleaning van to do their job. He passed a bored, tired-looking guy on his way into the elevator and nodded to him as he hit the button for the seventh floor.

His steps echoed in the hall in a way they normally didn't, even though the only person missing from the usual picture was the receptionist on the front desk. What really made the place seem empty was the lack of energy emanating from behind the closed doors of the offices on either side or beneath the floorboards from the identical sixth floor that also represented Kent, Kent & Morris. The frenetic hurry-up-and-wait buzz of a busy law office was noticeably absent.

He passed the closed doors of the other lawyers' domains and turned left at the end of the long main hallway. He was greeted by the familiar sight of his assistant's desk, immaculately clean as usual, but without Marie, who typically sat behind it, fending off walk-ins and other annoyances as she had for over two years. The longest he'd ever had an assistant.

He would miss her, he realized. She'd given him her unofficial notice by slapping an ultrasound on his desk along with his morning coffee. She'd always said she'd give it up and move back to Oregon to be closer to her family if she had a third kid. According to the note on the fuzzy alien portrait—*Baby Johnson No. 3, 14 weeks*—he estimated he had about two months to find a suitable replacement before she'd leave him high and dry. Knowing Marie, she would have already lined up a place to live, a gym membership and a favorite coffee shop, so he'd better get a move on. The thought of adding that to his plate made his headache even worse.

Behind Marie's desk, he could see the brighter light of his office spilling into the carpeted hallway. Through the partially open door, he could make out a cart overstuffed with cleaning supplies, but not the cleaner who went with it. He padded in, his footsteps falling lightly, caught up in the atmosphere of a library after-hours.

He was seconds from calling out to avoid giving the poor schmuck on the night shift a heart attack when he finally spotted the very person he was looking for.

Kneeling on the ground, their blond hair just long enough to obscure their face, someone in the same uniform as the one he'd seen downstairs was struggling to free a heavy, god-awful, familiar statue from the strap of a grubby canvas bag. It took him a slow, gear-cranking second to figure out what he was seeing, but once he did, it didn't take him long to size up the thief and form an action plan based on what he could see of the person's short stature and skinny limbs.

Innes wasn't too proud to abandon ship and call security, but in this case, he was pretty sure he could take the thief.

"Well, what have we here?" Innes drawled, crossing his arms and lifting his chin to the optimal angle for intimidation.

The kid's spindly fingers stopped fidgeting and his head snapped up, his eyes widening enough that the vibrant blue had a ring of white all around.

The beat of silence that followed while the guy realized how busted he was about to be was, uncontested, the best moment of Innes's weekend.

"Uh." It fell out of the kid's mouth, then he stood up and stumbled a few steps back as if putting distance between himself and his crime would make it null and void. With this new distance, Innes was able to get a better look at him. He wasn't any more physically impressive upright than he'd been crouched down, standing at least a couple of inches shorter than Innes himself, who'd never been granted that last growth spurt to push him to six feet like he'd been promised, like every Kent boy before him.

The kid's face was all angles and hollows, with a long, sharp nose and features that were too masculine to be called fey, but delicate all the same.

"Is that your name?" Innes gestured to the front of the uniform that hung limply from his skinny frame. "Charlie?"

The dark eyebrows that contrasted with his pint-sized Scandinavian good looks pulled into a thunderous frown. "Is there any point in lying?"

"Probably not." A false name wouldn't be enough to get this kid out of trouble if Innes decided to report him to his supervisor.

The kid considered his pitiful options for a few seconds, his jaw working obviously beneath his colorless cheeks and his lips set in a mutinous line. "Then, yes."

"Well. Good to meet you, Charlie." Innes smiled brightly and stepped closer, offering a hand to further discomfit him, but Charlie stepped back quickly, his fists clenching at his sides, fear etched in every tense line of his body. Innes let his hand fall instead, waving it in the direction of the abandoned bag. "I see you have expensive taste, if not the most aesthetic."

Charlie licked his lips and jerked a shoulder in a half shrug too stiff to be nonchalant. "Not my first choice, if I'm honest," he said. "I wasn't the one who decorated this office."

Innes's short laugh bounced off the ceiling of the office and resonated in the empty hall. "I suppose not. I didn't either, funnily enough, even though I'm the one who has to sit in it every weekday from nine to five."

He made a show of looking around the room, his eyes lingering on the pricey trinkets and state-of-the-art electronics. He took his sweet time, letting Charlie stew in uncertainty and nerves before he pinned him with the same look he used on clients who jerked him around and recalcitrant five-year-old nieces and nephews with sticky hands.

Charlie looked right back at him.

Innes had enough practice not to show any surprise, but he was impressed despite himself. Charlie was already too far gone into panic mode to pretend he was cool as a cucumber, but he wasn't letting Innes get him more riled up than he already was. Innes would have thought that would spoil his fun, but he had a feeling they were just getting started.

"Nice work in here," he said. "The surfaces have never been so sparkling clean. I guess you thought you'd do me a favor by getting rid of some of the clutter, hmm?"

"I—"

"Don't insult my intelligence by trying to deny it," he interrupted, injecting a shot of steel into his voice.

Charlie's eyes flashed with a brief ignition of anger, the first new reaction since he'd stepped farther out of Innes's reach. "I wasn't going to," he said through gritted teeth. "That would be pointless."

"Yes, it would," Innes agreed with an easy smile. "Forgive me for interrupting, then. I'm interested in what you have to say for yourself."

"Nothing."

This time, Innes was too surprised not to let it show. "Nothing?"

Charlie shrugged again, a more fluid motion, with the barest hint of attitude. "There isn't much to say. I tried to take something of yours. You caught me. What are you going to do about it?"

"I haven't decided yet," he answered truthfully. "That will probably depend on whether this is your first time or if you're experienced. Which is it? Is this prom night or third honeymoon?"

Innes's amusement grew along with the ruddy blush on Charlie's cheeks as he struggled to come up with an answer, probably one that didn't perpetuate Innes's metaphor.

"I'm not a thief," Charlie decided on, then winced. "Seriously. You don't have to believe me, but I was going to put it back."

"And there it is." Innes nearly called the police right then he was so disappointed. Just when he'd finally stopped being bored, Charlie had to go and ruin it by being predictable.

"I said you don't have to believe me!" Charlie's chin lifted, jutting obnoxiously into the air like it could stab Innes to death from across the room. "I'm only telling you the truth because my mother would be disappointed in me if I lied."

"You sure you're not trying to save your own skin? I'm really not the kind of person to fall for a sob story, so you're better off saving your breath."

"I don't care what kind of person you are. Not everything is about you."

"No, it isn't. Did I say or do something to suggest otherwise?"

"You didn't need to."

Innes felt a smile curl on his lips as he met Charlie's unwavering, challenging gaze. "That's a bit harsh considering you don't actually know the first thing about me."

"I'm a good judge of character."

"Are you?"

"Definitely. Learning which people I should avoid saved me a lot of beatings in high school."

"Bet you didn't make many friends, either."

Charlie clenched his fists, then released them just as quickly, his fingers wiggling like he was playing an invisible piano. "Enough."

"What about girlfriends? Were you too busy judging their character to get into their pants?"

This time, Charlie looked as confused as he was uncomfortable, but his chin went higher and his bony shoulders squared regardless. "No girlfriends. But I got really good at spotting the boys who wouldn't punch my lights out if I asked them if they wanted to trade handjobs in the bathroom."

Innes blinked, then let his body weight shift to his back foot as he observed Charlie. Interesting, surprising Charlie, who'd only been in Innes's acquaintance for ten minutes and had still managed to defy his expectations more than once.

"All right," Innes said, restraining himself from rubbing his hands together in anticipation. Taking a wide path around where Charlie stood, Innes crossed the room to the subtle liquor cabinet that stored his reward system for well-behaved clients. "Drink?"

"No."

The quick response wasn't a disappointment, because it wasn't a surprise. Actually, he would've been more disappointed if Charlie had accepted, since it said something about his self-preservation instincts.

Innes's real reason for asking was geographical in nature. With Innes all the way over by the wall, Charlie had a free path to the exit, should he get the gumption to try to make a break for it.

Innes hoped he wouldn't, almost as much as he hoped he would.

"Okay. I won't either," he said easily, then came back to the center of the room, turning one of the guest chairs in front of his desk toward Charlie. "Sit."

"No, thanks."

So polite, Innes almost purred. "Why not?"

"Fight or flight's a strong instinct. Sitting down feels like a bad move if I don't want to get mauled."

With a low chuckle, Innes tapped the top of the guest chair, then looked Charlie up and down. He took in everything, from the ragged cuffs of his pants and the knobby bones of his wrists, to his trim waist and pink, pursed lips. "Aren't your feet sore?"

"Always."

An interestingly candid response, and one Innes had been banking on.

Sitting down in the chair himself, he sighed heavily, deep in the fantasy that it was the most comfortable seat he'd ever enjoyed. A contented wiggle earned him a raised eyebrow. A second, over-the-top sigh got him a firmed line of tensed lips.

It was only a full-on groan of supposed chair-induced pleasure that made Charlie break: a small but unmistakable smile twitching on his mouth before it was quickly covered by a frown.

"Fine," Charlie said, in a flat tone that still managed to sound more amused than annoyed. "If it'll make you stop that."

"Stop what? The chairs are comfortable."

"You know wh— All right, never mind." He sat down in the other chair, helpfully turning it to face Innes. "This isn't going to go anywhere."

"You give up so quickly." He'd admitted to the theft without a fight too, but somehow Innes didn't think those two data points really added up to the conclusion of Charlie being a passive person. Not a chance.

"I'm not going to waste energy on arguing a stupid point," Charlie said, his jaw jutting out impudently. "I save it for what matters."

"And what's that?"

"Do you care?"

That seemed like a genuine question. After the sharp back-and-forths they'd already enjoyed, the tilt of Charlie's head and the slight softening of his icy eyes was starkly different.

Innes shrugged. "Sure. Call it curiosity for how the other half lives."

"Right. What do you want to know?"

Reading people was a skill Innes had learned well in his profession. Body language was as telling as a book, and Charlie's told a couple of chapters.

He wasn't as relaxed as he appeared. Sure, he slouched in the chair, his legs crossed at the knee like he didn't have a care in the world, but that same knee would probably have been bouncing up and down at a rabbit's pace if it was free to move, judging by the vibrating tension in Charlie's ankle.

What would he look like if he were truly relaxed? It would probably take a lot more than one conversation to find out, but Innes wanted to know. Even if it took throwing money at him to get there. Especially then, actually.

But one step at a time. He didn't want to scare him off.

"Who is Charlie?" Innes asked, with an all-encompassing gesture toward his guest.

Charlie's dark eyebrow rose again. "He's a very tired millennial with socialist political leanings and a shit job, who hates when people talk about themselves in the third person."

"Hmm, same. About the third-person thing. Can't say I truly fit any of the others."

Squinting, Charlie looked consideringly at him, like he'd done exactly what Innes had intended and had forgotten to be stressed about his fate. "Maybe one. How old are you, anyway?"

"A lady never tells."

The snort of laughter that followed wasn't attractive, necessarily, but it was a bit thrilling to hear from Charlie, who'd looked for the last few minutes like he didn't know the definition of the word *laughter*.

"You sound like my mother."

"Oh, is that what does it for you?"

"Does what?" Blinking, Charlie took a couple of seconds before it clicked. "Oh my god, no! What is wrong with you?"

"So many things. I'm a bag of issues stitched into the shape of a person." The second he stopped speaking, Innes started regretting. Why the hell had he said that? Too late to take it back. "But I'm kidding, obviously. I don't really think that's what gets you going. I've got other ideas for that."

"Why?" A small V of confusion had formed between Charlie's eyebrows. "Why are you even thinking about it?"

"I'm interested in people. In a way. I couldn't care less about being nice, but I like to know what makes them tick, because understanding motivations can usually help me later."

"So you just go around guessing at what people like in bed?"

That was blunt. He'd expected to have to tiptoe around it a little longer, but if he was honest, he preferred it this way. "Sometimes. I'd like to think I'm pretty good at it too."

He wasn't being entirely truthful, but when was he? Yes, he liked to anticipate what he could be up against, but only a select few got him thinking along these lines.

"Okay," Charlie said slowly, and Innes was sure he was about to make another *ew* face, but was once again surprised. "Enlighten me, then."

"Really?"

"I want to know how wrong you are."

Charlie was leaning forward, a new confidence making him draw Innes's eyes like a magnet. Still tense, of course, since he was far from off the hook, but not so fearful as before. Good.

"Some people might think you get off on being taken down a notch," Innes said. "You seem like a guy who's in control of himself, and an unobservant person might want to give you the opposite."

"Not you?"

"Not every CEO wants to be powerless for once, and not every meek housewife wants to put someone in their place. Humans are a lot more nuanced than that, but sometimes, what you see is what you get."

Charlie hummed, his expression as unchangeably intense as ever, but his legs moved, uncrossing in a gesture that was more telling than he probably knew.

Leaning forward in his chair, Innes dropped his final point, his thesis statement. "I think you want to be pushed, but only if you can push back."

Like this, both on the edge of their seats, there was so little distance between their faces. Enough that he could imagine he felt the disrupted breath of Charlie's lungs and see the kindling heat in his cool eyes. So close . . .

Until those eyes widened, and Charlie popped out of his seat, putting the chair between him and Innes. His eyebrows had crashed down again, but he wasn't shaking in fear like he had been before, so as he backed up, Innes stood and followed.

"So? Did I get it right?"

"Why would I tell you?"

Innes's office was one of the largest, but that didn't mean there was a lot of space to go. After a few unsteady steps, Charlie's back hit the bookshelf, and he stayed there, not moving an inch as Innes crowded him, not quite near enough to touch.

"That was the game, wasn't it?"

"I didn't agree to that."

Closing another step of distance, Innes noticed the growing flush on Charlie's cheeks, the flicker of his tongue wetting his lips, and the stutter of breath that didn't have anything to do with nervousness.

With slow, sure movements, he braced his arms on the bookshelf on either side of Charlie's shoulders.

"Didn't you? My mistake. I still think I won, though," Innes murmured into his ear, tilting his head so that his lips had a direct path to the soft-looking bit of skin where Charlie's jaw met his neck, should he choose to close the distance. Charlie shivered almost imperceptibly from the passage of air across intimate skin. "Do I get a reward?"

Charlie let out a puff of breath like he'd been socked in the stomach, frozen with his lips slightly parted and his eyes wide. After a few taut, charged seconds, Charlie's long eyelashes blinked, and blinked again, and his stunned, dazed look began to disappear. Replacing it, however, was not the expected sly flirtation, or even a bashful, interested cringe.

"Uh, how about no," Charlie said, using his forearms to nudge the inside of Innes's elbows so he was forced to straighten up or fall ungracefully against Charlie's chest. His flush rose and his fists clenched as Innes staggered back, completely thrown. "Wow. Talk about shit timing. Did you think I'd actually have sex with you while you've got the cops on speed dial?"

Innes raised an eyebrow, crossing his arms and hoping he didn't look as annoyed as he felt. "I don't even have my phone on me." Was that a smart thing to have revealed? It didn't seem to matter, since Charlie waved him away.

"Metaphorically."

"Well, literally, yes, I thought you could be interested. No harm in trying my luck with an attractive man."

"Jesus. I need an adult."

Innes snorted. "You are an adult." The pit of his stomach swooped with suspicion. "You are, aren't you?"

"What the hell, man? I'm twenty-four," Charlie said, indignant.

"Oh, good." That was a complication he sure didn't need.

The long slow morphing of Charlie's face from annoyed to disgusted was a thing of beauty. "*Gross.*"

"Okay, okay, I get it. I'm a nasty predator." Innes rolled his eyes. "You should probably hurry along back to Mommy."

Charlie's spine went even more ramrod straight, and his dark brows slammed down over his narrowed eyes. "Just like that? Really?"

"Really. I won't call the cops or tell your boss. I don't need the hassle."

He jerked his head in the direction of the entrance, and Charlie wasted no time, scurrying over to his abandoned messenger bag and slinging it back onto the cleaning cart, but not before setting the statue he'd tried to steal on the floor next to him with a heavy *thump*.

"There," Innes said. "We're square. That wasn't so hard, was it?"

"Wait."

Charlie's hand dug into the bag again, and he pulled out something else. A paperweight that landed next to the statue, gleaming in the light of the office.

Innes stared at it, more disbelief than anger making his voice go a little higher. "You little shit."

"You said I could go. Can't take it back now." Popping up from the floor like a toy on a spring, Charlie grabbed the handles of the cart in a white-knuckled grip.

"No, I won't. Now, scram." Innes let him push the cart a few steps, just for the drama of it all. "But, Charlie."

Charlie looked up from the rolls of paper towel and met Innes's gaze head-on.

"This is a one-time offer because I've had a shit day and misery makes me feel generous." Innes had no idea if that was actually true or not, but it was as good a reason as any. "But if I see you here again, we'll have a problem."

Charlie swallowed hard and nodded. "Understood," he said, and he continued to back out of the room, pausing only briefly on the threshold to tell Innes, "I hope your day gets better."

Innes looked at his watch and grimaced. "Yeah, too late for that. Ah, well. Tomorrow's another day. Better luck next time," he called after Charlie as he wheeled himself into the hallway.

"Thanks," Innes heard as Charlie trundled toward the elevator, and he grinned at the sardonic lilt to Charlie's tone. "You too, perv."

With a soft chuckle at Charlie's boldness, Innes walked over to the statue and paperweight sitting on the ground. He picked them up, weighing them in each hand as he contemplated the statue. He couldn't for the life of him remember where or when he'd acquired it, but he assumed—hoped—that it'd been a gift, or something brought in by the decorator. However well the ugly thing went with the aesthetic of the room, it was still an eyesore. It looked like a tacky and expensive reminder of someone's grand South-Asian vacation, promptly regifted and forgotten after the next Mediterranean cruise.

Such an insignificant little thing to have caused such drama, not to mention lead to the most entertaining conversation Innes had had in months.

He turned to the bookshelf, scanning the shelf filled with other meaningless eye-catching items and books he'd never read to try to find where the statue had come from. He looked for an obvious blank spot rather than trying to remember where it might have been, and sure enough, he found it, way up on one of the topmost shelves. Tucking the statue under his arm, he placed a foot on the bottom shelf, then thought better of it.

Charlie might have been small enough to scramble up there, but Innes was heavier. He also didn't have anyone who'd miss him until Monday morning, and he didn't relish being crushed by the physical manifestations of his wealth for the rest of the weekend. That would be way too symbolic for his taste.

Moving around a few things was easy, and he made space on a lower shelf for both the statue and the amber paperweight, of which he did actually remember the origin. It had been a birthday present from his parents. Pricey, decorative and generic enough not to have had any thought put into it at all. Relegated to the back of a tall bookcase so that he didn't have to see it again and get pissed off.

Dusting off his hands—Charlie must have missed a few spots on the shelf before he'd pilfered from them—he slumped to his chair and sat heavily, rocking the seat back. He let his head fall against the generously padded headrest and laughed.

"Ballsy fucker," Innes said to himself, still chuckling in an empty room.

He didn't stop laughing about it until after he got home and realized that he'd completely forgotten about the whiskey he'd meant to get drunk on.

# Chapter Two

**W**hen Charlie had graduated high school, he'd thought customer service couldn't possibly be as bad as having his soul sucked out of him by a job pushing the same button every damn day into infinity. It hadn't mattered back then if the money was better in some corporate-owned, sheep-operated nightmare factory.

Seventeen-year-old Charlie had been naive and hadn't known exactly how shitty the service industry could be.

These days, he was in a constant debate with himself over whether he'd prefer to be making a ton of cash in a job he hated 100% of the time, or continue how he was, making shit money in a job he only hated 75% of the time. On days like this one, he started to lean toward the first option. At least he could guarantee his misery, rather than being surprised by a whole pile of crap being dumped on him in a single shift.

"Any luck?"

Charlie looked up at Janine from the paper towel he was using to scrub at the streak of butternut bisque that stubbornly clung to his black pants. "No. Nothing for it. Good thing I have an extra pair."

"Yeah," she said. "Well, I hate to hurry you, but two more tables just came in, and Alice hasn't recovered from the lecture you gave her."

He winced, but she was gone before he could apologize. It wasn't her he should be saying sorry to, anyway. It wasn't Alice's fault that she was new and didn't know to shout her presence behind the kitchen doors, but it also definitely wasn't his job to get covered in scalding hot soup because nobody bothered to tell her the protocol and she wasn't quick enough to pick it up.

Sighing, he gave up, pitched the napkin and opened his locker, shaking out the extra pair of pants to try to deal with the wrinkles a bit. He hadn't worn them in over six months, and there was a reason why they lived in his locker for emergencies.

He'd found them at the thrift store, the perfect length and color, and with the tag still on them from a fancy department store he'd never shop at. They'd had some awful pleats in the front, but he'd converted them to look more modern, no sweat. The problem came when he'd had to replace the broken button, the reason why they'd been given away in the first place. The only matching button he'd had on hand was huge and dug into his stomach whenever he slouched even a little. He kept meaning to change it, but that would require time he didn't have.

While he was putting on the pants, Charlie swore under his breath, trying to get his verbal frustration out before he had to get back on the floor. The normal Thursday lunch rush was worse than usual because of the nice weather outside, so he'd been running around since 11 o'clock between the patio and dining room. He'd had a headache from squinting in the sun before eleven thirty. Now, it was noon, and between the newbie, the dishwasher breaking before they could get more teaspoons, and the pack of assholes at table three, he was well on his way to a migraine.

And of course it had nothing to do with the job he'd quit a week ago. Nothing at all.

Slamming his locker shut didn't help the headache, but it made him feel better to imagine he was closing it on the face of one of the obnoxious suits at table three. His vivid imagination was even able to put a genuine smile on his face as he entered the rodeo again.

"Alice," he said as he came up behind her at the pass. "You good?"

"Yes," she squeaked, then she cleared her throat and looked him in the eye. "I'm fine. You?"

*Atta girl*, Charlie thought. "All good. I've had worse. Remind me to tell you about my first shift, and the asparagus puree incident. Way worse than butternut squash, let me tell you."

Alice laughed, dimpling her cheeks in a way the randy businessmen would love. Despite her slow start, Charlie hoped she stuck around, for her sake as well as his. She'd make a killing in tips if she could get her efficiency as high as her cute factor, and that could only mean good things for him too, since if she got some regulars coming in, Stanley might give everyone that measly one percent raise Charlie had been asking for at every team meeting. It was a long shot, based only on her dimples, but he couldn't help but dream, especially since he was down a paycheck.

"Pick up, table ten!"

"Thanks, Jim," Charlie said, returning Jim's habitual wink, then he turned back to Alice. "Have you got a couple minutes?"

"In a bit, maybe? Have to drop these off, then Donna's going to show me how to roll napkins," Alice chirped as she hefted her plates, her grip surer than the time before, or the time before that.

"Thrilling. Okay, come and find me in the empty section in a few, I'll make it worth your while."

"Sure. Oh, table three wanted to know where you were, by the way. They're ready to order."

"Finally," Charlie groaned, digging in his pocket for his notepad and following Alice out the door and back to his section. The dick herd had been taking up their table for an hour already, apparently waiting for someone who might or might not show, getting steadily more hydrated with the free water while bothering Charlie about every tiny quibble they'd had with the menu and making comments about how much better their jobs were than Charlie's that they thought were subtle.

On a normal day, maybe Charlie could have brushed it off, made a couple backhanded compliments that wouldn't get him fired, and hoped that their need to compare dick and wallet sizes would outweigh their general assholery and they'd all tip well.

This particular Thursday, however, he was too busy worrying about the state of his bank account to have the patience for anything.

In the week since he'd quit his job at the cleaning service, he hadn't had any luck finding something else to fill his post-restaurant hours. That, on its own, was enough to make it hard to sleep at night, but given that he was also constantly wondering if the police were going to knock on his door, he was exhausted and tense way beyond his normal level.

They'd never find anything to prove he was a thief, of course, because there wasn't anything to find, but Charlie couldn't count on that stopping Innes Kent from going back on his word. It'd already been a week, and he hadn't had any trouble, but it would be a few more weeks before he'd allow himself to relax. Not to mention to forgive himself for making a stupid mistake.

Charlie looked down at the pen in his hand and realized that he was clicking it incessantly. He stopped at the edge of the wall that separated his section from Donna's and allowed himself eight whole seconds to breathe, shaking out the tension in his hands and trying to ignore the tightness of his shoulders. Charlie needed to get a handle on himself before the top of his head popped off or one of the other waitstaff stabbed him in the eye with his own annoying pen.

The table of five ordered some douchey salads and a so-five-years ago bruschetta, and Charlie was tucked in the corner of the empty section—closed for the slower lunch time—with Alice in only a few minutes.

It wasn't the best location, with the toilet flushing loudly through the wall as background noises, but he'd take what he could get.

"Okay, so you're doing great at this," he said, tucking his notepad into his jeans so his finger didn't fuss with the spiral binding. "Donna's an awesome teacher, but she's also too nice to give you the dirty details. I'm not that nice, obviously."

Alice's doe eyes widened. "Oh, no, I—"

"Don't worry about it, I'm really not. Here is your waitstaff survival guide. Lesson one: Don't admit you fucked up until you absolutely have to. It doesn't matter whether you did or not; if you apologize for something, you're immediately the one at fault. Be gracious, get them free shit, and be sympathetic, but don't let them think you're the one in the wrong." He clapped his hands, then winced as it echoed off the empty chairs, and probably out into where the guests could hear. Oh, well. "Let's practice."

"Okay." She still looked a little shell-shocked, but determined and not completely put off, yet.

"You get busy doing something else, and your first visit to the table is a bit delayed. What do you say first?"

"Um. Sorry for the wait?"

"Nope. They're suddenly reminded of the wait, when some of them might not even have noticed at all. What's better? 'Thanks for your patience.' Everyone likes a compliment, and you've just told them they're patient. Go, you!"

Her mouth pouted in sudden understanding. "Ooohhh."

"Someone says their extra side of potatoes is missing. Oops. Maybe they remembered to order it, maybe they didn't. The world may never know. They're pissed and they want their carbs. What do you say?"

"I'm guessing it's not 'Sorry about that.'"

"Ding ding! Correct. 'Oh, that's strange. Let me fix that for you.' Imply that this isn't normal, acceptable, or your fault. Focus on quick solutions. Everybody's happy."

"Awesome." Her fingers twitched at her sides, probably for her own notepad and pen, but there was no way she'd get everything down, not when he had so far to go and so little time.

"Lesson two," he continued. "Be what they want you to be. Younger patrons will want you to relate to them. Be real, and don't be afraid to make jokes. Don't ignore or look down on the teenagers, even if they can't tip much, because they will keep coming back, and they will bring more friends than any person should conceivably have. Sometimes quantity is better than quality, even if you're getting paid in quarters. Older patrons will want you to either be their granddaughter or their midlife crisis. You gotta get a feel for which is which, because boy, are their expectations different."

A short, high giggle escaped her throat, but other than that, she only nodded.

"Chameleon yourself into being any patron's favorite person. Now, lesson three. You find a better job than this one, you take it."

"Oh, no, I don't—"

He cut off her protests with a firm slice of his hand in the air. "Seriously. The amount of new staff who come in and out of this place should tell you a lot about what kind of place it is. The ones who stick around are awesome, if I do say so myself. But it's an unspoken rule: if someone wants to move on, everyone else will do what's necessary to cover those shifts. Get out while you can. Promise me, okay?"

"I promise." Her swingy, clean brown hair rippled with the force of her nod.

"Cool. Lesson four. Be psychic."

"What?"

"Yeah, sorry. I can't tell you much more than that. It'll get easier, but the best way to impress people is by giving them what they need before they even know they want it." The clatter of the kitchen and the murmur of the guests was nearly loud enough to drown him out, but she needed to hear this. "People are inherently selfish. Yeah, every once in a while, you'll get a big spender, but in general, you'll have to be so good at what you do that you'll guilt people into tipping well. Customers are generally the absolute worst, so don't feel bad if you're scamming them into thinking they're the best part of your day. They don't care about you, so give them the exact same consideration."

When Charlie heard the pointed clearing of an officious throat, he rolled his eyes right away, because he was positive he knew who it was. Brandon, probably wondering what they were doing in what he considered his section.

Except, when Charlie turned around, it wasn't Brandon. Instead, he was in a nightmare—the one he'd been having for a week where he looked up and Innes Kent was smirking at him, about to crush him into dust.

"What's lesson five?" Kent asked. "I'm dying to know."

With a little push to her shoulder, Charlie sent Alice scurrying away to learn how to fold napkins or whatever while he contemplated whether or not running out of there would cost him his job.

"How long were you standing there?"

Did it matter? Five seconds, five minutes. He'd heard enough to end Charlie's life as he knew it.

"Don't worry, I wasn't waiting too long. You don't even have to thank me for my patience."

Oh, god. That long, huh?

"Why are you here?" Charlie demanded, long past faking politeness. "Are you following me?"

"Of course not, I—" Tugging the front of his blazer into place, Kent looked over his shoulder, then back. "Can we chat? Somewhere private."

"Why should I?"

"So I don't go directly to your boss and get you in trouble?"

Maybe if this was the first thing Charlie had gotten in trouble for this year—hell, this month—Charlie would've pushed back a little more, but he was already on thin ice from the last staff meeting when he'd publicly challenged Stanley about the busted fire door. If his boss heard about this, he'd have a legitimate reason to fire him.

"Oh, for— Fine. Follow me but be quiet."

At the opening to the hallway, Charlie stuck his head around the wall and whisper-shouted in the direction of the pass. "Donna. Donna!"

"Yes, dear?" Donna said, looking up from the napkin she was folding. "I heard about your little spill, are you okay?"

"I'm fine. I need you to cover for me for a few minutes."

She blinked, then frowned sympathetically. "Oh, honey, are you ill? You don't look well; do you need the bathroom?"

"No!" Charlie said, loud enough that he saw flirty Jim in the kitchen look up from his work. He lowered his voice to a whisper again, intensely aware of Kent's presence behind him. "That's not the reason. I just need a favor, okay?"

"Yeah, honey, go ahead," she said, waving a weathered, red clay-colored hand in the direction of the toilets. "If anyone asks, I'll tell them you're working hard somewhere else."

"Thanks."

"You're welcome, dear! Feel better!"

"I'm not—" Charlie sighed. There was no point in trying to convince Donna that he felt fine, and maybe she'd bring him chicken soup to cure his nonexistent illness if she felt bad enough.

That was if he was still a free man tomorrow.

"Not that I'm not enjoying the view . . ."

Kent's smooth voice came from behind him, and Charlie realized he'd wasted enough time. Straightening so hard he nearly cracked a vertebrae, he tossed a look back that he hoped was scathing and not terrified.

"Follow me, and don't say anything."

Past the entrance to the kitchen and down the hall from the public washrooms, an emergency exit stood in the shadow of a burnt-out light. It wasn't private, but it was far enough away from where anyone could hear that it would have to do.

When he stopped next to the heavy fire door, he realized, too late, that he was the one cornered here.

"Well, hello, Charlie," Innes said, his lips tilted in a smirk that was as self-satisfied as his relaxed, muscular-arms-crossed posture.

"Kent," Charlie said, tonelessly, nodding once like this was a brief passing of acquaintances in the street.

"Innes, please. I feel like we know each other well enough by now."

"How do you figure?" Charlie glanced over Innes's shoulder, willing his coworkers to appear.

"Well, I've run across you unexpectedly twice now, once on my turf, once on yours. I quite enjoyed our conversation last time, I'll admit. I learned your name, now you can know mine, and we can have just as—" he paused, tapping a thumb against his lip in theatrical thought "—illuminating a discussion this time around."

"What do you want?" Charlie asked. His stomach was tight and swimming with nausea, so he didn't have time for Innes's gentleman-supervillain speeches or he was going to throw up on some very expensive-looking shoes.

"To talk," Innes said, his smile dimming, but not disappearing entirely. "And apologize. I thought I was reading the situation right, last time, and I wasn't. I'm sorry if I made you uncomfortable."

Charlie blinked, taking an instinctive step back and hitting the baseboard of the hallway's dead end with a jarring scuffing sound. The sting in the back of his heel was almost as annoying as the fact that he always seemed to be surprised and thrown off by everything Innes said. "What?"

"You heard me. I won't apologize for being a little intimidating, since you were trying to rob me, but I'll admit that I overstepped. Maybe because I was so impressed."

"Impressed? That I tried to steal from you?" Either this guy was crazier than Charlie had thought, or he was in a much shadier business and took networking very seriously.

"I don't think you realize what a big risk you were taking." Even in the dim light of an employees-only cubby hole, Charlie could see Innes's eyes sharpen as his face stayed passive and pleasant. "I'm a lawyer. A good one. If you'd actually done it, I could have crucified you and gotten any judge in the state of California to believe that I feed the homeless and rescue lost kittens while you trip old people in the street and steal from unsuspecting, upstanding gentlemen like me."

Helpless anger pulsed in Charlie's ears and throat with every beat of his blood. The image Innes was painting was the worst-case scenario he'd imagined himself a hundred times in the past week. The one where he went to jail. Or had to pay a fine steep enough that he and Ma were evicted, and then he'd have a criminal record to make it even harder for him to get a job, so they'd never get on top of the bills, and . . .

Charlie focused himself on the present by clenching his right fist so hard that he felt a knuckle crack, and he half expected his ma's voice to come from across the room, telling him to quit it or he'd get arthritis. He wanted to bite his thumbnail, wanted it hard enough that he could feel it between his teeth, but it'd been five years since he'd broken that habit, and he wasn't about to start again just because of a rich man's idle baiting.

"This isn't primetime TV," Charlie spat. "Considering that all the judges in this area probably already know you, and you've had to talk to them for more than five minutes, I doubt you could convince them that you'd let a homeless guy bum a smoke."

In a restaurant as busy as the one they were in, in the middle of the lunch rush, there was no such thing as silence. But what followed after Charlie's words was pretty close. Over clinking of silverware, the chatter of patrons, and the squawking of the cooks in the kitchens, Charlie could hear his own breathing and not much else, until there was suddenly low, snickering laughter.

"You're probably right," Innes said, palming the back of his perfect hair in a self-aware, self-deprecating cringe. "They all learned what kind of person I am years ago, but it wouldn't matter if they all hate me." With the *aw, shucks* smile still in place, he pinned Charlie with a finger pointed right at his throat. "I'd still beat the righteous fuck out of any counsel you could afford. You know that. And still, you're not even shaking in your sensible, arch-supporting shoes—"

Charlie bristled and pointedly didn't shuffle his feet. "You try walking around all day in loafers."

"So far, you've attempted to steal from me, maligned my character—"

"Are you a nineteenth-century lord?"

"Provided terrible service at this mediocre establishment—" Innes paused, tilting his head expectantly. "What, no rebuttal to that one?"

Charlie shrugged his stiff shoulders, making the heavy silver nametag on his shirt click against a button. "I mean, this place is mediocre."

"That's what I gathered from the people I'm supposed to be eating with right now."

In his shock to see him, Charlie had almost forgotten what Innes had to be here for. "Who—" The obvious answer clicked. "Oh, man, not the dream team? Yeah, I'm not about to give them five-star service. They asked me for the specials three times."

Innes winced, his lip curling. "They are insufferable, aren't they?"

"Why are you with them, then?" Charlie couldn't resist asking.

Innes's face smoothed into a blank, professional mask. "They're all under the impression that one of them is going to be hired on as an intern. They don't know which one yet, so they've stuck together to try to make backhanded compliments about all the others in the hope that I'll choose them."

"Is it working?"

"Not at all. We chose our intern a week ago, and she's more talented than any of them and their fathers combined."

"Then why are you here?"

Innes shrugged. "Free lunch."

"Oh, come on."

"I'm serious. It was actually simple chance. I was starting to think it wasn't worth it, but then you happened to be here."

The predatory gleam was back, and this time, it made Charlie remember the one part of their strange first meeting he'd tried to forget completely.

For a few minutes, though he'd never admit it to anyone, he'd considered taking Innes up on his blatant offer. He'd noticed Innes's attractiveness, and the way he'd responded hadn't only been because of his dislike of being outdone.

"Yep," Charlie said, as brightly as he could manage. "You just happened to find the guy who burgled, insulted, and inconvenienced you. Nearly burgled," he corrected himself. "So, why are you still here, taking me away from my job?"

"I'm going to make you an offer."

Charlie waited for the explanation. Then he waited for the punch line when no more information seemed to be coming. He waited for a mocking laugh or a sly smile, some indication that Innes was joking, but he looked absolutely serious.

"You already tried that. I said no." And Innes hadn't pushed. He had, in fact, let Charlie go without paying any kind of toll, legal or not. Innes had been annoyed, but not aggressive. And he'd apologized.

A pretty shitty apology, but it was something.

Innes huffed. "Relax, it's not that kind of offer, but one that is mutually beneficial." He pulled a business card out of his wallet, handing it over with a practiced, practical flick. "Call me when your shift is over. We'll talk details."

Charlie took the card without much thought to whether it was a good idea or not, squinting at it closely in the dim light. Innes's contact info was printed in black no-nonsense ink, but even Charlie, who didn't know a thing about business cards, could tell that the paper was luxe and the understated design was professionally done. "Details," he said, his eyes fixed on the card instead of Innes's always smirking, never straightforward face. "About an offer I can't refuse?"

"Oh, you could refuse it. However, I feel very certain that you won't want to." Innes reached out and flicked the card, narrowly missing Charlie's nose. "Does that thing hold the answer to the meaning of life?"

Charlie glared, holding the card up, pointedly not putting it away. "I just don't understand," he gritted out. "Why aren't you getting me in trouble?"

Innes met his glare with a cocky, unconcerned tilt of his head and a raking glance up Charlie's body that felt more assessing than sexual, like he was calculating value rather than noticing a person. "For all the reasons I've stated. You've been an absolute brat, and I could make your life very difficult, but you're still talking back and questioning everything I say with no apologies. You aren't afraid of me, or of what

I can do to you. Or if you are, and a smart person would be at least a little bit, you don't let that get to you. You've sassed me at every turn. And that is exactly what I need."

Innes turned to go. Charlie followed, reaching out a hand, but stopping short of Innes's elbow when Innes stopped and gave his hand, then Charlie himself a quelling glance.

"For what?" Charlie asked, taking the hand back but refusing to step away.

"Call me. We'll talk about it."

"Any reason why you can't talk about it here?" He glanced up the hall, wondering if the chance of them getting walked in on was the reason Innes was being so closed-lipped about his mysterious offer.

Innes sighed and pulled a smartphone from his pocket, checking it, then holding it loosely at his side in the same hand that sported a watch that looked as expensive as the phone. "Well, for one thing, you'll be missed, and I don't want to be interrupted when you have to go refill someone's drinks. Secondly, I'll be missed. Another few minutes and my absence is going to turn from making the boy's club sweat to making them annoyed, and I don't want to have to deal with their daddies getting all up in arms for treating them like the time wasters they are." With a lazy wave, Innes started down the hallway again, shouting back to Charlie without turning around, "Call me. I promise you'll be interested."

Charlie stayed rooted to the spot until Innes's footsteps had completely faded into the clatter of the kitchen and the dining room, stroking a finger along the edge of the card. He could feel it start to get a little fuzzy, a little less crisp and clean than it was when Innes handed it to him.

An offer. What could that possibly mean? Was Innes lying, trying to get him to say yes to sex again? Innes's practice—Kent, Kent & Morris, according to the card and the sign on the door Charlie himself had polished to a shine—had seemed completely legit, but maybe it was an elaborate front for drugs or something equally shady.

Or maybe it wasn't. Maybe Innes's offer was something he'd take without a second thought.

Charlie tilted the card, watching it catch the dim light in the semigloss of its surface. Resisting the urge to crumple it, he shoved it deep into his pocket, putting it out of his mind until later.

Blowing out a long breath, he walked to the end of the hallway, getting his notepad out of his other pocket, but he found his way blocked yet again, this time by Brandon, whose black shirt was already darker in places with sweat.

"Charlie," he said, with relief and a definite edge of annoyance. "Are you gonna get back on the floor? Donna's trying her best, but your entire section is twitchy as hell."

Charlie nodded, wiggling his notepad for Brandon to see. "Coming. I was dealing with a patron issue."

Instead of moving out of the way, Brandon glanced behind himself to where he must have seen Innes leaving, then raised both eyebrows at Charlie. "Back here? Dude need help getting his fly undone?"

Charlie shot him a half-hearted glare and gave him the finger as he shoved past, ignoring him as usual.

Brandon's humor was always at someone else's expense, and he hadn't yet figured out that adding *just kidding* onto the end of every cheap shot didn't make it funny. But each time Brandon's *fun* was directed at Charlie was one less time it was aimed at a new hire, like sweet Alice, or Donna, who was usually hurt by Brandon's jibes, no matter how she tried to hide it.

Brandon's attempt at wit had nothing on Innes's, who could've spent his entire lunch poking holes in Charlie's composure, but when Charlie finished his internal pep-talk, the whole table was empty.

Tucked under a bread plate was a fifty-dollar bill, a message that Charlie read loud and clear.

There was more where that came from.

His feet were killing him by the time he let himself into the apartment, and as he'd predicted, his skin was raw under his navel from the stupid button. At least now he had a good opportunity to fix them.

"Charlie? That you?"

He smiled and trudged to the living room. "Who else would it be, Ma?"

She laughed, her girlish titter tapering off as he made it to the sagging, flowered couch and collapsed on it.

"How was work?"

"Fine." He pressed his fingers against his cheeks, as if digging them in and scrubbing out the tiredness would make him more alert. "Same as ever. What did you do today?"

"Oh, not much." She sighed, looking out of the small window near her chair. "I called my friend Marsha."

Charlie frowned as he adjusted to a marginally more comfortable position on the lumpy couch. "You have a friend Marsha?"

She laughed again, reaching over the arm of her chair and patting his knee. "You remember, the lovely lady from the Dollar Tree."

Dollar Tree. The very last job Charlie's ma had had before he'd told her she didn't have to work anymore because he'd take care of them. Six years ago. The one she'd only had for about three months before she'd called in sick for a week straight, then broken down and told Charlie that she just couldn't do it anymore.

"Okay," Charlie said slowly. "And how was she?"

"Well, she didn't have much time to talk. She's still working there, did you know that?" She looked at him expectantly, and Charlie supposed he should try to show some kind of reaction beyond baffled exhaustion.

"Oh, yeah? That's cool," he said. He toed off his shoes and stretched his feet, wincing at the cracking of his joints. "And she remembered you?"

"Of course! She asked about you after I brought up her daughter. She was a sweet girl. I wondered if you might get along with her."

She looked remarkably pretty like this, he noticed. She always did when her blue eyes, so much like his, sparkled with enthusiasm, and her heat-set curls, tight and perfect around her face, trembled next to her flushed, smiling cheeks. *Pretty* felt like an odd adjective to use for a forty-five-year-old woman, but it was more accurate than *beautiful* or *handsome*. She was pretty like a young girl was, fresh and young looking, despite the tiny wrinkles starting to show around her eyes. Nothing could age her in spirit, not when she was as carefree as the girl she'd grown up as, wealthy and coddled.

With her familiar face so radiantly beaming, it was easy to ignore the way she linked him hopefully with every girl of appropriate age even though she knew that he—

She *knew*.

"That's nice, Ma," he said, inwardly shaking his head at her tendency to live in the past and bother other people with it as well. "Did you get a chance to put that laundry in?"

She gasped and clutched her pink-tipped nails to her chest, her lips with their matching color of lipstick rounding into an O of guilty shock. "I forgot! Oh, dear, I'm so sorry, Charlie!"

"It's okay, Ma," he said, even though his stomach was sinking at the thought of having to trudge back out of the apartment and down to the basement where the two washing machines that still worked lived. He couldn't put it off, though, since he only had a single pair of pants left for work, now that one of them was covered in squash and garlic juice.

"You're so much better at it, anyway," she said, fussing with the blanket on her lap, avoiding his eyes purposefully or not. "I can never figure out the buttons on the new machines; they're too complicated."

"I can show you again if you don't understand them," he said, patiently. That would only make the sixth time in the year since he'd badgered the landlord into getting them replaced after handwashing everything for two months.

"I cut out some coupons, though." She flapped a hand vaguely at the rickety side table across the room, the one that was still covered in newspapers and flyers that he'd begged her to recycle a week ago. He could do it himself, but he'd asked a dozen times already so now it was the principle of the thing. He did so many other things to keep their tiny, rundown home as clean and nice as it could be. The only reason it was so livable was because he worked hard to keep the roaches out and the mold at bay, and it felt like a kick in the pants to have to fight with her to clean up a stack of weeks-old papers.

He got up with another long groan. He didn't feel like getting annoyed tonight, and if he didn't get his laundry done before his second wind wore off, he wouldn't get to it before he fell asleep, and that would spell disaster for Future Charlie.

Future Charlie would thank him dearly. It was just too bad Present Charlie felt like doing nothing but collapsing into a heap of sweat and muscle aches.

He heard Ma's voice again as he shut their front door behind him, a cracked plastic hamper on his hip, but he guiltily didn't stop.

A few years ago, he would've loved to sit in front of her legs and rant about his day—Ma was nothing if not a great listener, even if the details sometimes escaped her—but that was then. Now, he didn't have the energy to double back.

One of the washers was mercifully empty, so he was coming back through their door in only a few minutes. Tonight, the risk that his unattended darks might be stolen was worth the half hour of downtime.

He stopped on the way back to his room at the sight of Ma, already asleep in her armchair, a Harlequin romance propped open on her chest. He smiled as he covered her with a blanket from the couch, kissed her forehead, then gave a firm push to the lever that kicked the footrest out. There was a chance she might wake up and go to bed, but these days, she slept in her chair more often than not. She said it was because it was warmer, but that reason didn't hold up in the middle of summer, or even nights like this one, warming up into spring. She'd never tell him, but he thought it was probably because the bedroom was too lonely.

His last task before he went to his bedroom was skimming through the coupons she'd cut out for him. As usual, they were good deals, but for luxury items, brand names they never bought, and never would. He dropped them into the trash can beside his desk before he collapsed onto his bed, curling up on top of the covers and listening to the sound of his breathing and how it fit into the rhythm of the blood pounding in his feet.

It wasn't always like this, he reminded himself as he pressed aching eyes into the cool fabric of his sheets. Most days, he didn't notice the tiredness as much. He leaned into the numbness and the way his body did all the things it needed to do—bills, food, clothes, clean, repeat—automatically with gratitude. It was only some days that a particularly awful shift would wipe the can-do attitude right out of him and leave him an irritable, frustratingly weepy mess.

But then his next shift would be better and Donna would bring him a warm muffin from her kitchen, or he'd have a half day off and his best friend Joy would make him laugh until his stomach hurt and nothing would seem quite so bleak.

He knew the cycle. He just hated being at this end of it.

He allowed himself five minutes to wallow in self-pity before he dragged his ass up, changing into some comfortable clothes and threading a needle with black thread. There was no way he was going to suffer through another shift of that stupid button digging into his abs. The only correctly sized button he had on hand was tortoise-shell, but he shrugged off his annoyance and sewed it on quickly, pitching the black one into the old margarine container with the rest. He'd find a use for it someday.

Once he was finished his most urgent task, he had a moment of indecision. He could do something else productive, cross something off his mile-long To Clean/To Fix/To Do list. Or . . . he could use the few minutes he had before the laundry needed to be changed to do something else, something that he *wanted* to do for a change. Before he'd even finished his own thought, he was pulling the cardboard box that held his current project out from under his bed.

It was almost finished. He'd done all the hard parts on his ancient sewing machine, praying that the delicate fabric of his mother's old dress survived the punch of the dull needle. It seemed fine, as sturdy as thin, flowing polyester could get, and the result was exactly how he'd pictured it: A two-layered shirt, the top part spilling down asymmetrically, the bottom darting in to make a natural waist, then flaring out again in a peplum style.

He could see Joy wearing it, could see how the dark red in the flowers would set off her coloring. The old-fashioned print would look charmingly out-of-sync with the modern cut of the blouse. Or that was what he hoped, at least. Charlie had seen so many interviews with designers whose clothes graced runways, and they always seemed to have the perfect adjectives and metaphors to describe the stuff their models were wearing. Charlie wasn't always sure they got what they were aiming for, but it didn't matter because they were confident in how they described it. Charlie tried to do the same, but that was tough when no one read about his work in magazines.

The shirt had been sitting in the box for weeks, only waiting for a hem. He didn't know why he'd put it off for so long, considering how much he loved hand sewing. It always reminded him of how he'd gotten his start, learning from his mother's careful hand. It was one of the only practical skills she'd been able to show him because Charlie's grandmother had thought all ladies should know how to mend a tear and darn a sock.

Charlie always smiled when he remembered his younger self, ever resourceful, using strips of old jeans and cheap thread to make wristbands with the logo of his high school's most popular screamo band on them. He'd spent hours sewing instead of doing his homework, sold the things for way more than they were worth, and used the profits to buy himself a machine. Wristbands became jackets and bags and anything he could stitch tour dates on until the band had tried to go pro and made him quit being their unofficial merch supplier.

He still sold some other stuff on Etsy, but nothing ever seemed worth the time and effort. He stuck to making clothes for himself, Ma, and Joy. At least that way he'd know the work was appreciated.

He snipped off the end of the thread when he finished, then folded the delicate blouse and left it on his desk. He'd give it to Joy the next time he saw her, and until then, the sight of it whenever he looked to that side of the room would make the rest of his week seem better.

The moan that burst from his mouth as he stood up was guttural and pathetic, devolving quickly into short grunts of pain as the feeling rushed back into his legs, pricking his feet with pins and needles. They'd only just started to wear off when he made it to the basement and pitched his damp laundry into the basket for hanging.

It was in the cranky old elevator, swaying a little on his feet with boredom, that he remembered the last item on his to-do list. The business card Innes had given him was still in his wallet, waiting for him to figure out what to do with it.

If he was honest with himself, though, he already knew. He'd pretended to consider not calling, but when it came down to it, if he was actually serious about ignoring it, he would have tossed it in the trash right away.

He sat on his bed to make the call, typing the number into his two-generations-old Nokia with steady fingers. He only realized it was nine o'clock at night when the phone was already ringing, and it was too late to wonder if he would be waking anyone up.

"Hello?"

"Hi," Charlie answered, his heartbeat spiking at the sound of Innes's voice. At least it didn't sound tired or groggy, like he was being woken up. "It's Charlie Nielsen."

"Nielsen. Good to know if I ever file that police report."

"Ha ha," Charlie said, rolling his eyes, even though Innes wasn't there to see it. "You don't think I'm actually worried about that anymore, do you?"

Innes's soft laugh came over the line. "Not really, no. I'm not in the business of making more work for myself. I'm busy enough as it is."

Charlie didn't say anything, thinking of his long day of combing through job advertisements in the morning, then working at the restaurant.

"I won't lie, I'm a little surprised you called," Innes said into the awkward silence, sounding perfectly self-assured, as usual. "I wasn't sure you'd be interested."

Innes made it sound like he'd pestered Charlie into taking his number in a bar, annoying him until Charlie had had no choice but to agree to make him go away. Charlie was pretty sure Innes never ran into the problem of other people not being interested.

Well, almost never.

"Yeah," Charlie said, giving away nothing. He didn't want to appear too eager or too bored, in case either of those reactions would change Innes's mind about whatever it was he wanted. "So why did you want me to call, anyway?"

"I want to give you a job."

Charlie hadn't realized how high his hopes were, or even what he was hoping for until he heard that. He was naturally skeptical about everything, Innes's unknown offer included, but for some reason, he'd been daydreaming that it would be for something legitimate.

"What kind of job?" Charlie asked, even though he was pretty sure he already knew.

"A lucrative one."

"I already told you, I'm not interested in having sex with you, and money isn't going to change that."

"Not *that* kind of job," Innes said immediately, with a tone of impatience like Charlie was an idiot for assuming the worst.

"Well, what then?" Charlie bristled. "I'm not going to be a drug runner for you."

"A drug run— No, nothing like that." Innes sounded like he was holding back laughter, which made Charlie glad they were having the conversation by phone, so he couldn't see Charlie's flaming-red face. "It's a real job. I'd rather talk about it in person, however. I'm much better at convincing people if they can see my pretty face—"

"You made me call you so that you could tell me you don't want to talk on the phone?" Charlie stood up from his bed, walking with quick, small steps to get out his frustrated energy without waking up Ma.

"To be honest, I didn't even think you would call," Innes confessed. "I figured getting you to come back to the office today was out of the question. I'm not sure anymore, though. You must be worse off than I thought."

Charlie stopped his pacing. He wanted to argue, but he couldn't when what Innes said was true. He had his pride. He would rather someone like Innes make the correct assumption that he had no money than make himself look foolish by pretending he wasn't struggling. There was no shame in poverty, in Charlie's opinion, but he didn't want to shout his bank balance from the rooftops.

"If you want to know more, come and meet me," Innes said, more gently than Charlie had heard before that moment. "Tomorrow, in the early afternoon, if you can."

Charlie adjusted his grip on his phone, and the plastic creaked in relief. "I could come at two," he said before he could think about it too hard. That would give him enough time to get to work at the restaurant by four.

"Perfect. I'll be expecting you. You know where my office is."

Innes's obvious smirk lingered in the silence after he hung up. Charlie stared at the retro physical number pad on his phone, wondering how big the mistake he'd just made was going to be.

# Chapter Three

**M**imi liked jazz.

Or so it would appear to anyone looking at her Twitter feed, where she'd just posted the second of two videos of someone he could only assume was a popular artist within the genre.

The *improvisational jazz genre.*

Innes was well aware that taste in music wasn't genetic and that his influence certainly wasn't enough to steer her toward some crisp classic rock, or even soul, which was jazz-inspired, but better in almost every way. He also knew, deep down, that there was no such thing as objectively good or bad music, and that what a person listened to didn't necessarily reflect on them as a person.

But jazz was *awful.*

With a fortifying breath, he pressed play on the second video, hoping against hope that Mimi's "song of the day" was better than he thought it would be. He lasted a little over thirty seconds before the constant, tuneless *noodling* that the admittedly talented clarinetist was doing simply grated too much for him to withstand a single second more. He would rather die, he thought, perfectly truthful at that moment, than sit through an hour of that nonsense.

There went a future gift idea out the window. Mimi would enjoy it, he supposed, but if the whole point of buying her an experience was hinting that he'd like to be the person who used the second ticket, then this goatee-sporting, fedora-wearing idiot was definitely off the list of potentials.

"I'd say that your two o'clock is here, but you don't have a two o'clock."

Innes looked up at Marie from the screen of his phone. Her arms were folded above where she had started showing her baby bump, and her perfectly penciled eyebrow was raised. "Ah," Innes said, closing the folder on his desk he'd been pretending to read and standing up. "That would be because it wasn't in the schedule."

Her nostrils flared and her eyes went cold as the shade of blue on her fingernails. (It was called Frostbite, she'd told him yesterday, when he'd questioned whether touching up her manicure was a good use of her time. He'd regretted asking immediately.)

"And why is that?" Marie demanded. "Are you taking care of your own timetable now? Or is this a booty call that I'm supposed to ignore, even though I'm ten feet away? I thought you quit doing that when—"

"Marie," Innes interrupted, coming around the edge of his desk and ushering her out the door with a hand hovering over her upper back. "It's fine. I'm well aware of the schedule and its utmost importance."

"You're sarcasming me, but that timetable keeps your days from becoming hell on earth."

"I believe you, and will make a blood offering to the scheduling program," he said under his breath as they reached her desk. Innes could see Charlie waiting at the end of the hall, his feet shuffling beneath him but his posture rigid and straight. "Marie, take twenty would you?"

She turned so forcefully in her surprise that she sent her office chair careening into the edge of the table. "But I already—"

"Don't worry about it," he said firmly, stepping back and gesturing grandly in the direction of the hallway, which would lead to the elevators. "Take twenty."

She narrowed her eyes at him, but eventually shrugged and grabbed her wallet out of her purse, calling over her shoulder, "Fine, but don't blame me if everything's on fire when I get back."

Charlie looked disconcerted as she passed him, but he hid it quickly under a mild scowl, his dark eyebrows drawing down in a belligerent line. He started down the hallway toward Innes just as Marie turned the corner.

"Good to see you," Innes greeted, holding out a hand.

"Sure," Charlie said, returning his handshake firmly.

Innes gestured to the office behind him but didn't lead the way in just yet. "Welcome to your final interview."

Charlie narrowed his eyes much like Marie just had. "There was more than one?"

"Every word we've exchanged since the moment we met has been us evaluating each other," Innes said with a shrug. "That's true for every human interaction, really."

Charlie's mouth twisted, and Innes was willing to bet it wasn't just a weird frown, but instead hiding a half smile. "Okay, Socrates. We gonna do this, or what? I don't even know what position I'm interviewing for."

"I need a favor before I tell you anything else. Sit here." He motioned to Marie's abandoned chair. "Don't let anyone into the office."

Charlie's momentary expression of nervous surprise before the blank mask came back made him look younger than he was. Innes watched with amusement as Charlie debated with himself, probably over whether or not all of this was worth it or maybe just an elaborate joke. His poker face wasn't as good as he thought it was, but it wasn't terrible. Innes just knew exactly where to look.

"But what if it's important?" Charlie asked.

Innes shook his head, already heading for the door of his office. "Doesn't matter. If nothing is on fire, I don't want anyone to come through that door."

"Wait, you—"

"I'll be back before Marie is," Innes called just before the heavy door swung shut. He stopped moving immediately, his feet stuck firmly to the floor so as not to make any noise. Turning his ear to face the door, he listened hard for Charlie's movements.

He was thrown back in time to when he used to listen at the top of the stairs for his parents' dinner parties and his college-aged brother's dates. He'd never heard anything he wanted to hear (and had in fact, learned more about his future sister-in-law than he'd ever wanted to know) but he was confident that this time, listening at the keyhole would pay off.

Charlie didn't move for a handful of moments, then Innes heard the sound of the chair rolling into place and a tapping, probably knuckles on the desk. Charlie's constantly moving fingers at work.

Innes listened for another minute, watching the softly-ticking clock on the wall until he decided he was safe to creep to his desk. This test for Charlie was important, but Innes really did need to finish reading that file.

He was almost at the end of it when the ding of the elevator sounded, and his 2:15 appointment walked in the door. Innes knew the guy, knew he was low on patience and high on self-importance. Perfect.

As quickly as he could while still being silent, Innes crept over to the door. For a second, he considered taking his shoes off, but he wasn't a child, for all he was more excited than he'd been in days. (Since he walked in on a scrappy kid stealing from him.)

"I have an appointment," Carl said, accompanied by the thump of a briefcase hitting the desk.

"Hello, sir," Charlie greeted pointedly, cool as anything. "If you could have a seat, he'll be with you in ten minutes."

"Ten minutes? But my appointment is at quarter after."

"Yes, he's running late, so you'll just have to wait a little longer."

Charlie was not above fudging the truth to keep Carl on the other side of the door, it seemed.

"I have other things to do today," Carl blustered. "Who's in there with him now? Can you tell them to hurry up?"

"No one's with him, sir, but—"

"Well, what's making him late, then?"

Innes barely managed to keep from hissing through his teeth. That was probably a big mistake on Charlie's part. Carl had sniffed out an inconsistency and wasn't about to let it go, so it would be up to Charlie to see if he could recover the situation.

"Well, I—" Charlie stuttered, then Innes heard the near-silent intake of a steadying breath. "Mr. Kent is otherwise engaged."

Innes couldn't help but punch a fist into the air in a small but ecstatic celebration. Charlie was a better faker than he could have hoped, slipping into a stilted and formal office dialect in seconds, based only on what he'd heard in movies if Innes had to make a guess.

"Well, what if I have to leave?" Carl was saying. "I don't have the time to—"

"Your appointment time slot is until 2:45, sir, but if you require more time, then Mr. Kent will schedule another meeting."

Charlie must have looked at Marie's computer screen. Clever. The attitude wasn't going to help him, though. That might be a problem in the future, but it wasn't something Innes was in a hurry to ask him to change, if only for the entertainment value.

Carl had decided to try his own forceful brand of honey-over-vinegar. "I'm just going to pop my head in," he said, his heavy footsteps approaching the door.

Innes was very tempted to move out of the way, but he stood his ground, waiting for Charlie's response, and sure enough, he heard the sound of the desk chair being pushed back, and Charlie's voice.

"Sir, I can't allow—"

That was good enough for Innes. He opened the door just as Charlie reached it, after having placed himself between the rock and the hard-headed place.

"Carl, good to see you," Innes said over Charlie, who whipped around and stumbled back two steps before slumping slightly in relief. "Come on in. Sorry for the wait, just off the phone with a relative who doesn't understand the concept of time zones."

With a crushing handshake and a waterfall of meaningless niceties, Carl was sent into the office, leaving Charlie alone.

"Wait here," Innes told him under his breath, thoroughly enjoying the peeved set of Charlie's mouth. "Have Marie get you a cup of coffee or something when she gets back.

"I have work. I can't stay here all day." Charlie looked like he was two seconds away from stamping his foot like a child.

Innes wasn't surprised to hear that Charlie was on his way to the restaurant, given that he was wearing the same uniform of sensible shoes, boring button-up shirt, and pants that had probably been black once but had been washed into pilled gray oblivion.

"You'll be on time for work, don't worry." Innes adjusted his body so that the door could close even more, and his head was firmly outside of it. "The firm bills in six-minute increments. You'd be surprised how much can get done in six minutes when you set your mind to it."

He shut the door on Charlie's baffled and confused face and turned his—almost—complete attention to Carl for the eighteen minutes required to solve the issue. He only allowed himself to be mildly distracted by what was going on in the lobby, especially when Marie's voice floated through the door and he knew that they were out there chatting. Or plotting, more than likely. The two of them together would be a force to be reckoned with, and Innes would never be late for anything. Ever. It was a good thing Marie was headed to Oregon, or he'd end up with his bowel movements timed to the minute.

Carl didn't spare a glance at Charlie—or Marie for that matter—as he passed on his way to the elevator, but Innes had his eyes fixed firmly on him.

"Congratulations," Innes said, grinning down at Charlie, who was sitting in one of the uncomfortable chairs against the wall, a paper cup of over-brewed pod-coffee dangling from his hand between his legs. "You passed the test."

Charlie's glare held only half the heat it had the day before when he'd been cornered in the back of the restaurant. "You know, pop quizzes aren't a thing anymore."

"Are they not?"

"No. I know you haven't been in high school in a long time—"

"Not *that* long."

"A long, *long* time," Charlie continued, ignoring both Innes and Marie, who was cackling and leaning back in her chair, enjoying the show. "But these days, you get some time to prepare. If I had flunked your stupid test, it would have been your fault."

"Well, it's a good thing you didn't, then."

Charlie stood up, letting his renewed displeased stare show how much he cared for Innes's flippancy. It was impressive, really, how he managed to look down his long, thin nose, when Innes had three or four inches on him.

"Are you done?" Charlie asked through gritted teeth, the muscle in his jaw working visibly. "Can I go to work now, or are you still having your little joke?"

This guy, Innes pondered, was probably the most suspicious and defensive person he'd ever met. "What joke?" Innes asked, opening the door to his office, showing the wide and inviting interior Charlie was so familiar with. "I'm entirely serious. I apologize for springing that on you, but I wanted to see how you would do under pressure, and I got my answer."

Charlie crossed his arms. "Most people would just ask me in the interview. I've got a great story about a kid going into anaphylactic shock after forgetting he couldn't eat strawberries even if they were in a salad."

Across the room, Marie snickered, and a certain amount of tension broke. Charlie still didn't look entirely thrilled with him, but Innes had yet to see Charlie at anything higher than reluctantly pleased on a scale from one to ecstasy. It was possible that Charlie didn't experience the full range of human emotion, which would be convenient.

"Time's ticking," Innes said, jerking a thumb at his office.

Charlie glanced at his sturdy digital watch, which made his arms look even skinnier than they were, then nodded and marched past him, with a quick "Thanks for the coffee" to Marie. He helped himself to one of the big wooden chairs on the other side of Innes's desk and sat bolt straight and composed until Innes joined him.

"What are you hiring me for?" Charlie demanded.

"Marie's job," Innes said. He held up a hand when Charlie perked up like a meerkat, outrage on his face. "I'm not firing her. I'm not stupid."

"Debatable."

"You haven't gotten this job yet, you know."

Charlie fell silent.

"She's going on mat leave," he went on. "Permanently this time, landing me without an assistant. That's where you come in, if you're interested."

He waited as Charlie tapped his fingers against the arm of his chair for almost a minute before answering. "Why me? I don't know anything about being a lawyer."

Innes waved this away. "Not necessary. Any jargon you need to know, you'll pick up, but we have paralegals for anything else. What I need is someone who can keep my life straight while also minding their own business. Someone to organize my calendar for me so that I don't have to worry about it."

"Why do I feel like there's a catch? And you still haven't answered my question. Why me, out of everybody who would apply for this job?"

Innes leaned back in his chair, observing Charlie and remembering all the things that had made him decide to give Charlie his number. He'd been thinking about Charlie all week, actually, and not just because he'd looked delicious in the sickening lighting of the exit sign the last time they'd met.

He looked incredible now too. Nearly vibrating in his seat with an intensity that made his blue eyes glow with intensity. That jawline too. Attractive at rest, it was simply edible when the planes of it jutted out with tension.

That Innes had probably missed his chance to taste it did sting. He could take no for an answer—he wasn't a good person, but he wasn't *that* much of an asshole—but the thing was, he rarely got a no in the first place. Rejection wasn't something he had much practice with, so he had trouble letting go. Another shot at getting Charlie to accept a different offer would be a balm to his wounded pride.

"Marie has been here for more than two years," Innes told him. "That's the longest an assistant has ever lasted in this office before quitting. The shortest was two weeks, but the average is about six months. That's the catch, I guess. The job itself isn't rocket science. You'll be paid handsomely to keep my schedule running on time, respond to invitations, take my clothes for dry cleaning, keep away people I don't want to talk to. Basically, make my life as easy as possible by taking care of all the things that aren't directly related to my job."

One of Charlie's long, thin fingers started to circle a knob of wood in the arm of his chair. Innes doubted he even knew he was doing it. "That doesn't sound so bad," Charlie said. "Why the quick turnover rate?"

Nothing good would come from lying, Innes figured. Not with Charlie, at least. "I can be demanding, and I rarely apologize for being rude. I expect anyone who works for me to reach a level of excellence rather than just competence. I'm not friendly, I don't have the energy to spend my niceness quota on someone who's paid to be with me. For these reasons, people tend not to want to stick around." Innes pushed back in his chair, crossing a leg over his knee, putting on his most innocent face, but not expecting it to work in the slightest. "Not to mention, it's difficult to find good candidates in the first place, despite the generous salary. Surprisingly, a lot of the coddled university grads who show up for the interviews are scared of me."

Charlie snorted, his finger stilling on the chair. "You? Scary? In what universe?"

A genuine laugh percolated its way up from somewhere in Innes's chest, the same place his fascination with Charlie, professional or otherwise, seemed to live. He snapped his fingers and pointed at him.

"See, that's why you are perfect for this job. You aren't afraid of what I can do to you, you don't take shit from anyone, and you're certainly not what I would call nice. You're feisty, resourceful and not afraid to break rules if you need to. You'll stand up to me instead of running sobbing from the room the first time I lay into you for breaking the copy machine."

Charlie raised an eyebrow, emulating Marie to a shocking degree of accuracy. "Why do I get the feeling you're talking about the one who only lasted two weeks?"

Innes was having fun, but the longer the conversation went on, the more he started to worry that he was letting the perfect assistant slip through his fingers. He sat up, leaning onto the richly stained wood of his desk and staring hard across it.

"I was lying before," he said, laying more cards on the table than he normally would. "This isn't an interview. I've known that I wanted you for this job since the moment you looked me in the eye and argued with me, even though you were sure you were about to get tossed in a cell."

Charlie rolled his eyes so hard his sockets must have hurt. "Well, I wouldn't say it was ever *that* dramatic."

"No." His index finger made a satisfying bump as he brought it down on the desk between them. "You wouldn't because you've generally got a level head. A bit of a temper, sure, but you know when to rein it in."

A flash of multiple emotions went across Charlie's face, including, but not limited to intense concentration, irritation and, strangely, humor, made Innes helpless not to ask, "What are you thinking of right now?"

Charlie drummed all four of his fingers against the knot of wood, then grinned wickedly. "I'm trying to come up with an insult using the word 'reins,' but everything that comes to mind sounds dirty even in my head."

Innes's second real laugh in under two minutes burst out of his throat, painful because he'd instinctively tried to suppress it and failed. "Charlie Nielsen," he said, shaking his head. "I heard everything I needed to know in your little tutoring session. You're perfect. Do me a favor and come work here."

It was a lucky thing skepticism was such a good look on Charlie's strong features. "I don't know. It sounds like you're offering good money, but I need something permanent, not something that I won't be able to stand in six months."

"So work for me until we're sick of the sight of each other, then I'll help you get your dream job. I have connections all over this city. And if I don't currently have the right ones, I can pull the string I've tied on someone who does. I want you for this position. You'll walk away a richer man and with a good reference and a favor to call in."

Innes let the silence unspool between them, counting the ticks of the clock on the wall as Charlie thought about it, his lips pursing and unpursing as he made Innes sweat.

"Making big decisions on the fly is a dumb idea," Charlie said suddenly, standing up from the chair. "You need to give me some time."

Innes stood too, triumphant in his victory, even if Charlie hadn't realized it yet. "Do I? You're awfully presumptuous. I am on a deadline here."

Charlie headed for the door, talking over his shoulder, "Come off it. You just told me how much you *want me.* Your assistant's baby isn't going to pop out tonight. You can give me twenty-four hours to make sure this is really what *I* want."

"Fine," Innes conceded. "You have my number," he told Charlie's retreating back, feeling more like a teenager trying to find a date to prom than he ever had.

After a few minutes, Marie came in and sat in the same chair Charlie had. "I like him," she said, smiling like a cat—no, like a *tiger* who hadn't been satisfied with the cream and had eaten the entire milkman. "He's nice, but not too nice. The sugar and spice to your blackstrap molasses."

"I agree." Pointedly, he opened the brief he was supposed to have read already and looked back up at her. "Do you need something, or are you finished making me hungry?"

"I'll leave you to it." She'd only just started seriously showing, but she still groaned as she got up, her hand on her lower back. "Have fun being boring, I'm going to call that florist you hate and send your nephew some ugly congratulatory flowers in your name."

"Which nephew? And congratulations for what?"

"Aiden. Didn't you hear? He resigned."

Innes paused in his paper-shifting. "Seriously?"

"Yep. He'll finish up his cases, but after that, he's gone and not even to another practice. Rumor has it, he's giving up on practicing law entirely."

"Huh."

Once the initial shock wore off, the news wasn't actually that surprising. Aiden was a passable lawyer who got the job done, but the inherited scent for blood in the water had skipped him over. That was probably a big reason why he'd managed to reel Elliott in, while Innes was still contemplating all the many, many fish in the sea.

Shaking that labored metaphor out of his head, Innes picked up his reading, but stopped almost immediately when Marie's words caught up with him.

"He works downstairs. You still have to get it delivered?"

She turned in the doorway, smirking back at him. "Seeing his face when the delivery person comes is half the fun. They are going to be *terrible* flowers."

"Marie," he called, just before the door closed. She poked her head back in, a sour look on her face. "I'll miss you," he said quietly. He went back to his papers without waiting for her response. A few seconds later, the door shut.

He hoped the flowers were truly awful. He'd used up his quota for expressing emotion for at least the next quarter.

She moved down the sidewalk at a slow, even pace, stopping first outside a small grocery store that had an inelegant bucket full of flowers in front of it. She brushed her hand over the top of the densely packed petals, then brought her hand to her face to smell the faint fragrance. Evidently, she found it pleasing because she smiled and dragged her hand over them again before moving on.

Next, a shop window grabbed her attention, but not for long. She glided past it, looking up at the mannequins with their carefully curated outfits that, while attractive, were too high fashion for any normal person to consider buying to wear all at once.

Her own clothes ruffled in the slight breeze kicked up by the warmer April weather and her smooth progress down the wide sidewalk. The blouse, with its spray of dark red flowers, and its asymmetrical, layered style, softened her square shoulders and fell loosely around her torso.

Charlie grinned, enjoying his handiwork as Joy steered her wheelchair back to their table, braking and looking at him with a half smile.

"Was that enough for you, Mr. Armani?" Joy asked, picking up her coffee with one hand and plucking at the hem of the shirt with the other, spreading it over her lap.

"It was perfect," he assured her. "You looked like a model, or like someone glamorous in a movie."

"Ooh." She lifted her eyebrows at him a few times, then blew on her latte. "Fancy. I hope it looks as nice under fluorescent lights as it does here. I'll wear it on Monday, get tons of compliments from everyone, and brag about my fashion designer friend."

Joy worked from home as an accountant a couple of days a week, but the rest of the time, she shamelessly showed off his projects to her coworkers, then he grilled her later for their reactions.

"Are you going to get food?" Joy asked, looking through the wide window into the café at the menu board. "They have chili again, but it's so warm, I don't feel like it."

"I'll stick with coffee today, thanks," Charlie said, fiddling absently with his nearly empty cup as he avoided her eyes by scrutinizing the drape of the shirt on the line of her biceps. It was perfect, so there wasn't much to distract him from her penetrating stare.

She reached out and tapped the table, forcing him to stop pretending he couldn't see her. "No luck on another job?"

Charlie hesitated. Normally, he kept nothing from her. They'd been friends since elementary school, when the social curses of being the poor, dirty kid and the girl who got held back a grade because she'd been out of school for a year after a car accident had left them alone every recess. Thankfully, having no other friends wasn't the only thing they'd had in common, so their relationship turned into something way better than *being with you is better than being alone.*

"I'm having trouble finding something that would work with my hours at the restaurant," he decided on, truthfully. "There's nothing with a good wage that doesn't want a ton of experience or a flexible schedule." Now, that was less true.

"Seriously? Nothing?"

"Well, the other day I saw an ad for what I'm pretty sure is a cockfighting ring assistant. I mean I know 'chicken catcher' is a job that exists but in the Westside? That's shady."

"Truly."

Charlie heard the metallic echoing sound of Joy brushing a finger along one of the metal parts of the wheel of her chair. It was the only fidgeting movement she ever did. Her customary near-perfect stillness was so noticeably different from his tapping and wiggling fingers and legs that he always knew when she was thinking deeply about something.

Sure enough, moments later, she sighed, then asked, "Have you ever thought about, I don't know, *leaving the restaurant?*"

He shook his head. "I can't, it's been my—"

"Only stable gig for years, I remember." She rolled her eyes masterfully, a skill she'd instructed Charlie in over a decade ago. "But just because you've been there for a long time doesn't mean it's a good job. Yes, you make good tips, but they treat you like shit."

"Correction. Brandon and Stanley treat me like shit because I don't let them get away with being assholes. Everyone else is fine." He grimaced at Joy's unimpressed look. "And Brandon is usually joking. Mostly."

"You know, most people don't have anyone who treats them like human garbage."

"Are you sure? I feel like that's Hollywood propaganda. People deserving respect, consideration, and a fair wage from their workplace? Total socialist myth."

"Stop." Joy poked him hard in the arm, then rubbed the same spot until it stopped hurting. "You're toeing the line where sarcasm becomes too real, and I am too tired for politics today."

"But we agree on everything," he pointed out.

"With each other, yeah. Everyone else is stupid, and it takes energy to get mad."

Charlie laughed, even though he worried about her. She knew how to handle bad pain days and had canceled their Saturday morning catch-ups more than once when she knew she couldn't do it, but he couldn't turn off his concern that she'd push herself too far to make sure he was okay. He didn't tell her, though, since she had enough unwanted worry to ward off from her parents.

He managed to keep quiet for another couple of moments before the urge to talk about the job offer from Innes overpowered any thought he might have had about keeping it to himself. He didn't have to tell her about how they met, after all, only that they had.

"There is one thing," he said, going for nonchalant and probably failing. "This lawyer in Century City, a real dickhead. He wants me to be his assistant. The job is mine if I want it, but I don't know."

"Excuse me, what?" Joy said, smacking her hand down on the table. "Why didn't you start with that?"

"Well—"

She flapped her other hand in his face. "Never mind. When did this happen? How did you get an interview? Why haven't you said yes yet?"

"Uh." He started counting off her questions on his fingers. "Yesterday. Because I'm awesome, screw you."

"You know I didn't mean it like that."

"And . . . I don't know." He shrugged. "It's different. I don't know if I'd like it, and I might have to quit the restaurant."

"How different?"

He told her about the meeting with Innes, everything he'd been told about the job, the guy he'd be working for, and the pay, which he'd only recently been informed of himself. That morning, he'd woken up to a text from Innes with a ballpark number that had made him fall out of bed with alarm. He'd told Ma it was nothing, while internally freaking out.

"And you haven't smashed the Send button on your acceptance email?" Joy asked incredulously when he told her.

"Nope. I have until three o'clock today to decide."

"What's there to decide? You get an amazing hourly wage, a job that you sound perfect for, and a chance to do what you've always wanted to do at the end of it."

When she put it that way, it seemed like an easy choice. The money was good, but the chance to turn his beloved hobby into a profession was even better.

He could get a paid internship at a label, maybe. Or a recommendation to a working designer, who could tell him what he needed to do and who he needed to talk to in order to go from a nobody with an empty bank account to a somebody with a paycheck big enough to take care of both himself and Ma.

"I don't know, Joy," he said, trailing a fingernail through a drop of coffee he'd spilled on the table. "Somehow it seems like I'd be selling my soul to the devil."

"Well, that's capitalism for you," she said pragmatically. "Any time you work for someone who isn't yourself, you're a gear in the machine that fills another person's bank account."

He looked up from the star he was drawing on the glass. "I thought you didn't want to talk about politics."

"I will never not want to denounce the evils of capitalism."

"Fair enough." With a tight sigh, he leaned back in his chair, hard. "It's not just that, though. I might have . . . done something."

"Done what?"

"Uh. It's better that you don't know, actually. Plausible deniability and all that."

Her eyebrows popped. "Well, you're talking like a lawyer already, so . . ."

If looks could kill, she probably wouldn't have felt more than a tap from his glare. "I'm not going to tell you, but I did something that he could've sent me to jail for, except he didn't. Then, he hit on me. Hard."

"Was he hot?"

"Like burning, but that doesn't matter. It was super weird."

"Naturally." Eyes narrowing, she pinned him with a look that actually might have done some damage. "All that weirdness, and you're asking me whether you should do it?"

"Yeah."

"Charlie. Baby. You've already decided." After a short, stunned silence, she went on, her voice firm. "If all that happened and you're still thinking about saying yes, then pretty much nothing in the cons list is going to make you give up on this idea."

Joy let him drop the subject after that. Charlie was willing to bet it was partly because she could see that he needed to work through everything himself, and partly because her paratransit ride arrived and she had to say goodbye for another week or two.

"Whatever you decide," she said just before she wheeled herself onto the lift, "make sure it's the best choice for you, not for anyone else."

There wasn't much doubt about who she was talking about. She knew how much he took care of his mother and how long it'd been his responsibility, just as he knew all about how she wished her parents would try to take care of her less. They'd often wished they could morph their three imperfect parents into four perfect ones, each with a little more of what the other needed less of.

But life didn't work like that, so Joy had been fending off her parents' well-intentioned meddling, and Charlie had been taking on more and more of a parent's role as he got older.

Charlie headed home to get ready for work, aware of every minute that ticked closer to the deadline. On the way, he tried to imagine how he'd make the decision if he wasn't in the situation he was in. Would he say *Screw it* and take a chance that he could have his dream job or play it safe?

Then again, if he didn't have the life he had, he wouldn't have tried to steal from Innes in the first place and he wouldn't have been offered the job. Who knew if he would've discovered how much he liked making clothes if he hadn't been bored with the single rubber ball he'd owned and lacking clothes that fit his legs after his one and only major growth spurt?

What-ifs wouldn't help him. He needed to decide what his current self wanted.

He thought of the table of jerks, and Donna's warm hand on his arm.

He thought of Innes's stupid smirk and the ordered desk from which Marie commanded a one-man army.

He thought of the rush of adrenaline he'd gotten when the door of Innes's office closed, and suddenly *he* was in charge.

His phone was in his hand and he was typing out an answer before he'd reached the end of the block. He only ran into one lamppost, and by the time he got home, Innes had responded:

*Welcome aboard.*

# Chapter Four

*Four days later*

"Oh, did I already tell you about who to call if the printer starts messing up?"

Charlie flipped through nearly three days' worth of crumpled pages in his notebook until he found the section about the printing room.

"Right here," he told Marie, who was sitting next to him in an office chair with a broken arm they'd pulled out of a storage closet on Monday.

"Oh, good. What about the fire escape plan, did I explain that?"

"Uh, give me a sec. Yes, got it."

"How to reset the phone?"

"Yep."

"And how Innes likes you to hand him any papers in landscape, not portrait?"

Charlie rolled his eyes. "Sure did."

Marie smirked. "I know, that's a weird one, right? But I mean, he's paying me, he might as well tell me how he likes it."

Charlie lasted about three seconds before he snorted and tried to hide his grin behind his hand. Marie looked at him funny for only a moment before she realized what he was laughing at.

"Jeez, that did sound a little bit dirty, didn't it? 'How do you like it, Mr. Kent, esquire?'"

"Ooh, baby," Charlie said, deadpan. "Do me in *landscape orientation*."

Neither of them could hold in their giggles after that. When Marie stopped laughing, she leaned back in her chair and rubbed circles over her small baby bump, particularly noticeable today under her pencil skirt.

"That was one thing I never had to worry about, working for Innes," she said with a sigh. "I got to wear all my best low-cut tops because my boss had no interest in staring down my shirt. A few of the grosser clients did, but they never stuck around long. Now, you." She raked her eyes over Charlie from head to toe. "You have more to worry about than me. You're just his type."

Charlie scraped his hair away from his face with his fingers, looking at the desk instead of at her. "He has a type?"

"Uh-huh. Small and feisty. The last one wasn't much taller than you, and he didn't take any crap either."

"You knew his last partner?"

"'Partner' is a strong word. I knew the last guy he had on his payroll and occasionally his desk, his coffee table, and the counter of his private bathroom." Marie mercilessly ignored Charlie's blush, only smiling wider.

"Sorry, payroll?"

"Oh, yeah." Marie's eyes went significantly wide. "Innes is a busy man, you see. He doesn't have time to go chasing after one-night stands or dates to all the Kent Foundation's functions. And that's straight from him, by the way. He doesn't make much of a secret of it."

"Wow."

Charlie would've liked to say Innes didn't seem the type to pay for sex, but he absolutely seemed the type. Not that he seemed desperate, just . . . willing to throw money at things for the sake of his own convenience.

If Charlie had that kind of cash, would he do the same? Probably not, but only because of his own inability to shut off his emotions. Innes could do what he wanted with his free time and his dick, as long as he was doing it to a consenting adult. And if Marie was so nonchalant about it, Charlie didn't think he had to worry.

She didn't seem to notice his woolgathering, too busy staring wistfully into the middle distance.

"He was nice," she sighed. "I liked him. Innes bitched at me for a month after they split, and he hasn't been in the best of moods ever since. I hope, for your sake, that he finds a replacement soon."

Shifting in his perfectly comfortable chair, Charlie fought the familiar, forbidden urge to bite a fingernail. He supposed he should feel the same way, but imagining Innes finding some random guy to bone after so recently pursuing him made him feel . . . used? A little uneasy, maybe.

"I guess I shouldn't joke about that," Marie said ruefully, probably interpreting his silence as discomfort with the subject.

"No, no, it's fine."

"I'm not serious anyway. He's too classy to hit on an employee, although he might try it the second you turn in your resignation."

"What makes you think I'll resign?" Charlie challenged her, with a lot more confidence than he felt.

She shrugged easily. "It's just probability at work. I got the scoop from the receptionist one floor down: this office was like a revolving door before I got here, and only about a quarter of the people who didn't last were fired. The rest of them walked out."

"I'll just try to be like you, then."

He liked Marie. When she'd called him the day after he'd accepted the job, asking him if he could start immediately, he'd been worried that their similar assertive personalities would clash, but the last few days had been interesting and sometimes even fun, if completely exhausting. He hadn't expected to be working two jobs quite so quickly, but Marie was eager to pass him the torch.

"Innes isn't so bad," she assured him, managing to look at least ninety percent sure of what she was saying. "He isn't nice, but he's rarely cruel, as long as you do things his way most of the time and know when to pick your battles."

He nodded. "I can do that. And I won't even have to use my masculine wiles to get him to like me."

Marie snorted, then stood up, groaning and massaging her throat. "Charlie, one more thing you should know is that pregnancy is enough to make someone believe in religion."

Charlie stifled his smile. "I'm guessing it's not because of the miracle of God's creation?"

"No. It's because it's so easy to imagine that childbirth was God's punishment of woman's evil sinning ways." She gave her stomach one final pat, then checked her watch. "Did I show you how to use the laminator?"

"Oh, yeah." He already had a couple of things he wanted to bring from home, which Marie had told him was absolutely forbidden, with a wink large enough to be seen from space.

"The paper guillotine?"

"Yes, and I'm terrified of it, but I'll manage."

"Damn, we are good." She lifted her hand for a high five, which Charlie stood up to return. "I'd planned on another half day to get through everything, but I don't think you need it."

"I think I have everything I could possibly want to know in here." He patted his notebook, leaving it on the desk.

"Well, in that case." She checked her watch again. "Would you mind terribly if I left you to it?"

"Not at all." Even he could hear that his voice was half an octave higher than normal.

"I can see you panicking," she teased, but she also smiled kindly at him as she put on her cardigan and grabbed her purse from the desk drawer. "I could stick around if you want, but honestly, this is the type of job where you can only learn so much before you have to jump in the water and hope you're good at swimming and spinning three plates at the same time. I think you will be."

"Thanks." Her faith in him was a welcome confidence boost. All the million things she'd told him to remember suddenly seemed a lot more daunting than they had when he'd first heard them.

"Innes doesn't have another appointment for the rest of the day, and if he needs anything, he won't be shy to tell you. Feel free to make the space your own, too. I have things the way I like it, but it's all yours now. You have my cell phone if something goes horribly wrong."

With a final wave, she disappeared around the corner to the main entrance of the floor. He heard the sound of the elevator a few minutes later.

The hallway he now called home was never really quiet. In the last two and a half days, he'd found out he could hear the comings and goings of the other two lawyers on the floor, the paralegals who scurried back and forth between offices, the reception in the lobby, and sometimes even the faint sound of Innes on the phone or with a client.

All of that faded away with the realization that Charlie was alone and in charge for the first time. The absence of Marie's clicky heels and her no-nonsense voice explaining how he did this or that was weirdly heavy. There was no clock ticking loudly, thankfully, since it'd be a pain in the ass to have to qualify to buy a gun to shoot it off the wall.

Another ambient noise of the building was the radiator, which had developed a subtle rattle Marie had complained about multiple times.

*"I asked facilities to come and look at it two weeks ago,"* she'd said. *"Why is it even turned on, anyway, is what I'd like to know. It's April, for crying out loud."*

Charlie didn't mind it as much because it reminded him of home. The ancient furnace that belched heat up through vents in the mild Januarys of LA sounded similar, and he tuned it out easily. That was one problem already dealt with.

It was a funny thing to give him the kick in the pants he needed, but he'd take what he could get, even if what he got was a loose bolt in a radiator. With a quick, deep breath, he stood up and shook away the last of his nerves.

He could do this. Marie believed in him, Innes had taken a chance on him, and it really wasn't as scary or new as he thought. Hadn't he been taking care of his mother's business since he was twelve?

He looked around the room. *"Feel free to make it your own,"* Marie had said.

Surveying the desk, he spotted a jar of pens that was nearly tipped over on its side from the mass of cables that had taken over. Deliberately, he snatched it up and placed it in a better location, closer at hand for when he wanted to write himself a note or scribble the shape of a sleeve or a skirt so he didn't forget.

It wasn't much, he thought, smiling down at the jar, standing out as plain and serviceable among the expensive stationary, equipment, and gadgets.

For a start, though, it would do just fine.

Charlie was a very fast walker. Innes had noticed it before, but he was reminded again when Charlie opened the door only five minutes after he'd been sent on a coffee run. Had he literally run all the way there?

"That was quick," Innes pointed out, accepting the cup Charlie handed him, which was marked on the side with Innes's preferred order. He hadn't even had to tell Charlie what it was, since Charlie had memorized it after just one other trip to the café down the block.

"There was an annoying person in front of me in line," Charlie said, his voice only a little bit breathy from his pace.

"Ah." Innes sat back in his desk chair, his finger making a hollow tapping sound on the top of the cup. "Don't rush on my account."

Pausing in the act of wiping his hands with a napkin, Charlie stood straight, his eyes round with a benign innocence that made Innes want to laugh. "I wasn't rushing."

"You were. I appreciate it, but please don't bother, and definitely don't lie about it."

If Charlie was stiff before, he was positively glacial now. "I wasn't—" He stopped at Innes's quelling look and couldn't quite hold back a pout, whether he was aware of it or not. "I was just doing what you asked me to."

That was exactly what he'd done since Marie had left him to it the last few days. Innes had been expecting some growing pains, some arguments, even, when he lost his cool and snapped at Charlie for not being able to read his mind and do everything like Marie, but it hadn't happened. Innes hadn't yet figured out if that was a good thing. Seemed suspicious.

A little honesty would be the perfect icebreaker.

"Here's the thing," he began, setting the coffee on the desk, only for Charlie to pick it up and move it a foot to the side, away from the edge.

At Innes's raised eyebrows, Charlie crossed his arms, his slightly pooched lips firming into a stubborn line. "You make bigger gestures than you think when you're talking. It might get spilled, and I'd rather clean it off the desk than the carpet."

That . . . made sense, actually, but he wasn't about to praise Charlie for that level of micromanagement. Not yet at least.

"Here's the thing," he repeated, graciously leaving the to-go cup where it was. "I could get a coffee maker in here, easy. Sending you out to Starbucks is basically an excuse to get you to go for walkies so you don't lose your mind working on the consent form update list." Charlie winced, his experience with the consent form update list clearly fresh in his mind. "And so that I can make a personal call without worrying I'll be interrupted."

It wasn't a great reason, admittedly. He'd been hoping that some privacy would give him the boost he needed to call Mimi, but lo and behold, Charlie was back, and his call history did not include his daughter's number.

He wouldn't try that tactic again. Charlie would be in and out of here far too much for him to be quite that shy.

"Why didn't you tell me that before?" Charlie accused more than asked, with deep disapproval etched into the corners of his mouth.

"Because no one's ever cared enough about this job to take less than ten minutes to go all the way down the block and run back with a scalding-hot beverage in their hands." Innes let out a tight sigh, deciding not to worry about how condescending it made him sound. "To be honest, Charlie, I think you're overcompensating a little."

Eyes slitting, Charlie puffed up in indignation. "I'm trying to do a good job. I don't know anything about being an assistant, I need to—"

"Who ever said you weren't doing a good job?"

That took the wind out of his sails, and the air from his lungs, apparently, since he collapsed into himself. Innes waited a few seconds before lifting his eyebrows to prompt him.

"No one," Charlie grumbled. "Yet."

"This is me, saying the opposite." When that got him only a sideways glance of exasperation, Innes leaned in, avoiding the coffee cup by his elbow. "Charlie. You're doing a good job. And you do know things about being an assistant, actually. We haven't had a single disaster in what, four days?"

"Well..."

From the crimping of Charlie's shoulders and the regret on his face, Innes could tell he was thinking about yesterday, when Bob Morris had come from upstairs and Charlie had addressed him far too informally, considering he was a senior partner. *And you are?* was apparently not a question Bob was asked often, and never in quite so unimpressed a tone.

"Okay, then. One disaster." And a highlight of Innes's week, but he wasn't about to say that. "But it doesn't matter, does it? I'm certain it won't happen again. I bet you looked at pictures of all the partners this morning, didn't you?"

"Yeah," Charlie admitted, with the hint of a smile.

"Right. So don't worry about it. Relax." Leaning back in his chair again, he took his own advice. "And for god's sake, don't pull a muscle speed walking."

Charlie glared and huffed but said nothing else as they settled down to some business. Sitting next to each other thanks to a dragged-over guest chair, they drafted an email Charlie would flesh out and send later that day. It was the kind of time-wasting exercise that he'd be glad to let go of when Charlie had the comfort he needed to be more independent.

As it was, it took more time than Innes was used to. A lot more time, but only because Charlie asked so many questions, getting off on tangents to get more information. It was different from Marie, who preferred to do things her way and by instinct, until she was told otherwise.

Charlie's way wasn't bad. Merely different. As much as Charlie was getting used to being his assistant, Innes was getting used to having him.

"So, if this was a meeting about a donation, instead of fiscal year-end, would it need to be longer or shorter?" Charlie asked, interrupting a very simple request that could've segued into a wrap-up if Charlie wasn't so detail-oriented.

"Shorter, hopefully."

Charlie lifted a brow. "Hopefully?"

Recognizing that he wasn't going to get out of that line of questioning, Innes fortified himself with a drink of coffee and leveled with him. "Here's a not very well-kept secret: There's a reason why I'm the events guy in the Kent family, and not the one actually making the decisions and talking to the accountant. With my personal finances, I can't get out of it."

"I wouldn't have thought you'd be bad with money."

"I'm not." Innes fumbled the cup a little, disproportionately offended. "I just don't like it. That kind of talk puts me to sleep, so I hired a very talented woman to think about it, and I pay her very well."

As Innes watched, Charlie's expression sharpened, and he made another mark on his ever-present notepad. Innes read as best as he could upside down.

*Accountant—gift after tax szn, whts TOO $$$?? Look it up!!*

"So," Charlie said, punctuating his writing with a couple of harsh slashes underneath. "As few meetings as possible with your money person."

"I suppose. I do need to actually give it my attention a few times a year."

Tapping on the notepad, Charlie thumbed the end of his pen but didn't click it. "Short bursts? Instead of a couple long ones?"

"Yeah. That'd be great." While they were on a related subject . . . "And don't schedule quite so many appointments for Mondays."

Yesterday had been hectic, and Innes was still recovering. He probably would've been able to handle the same number of appointments on a Thursday totally fine, but he'd admit he was a bit of a cliché when it came to the Monday grind.

There was no note made this time, but Innes could literally see him committing the details to memory, before offended annoyance wiped the look of concentration away.

"Why isn't that in the manual?"

Innes shrugged, wondering himself. He'd have to submit an update. "It's a preference, not a rule."

"All your preferences are rules."

"I was trying to be nice and not overwhelm you at the beginning."

Sitting back in his chair, Charlie seemed to grow in confidence under the mild constructive criticism instead of wilting or getting mad. "I can handle it, I promise. You already told me you're not a nice guy to work for." He drew a little circle in the air with his pen, directed at Innes's chest. "And so far, you're not that bad. I'm a little disappointed, even."

"You want me to be meaner?"

"'Want' is a strong word. But I expected it. And I've had mean people in charge of me before, so you really can't shock me or make me run away that easy."

"Authoritarian parent?" Innes asked, mostly to see that cool exterior crack, but Charlie only let out a loud, crude laugh.

"God, no. My ma wouldn't hurt a fly. I spend a lot more time telling her things than she does for me. If it were up to her, she'd watch TV until 4 a.m. every night. I'm the one enforcing curfew, since our living room wall is basically a mirage. I'd be out there with her if I could, but sleep is a more tempting siren than reruns of *Seinfeld*. Barely."

The monologue of unnecessary information ended with a sappy smile, the softest expression Innes had seen on Charlie's face so far.

"You're close with her?" Innes found himself asking. Was it the novelty? Maybe. A mutually affectionate parental relationship? Imagine!

"Yeah. She's all I have, family-wise. I'd do anything for her."

His description was so different from everything Innes knew that it was a wonder Innes found himself thinking of his own experience with having a child. Could he really count it as *having* if he'd barely seen her since she was eight?

A few years ago, he might not have felt anything about that fact. A few months ago, even. He didn't know what had changed. Age? Loneliness? Charlie's brief but powerful influence? It didn't matter, but he felt a pang. An honest-to-god feeling, when he'd been doing a pretty good job of ignoring impulses of the kind for years.

That couldn't lead anywhere good, but oddly, he wanted to follow it.

"Anyway," he said, wiping away the topic with a gesture—a little bigger than he'd been expecting, damn it—of his coffee cup. "One more thing before we move on with the day. I've got a gala thing next month, and I'm using it as an excuse to replace one of my formal suits. I've got it narrowed down to a couple, but the details are making me go cross-eyed after staring at them for so long."

Charlie sat up so fast, his chair slid a little. "You want my opinion?"

"Sure." Amused, Innes opened his computer browser to click through the options. "Obviously, the finished product will look different with the tailoring, but you get the—"

Charlie's finger snaked over Innes's shoulder, stopping shy of the screen. "This one. Definitely."

"That was quick."

Sitting back, Charlie didn't take his eyes off the screen. "What's to debate? The other one is a little vintage, which is hot right now, but this one will make your shoulders look incredible. Is that a green tint, or is your screen color set weird?"

"It's green. A little bit. It's not too much?"

Charlie was already shaking his head. "Perfect. You can pull it off, for sure, and your eyes will go hazel in the right light. Trust me."

Innes fought a smile, and lost but valiantly kept it small. It wasn't much, but it was one of the first indications he'd had that Charlie did find him attractive. Lingering looks could have been wishful thinking, but he'd known he wasn't wrong. Nothing to be done about it now, but he did love being right.

"Okay," he drawled, looking over his shoulder at Charlie, who was turning a delicious shade of pink. "If you think so."

Bless him, Charlie ignored him, picking up his notepad and pointedly flicking to a new page. "Anything else?" His voice was a tad higher than normal, so Innes gave him some mercy.

"Give me my afternoon, and that's it. Quickly, though, since you've got a meeting to schedule."

"A short one."

Innes paused, then picked up the coffee cup, hiding his smirk behind it. "Yes."

It was an adjustment, sure, but Innes thought they were getting along quite nicely.

"Oh, thank god," Innes said when the woman sharing the elevator with him got off on the third floor. It had nothing to do with her. She'd seemed a nice lady, who was probably close to getting sole custody of her children, if his assessment was correct.

Her clothes were clean but comfortable and not new, so not used to dressing professionally. The floor she'd disembarked on housed a family law practice with a good history of winning cases. She'd also had a spring in her step and a polite not-*all*-men-are-pigs smile for him when he'd asked her to hold the door for him.

The reason for his gratitude was because he wanted more than anything to be alone for two seconds so that he could stretch his damn back in peace. He'd done a lot more sitting than usual in court today, which had turned the tiny twinge he'd been trying to kick since the tense car ride with Mimi into a full-on spasm.

He thanked whatever deity he had no business believing in that it was Friday, and he had the rest of the weekend to recover.

Groaning unattractively, Innes leaned over and reached as far to the floor as he could manage, which wasn't far. Athletic, he might be. Flexible? Not so much. It wasn't a long-term solution, by any means, but it allowed him to relax just a little bit, and if the elevator doors opened unexpectedly, he could straighten up quickly with his briefcase in hand, pretending he wasn't getting as close to yoga as he ever would.

The elevator slowed to a stop before his back could improve much at all, but he managed not to slouch past the receptionist at the front desk. He dropped his polite grimace of a smile the moment he reached beyond her sight but didn't slow his pace until he was around the corner.

Once he made it, he slammed his hand against the wall and leaned there for the space of a few slow but shallow breaths. His new posture wasn't necessarily less painful, but it at least hurt in a different way. He could pretend he was letting it get better before making his final journey, which was only maybe twenty feet to the carpeted floor in the middle of his office but could have been a mile.

Gently, he arched back, scrunching his vertebra together to see if— *There* it was, a pop loud enough that the receptionist might have heard it if she knew what she was listening for. It wasn't a cure, but he could stand up straight and walk without stooping like an old man, and that was something.

"Shit," he said under his breath. He hadn't had a day this bad in months.

Finally hearing something other than the buzzing in his ears meant that he became aware of a screeching, grinding squawk from the end of the hallway. He looked up and saw Charlie putting his entire meagre strength into pushing his desk across the room.

"What the hell are you doing?"

Charlie's head popped up, then dropped down again as he continued pushing. "I'm moving the desk."

"I can see that." Innes left the wall, hoping that Charlie had been too busy to notice his moment of weakness. "Any particular reason why?"

Charlie stopped shoving with a final heave, then shook out his hands. "Every time someone walks by, I look over. It's gonna give me neck problems if I do it for more than a week."

"Have you ever thought of *not* looking?"

"Yeah, and that totally works." Charlie's epic eye roll looked almost painful in its intensity. "Ask any teenager who was ever told not to look at porn on the internet."

"Fair enough."

Charlie returned immediately to moving things around, rearranging the computer and keyboard to exactly the position he liked. Innes supposed it made perfect sense that he would want to have things his way. Today marked a full week since the last time Marie was here to help him, and he didn't seem the type to accept things simply because that was the way they were.

Innes had been staying out of Charlie's way for the most part, and it seemed to be working, since the transition between assistants had been remarkably smooth. He decided not to mess with a good thing, tightening his grip on his briefcase and starting the last short walk to the door. The realization that the new position of the desk meant that he had to change his usual path made him pause, more of a stutter than an actual stumble.

From behind him, he heard, "The pathway is smaller."

Innes looked back at Charlie, who'd stopped again, and was gazing at him with a defiant glint in his eyes. Innes looked from the wall to the corner of the desk. Sure enough, they'd lost about two feet of space now that the desk was perpendicular to the wall.

"It's wide enough to be accessible," Charlie continued, quickly, as if to interrupt Innes before he came up with reasons why two feet less space was unacceptable. "I measured. There's room for all standard wheelchairs, though a couple of the big power ones will be a tight fit. I can move it back if there's an issue."

"No. It should be fine." Innes hadn't even considered that. Did that make him an asshole, or just unempathetic? Was Charlie particularly smart for considering accessibility, or was that something that normal humans made concessions for all the time?

Innes shook his head, clearing those questions for a time when a bottle of extra-strength painkillers wasn't screaming his name. He opened his door and was almost through it to freedom before he remembered the top item on his to-do list, which he'd probably forget about until next week if he didn't accomplish it right away.

Hanging outside of his doorway, he asked, "Have you decided what you want when you leave here? Obviously, I'm not anxious for you to go, but if you have an idea, I'd love to know so that I can make sure I save the favor of the best person for the job."

Charlie squirmed for a full ten seconds before speaking.

"Do you know anyone in the fashion industry?" He fidgeted with his cuff, looking at the worn-out fabric instead of at Innes. "I'm a designer when I can find the time. I'd take a job, or even a paid internship pretty much anywhere that can guarantee upward mobility for people who have talent."

At the end of his little speech, he looked up and glared at Innes, as if daring him to disagree.

"Wow. Really?" Maybe if Innes wasn't so tired and genuinely astonished, he might have filtered his reaction better.

Charlie's fiery temper—which Innes was learning was always a single puff of oxygen away from roaring—sprang to life.

"Why are you so surprised?" Charlie barked, a touch shy of actually shouting. "Because I'm not some effeminate gay who wears Gucci and talks about celebrities all the time? That's stereotyping. Just because I like making stuff doesn't mean I have to fit into your pigeonhole."

Innes held up a defensive hand to stop the tirade. "Cool your jets. I'm *surprised* because you look like a hobo all the time. Do what you want, I couldn't give a shit. Speaking of which, don't come to work looking like that anymore, or I'll fire you." Charlie's anger switched to panic as quickly as it had been ignited in the first place, but Innes didn't make him suffer for long. "Take the company credit card, and buy yourself some nice things."

"I can't, that's—"

"This is not charity, this is necessity. This isn't something I'm forcing you to do because I feel like it. I've been meaning to bring it up for a while. When you sit out here, you represent the firm, and you represent me. That warrants something better than a potato sack."

Charlie chewed on his lip, but eventually nodded, his hand twitching at his side.

"Good," Innes said, then he turned to leave, pausing at a twinge in his back.

"Mr. Kent."

Innes sighed and turned around yet again, ready to snap at Charlie to let him go about his day, for God's sake—

By some sleight of hand, Charlie had produced a bottle of painkillers, which he shook tantalizingly. They were even the good ones, with the muscle relaxer in them. Innes looked from the bottle to Charlie's impassive face, then reached out and took them. Charlie produced a bottle of water from one of the many drawers in his desk, warm but still sealed. Innes took that too, tucking it under the arm that was holding his briefcase.

"Thanks." It was the closest he was likely to get to an apology from Charlie for jumping down his throat about the fashion design thing, and he'd take it.

"No problem, Mr. Kent. Marie mentioned you might need them."

"You'd better call me Innes. Too many Mr. Kents around here, not to mention a Ms. or two."

"All right. Innes." Charlie looked like it had physically pained him to call Innes by his first name. "I'll work on it," he promised, then he turned back to the desk, effectively dismissing him.

Innes couldn't argue with that, not when he had a flat surface calling his name.

The sound he made when he finally made it to the carpet in front of his desk was orgasmic, and he was too far gone to care that Charlie almost certainly heard it. It hadn't quit hurting altogether, but it was a satisfying pain now, the kind that happened after a good work out or good sex.

"Damn it," he told the ceiling. Now he was thinking about sex and Charlie together.

It wouldn't normally bother him to notice in an academic sort of way that his employee was attractive. He wasn't blind or brain-dead. The problem was that this time, the person he was ogling wasn't just another boring, totally straight dude-bro who'd probably be gone after two months of being mediocre at the job. This was Charlie, who managed to be the most interesting person Innes had had the pleasure of getting to know in years, and who was also damn talented at his new job.

He'd trained up quicker than anyone else who'd held the position, including Marie. Innes saw him paging through the gigantic *What You Need to Know* binder nearly every time he passed by, but he never seemed to need to refer to it when Innes asked him a direct question. The binder was helpful, but it didn't hold the answers to life or contain the key to keeping Innes happy, and every time Innes had asked Charlie to change something or do something else more to his liking, Charlie had adapted amazingly well. He hadn't even put up a fuss when Innes had asked him to close the office door with a little less zest for life.

Only two weeks in, and already Charlie was exceeding expectations . . . and giving Innes pants-feelings he had absolutely no business having. *Ah, well*, he thought. He'd gotten bored with almost every other romantic entanglement within a couple of months, so it most likely wouldn't be an issue. (He refused to think about the single exception: his longest lasting relationship that wasn't even really a relationship. He'd paid Elliott for sex and companionship for two years before they'd combusted, and Charlie had all the personality traits that he'd liked in Elliott, with few of the ones he hadn't.)

Innes sighed, plucking his phone out of his pocket so that he could at least be productive while he was incapacitated.

He was caught up on work emails, but his older brother—sixteen years his senior, so hardly young—had called him while he was in court today, so he called him back. Boring, as usual, asking him his opinion on how to proceed with one of the many donations the family foundation made. Innes made the appropriate noises and allowed his brother to talk himself into the decision he'd already made before he'd even called.

Never let it be said that Innes did nothing for his siblings. The fact that he hadn't seen any of them outside of work in close to a year meant nothing. He cared as much—or, more accurately, as little—as he always had.

Once his brother had released him from his suffering, he stared up at his phone, which was backlit in an angelic sort of way by the light fixture above him. It looked relatively harmless for all the trouble it caused him.

The stress it was causing him that afternoon, however, was of his own making. He was being as indecisive as his brother about an issue that he would do better to get cleared up.

He snorted. As if over ten years of being an absent parent could be cleared up in a phone call.

He needed to call Mimi. She hadn't responded to the apology text he'd sent after their last fight, and while he didn't expect her to suddenly forgive all of his past transgressions, he wanted to know where they stood.

The sound of the dialing phone grated on his nerves, and he almost hung up during every pause between rings, but somehow, he made it through to voice mail, then realized he hadn't given a single thought to what he might say.

He cleared his throat. "Hi, Mimi. I hope you're doing well. I know I haven't called in a long time, but I wanted to, uh, call, I guess." *Oh, yes, great,* he thought. *Remind her of how bad you fail as a father, then say something inane. A one-two punch of excellent communication. Come on, Kent, you're a damn lawyer. Act like it.*

"I felt terrible about how our visit ended last time. You had a bad week, and I'm sure I didn't help by being an insensitive asshole." Never mind that he didn't even know how he'd pissed her off so much. "You don't have to call me back if you don't want to, but I hope you know that I care about you and I only ever want what is best for you."

He cleared his throat again, blinking up at the ceiling with its too-bright light. "You've grown into an amazing young woman. You don't need me to tell you that, and I have no right to be proud of you for it, but I wanted to say it. And I hope that next time you come to a Kent family barbecue, you'll stay long enough that I can see you too. Text me. If you want. Bye."

He closed his eyes after the screen went dark and let himself breathe. If Charlie or anyone else came in, he could always pretend it was only his back that was hurting him.

Later, at five minutes to five exactly, Charlie knocked and came in. Innes was already at his desk by then, his maudlin moment behind him but not entirely forgotten. He hadn't gotten very much work done at all, but at least the painkillers had done their job.

"What do you want for lunch on Monday?" Charlie asked, his pen and notepad at the ready.

Innes swiped a hand over his face. "Surprise me. I can't think that far in advance."

Charlie didn't look up from the note he was writing. "You have that Kidney Disease brunch Sunday at noon."

"Oh, joy."

"Do you want me to cancel for you?"

"No, it'll be fine. Not like I have anywhere to be Saturday night."

That made Charlie look up, the beginning of a frown creasing his eyebrows in the center, but he stuck to business. "Your sister-in-law called, something about the foundation—"

"Solved. She was only pestering me on behalf of my brother."

Charlie's frown got bigger. He stuffed his notepad and pen into his pocket and crossed his arms. "Everything all right?"

"Absolutely." Innes stood up, walking away from the heavy, stifling desk. "I wanted to talk to you, actually."

"Anything wrong?"

"No, no." Innes beckoned him in, waving at the chair in front of him and perching on the desk. For once, sitting up and towering over Charlie had nothing to do with intimidation techniques. All he was trying to achieve this time was an atmosphere that was different from that first interview, a full two weeks ago today. It seemed ridiculous that Charlie could be so well-integrated into his life in only a fortnight.

"How are you doing?" Innes asked when Charlie was seated, though not settled.

"With what?"

"The job. How are you finding it?"

"Fine," Charlie said, too quickly to be anything but a brush-off.

"Are you sure?" It wasn't that Innes didn't believe him. He simply wanted to pull a genuine response from Charlie that wasn't defensive and suspicious.

"Yep." Charlie's knuckles were white on his skinny knees. "Why? Is there something wrong?"

"No," he denied again. He shifted on the desk, leaning forward so that he wasn't so far away from the chair Charlie occupied. "You're doing remarkably well, actually. But at this point, people usually start having regrets. The new-job sheen starts to wear off, and they realize that I actually *am* as much of a bastard as I seemed in the interview stage. If I'd coddled them at all in the beginning, I usually would have stopped by now, and they'd have the entire weekend to question their life choices and decide if the paycheck or the line on their résumé was worth it."

"Oh." Charlie brought a hand close to his face, stopped, then dropped it again worrying his nail beds with his other hand, his gaze flicking up only briefly to Innes. "Well, the answer is still that I'm fine. I like it, actually, more than I thought I would. My friend laughed at me the other day because I told her I didn't think being in charge of a whole office would appeal to me. Then she wouldn't stop laughing long enough to tell me why she thought it was so damn funny."

Innes laughed. "Your friend is right. It's pretty ridiculous that you think being in charge isn't the thing you're best at."

"I don't consider myself to be a leader."

"You don't have the charisma to convince a whole group of people to drink your Kool-Aid, but you do care. It doesn't matter what it is, you have an opinion about everything, and you care that your opinion is taken seriously."

"Huh," Charlie said, tapping a finger thoughtfully on the back of his other hand.

Innes hadn't noticed until that second, but in the time between when he'd called Charlie in and now, Charlie had relaxed enough to bend his spine into a slight curve, leaning back into the chair in a way that almost made the giant wooden monstrosity seem comfortable. Innes supposed it might be to someone whose back didn't normally touch any chair they sat on.

The slight relaxation was a good look on Charlie. He seemed paradoxically larger, now that he wasn't tensed up and pretending to be taller than he was. His legs had fallen open a few inches, and his head was tilted to the side, emphasizing his clean jawline and stubborn chin.

"I'm tired," Charlie said, interrupting Innes's daydreaming.

The thought of how attractive Charlie would be if he was even *more* relaxed had Innes struggling to follow the non sequitur. His only response was to raise his eyebrows, allowing Charlie to do the explaining.

"I'm doing fine, but I'm tired all the time." The slouch remained, but some of the tension crept back in, primarily in the space between Charlie's dark eyebrows. "I don't think it's affecting my performance, but sometimes I feel like I could fall asleep in the middle of a conversation."

"Why is that? Too much cheese before bed?"

"I don't get much time to sleep between this job and the one at the restaurant."

The heels of Innes's shoes scraped against the wood he was leaning on with his surprise. "You still work there? Why? I would have thought that the salary for this job is more than generous."

Generous enough that Innes hadn't once worried that Charlie would return to his brief life of crime, especially considering Charlie's gaze never landed on the wall of trinkets for longer than a second.

"It is. But I don't know how long it'll last. Maybe next week I'll decide I can't stand this new gig, or you, and want to walk out the door. Three weeks doesn't seem long enough to get that reference you promised me, so I need something to fall back on. Plus, the tips don't hurt. Everything goes into my rainy-day fund. If I can save enough from this job and that one, I'll be prepared for a monsoon."

Innes supposed that made sense, but he couldn't help picturing Charlie toiling away into the night like Cinderella. "Understandable. But don't you think you deserve a bit of a break?"

Charlie shrugged. "It's only work. I've been doing it all my life."

"Working?" Didn't that make the Cinderella image even clearer?

"Surviving."

The bare, honest truth in Charlie's eyes sent a bolt of shame through Innes's center. Of course, it wasn't his fault that he'd been born into a family already wealthy for a few generations before him. Not to mention, his life hadn't been entirely sunshine and roses every second. But the realization that Innes would never know the same hardships that Charlie had already experienced before he'd reached his midtwenties made Innes's stomach flip over.

His white, upper-class guilt wouldn't fix anything, however, so he straightened up and sat down in the chair behind his desk again, stepping back from the conversation in a tangible way.

"All right, Destiny's Child," he said flippantly. "Do what you want, but don't burn yourself out. You can't work anywhere if you drop dead from exhaustion."

"Understood," Charlie said, his features organized in an expression that, to a perfect stranger, would look neutral and civil. Innes knew better.

For the first few days of Charlie's employment, Innes had been worried that he was wrong and that Charlie wasn't going to be the sarcastic, disrespectful brat Innes had thought he'd be but would turn out to be polite and completely boring.

Then he learned how to recognize the blatant, unrepentant sass Charlie was capable of exuding with a tip of his lips or a tiny lift of his brow. Inspiring, really.

"Anything else you want to talk about while you've got an ear?" Innes asked. "A question? A procedure you don't get? The recipe for that goulash you brought on Tuesday? That smelled damn good, by the way."

"I kind of thought you'd be working more," Charlie blurted.

The finger Innes hadn't realized he was tapping on the desk stopped abruptly. "More than forty hours a week?"

Charlie frowned, not at Innes in particular, but at the papers in his in-tray, and the expensive computer that he used. "I did some research before I took this job."

"Smart."

"Some websites I checked said that a lot of lawyers work seventy- or eighty-hour weeks sometimes. I know I've only been here for two weeks, but it kind of seems as if . . . I don't know, I thought you'd be busier."

Innes nodded. "It's a common thought process and one that's not entirely wrong. I am where I am because I put in the hours, but now that I have, I can relax a little bit. You'll notice that a lot of the scheduling you have to take care of is for things outside of my job. I like it that way. I take the cases that interest me, and fill up the rest of my time with work for the foundation. I take on the bulk of the social engagements so that I rarely have to deal with the practical side. Appointments with the accountants and such. No seventy-hour work weeks for me, thank you. Not for a long time."

"That must be nice."

After knowing a little more about Charlie's work ethic, and how much "surviving" he'd done, it was easy for Innes to pick out the trace of bitterness in Charlie's voice. He didn't try to deny it.

"Absolutely. I know what it's like, and I don't miss it. My nephew, Aiden, worked that much for four years until he got an ulcer and his mother made him take fewer cases."

"Ouch."

"Yeah. The lawyer thing is a bit of a tradition. Half of us have ended up here at some point or another."

"Big family?"

There might have been people in the world with more earnest eyes and open expressions, but Innes hadn't met them. When Charlie wanted to look approachable, his magnetism was off the charts, and even knowing that didn't make Innes any less susceptible.

"Yes," he found himself saying, even though he didn't normally like to talk about it. Charlie didn't seem like he was trying to pry, however, and those eyes . . . Innes was powerless. "One sister, two brothers, all of them married with multiple children."

And one daughter, but he wasn't about to tell Charlie that. Not yet, at least. Innes had a hard enough time admitting it to himself, when he knew he hadn't done enough to be called a father. Charlie seemed the type to have opinions about that, and Innes wasn't sure he'd disagree with them.

"Wow," Charlie said, unaware of the mental editing Innes was doing. "That's a lot."

"It gets worse. Now, those kids have begun to breed. I'm a great-uncle, actually. It's pretty awful."

"Wow. You must be fun at Thanksgiving."

"I will never admit to having paid a few of them to leave me alone for all of Christmas."

Innes hadn't heard much of Charlie's laugh. It was a nice one, a bit restrained, not terribly loud, but genuine. Like Charlie.

"How about you?" Innes said, recalling his manners and conversational skills. "Siblings?"

"Just me and my ma. Are you close with yours?"

Innes recognized a change of subject when he heard one. Part of him wanted to push, but the rest of him that was tired and ready for the weekend refused.

"My family? Not really. Never had much of a chance." He almost stopped there. He wished he could have stopped there, but the combination of Charlie's encouraging look and the realization that he hadn't ever actually said any of this out loud was a heady mix when he was already brain-dead from his back spasm and his call to Mimi. "They're quite a bit older than me, you see. All of them were off to college by the time I could hold an intelligent conversation. They always seemed to be a few milestones too far ahead for us to relate to each other."

"That's too bad."

"It is what it is." He tilted his head consideringly. "My parents are dead."

"I'm sorry."

"Are you? That's nice. I try to be." He ignored the way Charlie's eyes widened in surprise. "We get along nicely this way. Their memories are better at returning my calls."

Charlie didn't appear to know what to say to that. Perhaps he was adjusting his worldview to account for people like Innes, whose parents were no more than people who lived in the same house as him for eighteen years. Or maybe he already knew what that felt like, and he was holding back a platitude that he knew meant nothing. Charlie never had said what happened to Daddy Nielsen.

"Well," Innes said, standing up and unplugging his phone from the charger on his desk. Charlie watched him until he'd walked all the way across the room before standing up as well, approaching the door Innes held open for him. "That was enough share and care for one day. Get out before I tell you all about how the kids laughed and called me names at my first dance recital. It was a horrifically scarring experience, and you'd never be able to be mean to me again."

Charlie rolled his eyes as he passed. "That'd be a tragedy."

"Enjoy your weekend," Innes called through the open door.

"Not much of a weekend when you work two twelve-hour shifts in a row," Charlie said wryly as he packed up his messenger bag, stuffed with who even knew what.

"Fine. I'll amend that to: don't collapse from exhaustion this weekend. See you Monday."

He should have closed the door, then. He was going to, but then Charlie reached a little farther across the desk than before, tilting forward so that his ass drew Innes's eyes immediately.

Under thin, well-fitted slacks, it was easy to see that it wasn't generous by any means, but it looked tight. Firm. The muscle would give delightfully if Innes got his hands on it and squeezed—

Charlie turned around, and Innes's gaze took a little too long to snap back to his face.

Oh, shit. Totally caught.

It could've been awkward. He didn't make a habit of lusting after his employees for a very good reason, and that was because it put both of them in a weird position. But as always, Charlie surprised him.

Instead of a pointed glare or a discomfited grimace, Charlie tossed him a smirk. A wicked one.

One of his hips cocked to the side as he slung his bag over his shoulder. "Don't you have work to be doing?"

"Nothing I can't put off for a minute."

Charlie's dark eyebrows climbed. "A whole minute, hm?"

"If the distraction is good enough." He shrugged, beyond embarrassment, too busy being intrigued.

"Nice to know." With one last hitch of his bag on his shoulder, Charlie nodded and headed down the hall.

Innes watched him go, then regretfully closed his door on the best view of his day. Work really was calling him.

He checked his phone one last time before taking his seat. Nothing from Mimi yet, but that wasn't a surprise. It was still early enough in the day that he could pretend she was in class. That excuse wouldn't last all weekend, however, and he didn't look forward to obsessing over it.

A text came in as he was looking at the screen. His chest clenched, but it was Charlie. *Kidney disease brunch on Sunday,* it read. *Don't forget.*

Strange, Innes thought as he looked around his lavish, empty office. Charlie seemed to make the room smaller.

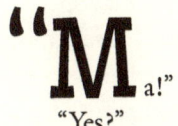

# Chapter Five

"**M**a!"

"Yes?"

"Have you seen my socks?" Charlie dumped the contents of the laundry basket he'd been holding onto his bed, then started tossing socks over his shoulders.

"What?"

"My socks!" He winced at his own volume. He hated to be *that neighbor* at such an early hour, but this was important. "The fancy ones, you know?"

"What?"

Charlie sighed and quit pawing through the sea of black and gray on his bedspread. There was no way the pair he was looking for would be among them. When he'd taken the firm's credit card, as Innes had instructed, and taken himself shopping, he hadn't let himself go crazy. He'd chosen the top end of department store clothing, rather than the bottom end of something more customized and pricey. He knew his body type, how to work it, and which fabrics and fashions would last the longest.

His one extravagance had been four pairs of silk-blend socks, soft as butter and black as night. They had cost so much that he was intensely aware of each pair and their location, which was always either in his drawer ready for wearing, in his hamper ready for washing, or in the case of the last clean pair he had left, draped gently on his shoes ready for walking out the door.

Or so he'd thought.

"Ma, have you seen them?" Charlie asked when he got to the living room.

She blinked up at him from her chair, two wayward Velcro rollers in her hair. "Seen what?"

He reached over and gently unraveled the rollers. "My socks, Ma. They were on my shoes. Did you move them?"

"Um." She thought about it, twisting one of the new curls around her finger, fixing it just so, as if someone other than her and Charlie were likely to see them. *Seclusion is no excuse for poor grooming, honey,* she always told him on his rare lazy pajama days, in that special tone of voice that told him she was quoting the posh conservative grandmother he'd never met.

"Any idea at all," he urged. "I really have to leave, so if you don't know where they are, I'll go without them." And be uncomfortably aware all day of the scrubby cotton of his old socks.

*How quickly luxury becomes necessity,* he thought.

"Oh, I remember," she said brightly. "There were some socks over there, and I thought they must be mine, so I threw them in with my laundry last night."

"Nooo, Ma, why would you—" He cut himself off. There was no use asking why she could never remember his system—black and gray socks for him, white socks for her, so they didn't get mixed up—because he already knew the answer: remembering things wasn't something she was good at. "Never mind, I have to go."

"Already?" she asked as he ran around the small apartment like an abnormally efficient headless chicken.

"Yep." He slung his lunch cooler to the floor and sat down next to it, shoving his feet into the awful, scratchy socks. "It's been three weeks of this, remember?"

"Has it been that long?" She reached out and patted his head as he tied his shoes. "Good for you, darling. What is it that you do at the doctor's office?"

"It's a lawyer's office, and I—" He stood up, hitching his messenger bag back onto his shoulder. He kissed her cheek. "I'm sorry, I gotta go."

"All right."

He was almost out the door when her voice drifted from the living room. "Your father would be so proud of you."

He stopped in his tracks, the hand he'd braced on the doorjamb curling into a fist. He said nothing. It was better to pretend he hadn't heard than to get into that old anger when he was already running late.

The moment the elevator doors at the office opened to Innes's floor, he was turning sideways to fit through them, power walking down the empty entrance hall and all but jumping into his chair, sending it rolling a few feet.

It was still spinning when Innes's door opened, startling Charlie into typing his password wrong on his keyboard. Innes almost never showed up a moment before he had to.

"I'm not late," he told Innes, whose arms were crossed over his chest like a disapproving parent.

"No, you're not. You are, in fact—" he checked his watch "—twenty minutes early. A slight downgrade from your usual twenty-five."

Charlie stopped typing in the right password, surprise stilling his fingers for just a moment. His schedule wasn't a secret, but why did Innes care? "Yep."

"Remember what I said about not burning yourself out?"

His busy fingers switched to the button of his mouse. "Yes, but this doesn't count."

"Why not?"

"This is part of my job."

A knock of knuckles on his desk made him look up to Innes. His arms were still crossed, and his face no longer pleasantly bland but somber and on the verge of annoyed.

"No. It's not," Innes said. "You know I never have appointments at nine in the morning because *you* make them, and you are well aware that I can't talk to people that early. You're always completely caught up with voice mails by nine thirty. Why do you insist on getting here so goddamn early?"

"Well, what if there was more traffic on my way here?" It was only logical. The earlier he left home, the less likely it was that he'd ever break his perfect record.

"Then you'd be late. Big deal!" Innes did the closest thing to dramatic jazz hands that he'd ever do. "The next day, you wouldn't be. And do *not* pretend that you wouldn't stay late to make up the time, even if there was nothing to do."

He didn't try to deny it. It was a fair call, and he was a crappy liar anyway. He stayed stubbornly silent, hoping that Innes would let it go, but not really expecting that to be the case.

"Look, Charlie boy," Innes said, leaning over on the desk.

"Don't call me that."

He squinted. "You sure? Fine, then. Charles?"

"Ew, no."

"What about Chucky, can I call you that?"

Charlie's grip tightened on the arm of his chair. "Not if you want to live."

Innes pressed a hand to his chest, acting wounded. "Harsh. But fair." The hand went back to the desk, his sturdy fingers drumming a pattern on the desk, drawing Charlie's attention to how clean and well-trimmed they were, and how strong they looked. "We've completely left the topic."

Charlie nodded. "Absolutely. The topic was Seattle. This—" he waved a finger between them "—is Las Vegas. Does that mean we can stop talking about it and go back to work?"

Innes's answering smile was wide and infectious. "No, I remember where I was going with it. The thing is, I am selfish enough to want to keep you as long as I can. Getting a new assistant is annoying, and getting a good one is difficult."

Charlie tamped down the warm and fuzzy feelings he got from Innes's approval. He wasn't a kid, he didn't need a pat on the head to know he was doing something well, but he couldn't help but appreciate the confirmation. It was an intoxicating feeling, especially combined with the way Innes was surging into his space. Not crowding him, but getting closer than he normally did, close enough that Charlie could see the individual flecks of encroaching silver in his hair, subtle, yet noticeable against the dark brown.

"I can't tell you what to do when you leave this office," Innes continued, seemingly oblivious to Charlie's struggle to keep his gaze on Innes's eyes at this distance. "If you want to work yourself into a coma, fine. I might not like it, but there's not much I can do about it. What I *can* do is make sure you don't work too hard while you're here."

Breaking out of his embarrassing stupor, Charlie narrowed his eyes. "How?"

"I don't want to see you here any earlier than five minutes to nine." Innes straightened up, tugging at his cuffs nonchalantly. "Also, your half hour paid lunch is now an hour."

Later, Charlie would deny that he nearly fell out of his chair. "No. Absolutely not, I'd never get any work done."

"That is a bald-faced lie and you know it. It might mean you'll have to cut down on the completely unnecessary dusting I *know* you do."

"The cleaning service only does it once every two weeks; it's barbaric."

Innes was obviously enjoying himself. A smile tugged at his lips, but he managed to keep it more or less in check as he pointed to his expression. "You see this face?" he said. "This is my Go Cry About It Face. No more than five minutes. One hour for lunch."

The tone of his voice was so final that Charlie jumped out of his chair, nearly knocking over his cup of pens in his outrage. "Come on, fifteen minutes at least. And how about forty minutes for lunch?"

"Nope." Innes crossed his arms again, not even attempting to hide his smirk anymore.

"Fifteen minutes and forty-five."

"No deal."

"Ten minutes and forty-five, and I won't dust anymore."

"Done." Innes's smirk had turned into an all-out grin. "And before you think about trying to hide the fact that you're coming in earlier than ten minutes, just know that I have access to a list of who entered the building and when. If I catch you in here at quarter to nine a single time, I will personally have your key card deactivated, so you'll have to enter the building when I do."

Charlie could feel how wide his eyes had gotten. "No."

"At 8:58."

"You bastard."

Next to him, the phone started to ring, and he reached for it automatically.

"Don't answer that," Innes commanded.

A strangled, aggravated noise escaped him. "Why not?"

"The office opens at nine, not a minute before that."

Charlie collapsed back into his chair, exhausted before he'd even begun to work. "Why are you doing this? I thought you'd be happy that I'm trying to be a good employee," he railed at Innes's retreating back.

Innes turned around, his amusement gone and something like sympathy on his face instead. "You are a good employee. That's why I'm doing this. I know you don't see it as a reward, and that's okay because it isn't one. It's purely self-serving."

With that, Innes left without waiting for a response, leaving his office door wide open.

Slumping down in his chair, Charlie felt the minutes stretching out before he could do any work.

Fine, then. He pulled out his phone. *If he wants me to slack off, I'll do it.*

Joy would probably be at work, but if she got a minute, she'd check her phone.

*My boss is being an asshole,* he texted her. No reply came right away, which left him with way too much time to think about Innes. And the suit he was wearing this morning.

It was a good one. Modern, a lighter gray than usual, with the subtlest pinstripe possible, and a collar that made his shoulders broader than a mountainside.

*A hot one tho,* he added to the text. *Jesus take the wheel, he looks edible today.*

He'd get teased for that later, but if he was going to bug Joy at work, the least he could do was give her something to poke at him about.

He sent a tongue emoji for good measure.

When he next looked, the clock had only moved by a minute, and a notification had popped up in the corner of his screen, telling him he had new emails waiting for him. Maybe, if he was really quiet, he could—

The phone rang again. Charlie almost picked it up out of habit before Innes's voice came out of his open office door.

"Don't answer that."

Charlie failed to hold back another tortured sound.

"Then it's just a matter of combining the two files. You hit Merge and click Done—"

"Oh, *there* it is." Charlie followed Marie's directions quicker than she could actually say them, eliminating the second Mr. Ranveer Sahni from the client file system. How it had gotten there in the first place was beyond him, but at least now he knew how to fix it. "That was easy. God, I feel dumb now."

Her laughter echoed down the phone line. "No problem. It's one of those things. You only have to do it a few times a year, so it's easy to forget in between."

"Good thing I have you to help me, then."

"Sure is. To be honest, I'm surprised I haven't heard from you more often."

He twisted the cord of the phone absently in his hand. "Are you, now? Should I be offended?"

"Oh, you know that's not what I mean. You're amazing, but there's a lot to learn in the first month of any job. Not hearing from you means that you're handling everything better than expected."

"Well, I try. Most things I can ask the internet about if I can't figure it out myself. Thanks to Google, I have mastered spreadsheets so hard." He spun around in his chair until the cord stopped him. "I didn't want to bother you too much, with the move and everything. How's the job search coming?"

"It sucks, but at least we have a place to live now." There was a clatter on her end, then the sound of distant whining. Marie went silent for a long moment, then sighed. "Oh, lord, that sounded bad."

"Any broken bones?"

"Probably not. It would be way louder. The lamp in the living room, however, might not have survived."

"Yikes."

She groaned. "Sorry, I have to go. Things are way too quiet in there."

"Don't worry about it. Mondays are always crazy, no matter which state you live in."

"Oh, before I forget, did you remember to buy a birthday gift for Mimi this month? I hope you used the personal card, not the business one, and—"

"Wait," he said, his chair clunking into the upright position. "Who's Mimi?"

The silence that followed was surely just as tense as the one Marie was hearing from her kids. "Um," she hedged, sounding more tentative than he'd ever heard her. "I don't know if it's my place to talk about it. It's a bit of a sensitive topic. You could ask Innes about it, but it would be easier to just trust me and not bring it up."

"So," he said, drawing it out and gripping the phone tighter to his ear. "A mystery person who I have to buy a gift for, hoping that they like it, even though I've never met them and have no idea what they might want or need."

"Essentially. Christmas too, if you last that long. And maybe a special occasion not otherwise specified, but only if Innes requests it. I put the date and a reminder in the calendar ad infinitum.

Off in the distance on Marie's end, someone had started crying. Hopefully one of the kids and not her husband.

"Oh, crap," she said. "I really have to go. But call again if you need it!"

"Thanks for the heads-up."

"My pleasure. *Micah*, I swear to *God*, if this is about the earthworms again, I will—"

Charlie would never know the end of Marie's threat, but he prayed for Micah's sake that the earthworms were not involved in the current crisis.

He set the phone back into its cradle and clicked to Innes's calendar. He had stared at the program every weekday for three weeks, checking and rechecking the daily, weekly, and upcoming schedule. He wondered how he could possibly have missed an unexplained entry, but sure enough, he clicked through to the next week, and there it was. Next Tuesday. A recurring event color-coded gray, which was probably why he hadn't seen it. He'd assigned every shade of blue there was on offer, but nothing he entered in was ever gray.

"Great," he said, then he sighed long and loud, tapping his fingers restlessly next to the mouse. He now had—he checked the calendar again—five and a half business days to choose, purchase, and mail a gift to a person he knew nothing about. That was just so awesome, and exactly what he needed on the day he hadn't worn his nice socks to work.

"It's fine," he told himself, exiting the calendar with a little more force than necessary, then shaking out the tension in his fingers. He had once created a prom dress, from pattern to final product, with only a pair of dull scissors, eight yards of taffeta and a needle and thread. If he could do that, *and* manage to raise his asking price by two hundred bucks on the night of the dance, then he could do anything.

All he needed was more information. According to the date of birth Marie—or one of the previous assistants at least—had left in the calendar entry's notes, the mysterious Mimi was turning nineteen. That made his list of potential gifts much shorter but didn't help much in the way of logistics or personality. The next step was finding out as much as possible with the resources he had available.

Casting his mind back, he remembered that this wasn't the first time he'd heard the name in the context of the Kent, Kent & Morris Law office. There was a file in the drawer of receipts labeled Mimi, as well as an entry in Innes's electronic contact log. He'd noticed both because neither of them had a last name attached, and his completionist brain had had trouble handling it.

He scrolled through the long list of clients, connections, and camouflaged booty calls—as if anyone would be fooled by an entry labeled *Jason McCheeks*, especially when it was accompanied by a winky face Charlie had been forbidden to remove—until he got to the *M* section. He let out a small whoop when he noticed that the address field was filled out, along with an Active Through date that hadn't passed.

"Nice," he told himself, copying the information for later.

His last step was the pile of receipts. He'd have to go through them in more detail when he had a better idea of his shortlist to make sure there was no repeat gifts, but the collection of items didn't give him much help. They spanned a huge range, from concert tickets, to electronics, to home decor, to restaurant gift cards. (He was totally judging the Ghost of Assistants Past who copped out with a hundred-dollar certificate to Chili's.)

Charlie leaned back in his chair, watching the clock tick down to when Innes would be back in the office from court. He had other things to get done today—though he needed to cross *dusting the back of the computer monitor* off his to-do list since he was sure that Innes would somehow *know*—and he shouldn't spend too much time on this one task that would likely mean little in the long run.

He shouldn't. But the same part of his brain that made him redo a wonky seam on a project, even though no one would ever see it, made him want to do this right. He couldn't send some impersonal brush-off gift. He simply *couldn't*. But without a clue who this person was or even a last name he could use to stalk them on social media, he didn't have a hope in hell of picking something that would be appreciated more than a boring wall hanging with a cheesy quote on it.

There was nothing for it. His self-preservation instincts that were telling him to follow Marie's advice and leave it alone were being completely overpowered by his reputation as Best Personal Assistant Ever.

Who cared if that reputation was only known to himself and his boss?

Innes liked to think he was pretty good at reading people in general, but when it came to Charlie, he was past simply being an expert. He was approaching PhD-level knowledge in how to predict his actions based on body language alone.

When Innes got back to the office Monday afternoon, Charlie didn't give his usual lazy wave of acknowledgment that meant *all systems normal*, nor did he nod curtly in a way that typically indicated a busier day than expected but nothing to panic about yet.

This time, he sat up straight in his chair, widened his eyes at his computer screen and pointedly did not look over at him. It made him resemble a particularly caffeinated prairie dog.

Innes almost turned around right there and went back to the courthouse. That look generally meant that Charlie had something that couldn't wait, a time-sensitive, often terrible task that needed to be done before the end of the day, and damned if Charlie was even going to let Innes take a bathroom break before it was crossed off the sacred To-Do List.

Instead, Innes walked faster into his office and shut the door right away. There was no avoiding Charlie's efficiency when he was in that mood, but at least this way, Innes could be sitting down and comfortable before the interrogation started.

He watched the ball bounce around on his screen saver while he waited for Charlie to decide he'd had enough time to regroup. As he watched it pinging every which way, missing the corner of the screen each time, he cast his mind back to the days before Charlie, and before Marie, for that matter, when he used to run his own life, free to do anything or talk to anyone he wanted without worrying what the repercussions would be if he was late.

It might have been fun to mess with the assistants who couldn't grow a spine and tell him he needed to be somewhere rather than politely suggesting it, but it sure was easier to function like an adult when he knew he couldn't get away with that kind of bullshit. He was way more productive when he wasn't plotting how to get out of his next appointment.

Charlie's knock was more of a warning before he entered regardless of permission than a request for entry. He didn't seem to check much more than whether Innes was alive and conscious before he was launching into his round-up.

"You've got a three o'clock and a four o'clock. Three o'clock should be easy, it's their second time working with the firm, so they know the drill. You didn't represent them, though, Bob Morris did. No indication for the switch, but it's probably due to your specialities."

"All right, I won't pretend I recognize them, then."

"Best not to. You hungry? I can get Thai if you need it."

Innes rubbed his stomach, which the salad he'd choked down from the deli around the street from the courthouse was doing a poor job filling up. "Probably shouldn't."

Innes could see him filing that piece of information away for later. If he was lucky, that would mean Charlie would call up the personal trainer who'd been on hiatus for months. Unlucky would mean he'd be seeing a lot more salad in his future, and Charlie would stop asking if he wanted noodles for lunch.

Charlie continued, "I spoke to your sister-in-law—"

"Which one?"

"Catherine." Charlie's eyes narrowed at being interrupted, but he didn't dwell on it, which was a sign of how important whatever was eating at him was. "It's your great-aunt Jocelyn's birthday."

"Jesus Christ, is she still alive?"

"Catherine put your name on the card for a spa day in Pasadena."

"She should tell them to be careful they don't lose her in the mud bath; she's even shorter than you are, and weighs half as much."

"Messages are all returned, emails are answered or queued for tomorrow, also, who is Mimi?"

Innes blinked at the strange sound of that name in someone else's voice.

A week ago, he'd given up trying to think of some amazing gift idea that would change everything and decided to do what he always did: let his assistant handle it, then kicked himself for being too chicken-shit to pick something.

Somehow, it always happened without him. He couldn't remember exactly how, but he'd made enough of an impression on the first assistant who'd nearly missed Mimi's birthday that no matter how long the current one stayed, they knew to tell the next in line about that special day in May, without knowing that Innes's indecision was just as regularly scheduled an occurrence.

"I'm not sure that's any of your business," Innes said, quiet enough that Charlie leaned in to hear him before immediately bristling.

"It is if I'm the one picking out a gift for them."

Innes fisted his hand on the arm of his chair. "What more could you possibly need to know? You have the address, I assume. Age. A credit card. Pick something and send it."

"It's not as simple as that."

"Why not? It's not your business." For the first time since the beginning of his employment, Innes was starting to seriously regret that he'd picked the guy with a stubborn streak wider than the state of Texas.

"You made it my business when you put this in my hands," Charlie said, his chin tilting in the telltale sign that he was digging in his heels for the long run.

Innes scoffed. "And you're suddenly ticked off that you have to handle my menial tasks? In case you haven't noticed, that's your job."

"Yes, it is. And I'm damn good at it. But I can't complete any task to the best of my ability if I don't have all the information. I have no idea who this person is. They could be your secret baby mama, for all I know. What if I sent something offensive, like a multi-window picture frame with 'family' on it in big cursive letters—"

"Stop that thought right now," Innes said, barely keeping himself from leaping out of his chair to cover Charlie's mouth. He sighed, leaning his forehead on his hands.

He'd lost this argument before it had even started. He'd known what Charlie's rebuttals were going to be before he'd said them because they were all great points. A logical conclusion would be that Innes should have told every assistant he'd had as much as he could.

Clever. Reasonable. Awful.

Jamming his hand through his hair, he took a bracing breath. There were worse things in the world than having to talk about one of his most closely guarded insecurities.

"I'll tell you what you need to know and nothing more," he said through gritted teeth. "Don't expect an essay or a tender heart-to-heart."

"Wouldn't dream of it. You might get some feelings on me," Charlie snarked back, as if he hadn't somehow hypnotized Innes into talking about his parents a week or two before.

"Fine. First of all, Mimi is my daughter." He paused, giving Charlie time to go absolutely still in surprise, then recover with admirable speed. "No, I am not married, nor have I ever been married. You could say we're estranged, but that is the only thing I'll ever hear you say about it. No speculation, no wondering out loud to anyone, even people in this office. You can do the math or make guesses in your head all you want, but keep it there, or you're out. No reference, no two weeks' notice, nothing."

"Understood."

His little speech had been a knee-jerk reaction, the lawyer in him covering all his bases, but there was no part of him that thought for a second that it would be a problem. The grave but neutral look in Charlie's eyes was a bonus promise that nothing of their conversation would leave the room, but he hadn't really needed it to be confident.

"Okay," he said, leaning back in his chair now that the important bit was done, leaving only the icky share-and-care portion. "You're going to ask the questions since I have no idea where to start."

Charlie pulled out his notebook, flipping to the right page. "She's turning nineteen. Does that mean she's a student?"

"Yes."

Charlie had already gotten a pen out and had it poised on the paper, but when Innes stubbornly said nothing else, he looked up, his entire face arranged in an obvious, unimpressed *really?*

When Innes only blinked innocently, Charlie followed up with, "And? Where does she go to school? Does she like it?"

"Stanford."

"Nice."

"Yes. She got a good scholarship too." This part, at least, was fairly easy. It was no great hardship to share one of the things he was most proud of. "With no help from the Kent name to make her seem more impressive. Can't say that about all the nieces and nephews. To answer your other question, yes, I think she likes it. At least as much as any student likes being broke, stressed, and tired all the time."

Charlie paused and looked up from the notebook with a crease of confusion in his forehead. "Is that what college is like?"

"For most people, yes."

"Huh. Kind of makes me glad I didn't go."

"It's a lot more fun than it sounds." Or at least, it had been when Innes had been an undergrad, free from the disapproval of his parents, the indifference of his siblings, and the responsibilities of young-absent-fatherhood for weeks at a time. The stress of getting papers done had seemed like nothing compared to the thought of having to see Theresa any time he wanted to visit his baby daughter.

"I'll take your word for it," Charlie decided. "What's her major?"

"Undeclared, but probably political science." She was resisting the pull toward pre-law tooth and nail, but according to his sister, she was born for prosecution, if their friendly argument over who stole the last roast potato at Christmas dinner was anything to go by. Innes could only imagine how her mother felt about that.

Charlie hesitated before the next question, fiddling with his pen before tapping it decisively against the paper. "What surname should I put on the package?"

"Greenlaw. Though I can't imagine there will be many Mimis in her building."

Charlie's lip twitched with a smile. "You never know. Is that a nickname?"

"Yes, but don't put her full name on the card, or you'll get the package mailed back with itching powder sprinkled liberally through the whole thing." At Charlie's startled look, Innes smiled. The details were coming out a little quicker now, and this was a fun one for him. "The name on her birth certificate is Miriam. She hates it, almost as much as her mother hates the name Mimi. I think she switched to that one when she was eight years old just because her mother made such a fuss about it. She's contrary like that."

Charlie got as far as opening his mouth to make a comment, likely something about her taking after him, but he obviously thought better of it, diverting at the last moment to the rest of his list.

"What's her usual style?"

That one gave him a little trouble. "Comfortable," he decided. "Casual. I've never seen her wear a dress or high heels, even for special occasions."

"Favorite TV show?"

"Magic School Bus."

That made the eyebrow go up.

Innes shrugged. "Or at least it was the last time I asked. No doubt it's changed by now."

Charlie looked at him for a long couple of seconds, smooth, bland interest wrinkling up into distinctly curious concern. Innes started to get hot under his necktie immediately, but he'd already shared too much. He couldn't threaten to fire him again if he didn't stop making that face because that would only make him look like he cared. Then Charlie would feel bad for him, and being pitied was far, far worse than anything else people might think about him.

After a short stare-down, Charlie was the first to break the silence, his voice firming into his most professional tone. "Shirt size?"

Innes frowned, pulling at his collar. "Medium, maybe? Smaller than Marie in the . . . chest area." He suppressed a shudder. He didn't make a habit of noticing the torsos of women, and even less so his own daughter's.

"Got it." Charlie clicked his pen and tapped it a couple of times on the notepad before stuffing them both into the pockets of the new, slim-legged pants that Innes had been admiring since they'd first appeared last week. "Anything else you want to mention before I put in an order?"

"Use the—"

"Personal card, not the business one, I know." The *you idiot* went unspoken.

"That's it, then."

As soon as Charlie headed for the door, Innes reached for the phone on the corner of his desk, intending to call his favorite Thai place. He *needed* it, and Charlie would only disapprove loudly now that he knew Innes wanted to watch his diet a little more.

Innes hissed in pain as his back spasmed the moment he sat up. Charlie turned around immediately, then wordlessly went to the attached bathroom for some painkillers.

"It's not that bad," Innes tried to tell him. "Just a twinge. It'll go away if I walk around for a minute."

"Sure," Charlie said wryly as he returned, the jar of pills and a bottle of water in hand. Instead of leaving after Innes took them, however, he perched on Innes's side of the desk, his slim thigh only a few inches from the arm of Innes's chair. "You know, you really should go to the chiropractor or something."

Innes had to swallow quickly to respond. "Chiropractors are pseudo-science nutjobs."

He sighed but still didn't get up. "Fine. Go to a doctor, then."

It took all of Innes's strength not to grumble like a cranky child. "I did."

That earned him a look of equal parts suspicious and surprised. "When?"

"When I was twenty-five."

"So, over ten years ago." Charlie crossed his arms, using his small height advantage to condescend aggressively at him. "And what did they tell you?"

"To stop working out so hard and to come back in six months for a follow-up."

Charlie's head fell into his palm. "And did you do either of those things?"

"No."

"And is there anything I could possibly say to change your mind?"

For the first time in what felt like hours, Innes gave in to his urge to grin. "No."

For his cheekiness, he was rewarded with the ghost of an indulgent smile on Charlie's thin lips, and the rush of a job well done gave him the motivation he needed to stand up, to try to stretch out a little.

Except that Charlie was motivated to stand at the exact same time.

In the small space between the desk and the chair, Charlie and Innes slapped into each other from chest to knee, a wall of warmth that lasted only a split second. Charlie stumbled back, but he didn't go far, steadied by Innes's hands on his elbows.

It was nice to look down at someone for once. Maybe, if Charlie had been taller than him, Innes wouldn't have had the same view of Charlie's tongue darting out to wet his, or his eyes going wide with long lashes fanned. Taller or shorter, Innes only knew that he wanted to have this view around for a while, and keep the bend of Charlie's elbow in his palms for longer.

But he couldn't get anything he wanted.

Charlie jumped back, one hand adjusting his belt an inch to the left, the other twitching at his side, like he could shake out the brief moment of sexual heat Innes was sure he didn't imagine.

"Can you at least get a more ergonomic chair?" Charlie asked, pointedly.

They were ignoring it, then. Fine with him, if Charlie wanted it that way. He straightened, rolling his shoulders and attempting to unclench the muscles near his spine.

"I like this one. It's the right height and the arms are the perfect width."

"Uh-huh. It definitely isn't because it matches the godawful aesthetic of your office in a way you secretly love."

"Nope."

Charlie let out a put-upon sigh and took the bottle of painkillers back, heading for the bathroom. "Fine. But I am not getting you opiates when these stop working." He rattled the pills from outside the door, then shouted the rest from out of sight. "You're bad enough now, I don't need to know how terrible you are when you're jonesing for your next hit."

"Your concern is touching."

Charlie flipped him off as he went out the door. Innes's back spasmed one more time, to drive home the point that he was determined to ignore.

# Chapter Six

"And then she tells me, 'Maybe it's your job!'"

"Oh, not this again," Charlie moaned into the phone, hoping for Joy's sake that the conversation went a different direction, but knowing from experience that he could guess what came next.

"Yes, this again. 'It's too stressful! You should quit and move back home!'"

Charlie stopped on the path of the park he was wandering through. "Joy. She didn't."

"She did." Charlie heard the stormy wind noises of a heavy sigh over a tiny microphone, followed by a short coughing fit. After she got it under control, she sounded a lot less righteously angry. "It's impossible, because I know she means well. She worries about me. They both do. And it's not as if I don't understand their concerns. I couldn't have gotten through this week without her here."

Joy had been fighting a bad cold since Monday, which had sapped her already low energy stores. Getting up and into her chair had been a chore, and there was the constant worry that it would turn into pneumonia and become a lot more dangerous. She hadn't been much better by Tuesday when he'd stopped by her apartment, but she was doing well enough now, and her mother was heading home.

"I'm sorry I couldn't visit more," Charlie said, moving off the path so a stroller could go by. "I feel awful, but between the office and the restaurant, it was—"

"Don't even worry about it, babe. I was happy to see you even once. You being busy is a good thing; it means you're happy. I know you, if you get too much time off, you start going crazy."

"Yeah." He looked down at the grass, hard and dry beneath his work shoes.

"What's that tone? You doing okay?"

He looked farther up the path at a bench that was miraculously empty, even at noon on a Friday. He wanted to sit, but he knew he'd regret it when he went back to the office to sit some more at his desk.

"I'm tired," he said. "Not in the same way I was when I was working at the restaurant more, this is more of a mental tired. This is harder, weirdly, than being physically exhausted."

Joy hummed sympathetically. He used to worry that complaining about his aches and pains would make Joy resent him. She'd broken him of that thinking, explaining that even if she had a bad day where she envied anyone over a stubbed toe or a sprained ankle, that was her business and not his problem.

After a few seconds of silence, Joy asked, "Do you think it's time to relax a little?"

"Maybe."

"Hey, who is this and how did you manage to steal my serial workaholic best friend Charlie's phone?"

"Funny." He switched his phone to his other ear to distract himself from wanting to chew his fingernails. "I don't know, I'm just getting it from all sides. You've been telling me to quit for ages, Ma would like me home more to keep her company, and Innes was on my case about it weeks ago."

"Was he? Is that a thing bosses normally do?"

"Possibly not, but he's not the most normal boss. He pretends he's not interested in the lives of other people, but he's actually nosy as hell. Then he won't talk about himself until I give him The Look."

She gasped. "Oh, no, not the patented Charlie Nielsen *You Can Tell Me Anything I Won't Judge Look.*"

"The very one."

Joy laughed, a welcome sound after she'd been so low. Charlie smiled at the infectious giggle that never failed to make him feel better.

"You like this guy," she said when she was finished.

"What?" If he'd been walking, he would have probably tripped on nothing. "Well, I guess so. He's my boss, so I can't hate him or I'd be miserable."

She made a buzzer noise. "False. You hate Stanley."

"Rebuttal: Stanley might be the owner, but he's never actually there to boss me around, so while I do hate him, I'm not miserable."

"Well, not for *that* reason, you aren't."

He didn't deny it. Stepping back onto the path, he headed for the office, using the silence Joy allowed him to think about whether or not it was a misery he could withstand for the sake of a paycheck.

"Have you had any time for more designing?"

He winced. "Not yet. How's work going, sick days aside?"

Joy gracefully let him change the subject, and he listened to her job updates as hard as possible while he was distracted by the fact that nothing had really changed. He was getting paid much better than he had for cleaning, and his schedule wasn't so messed up, but really, there was no good news to share. No more time in his schedule to let his mind run wild, then to put it all on paper, then fabric.

Until he gave up the restaurant, there would be nothing, except Joy's periodic gentle prodding that made his heart hurt and warm up at the same time. She cared so much about him and wanted the very best, and he wished he could give her that, if only to help her stop worrying like he worried for her.

But he wasn't ready to make that leap. Not yet. He wasn't a big believer in signs from the universe, but everything was still too much the same as before to make him think something should change.

On the other end of the phone, Charlie heard a raised voice, far enough away that it was still faint.

"I put it in your bag, Mom," Joy shouted back, her hand covering the mouthpiece.

"Am I keeping you?"

"Not really. Oh, hey, I'm wearing that dress you made me."

Charlie smirked and shook his head at her unsubtle subject change. If she wanted to avoid her mother, he'd be a good friend and enable her. "Which one? There's so many."

"The one with the straps that are hard for me to do on my own."

Charlie groaned, punching the button for the crosswalk with a little more force than necessary. "Oh God, why are you reminding me of that stupid thing? I still kick myself about it—"

"Because it's a great dress and it looks good on me. It's just a little logistically challenging, but Mom's here, so I might as well take advantage of her nimble fingers and fully functioning spinal cord."

"Nice."

There was more shouting in the background. "Coming, Mom! I'll send you a selfie later. For now, I'd better go back to helping Mom pack and trying to explain to her why my job is so important to me. Maybe the twentieth time will be the charm."

"I believe in you. If anyone can make her understand, it's you."

He hung up just as he entered the lobby of the building, and was sitting down at his desk when his phone rang again. It was a text message this time.

It was Alice, the new—or not so new, now—waitress from the restaurant who'd done him a huge solid by taking most of his day shifts for him.

*Heh charloe,* she'd texted.

He frowned. She wasn't normally the type to have spelling errors or even many short forms in her texts. While he was looking, another message came in and his stomach clenched.

*im soooo sorry but i got hut bya car today and my arm is niot gud*

She followed that up with a picture message, which Charlie assumed was photographic proof of her injury, but it was too blurry to tell.

*Sorry to hear that,* he told her. *Are you okay?*

*Ya!! Painkillers r great!!! shoudd be bsck monday.*

That was a relief at least. She was a nice girl, and he wouldn't wish an injury on anyone, but more worrying was the thought of having to cover any more shifts next week. Stanley kept telling him that he'd try not to schedule him for shifts that started earlier than five thirty, but somehow, they kept showing up.

Asshole. He'd been doing the same thing to Donna for years, when she had grandkids depending on her to pick them up from school, who were her motivation for never complaining too much.

*Well, take care of yourself,* he sent back, along with, *I'll work it out somehow.*

She sent him a sad face, then his phone went silent. With a growl of frustration, he stood up and marched himself into the office, where

Innes was listlessly poking at an "Asian-inspired" salad from the café downstairs.

"Hey."

Innes pushed the salad away. "This is an insult to the entire continent of Asia," he said, his lip curling in a way that somehow managed to look disdainfully hot, especially since he was wearing that one suit jacket that did amazing things for his shoulders.

"That bad, huh?"

He shuddered. "So much worse than you could imagine."

Charlie had discovered that Innes was a bit of a foodie, which made complete sense from what Charlie knew about him. He suspected it was a by-product of Innes being rich all his life and enjoying flaunting that wealth more than he'd ever admit out loud.

"I won't order it again," Charlie promised, holding back his *told you so*. He'd suggested the veggie wrap, but Innes had turned up his nose at that.

"Can I help you?" Innes asked, in a flat way that Charlie took to mean he hadn't hidden his satisfaction as well as he'd thought.

Charlie took a steadying breath, then burst out, "Would it be okay if I left a little early today?"

Innes's eyebrows popped up just a little, but he didn't think long before he said, "Sure."

His stomach swooped with relief. It'd take a while to get the panic out of his system, but at least he could stop worrying about losing either of his jobs.

"I'll take a shorter lunch on Monday," he promised.

"Don't bother. You've earned it."

The warm, expanding feeling in Charlie's chest that he was starting to get familiar with had him fighting a grin. "Thanks."

"Can I ask what for?" Innes asked, predictably. As much as he claimed he didn't care about the boring parts of other people's lives, he still needed to know. Charlie thought it was probably a lawyer thing, the urge to ferret out every detail to create a useful and complete picture.

"My other job," Charlie told him. "I had it covered, but it fell through. Sorry."

Innes waved an impatient hand at him. "It's really not a big deal. You know my feelings about your other job, but I won't keep you from it, and I don't want to get you fired. You'll be in a crappy mood about it for ages if I did."

Charlie snorted. "Like I'm a barrel of laughs every other time?"

"Oh, I bet you can be plenty of fun."

The difference was so subtle, Charlie nearly barreled on with another meaningless quip before a warmth in Innes's voice that hadn't been there before stopped his normal respiration with a pulse of answering desire.

"Sure," Charlie said, with a sudden breathlessness that he hoped wasn't audible. "With the right incentive, I can be fun for hours, even."

"Hours, huh? That's something I'd like to experience."

Innes must have been aware of the line they were skirting. Without knowing his thoughts and feelings, Charlie could take a guess that the sharpness in Innes's eyes meant he hadn't missed the turn the conversation had taken toward the truly suggestive. They'd both slipped into it so easily, like the tension was a tepid bath that was slowly rising in temperature, and neither of them wanted out.

It was dumb. Charlie never should've responded to Innes's first volley.

But it was also *enjoyable*. This game they were playing was one he hadn't indulged in in too long, and especially not with someone who could match him like Innes.

Then again, that was exactly why he shouldn't play with fire.

Charlie hummed, breaking their eye contact by watching his own fingers mess with the coil on his notepad. "Sadly, I don't have time for any fun these days."

"Not even solo?"

Charlie stopped himself from rolling his eyes, meeting Innes's laughing ones instead. "That doesn't count."

"Maybe not when you do it. I see no reason to let isolation mean abstinence from joy."

"I'm far from joyless."

Innes's chair creaked subtly as he sat back. "Is that right? You must be spending some of your time entertaining yourself, then."

At some point in the last few seconds, the mood had switched again, as subtly as it had before. They were back to the playful, cutting banter they typically had, even if the subject matter was closer to the edge of inappropriate than normal.

"Oh, I'm pretty good at self-amusement," Charlie said in a dry drawl. "Lots of practice."

"Well, you know where to find me if you get bored of solitaire."

This time, Charlie really did roll his eyes, even if the teasing wasn't as absurd to contemplate as it should have been. "Thanks. That's real sweet of you to offer."

With a soft grunt, Innes's face pulled into a petulant scowl. "Please don't talk about sweets, I would maim for a brownie right now."

"Only maim? Not kill?"

Innes lowered his head, peering at him like he was looking over invisible reading glasses. "I have better self-control than that. But if we're talking cheesecake, I can't be held responsible for the death of anyone who got in my way. You want to know a secret?"

"Will it get me assassinated by the cheesecake mafia?"

Innes continued as if he didn't hear or care about Charlie's response. "Tim, the paralegal who always smells like mouthwash and feet? You know the one. The only reason he still works here is the cheesecake he brings to holiday parties. The man is useless at personal grooming but, damn, can he bake."

"You're a disgrace," Charlie said easily, shaking his head and pulling out his notebook. "If the hunger pangs aren't too much for you to handle, can I give you your afternoon?"

"If you must." Innes leaned back in his chair like he always did when he was doing something other than actually working.

"It's not much, actually. Scheduled phone call at 2:45 with Mr. Rosenquist. Three emails that I can't answer myself. And you already know the other stuff you have to do before the weekend."

"Unfortunately."

Charlie flicked the pages on the bottom of the notepad, anticipating exactly how well the last thing he had to say would be received. "Also, your great-aunt Jocelyn is back from her spa vacay and wants you to drop by today after work."

Innes groaned, clapping his hands to his face and mumbling through them. "Christ, I forgot about that. Call and reschedule, I'm way too tired to deal with her bullshit today."

Charlie sucked in a breath through his teeth. "You don't want to do that."

Innes stilled but didn't take his hands away from his face. "Why?"

"Because your great-aunt Jocelyn is a total old person cliché and goes to either bingo, bridge, or the Navy Club every day except Tuesdays and Fridays. You hate Fridays and you're always tired of seeing people by the end of the week, but while you might not want to see her today, you're going to want to do it even less on any given Tuesday. That's your chest and shoulder day at the gym, and you always limp in here like you're Jocelyn's age, then basically crawl home."

Innes sat up and leaned over his massive desk, extending his hand, palm up, and making a wiggly come-hither motion. Charlie reluctantly stepped closer and reached out his own hand when it became clear that was what he wanted. Innes grasped Charlie's long fingers in his strong ones and squeezed, looking up with a pathetic pout on his face.

"Where have you been all my life?" Innes said.

Innes's palm was warm. It was broad and dry against the bottom of Charlie's knuckles, uncalloused and unmoving. It occurred to Charlie that they didn't really touch each other. They were past the handshake stage, neither of them were particularly touchy people, and most of their interactions happened across the room from each other.

One of the few clear memories he had of Innes touching him at all was the first time they met, when Charlie had stood, frozen and a little bit captivated by the way the inside of Innes's arms had brushed his shoulders and his lips had almost-but-not-quite touched his neck, *Bad!* and *Wrong!* screaming in the back of his mind but excitement and lust keeping him in place.

This was different. Kind of. He didn't feel any of the danger or subtle creepiness of the first time, only a zing of awareness of completely non-intimate skin brushing skin, but there was definitely a touch of flirting, which, as much as he wished he could ignore it, made him want to tease right back.

"Well, first there was infancy," he said, taking his hand back and using it to tap thoughtfully on his cheek. "Then elementary, then high school. I mean, you've got a lot of life on me, so—"

Innes scoffed, jamming his pointer finger into the wood of his desk. "Oh, shut up, I'm only ten years older than you."

"Twelve, actually, which means that you're *technically* closer to my mother's age than mine."

"Stop. I can't take it." He put his head in his hands, probably missing Charlie's delighted grin.

"You're sooo old."

"I am not *old*, now get off my lawn, whippersnapper." As Charlie turned to go, Innes called after him, "And don't cancel that appointment."

"Sure thing," Charlie said, leaning around the edge of the door. "Next time, I'll pencil her in after your afternoon nap."

As he closed the door, he heard something—probably one of Innes's water bottles—hit the back of it and laughed. He was still chuckling when he turned around and jumped back.

A man with a thunderous frown was standing two feet away from him.

Charlie slapped his notebook to his heaving chest, but recovered enough to ask, "Hello, can I help you?"

"So, you're the reason we haven't heard screaming from up here in three weeks," the man said, raising an eyebrow in a familiar way.

"Uh." Charlie swallowed and straightened, shaking off his embarrassment at being so startled. "Just finished four weeks, actually, as of today."

"Excellent. Aiden Kent."

The man extended his hand to shake, which Charlie returned. "Charlie Nielsen."

According to his research, this was the nephew with the ulcer, which made how familiar the guy seemed make sense. He and Innes didn't exactly look identical, but Charlie could see something in Aiden's face that might have reminded him of Innes if their default expressions weren't completely different.

"Likewise. I don't have an appointment or anything. Could I just poke my head in? It's a family thing, not work-related."

"Let me check." He opened the door, considered simply talking around it, but thought better of it and stepped inside and closed them off. "Your nephew is here. Do you want to talk to him?"

Innes didn't look up from his computer screen. "Which one?"

"Aiden."

Innes's groan was long and hearty, but hopefully not loud enough to be heard outside the door. "Fine," he said eventually, still staring ahead, and not at Charlie. "Rescue me in four and a half minutes. That's how much energy I have to spare for him today."

That was better than he'd expected to get, so he opened the door all the way and gestured for Aiden. "He has two minutes."

"Thanks." Aiden nodded at him and started into the room but paused when he saw the water bottle still on the floor. He raised an eyebrow at Charlie, who wondered how much Aiden had heard of the teasing banter that had come before. He shut the door quickly once Aiden had gone all the way in, and took his blushing face back to his desk to cool off. Tomato was not his color.

He watched the clock the whole time they did their business in the office, knowing that Innes was absolutely serious about the four and a half minutes. Thankfully, Aiden was out in three, closing the door behind him with a *snap*.

On his way past the desk, Aiden paused, his hand coming up to fiddle with his watch as he lingered in the middle of the hallway. He looked at Charlie and seemed like he was about to say something, but after a handful of seconds and a single, quick indrawn breath, Aiden shook his head and nodded goodbye. He left with a small smile, which changed his face dramatically to something softer, more approachable.

*Nice guy*, Charlie thought. How did someone so normal end up with an uncle so bitter and self-absorbed? And why did Charlie feel like he preferred his Kent men without any sweetener?

According to his computer clock, there was still at least twenty minutes before someone else showed up. Normally, that time would be eaten up by whatever it was that Innes did for his job. Charlie didn't tend to ask.

But today had already been a little weird, so he wasn't exactly surprised when Innes called for him.

Hurrying to the door, he poked his head inside. "Yes?"

Innes's pleasant voice was muffled by his desk, since he was slumped with his head on top of it. "I need you to do me a favor, and also never talk about it again. To me or anyone else. Please."

"What's the favor?" Closing the door behind him, Charlie approached the desk, real worry slithering down his spine.

When he'd left the room last time, Innes's groans and complaints had been in good fun. A show he put on, part of the back-and-forth that kept them both entertained. Whatever had happened in the three minutes Aiden Kent had been in here had turned those theatrics into something real.

"I need you to go to a store." Innes's hand fisted on the desk as he shifted, his lips stiff. "Don't care where, just get me a heating pad. Those microwavable things. Or one of those stick-ons? Anything."

"Your back."

Innes visibly swallowed, his eyes glued to the carpet in front of the desk. "Yes," he said. His mouth barely moved as he said it, like he could make it not the truth if he said it quietly.

"Yeah, I can do that."

"Take the—"

"The card, yeah, I know." Instead of turning right away, he kept staring at the jagged line between Innes's eyebrows that hadn't been there ten minutes ago. "What happened?"

"Age. Hubris. Whatever." Even the little fluttering motion of his hand looked like it cost him.

"No, I mean . . . was it your nephew?"

"Not really. He was only a messenger. It's not his fault his mother is a rabid dog."

Was that a term of endearment in the Kent family? Innes didn't even look that mad about whatever it was.

"Do you need help?"

Innes's eyes swiveled in his direction like some kind of crab poking out of a hole. "With what?"

"I could . . . rub it?"

"Oh, Charlie. I thought you'd never ask."

If Innes hadn't looked so pitiful, Charlie might have hit him. "Shut up, I'm serious. If you think it would help, I could try to make it better."

Half expecting yet another charged, over-the-top comment, he was treated instead to silence. The details were in Innes's micro-expressions. The way his eyes shivered in their sockets, and the corner of his mouth moving slightly, like the argument he was having with himself was a lively one.

Then, quietly, Innes asked, "Would you?"

"Yeah. I don't mind." Or he didn't, until he made it to the side of Innes's chair and his brain caught up with what he'd offered, and all it meant. "Uh, take your jacket off, I guess."

"Easier said than done."

Innes struggled with it, moving slowly and as little as possible. As soon as it was off one arm, Charlie took over, whisking it away and folding it to rest on the desk beside Innes's.

It was awkward, and not simply because he was about to put his hands all over his boss. The big chair and its jutting arms were difficult to work around, but he could do it. He would do it, since he'd offered, even though . . .

Putting his hands on Innes's lower back wasn't as bad as he'd thought it would be. It was what came after that was a little tricky. As he started kneading, his fingers skipping ineffectively over the matte cotton of Innes's shirt, he could only curse his lack of experience. He didn't know what to do except kind of push? He didn't know how hard to prod or how fast to go, but he did know there wasn't supposed to be a distinct lump of knotted muscle that made Innes hiss when he pressed on it.

"Is that it?" Charlie asked, letting up, then testing out a gentler pressure.

"Sure is. My boon companion all these years. It comes and goes, but that's where it happens, usually."

"Holy shit." He couldn't imagine, but trying to gave him the boost of sympathy and confidence to take the massage to the next level. "I don't want you to take this the wrong way, but do you want to take your shirt off?"

Innes hadn't been moving much, but after that, he went utterly still. "Is there a right way to take that?"

"I mean, so I can do this on your skin. It'd be easier, I think."

A pause, during which Charlie was especially aware that he hadn't taken his hands away. Innes's voice sounded a little strained when he next spoke. "Would you be okay with that?"

He shrugged, even though Innes couldn't see it. "I offered."

"Then yes. Please."

"Okay. You don't even have to take it off, just lift it up. I'll be right back."

Running out to his desk took only a few seconds, since he knew exactly what he was looking for and where to find it. The tube of moisturizer was a gift from Joy on his last birthday, to ease his chapped hands after working with rough fabrics and taut threads and washing them at the restaurant so many times.

The crisp citrus scent of it overpowered him as he coated his hands thoroughly, using it as a distraction from the fact that Innes's bare skin was right there. He'd hoped it might help him feel like there was still a layer between them, but when he put his palms back on Innes's spine, it melted away, and it was painfully apparent that he was touching naked skin.

Having a job to do helped, though. With a goal in mind, it was easier not to notice that Innes's skin was hot, not simply warm. His hands were almost too busy moving for him to notice that Innes had a freckle on his back. To the left of his spine, right above his shiny leather belt, slightly raised and no bigger than a sesame seed.

Sure, his cheeks flamed, but his task kept him from feeling things he shouldn't.

The whole time, he watched the clock. When there was five minutes left until the next appointment would even think about showing up, he stopped, but did it slowly, gentling his strokes so it wouldn't seem so abrupt, since he thought if their positions were reversed, he'd want some warning before the end.

If their positions were reversed . . .

The image, and the way he was almost petting Innes's skin, made everything he wasn't supposed to be thinking about rush in.

Peeling his hands off and pulling Innes's shirt back down felt almost more intimate than the touching. There wasn't the high stakes of helping someone anymore, especially when he smoothed down the soft fabric of Innes's shirt. It stuck to his back, a little darker where the moisturizer dampened it. His skin could probably still feel the imprint of Charlie's hands.

It was only when he was finished that he looked up, and saw Innes's face turned toward him. Their features couldn't have been more different—with Charlie's thin sharpness and Innes's bold, strong and broad lines—but making eye contact was like looking into a mirror.

The same want was there. The tug of something shivery and as warm as blood-flushed skin, that wouldn't go away no matter what he did.

"There," he said, stepping back and rubbing the rest of the moisturizer into his palms. "I did my best."

"It helped, I think."

Despite how little he knew about unknotting tense muscles, Charlie thought that was probably true, since there was less vibrating, miserable tension in Innes's body. "Well, even if it didn't, you smell pretty, now." He brandished the tube with its adorable floral designs.

"My lucky day," Innes drawled, but the smile was a lot less tight than before.

"I'll run out and get that heat pack."

Innes waved his hand as he sat up straight, a little tentatively still. "No, don't bother. I'm fine now."

"I'm going, you can't stop me."

But at the door, he did stop.

"Charlie," Innes said, in a voice soft enough that Charlie almost didn't want to look back and see the expression that matched it.

But he did, and it was just as uncomfortably earnest—and fascinating—as he'd thought. He had to clear his throat to speak again. "Yeah?"

"Thank you."

"No problem."

Closing the door behind him, he tried not to worry about how much he wished he could say, *Anytime*.

Not even silk socks could make Friday dinner rush any fun at all. Charlie had to admit they helped a little, compared to his regular scratchy cotton ones with the huge seam across the toe, but that wasn't enough to keep the soreness away. It might even become a blister if he was really unlucky.

That was what he got for not working at the restaurant for six whole days. It'd been a welcome break, but he was paying for it now with raw heels, snide comments from Brandon, and far more pointed ones from Stanley, who of course had to choose the one weekday Charlie was around to make one of his unannounced visits.

As Charlie dropped a couple of plates off at one of his tables, he wiggled his toes in his shoes, relishing the cool breeze around his ankles. As he headed back to the pass for his next order, his mind started wondering how difficult it would be to make his own socks with sale silk-blend fabric. Probably more trouble than it was worth, but the socks he'd fallen in love with weren't known for lasting a long time or being durable at all, and he was bound to run out sooner rather than later. If he could throw together a bad substitute, it might still—

Later, he'd alternately curse and thank his weird obsession with silk socks for being a catalyst. He was lost in thought and didn't watch the edge of the wrinkled carpet carefully enough, so when his foot caught the edge of it, he didn't react fast enough to keep from falling over into the wall sideways.

Quicker than he could even swear up a storm from the dull pain in his shoulder, Brandon came around the corner and tripped over his legs, sending himself and the tray of three full plates crashing to the floor.

Charlie went down as well, his knees crushed uncomfortably under Brandon's legs. After a lightning-speed check that none of his parts were too badly bumped or broken, he started yanking his feet back under him, then stood, wobbly but upright.

"I'm sorry!" Charlie said, whipping around.

"What the hell is wrong with you?" Brandon shouted, his nostrils flared with rage.

Any of the patrons nearby who hadn't already looked over at the spectacular sound of dishes breaking turned in their seats at the sound of Brandon's voice.

Charlie winced, hating being the center of attention. "I didn't—"

"What on earth is going on here?"

It was Stanley, puffed up in his ill-fitting suit and glaring, annoyingly, at only Charlie, not sparing Brandon a glance.

"He tripped me," Brandon said, pointing a finger at Charlie like a child tattling on a playmate.

"It was an accident," Charlie said, trying hard to remember that it *was* his own fault. "I didn't see you."

"I was right there, how could you not see me? Are you an idiot?"

Charlie's fists clenched, and he discovered a raw patch on his palms from his landing. "I just didn't, okay? I'm sorry. Won't happen again."

Stanley grunted. "No, it damn well won't," he said, then he snapped at Charlie and pointed to the mess of food and broken china on the floor. "Clean this up."

Charlie straightened up from the wall and nodded, resigned but annoyed at being ordered like a dog with a hand command. "I need to get a refill first, let me get a caution sign—"

"No. Now," Stanley barked.

All the report cards Charlie had ever gotten with the comment *hard worker but issues with authority* came to mind as his jaw clenched and he fought the urge to argue simply *because*.

"Sure thing," he said through gritted teeth.

He got to work immediately, kneeling down to start loading the biggest pieces onto the abandoned tray. Brandon, who hadn't left yet, took that moment to walk through the mess, stepping with deliberate care into a puddle of runny pasta sauce and flicking it off his shoe as he passed, right into Charlie's face.

It was the most overtly nasty thing Brandon had ever done, after years of constant needling, general unhelpfulness and insults disguised as jokes.

"Hey!" Charlie yelled after his shock had worn off. Brandon didn't stop, didn't even turn around as he headed back to the kitchen. Stanley was still standing there. Charlie turned to him and asked, "Did you see that?"

"See what?"

Charlie's anger had always burned hot and messy. His temper sometimes got the better of him because he had a hard time getting back to rational from the crazy, feverish energy being *that mad* gave him.

This time, his rage froze him. He was crystallized calm, the heat centered somewhere but not fuzzing up his brain at all. He could see everything so clearly.

He was fed up with being treated like dirt. They were all treated like dirt, but Charlie especially, and that wasn't his persecution-complex talking. Charlie had had the nerve to complain about their hours, their pay, their break room. He'd gone to bat with Stanley about little things and big ones, speaking up when other people wouldn't—like Brandon, who didn't care if anyone else was struggling to pay rent—or couldn't—like Donna, who had two grandchildren living with her and couldn't afford a lost job. In return, he'd gotten the gratitude of most of the other employees, but also the worst shifts, the grossest jobs, and not an ounce of respect. The only reason he still worked there was because Stanley was too lazy and greedy to spend the time training someone when he didn't have to.

"I quit," Charlie said. Perhaps Volcanic-Pissed Charlie would have felt the need to shout it, but Hypothermic-Furious Charlie only got up and snagged a Wet Floor Watch Out sign for the pile of muck.

"What?" Stanley said, his face purpling. He'd obviously heard Charlie perfectly well.

"I quit," he said again, crisp as a new twenty-dollar bill. "I'm leaving. Right now."

"You can't do that. You have to give notice!" Stanley blustered, his shiny shoes squeaking on the rubber mat outside the pass as Charlie shouldered by him.

"Nope. No law in California about giving you two weeks to find some other poor bastard to do your dirty work. And it's not in my contract." Charlie turned around, walking slowly backward toward the locker room and his freedom. "You know how I know that, Stanley? Because I've been waiting for this day for *years*. And now I can finally tell you exactly what you can do."

"Charlie, you're a—"

"Take your butternut bisque and your god-awful double-breasted jackets and shove them into the broken toilet in the breakroom, you asshole."

He could hear Stanley shouting down the hall at him, but he was too busy walking on air to care about it. He glided into the locker room to get his stuff as quickly as he could.

"Donna," he said. She was still changing her shoes to start her shift. He slung his small bag of extra clothes and expired granola bars next to the bench and held his arms open for a hug, which she returned immediately, though her smile was confused.

"Yes, dear?"

"I'm outta here, for real this time."

"Oh, honey!" Donna exclaimed, hugging him again with purpose. "Congratulations! It's been a long time coming."

Charlie smiled into her shoulder. He felt a pang of sadness that he might not smell the coconut oil in her hair again, but he still felt lighter than he had in months and was starting to get worried he'd get stuck on the ceiling.

"Stanley will probably make you work extra hours this weekend to take up the slack for me and Alice," he said when she let him go as far as her outstretched arms. "God knows he wouldn't actually pick up a tray and help out himself. If you need someone to look after the kids, please call. You're the only reason I feel a little bad for walking out like this."

"Don't worry about me, dear," she said, her eyes crinkling. "Promise you'll visit once in a while, though. Make that little asshole Brandon bring you fresh ice water every ten minutes."

He laughed and hugged her again, then waved to everyone he passed on the way to the exit. (Everyone except Brandon.) Most of them had already heard that they'd be down a server for the rest of the night, which got him mixed reactions, from a full-on scowl to a small but enthusiastic thumbs-up.

He burst out into the night air, still high on the rush of quitting the job he'd had since he only a couple years out of high school. He did a little mental math, calculating the time spent wasting away his hours for Stanley.

Four years.

That was a hell of a long time doing a job he hated, for a boss he loathed, serving customers who didn't give a shit about him or any of the other staff. Part of him cringed at the blow his résumé would take, but even if he'd been on his best behavior tonight and quit the proper way, with two weeks' notice and everything, there was no way he was getting a good recommendation from Stanley. Not after all the arguments they'd had.

Maybe he could get flirty Jim from the kitchen to impersonate someone in charge if he needed it. For now, he didn't want to think about it, and it was surprisingly easy to put the worry out of his mind. He suddenly had more hours of free time than he knew what to do with.

The mature, adult thing to do would be to get a head start on the chores he'd carefully scheduled for next week, but Charlie wasn't going to do that. He was going to take his suddenly free evening and do whatever the hell he wanted.

The thought had him floating all the way back home. He did convince himself to be a little responsible, though, by cooking up some spaghetti for him and Ma.

When he put the bowl in her hands, she asked, only then realizing something was different, "What are you doing home so early?"

He had to give her a bit of credit. He thought he'd get *Why are you home so late?*, even though he'd made a point of calling before he started work to tell her of the change of plan.

He sat heavily on the nearest couch cushion, leaning over to squeeze her arm. "I have something to tell you. I quit my job today."

"The doctor's office?"

"No, Ma. It's a lawyer's office."

"Oh, yes, of course. My father was a lawyer, did I tell you?"

"Yes, you did." More than once, and another few times since he'd gotten the new job. Charlie hadn't known his grandfather, but he suspected his grandmother had bailed them out of a few tight situations when he was a kid. He had a vague memory of Ma making a call from a pay phone down the street, and an older woman in pearls taking a cab to meet them at a grocery store.

But that couldn't take away the blame he placed at her feet— and his grandfather's—for raising their daughter with no practical skills or ability to cope with stress, leaving her powerless in the grip of whatever undiagnosed learning challenge she had that made remembering so difficult. They should have had it diagnosed, but it was too late now for Charlie, whose urging had never gotten her to open up to a doctor.

"I didn't quit that job," he told Ma. "I quit the restaurant."

"Oh, no. Why?"

"Because it was an awful job." He took a deep breath to hold back his annoyance. He'd always kept the worst of his complaints to himself so that she wouldn't worry or feel guilty about not contributing, but he'd told her enough about how much he hated the restaurant that the comment irked him. He had distinct, happy memories of sitting at the foot of her chair with her hand carding through his hair while he poured out a sanitized version of his woes.

Ma was a great listener. She just wasn't a great remember-er.

"I'll be home in the evening, now," he said. "I'll make you dinner more often. We can watch your shows together like we used to." The soaps would still have some of the characters he remembered, even if they were five years old, and had each been through two marriages and a kidnapping.

"Wonderful!" She clapped her hands together and smiled at him, all trace of worry gone.

"Yeah, it is." Her smile was catching, and his excellent mood came back in full force. His spaghetti tasted even better than it normally would because he was eating it at home on the couch with his mother, not quickly in the break room out of a stained Tupperware.

"I'm glad I said no to Mr. Flores today, then."

Charlie blinked at the detour into uncharted conversational territory. "What?"

A small, girlish smile flitted across her pink-painted mouth. "We were talking today in the lobby, and he invited me to get a coffee, but I told him I wasn't interested. Good thing, because I wouldn't have had time for it anyway, now that you're home."

Truthfully, Charlie didn't really know if Mr. Flores was nice or not. Once, he'd taken Charlie's garbage to the dumpster for him when he'd seen Charlie racing down the stairs, late for his shift at the restaurant. Since then, they always waved to each other as they passed in the hall, so Mr. Flores probably wasn't a complete asshole.

"You should've said yes," Charlie urged, nudging her with a soft elbow. "He seems nice, and I won't be home all the time." He was also confident he'd survive a few hours home alone, but that wouldn't have been helpful to point out.

"I couldn't do that."

"Why not?"

"Oh, you know."

The answer was a vague sigh of words that didn't get close to the true reason, which Charlie knew very well.

His father.

"Okay," Charlie said, standing up from the couch with a smile plastered on his face to try to retain his good mood.

It didn't work for long.

"Your father always wanted to own a business," Ma said a little later.

The scrub brush Charlie had been using to wash out their bowls clattered to the bottom of the sink. He squeezed his eyes shut, committing his happiness to memory before it was spoiled.

Ma didn't seem to care that he hadn't responded, or even that he wasn't in the room to talk to. "I always told him he could do it if he set his mind to it. He was like you that way. Stubborn, and he always wanted to take care of me. Never let me work, so he never took the risk to go out on his own."

Charlie slumped to the kitchen door, leaning against the jamb with his forehead pressed to the scratched, yellowed varnish. The heavy, cold pit in his stomach felt even worse than it would have been if he'd sunk there from baseline. From the high he'd been on, it was almost unbearable, but he still had to listen. He couldn't close his ears at will or hide in his room until she was finished.

"I regret that," she said, so softly that he could barely hear it. "I should have pushed him more. Maybe he would have been happy if I had. We didn't need money. All we needed was each other. And you, when you came along."

He bit his lip, hard enough that he'd have a bruise the next day. Sure, they hadn't needed money. Not until Charlie's father was gone, and Charlie had walked into their tiny kitchen to see his mother crying over bills and handwritten budgets with red ink all over them, completely lost after nearly thirty years of having everything she'd ever needed handed to her.

His lip protested the rough treatment, but the alternative was opening his mouth, and in his current state of mind, that would be a mistake. There were some secrets that didn't need exposing, even if the rosy view of what his father had been was an image he badly wanted to tarnish with what he knew.

The sound of the TV turning on freed him, its mindless drone alleviating the burning desire to start wagging his tongue. He left the bowls in the sink for later, knowing that he'd regret it when he was scraping off tomato sauce, but suddenly too tired to stand. In his room, he sat at his little desk instead of on his bed, only turning on one light: the warm, dim glow of his sewing machine. It made his eyes sting to look at it, but he looked anyway.

He was weary but still too keyed up to relax. He knew he wouldn't sleep for hours, but for once, he didn't need to worry about getting up early for work. Tomorrow was Saturday. He could wake up when he wanted, get some housework done and see Joy, tell her in person that her months of badgering had finally paid off.

He wanted to text her now, but a look at the clock told him that she'd probably be asleep already, early-riser that she was. He took out his phone regardless, spinning it between his fingers, then opening it up to scroll through his contacts.

He didn't have many. No family, only one close friend, a couple of people from his—now former—job. Some household services, like the fridge repair guy the landlord always made Charlie call himself. The clinic he called to make appointments for Ma a couple of times a year, giving them her history himself because she got too flustered to answer correctly.

And Innes Kent.

They texted sometimes, on weekends mostly, when Innes's schedule suddenly changed on Charlie's day off and it couldn't wait until Monday. Short, to the point, and nothing particularly personal, except the occasional comment from Innes about how pleased or annoyed he was to be adjusting his appointments.

Charlie wasn't sure what made him type out a message and send it without too much thought, but it was done before he could second-guess himself.

*I quit the restaurant today.*

There it was, in black and white. (Well, black and really light blue, as close to monochrome as his old phone could get.) No turning back. For the first time since his teens, he only had one employer, other than himself.

His phone pinged almost immediately. Charlie nearly dropped it in his haste to read what Innes had said.

*Interesting. Why the sudden change of heart?*

Charlie grinned. *Nosy*, he thought.

*I got tired of being treated like garbage for a waiter's wage. I'd much rather be treated like garbage for what you're paying me.*

*I'm shocked!!!* he received right away. *I do not treat you like garbage. If anything, I treat you like recyclable plastic. Useful, durable, and highly practical.*

*Oh, stop. You'll make me blush.*

He spent the next few minutes debating whether he should send an eye roll to make that sound a little less like flirting than it did. Or was he overthinking?

Another ping of a new message. *Well, in any case, I'm glad. Now I have you all to myself.*

This time, Charlie did actually blush. Alone in his room, he buried his flaming cheeks in his hands, embarrassed as much by the fact that he was blushing at all as by what Innes had said.

He couldn't bring himself to respond. He went to bed instead, staring at the ceiling for a long time, thinking about the weekend he'd have free, the clothes he'd make with all the time he had, and what the hell he'd say to Innes on Monday when he was trying desperately not to think about what it might be like if Innes really did have him all to himself.

# Chapter Seven

"**Y**our parents' legacy is important."

"Yes, Catherine, I understand that, but the bottom line is that I don't want to go, so I won't be going."

Innes hated how childish he sounded whenever he spoke to his family. He wasn't even related by blood to Catherine, and she still managed to bring out the worst in him.

"This dedication is a huge honor," she said calmly, as if he hadn't already told her that he didn't give a single crap.

"So your son has informed me. Terrible tactic, by the way, sending him in first. I'm not sure what you were trying to achieve, but he hasn't been able to convince me of anything since he was small enough to be cute and the only thing on the line was an extra popsicle."

Aiden was also so awkward around Innes that he could barely look him in the eye, but neither of them were going to tell the rest of the family why that was, not when it seemed that Aiden and his boyfriend—Innes's ex-sugar baby—were getting serious.

Aiden had not only managed to demand Innes's presence at a statue dedication in a way that would guarantee Innes wouldn't be there, but he also managed to annoy him further by touching on a sensitive issue.

"*Careful with him,*" Aiden had said, jerking his head toward the door.

"*Who? Charlie?*" Innes had replied incredulously. "*He needs no protection from me. He's like a puffer fish. Small, but spiky when poked. I poke him often, just to see if he'll actually blow up one day. Don't tell him I said that.*"

*"Yeah, well, as long as any poking remains metaphorical, you're fine."*

*"Aiden, does having one degree of separation in sexual partners suddenly make you interested in everyone else I plan to sleep with for the rest of time?"*

The look of revulsion on his face had made the whole conversation worth it. *"God, no."*

*"Then keep out of my business."*

Catherine's voice brought him back to the present. "I really didn't think you needed that much convincing, or I would have come myself the first time."

"Catherine, you worked at the firm with me for how many years?"

"Well, it must have been . . . eight years or so before I retired."

He hummed in agreement. "Must have been. And in that time, have you ever known me to be sentimental about my dear, departed parents?"

By the long, tense silence that followed, he decided he'd already won. The answer to his question was an unequivocal *no.* Not even at their joint funeral, when he'd stood like a stone next to his brothers and sister, unable to summon a single tear. He hadn't been happy. He wasn't a sociopath. But he hadn't exactly been sad, either, though he regretted that his nieces and nephews had lost both grandparents so young.

"I just thought that after all this time," she said, as gently as she might to one of her own children, "you might be able to forgive past hurts."

He hummed again. "Ten years, right? That's why they're suddenly making a big deal out of their memory? No, not enough time yet. Try back in another decade, see how I feel then."

"Innes! How could you be so flippant? They were good people, they gave you everything you ever could have wanted."

"Please don't turn this into an Oscar-winning family drama," he snapped. "My parents provided everything they could for me. That just didn't include anything beyond money and indifference. Excuse me if I'm not on my knees thanking them for failing at family planning and taking it out on me."

"Innes—"

"I'm not going," he said tonelessly. "Is there anything else I can help you with today, Catherine?"

She sighed, resigned but not above pulling a Disappointed Mom. "No. I'm sorry you feel that way. I'm sure they wouldn't want you to think they didn't love you."

"Oh, I'm sure they wouldn't either. That would have been terrible for their image."

He hung up before she could splutter a response. His cellphone hit the desk with a thud, and he pressed his fingers into his eyes.

Yes, that was *exactly* how he wanted to end his day. All but yelling at the one in-law he actually liked and whining about his poor-little-rich-kid life and his parents who used up all their love on the first three kids who were actually on purpose.

He'd never once been called a happy accident, but he wondered if Mimi had. For all Theresa's faults, she loved Mimi. That had never been in question, even if he didn't always agree with her idea of what love meant. He wouldn't have any suggestions, anyway.

But what had Mimi been told about how she came to be? Had the story evolved over the years to include new, adult details? When had she learned that she was the product of a drunken mistake? Surely she knew by now. If she hadn't been told, she would've figured it out.

At least Innes had never pretended. In public, or private, he never feigned affection for Theresa, or tried to convince anyone that Mimi had been planned. In his mind—and his experience—that was worse. At least this way, she'd never have to search for the reasons why things were how they were, and she'd hopefully never land on the reason being herself.

He'd never been sure any of the things he'd done were right, but he could hope that the choices he'd made meant Mimi never thought it was her fault. None of it was, and she deserved to be aware of that, even if he'd never had the guts to talk about it.

Innes put his hands down and his vision cleared as he shouted, "Charlie!"

"Yeah?" Charlie said at the same volume. God knew what the clients down the hall thought they were doing.

"Coffee. Now."

The resulting rustling and thumping from outside were pointedly slow and precise. Innes stared at his ceiling as he listened, counting the ticks of the clock on the wall. His phone rang again just as his coffee came in with his assistant attached to it. He groaned, long and lusty, but picked it up from the desk anyway. He really needed Charlie to start screening more of his personal calls.

When he spotted the caller ID display, he sat straight upright, clearing his throat and answering as quickly as his thumb could hit the button.

"Kent speaking." He smacked his palm to his forehead the moment the words were out of his mouth. *Way to set the tone for the rest of the call, dummy,* he scolded himself.

"Um, hi," Mimi said. "It's, uh, your daughter."

"Hello, Mimi. What's up?" Out of the corner of his eye, he saw Charlie freeze in the motion of putting the coffee cup down. Then, fast as lightning, Charlie picked up the little calendar stand that perched on the edge of his desk for clients who signed forms in his office. He plunked it down in front of Innes and pointed to the date.

May the ninth.

"Happy birthday," Innes blurted before Mimi could get a word in.

"Thanks. Nineteen is a pretty cool age. I looked it up, and I can drink legally in Canada now."

"Useful," he said. "Are you planning on going to Canada any time soon?"

"No. It's just interesting to know."

"Right."

Mimi rarely called him. The last time she'd called him was . . . actually not that long ago, when he thought about it. And that time, he'd gotten in the car, driven her to the airport, and they'd gotten into a colossal fight.

He looked up, panicking, but Charlie had turned around and was running—actually running—out of the office. Innes only had a second to be appalled before Mimi was taking his attention.

"I wanted you to know I got your gift," she was saying. "It came yesterday."

"Great, I'm glad. Did you wait until today to open it?"

"No way. I could never wait that long, not even on Christmas."

He could hear a smile in her voice, and it made his chest clench. He hated it, it was uncomfortable, but he also never wanted it to stop.

"Ah. I'm the same, I'll admit. I never got the point of drawing it out." He looked up when Charlie came tearing back into the room, a piece of paper flapping in the breeze he'd created, which he then slapped down in front of Innes.

It was a receipt.

"Yeah, I get that," Mimi said. "And I wanted to thank you too. The present is great. Really awesome."

Innes skimmed the page quickly. It looked like Charlie had gone with a theme this year. *College Survival Pack* or something. On the list was a package of expensive ergonomic pens, a cookbook for microwaves, some noise-canceling headphones, a variety pack of gourmet popcorn, and a thermos that looked like it could survive a nuclear winter.

"I'm glad you liked it," he said, then he covered the microphone and mouthed, *Thank you*, at Charlie, who let himself out with a nod. "What's your favorite part?"

"The cookbook, definitely. The food here is so mediocre, and I'm sick to death of instant ramen. I've already tried three of the recipes, and they taste like real food. It's awesome."

"Excellent. You'll have to let me know your favorites."

"Sure. Aunt Catherine said that you like to cook." She paused and a fuzz of static filled the awkward silence. "I thought maybe when I'm home next, you could teach me how to make actual food, no microwave."

*Aunt Catherine.* His chest cramped again, this time with disappointment that the rest of his family had been let into her life sooner than he had. He had only himself to blame, but it was still a bitter pill.

"I would love that," Innes said hesitantly. "I just don't know if your mother—"

"My mother can suck it up," she said fiercely. "She's still on my case about transferring to Pepperdine, so I'm really not in the mood to think about what she wants."

That was a big change. Although probably not a recent one. Innes's brothers and sister had stepped away largely for the same reason Innes had: Theresa, and her inability to deal with her jealousy in a way that didn't also hurt Mimi.

But if Mimi had distanced herself that much, perhaps he could take the opportunity to pick up the slack. It would be the smart thing to do, but his whole being cringed at the thought of someone else being in his space. Someone he couldn't ditch the moment they learned something intimate, like where he kept his measuring spoons.

"Okay, then," he said, thinking quickly. "Well, how about this. I'll do you one better. Have you ever been to San Francisco?"

"Duh. It's like an hour away, and the bars are way better."

"Fair enough. So, you like the city?""

"Sure. Well, one time my friend's boyfriend who's a senior came with us and his gross friends hit on me all night, but it's usually fun."

Innes grimaced. He remembered being a college student, and he hated the thought of someone like his past self annoying her. "Gross is right. How about you let me take you there, maybe make a weekend of it. Celebrate your birthday properly. Being able to drink legally in Canada is a big deal, you know."

She laughed. He'd made her *laugh*. He was starting to get used to the warm, pulsing clench in his chest, and that prospect was as terrifying as it was thrilling.

"Sure," she said. "When?"

He was online looking at plane tickets within minutes, hanging up with Mimi with the promise that he'd take care of everything and pick her up the weekend after next.

Truthfully, he would take care of nothing. Charlie would be the one to worry about it, which only served to make him feel more guilty than he already was.

Mimi was only giving him a chance because of the thoughtful, useful birthday present she *thought* he'd gotten her. In reality, he'd only grudgingly given his assistant enough information to go on so he could make an accurate guess. Innes had thrown his money at the problem and successfully solved it, far better than he could have hoped.

He jotted down the relevant details of the trip and went out into the reception area, coming to a stop in front of Charlie's desk with what he hoped was a penitent expression.

"Thank you," he said, fiddling with the piece of paper in his hands.

"You're welcome." Charlie crossed his arms. "It's my job to help you in whatever area you require."

"It's not in your job description to be a mind reader, and yet you consistently go above and beyond. I'm thanking you for putting in the work to get Mimi a nice gift."

"She liked it?"

Innes fought a smile. "Very much. You put the rest of my assistants to shame, I think. She's never called to thank me before."

Charlie shook his head dismissively. "It wasn't exactly a high standard to beat. For her fifteenth birthday, whoever your assistant was gave her a power drill. Can you imagine being that age and getting a home renovation tool as a gift? Totally stupid."

Innes hummed, regret pooling in the pit of his stomach. He'd always thought he'd done the right thing by pawning off birthdays and Christmases. Apparently, that wasn't the case.

Charlie seemed to realize what he'd said and scrambled to distract him. "Hey, I know fifteen was pretty far back for you, so don't feel bad if you can't remember what it was like."

Innes appreciated the attempt to cover the awkwardness with a joke more than he ever would an actual apology.

"Careful, smart-ass, or you might not receive the full benefits of my gratitude," he warned, but Charlie would know he wasn't serious.

"Meaning?"

"Let me take you out to dinner."

Charlie's chair made a thunking noise as he sat straight up. "Uh, what?"

"To thank you properly. What are you doing tonight?"

"Nothing, but—"

"Great. It'll be a joint 'thanks for saving my bacon' and 'congrats on no longer being a waiter' dinner." He put the piece of paper with the info for next weekend on the desk. "You can make the reservation, and while you're at it, you can make a few more. I'm going to San Fran. I need flights, hotel, rental car, the works."

"Got it," Charlie said, numbly. He picked up the paper on autopilot, apparently too bulldozed to put up much of an argument about dinner. Perfect.

Innes was whistling as he went back to his own office. His day was getting better and better.

"What did those peas ever do to you?"

Charlie looked up from mashing his peas into a bright green mass on the edge of his plate. Innes had been watching him do it with growing amusement ever since they'd gotten their meals—steak for him, chicken for Charlie.

"Are they not to your liking?" Innes pressed.

"No, they're fine, they're just, uh," he stammered, taking a forkful of the ones he hadn't destroyed, but not bringing it to his mouth. "They're different from what I'm used to."

Innes frowned down at them. They looked pretty standard to him. "All right," he said and left it at that.

Or at least, he tried to.

"You know I'm not going to make fun of you for not eating your vegetables, right?" Innes said after another minute of watching Charlie try to subtly hide the rest of his peas under the remains of his chicken.

Charlie looked up again, biting his lip and putting his fork down with a clatter. "I know," he said, close to pouting. "Would you stop looking at me and pay attention to your own damn food?"

"I will when you stop being more interesting than my boring old meat and potatoes." He leaned back in his chair, grinning. "Now, are you going to tell me what those peas have done to mortally offend you?"

"They're really small!" Charlie burst out, loud enough that the man at the table next to them looked over momentarily. "And . . . fresh, I guess. I'm not really used to fresh peas."

"As opposed to frozen? I didn't think there was much of a difference."

"Not frozen," Charlie said, shifting in his seat. "Canned. I've been eating them that way my whole life. They're cheaper than the frozen ones."

"Ah." Innes suddenly felt like a dick for pushing.

"The peas I'm used to are huge and grainy and they taste like the inside of a tin shed, but I guess I like them that way. It's weird." Charlie picked his fork up again and poked at his chicken. "Now that I have a little bit of wiggle room in the budget, I could probably get myself some frozen peas, or some brand-name pasta, but I don't think I would, even if I was suddenly a millionaire. I'm stuck in my ways, I guess."

"Probably not as much as you think. You transitioned to an office job pretty well," Innes pointed out.

Charlie grinned. "I did, didn't I?"

"Such modesty! Such tact!"

He poked his fork at Innes. "Shut up. You said it first, not me."

Innes used a single finger to push aside the tines of Charlie's weapon. "You are a very aggressive person, did you know that?"

"Assertive," Charlie rebutted, his mouth suddenly full with more food. "And yes, I am aware. I've been called some synonym of that by every teacher I've ever had."

"No, I think 'assertive' is far too tame a word for you. Sometimes I think you must have been raised by a particularly angry tiger in the wild."

"Grr," Charlie said, attacking the last of his chicken with his knife. "I don't see why a bit of aggression is a bad thing. Aggressive people take care of the things passive people wish they could. I'm not mean about it."

"No, you're not, which is why I think you're not as cutthroat as you think you are. Ergo, assertive, not aggressive. You win."

"Oh, 'ergo,' huh?"

"Yes. Tell me, are you wowed by my impressively large vocabulary? It's even bigger if I really let loose, I promise."

Charlie choked on his food, smacking his silverware to the table as he fought to keep it in his mouth. The coughing fit didn't last long, and then Charlie was only overcome by laughter.

"That was so bad," he gasped through his giggles.

Innes hummed thoughtfully. "No, not my best, I'll give you that."

"What's your best? No, wait, screw that. I want to hear your worst."

"Well, if we're going by the least intelligent, then I guess the worst would be the few times I've asked 'I'm rich, wanna fuck?'"

Charlie's smile disappeared. He cleared his throat and picked up his napkin, using it to wipe his mouth, then putting it in his lap to fiddle with under the tablecloth.

Innes quickly tried to think of some lighthearted comment to ease the sudden tension, but in the next moment, Charlie broke it instead.

"Okay, is this weird?" Charlie blurted. "I'm feeling like this is weird."

"What's weird?" Innes widened his eyes and blinked like a woodland creature in a cartoon.

"This." Charlie flapped his hand between them, still holding the napkin and narrowly missing a glass of ice water. "Us, having dinner and chatting and laughing. It's weird."

Innes shrugged. "People have meals with their colleagues all the time."

"One, you're not a colleague, you're my boss." He jammed a finger into the white tablecloth, then added a second with a dull *thud*. "Two, that's the occasional coffee or a business lunch. Not dinner in a really nice place where they just dimmed the lighting for a more romantic atmosphere. Don't try to pretend you don't know what I'm talking about."

Innes gave up the act. "I enjoy your company. That's a rare occurrence for me, so why shouldn't I take advantage while I can? Also, you chose this place, so don't blame me if they start bringing out the candles."

"Oh, I see," Charlie drawled. "You're using me for my stunning conversation skills. It has nothing to do with your . . . vocabulary."

"Exactly right. Dessert?"

"No."

Innes signaled for their server to bring the check. Charlie remained silent throughout the process of paying for their meal, allowing Innes to foot the bill entirely. Innes counted that as a win.

A few weeks ago, Charlie's pride probably would have demanded he help at least a little bit, even if his wallet couldn't handle the strain. Today, Charlie hadn't even tried to pick a cheaper restaurant or order the least expensive bare salad on the menu. Instead, Charlie fixed his sharp eyes on their server, like he was fitting them for a new suit, which—knowing Charlie's interests—he probably was.

Charlie's only interference, once the transaction was over, was to nudge the bill toward himself. Innes saw his eyes snap to the bottom of the receipt to check how much he'd written in for a tip. Rude. Apparently, the number was satisfactory, because Charlie smiled and sat back in his chair, looking pleased.

They didn't stay much longer. They'd come straight from work, fighting the rush hour traffic to make their reservation, but it was still early in the evening. There were more customers entering the restaurant than leaving it, so when they made it outside through the separate exit, there weren't many people around.

"This was nice," Charlie said out of the blue, stopping outside of the beam of light coming from the door.

"I'm glad you think so. I agree. I really am grateful to you for all you've done."

"Do you take all your best assistants out for dinner?"

Innes sighed. "This again?"

"I'm curious!" Charlie raised his hands in defense, turning to face Innes head-on. "Did you show Marie this kind of gratitude?"

Innes tilted his head, all desire to tease or shy away from the tension they'd been brewing suddenly gone. Charlie was looking up at him, his lips slightly parted, his intense gaze softened by the dim light and an emotion that Innes could swear was anticipation.

Taking a deliberate step closer, he asked, "Do you really want to know the answer to that question?"

In the pause that followed, Charlie didn't step back. He kept on staring, until the moment he swallowed hard and said in a near whisper, "Yes."

"The answer is no. I didn't." They were standing so close that it was easy to lean down and purr into his ear. "Just you, Charlie."

He forced himself to stay utterly still. If they were about to make a mistake, he wanted to make absolutely certain that it was one they made together, and that Charlie would know in his heart that neither of them had been smart enough to say no or think better of it.

He didn't have to wait long. Charlie reached out a hand to clutch Innes's waist under his blazer, and closed the distance between them, surging up until their lips met and finally, *finally,* they were pouring all the heat that had been smoldering between them into an explosively slow, thorough kiss.

Charlie had talented lips. He didn't allow himself to be led, but actively participated in every tilt, every plunge of tongue, every tug of lip. His hand squeezed convulsively at Innes's side, gripping harder when Innes cupped his sharp jawline, pulling him in even though they were as near as they could get.

When they had to stop to pull in a few deep breaths, Charlie let his head fall to Innes's shoulder, panting hard enough that Innes could feel the warm gusts through his shirt on his chest.

"Charlie," he said, as calmly as he could manage with his lungs working like he'd run a couple of blocks at top speed. "When you made a reservation at this restaurant, did you happen to notice it was attached to a hotel? An expensive hotel, in fact."

"Uh-huh." Charlie sounded dazed. He didn't look up, but a small shiver tracked its way down his spine as Innes watched.

"I don't want to come across as too *aggressive.*" Taking his hands from Charlie's nape, he grabbed Charlie's hips instead, jolting him into making a short, pained noise of passion. "But could I perhaps interest you in getting a room and—"

"God, yeah." Charlie stepped away on unsteady legs, grabbed his hand, and pulled him away down the sidewalk. "Let's go."

Back into the hotel they went—to the lobby this time. Charlie took the lead, which was a rare but not unwelcome experience. It gave Innes both the time to admire the way Charlie's pants fell against the back of his legs as he leaned into the reception desk, and a great view of his ass when he twisted around to snap at Innes for his credit card.

Innes was able to focus long enough to get the room keys, but Charlie had already started power walking to the elevators, so he missed the teasing tilt to the receptionist's polite smile at his impatience.

They'd barely made it inside the room before Charlie was fumbling for Innes's buttons, backing him up into the room and closer to the bed.

"Been a while?" Innes asked, stopping their progress before he toppled over, thankfully.

"Yep." He didn't look up, yanking Innes's shirt out of his pants instead. "Too long."

"Mmm. Me too." Innes snagged Charlie's hands, pulling them away from his belt buckle and holding them between their bodies. That did grab Charlie's attention, and Innes had to suppress a laugh at the grumpy kitten frown he got for his efforts.

"I think it would be a waste of admirable patience for this to go too quickly," he said, adjusting his grip on Charlie's wiggling fingers so that he could stroke the back of Charlie's palm with a thumb. "We have two options here, both of which I am perfectly willing to try. Option number one: We try to make this a game of sorts. See how long we can last even though both of us are on a bit of a hair trigger. Could be interesting. Could be that we both fail miserably, but we'll at least have fun trying."

Charlie tugged his hands away but didn't go back to feverishly undressing either of them. "Sounds exhausting. What's the other option?"

"We forget about trying to hold back." Innes took over where Charlie had left off, undoing his belt and slowly shedding everything as he spoke. "We both get off, get it out of the way. Then stick around and see how long it takes us to be ready for round two. I don't know about you, but I'm pretty confident that we won't have time to get bored in between."

Charlie devoured every new piece of bared skin with a hungry gaze and a wicked smirk. "We do have this room until tomorrow at eleven."

"Well, fuck, we better use it."

Charlie cackled and whipped his own clothing off faster than seemed physically possible. Innes only had a second to fully appreciate the view before he was being pushed onto the bed and straddled.

Somehow, the fact that neither of them was completely undressed made it hotter. He was pretty sure he had a sock dangling from his foot, and Charlie was wearing boxers, but that didn't matter when Charlie rolled his hips and they both arched into the sweet, uncomplicated pleasure of their bodies rubbing together.

It took minutes for Charlie to ride them both over the edge and collapse onto Innes's chest, planting a messy, eager kiss on his lips in the aftermath.

Innes felt way too good to be embarrassed about anything. "Inelegant," he said, getting his breath back. "But effective."

"Ooh, tempt me with that vocabulary again," Charlie purred, then he started dragging his lips down the side of Innes's neck, kissing and licking his way to his chest. "It really is bigger up close."

Charlie gave his hips a final push, his smile sated, but still energized.

"God, stop it," Innes groaned. "Give me a break, would you?"

Charlie rolled off, and they lay panting next to each other for a few minutes. It wasn't dozing, but they weren't completely with it either. Innes stretched, kicking off the tenacious sock and marveling at how much he'd missed this.

There was only so much satisfaction he could get at home alone. He could take care of business, but the burn was hollow when he wasn't also congratulating himself on a job well done and basking in the body heat of another person.

Eventually, he forced himself to get up and deal with the mess. When he came back from the bathroom with a warm cloth and a good head start on his second wind, he let himself get the long look at Charlie's body that he'd missed before.

He was just as gorgeous under his buttoned-up work clothes as Innes had thought he'd be. He was wiry, surprisingly muscled for being so slight, but in the way that was obviously not from weightlifting and protein powder. It took strength to clean toilets and heft plates every day, after all, and the resulting lean power suited him more than bulging biceps would.

Innes followed the trail of freckles that decorated Charlie's fair skin all the way up to his face but stopped there when he realized that those dark eyebrows—the same color as Charlie's body hair, a fact Innes was unlikely to be able to forget—were pulled into a frown.

Sauntering over, he sat down and leaned over, kissing the tension away from Charlie's lips.

"You need to bail early?" Innes asked when he pulled away. He didn't let the disappointment into his voice, keeping his face carefully neutral. This was Charlie's chance to back out and run away, and he wasn't going to try to convince him either way.

After a beat of intense concentration, Charlie seemed to shut off the thinking side of his brain. He smiled, pushing Innes away and sitting up.

"Not a chance," he said, grinning, then, abruptly, like he was issuing a challenge, asked, "Do you want to fuck me?"

Innes blinked. "Yes. I do. You're not going to have a problem with that? I seem to remember you being annoyed when you thought I was pinning you to a stereotype."

Charlie scoffed. "What, you think because I'm a small guy, I'll resist the fact that I like to bottom because of some moral reason? I'm too selfish for that."

"How lucky for me." He pulled Charlie in by his chin for another hard, quick kiss, then Charlie was leaping up and almost skipping to the bathroom with way more energy than he should rightfully have.

*Ah, to be on the sunny side of thirty again,* Innes mused.

He looked around the room, feeling like a tool for wishing he could check his phone, until he heard the shower turn on and figured Charlie would be a while. He contented himself by looking up tourist attractions in San Francisco.

A gurgle announced the water shutting off.

He was shoving his phone back into the pocket of his discarded pants when Charlie came out of the bathroom. He was rosy pink all over, dry except for the very tips of his hair, and naked as the day he was born.

Innes crossed the carpeted floor to meet him, curling his arms around Charlie's waist and capturing his mouth, saying without words but with crystal clarity, *This time, I'm in charge.*

He backed Charlie up into the nearest bare wall, pinning him there with a forceful but painless shove that made Charlie moan a little into Innes's mouth. He reached down, trailing a hand up the side of Charlie's thigh, warm and dewy from his shower. He didn't linger there. He took Charlie in hand, biting his own lip at the lovely choked-off sound it produced. He cherished that sound and the ones that followed, precious sips of Charlie's exposed need getting harsher and more real.

He felt more than saw Charlie reach out to return the favor, but he used his free hand to grab the first wrist he could reach, shushing Charlie's half-hearted protests.

"There's time for that in a while," he said, stroking his thumb over the drop of gathering wetness and using it to ease the way. "Right now is about you. Just you."

Charlie let his head fall back against the wall, exposing his long neck, ruddy in blotches from exertion and his rising temperature. Innes licked a stripe all the way up a jutting tendon at the same time as he twisted his hand, wringing a cry from the throat he wanted to take a bite out of.

He chuckled. "You're still so pent up, aren't you?"

"Yeah," Charlie panted, his head rolling on the wall, almost close enough that he could press his fevered cheek against it, but not quite. "So fucking do it already."

"So impatient," he scolded, rubbing his thumb in a place that made Charlie gasp. "I thought we were going to take our time."

"New plan. Do it now, I don't want to wait." Charlie clutched at him, digging his fingers into Innes's hips.

"Fine, we'll do it your way."

He took a half step back, considering. The hotel bed was large and serviceable. So was the armchair in the corner, though the reading lamp might brain them if he tried anything. He looked back at Charlie, still so pink against the cream wall, and decided he liked the view too much to change the locale.

"Turn around," he said, then he guided Charlie by his shoulders until he was pressed against the wall, braced on his forearms. He let his hands drift down the slim muscles of Charlie's back and sides, like a particularly ineffective massage. He didn't stop until he got to the lean padding of Charlie's ass. Not especially ample, but enough of a handful that Innes could squeeze, drawing a hiss that made him smirk and prompted him to kiss the space between Charlie's shoulder blades.

"Come on," Charlie rasped.

"One minute." He stepped away completely, noting the way Charlie shivered and loving it. He retrieved a condom from his wallet, along with a pack of lube. When he'd put the supplies in there before leaving the office, he'd wondered if he was jinxing himself. It was a good thing he wasn't superstitious enough to leave them at home.

Putting both on the sturdy table within reach, he crowded Charlie again, jostling him enough to make him lose his balance and nearly face-plant into the wall. Charlie didn't seem to mind, however, letting out a sort of discontented growl and reaching behind himself with one hand, squeezing Innes's thigh.

"Soon," Innes murmured, then he helped himself to a nibble of Charlie's freckled shoulder. "I'm going to give you what you need."

Soon, but not yet, he decided. Condom first. Instead of efficiently taking himself in hand to get ready, he seized Charlie's hips and held them still as he gave one good grind of his hips in the damp crevice of Charlie's ass.

Charlie jerked, whipping his head and around stuttering, "What—what are you—"

"Relax," Innes soothed, realizing that Charlie couldn't see much from his position against the wall. He must have thought Innes was jumping the gun. "I'll get you ready for the main event, and glove up, don't worry. Give me a minute."

He made a feast of the side of Charlie's neck while he rubbed himself to full hardness against Charlie's lower back. Charlie was distracted enough by it that he lost a bit of his impatience but none of his passion. He moaned and whimpered quietly every time Innes sucked or bit a faint mark, and tensed every time Innes hummed his satisfaction.

When Innes started leaving his own trail of moisture against Charlie's tailbone, he pulled away, ripped the condom open ,and rolled it on quickly. The lube came next, a generous amount poured over the tips of his fingers.

Stroking his free hand down the center of Charlie's spine, he leaned in to croon in Charlie's ear, "You've waited so long."

"Yeah," Charlie groaned.

"I've been so mean, making you wait. Should I be even meaner?"

"No," Charlie burst out, his arms shaking with tension. "No, no—"

"Fine. No more waiting."

With sure fingers, he smeared the slightly warmed lube over Charlie's scorching-hot hole, ignoring the small hiss it caused and starting a slow, gentle massage.

Charlie let his head fall against the wall, but he didn't lose any of the tautness in his limbs. Innes circled his fingers again and again, pressing a little more each time, but nothing seemed to change much, even after a few minutes.

He frowned, thinking he must be out of practice. Tentatively, he used his middle finger to prod deeper, gathering the lube to make it easier, but instead of starting to give, Charlie clenched tighter with a quick indrawn breath.

All impulse to tease disappeared.

"Charlie," Innes said. Charlie twitched at the sound. "Relax."

"I am. Do it." Charlie's voice was strained, and not with want.

Innes spent another few seconds attempting to coax Charlie's body to accept him, but he gave up when he heard a soft grunt of pain.

"Charlie, seriously. Relax, or you'll hate me tomorrow," he cajoled. There was always the possibility that that would happen anyway, regardless of how sore either of them were, but he was choosing not to think about that.

Charlie snorted. "Hate your dick, maybe."

"That dick is attached to me, I'll have you know. Now, come on. Take a breath, calm down a little. Enjoy this."

Charlie let out a frustrated breath, hiding his face in the crook of his arm. Innes started rubbing again, then gave Charlie's shoulder a gentle shove, hoping a jolt would help him get out of the frozen state he was in. It didn't work.

Innes stepped back, taking his hands off Charlie completely. "Do you need to move? Does this not work for you?"

"No, it's fine," Charlie snapped. "Just do it, I don't care."

"Well, I care," Innes said, harsher than he'd meant to. "Tell me what you need, or I stop right now."

Innes waited. *Funny,* he thought as he watched the battle Charlie waged with himself play over his face. How interesting that Charlie would choose now to worry about showing weakness when the very role he'd chosen to take was considered the weaker one by many. Not by Innes, but others would question why Charlie felt the need to prove himself by taking the pain when he'd already been eager to take Innes's cock.

As always, Charlie continued to surprise him.

Seeming to come to an agreement with himself, Charlie lifted his chin, staring confidently at Innes even while he stammered, "I need to—to be—"

"Bent over?"

"Yeah."

"That's fine."

Innes guided him off the wall on shaky legs, only going as far as the table next to them, clearing the condom wrapper and rescuing the lube packet first. He persuaded rather than pressured him to lie down so most of his torso was on the table, his face insufficiently cushioned by an embroidered runner in the center.

"Good?" Innes asked, placing his hands on Charlie's sides, running his thumb across a jutting hip bone.

"Yes."

In this position, it was easy for Charlie to look back so Innes could see his face. It was more intimate than he'd expected.

This time, after a few more minutes of gradual pressure, when Innes tried to breach him, Charlie's body accepted it.

"That's right," he soothed when Charlie grabbed at the table with white knuckles, even as he obviously made a conscious effort to unclench. "Let me make you feel good."

Charlie was as responsive in this as he'd been to everything that came before, sighing and humming with every push of Innes's finger. His hand curled into a fist when Innes added the second one, straining into the lacquered wood of the table.

Innes might have stopped there and moved on to the main event—Charlie probably would have preferred it—but he prided himself on being nothing if not thorough.

When Charlie was ready, he added a third, grinning at Charlie's widening eyes.

"How many is that?" Charlie asked, his fist grinding down and squeaking with sweat.

"Three."

"You fucker, could you do it already?" Charlie exploded, but he was grinning this time, not genuinely annoyed.

"No appreciation," Innes said, tutting. "Try to be nice, what does it get me?"

"If you want to be nice, you would stick—"

"Yes, yes, I'm going."

With one hand on the middle of Charlie's back to anchor him, he guided his cock to Charlie's hole, pressing inside as slowly as he had with his fingers.

Charlie groaned, a throttled sigh of satisfaction.

Innes chuckled. "Why, thank you. There's the appreciation at last."

"Shut up and fuck me."

Innes didn't argue, wasting no time in sinking in the rest of the way and setting a driving rhythm designed to send them both to the edge of pleasure with no trouble. For all that it had taken so long for them to get to where they were, it took a surprisingly short time to reach that edge, poised to fall right off.

Charlie's noises picked up in pitch and speed, and he reached back again, blindly. Innes blinked, fighting through a haze of beating lust, and grabbed on, tucking both their hands up by Charlie's shoulder while he kicked his pace into another gear, slamming into Charlie hard enough to make the table wobble.

Their hands stayed joined until Charlie seemed to hit a plateau, whining and gritting out, "More, now, right now."

Innes retrieved his hand and reached for Charlie's cock, stroking it quickly, aided by the way it leaked with how close he was, until Charlie was coming with a shout, and Innes lost all coordination as he followed.

He managed to keep from squishing Charlie against the table, but barely. He slumped over him instead, breathing hard and watching a cloud of condensation grow and shrink next to the tablecloth under Charlie's panting mouth.

Innes was the first to recover again, straightening up and dealing quickly with the condom. He had to peel Charlie, grumbling, off the table and shove him toward the bed so he didn't fall asleep half-standing up in the middle of the room.

*So much for youthful stamina,* he thought, noticing the way Charlie's blinks got longer and farther between.

They managed to pour themselves under the covers, silently agreeing not to leave right away. Thankfully, they were both too hot and sweaty for Innes to have to even think about whether he should be offering a postcoital cuddle.

He did look over at Charlie before he drifted off and couldn't help but burst out laughing.

"What?" Charlie asked, waking up enough to be annoyed.

"Your face."

He pointed. The pattern of the embroidery on the table runner was pressed into Charlie's cheek in swirls and a couple of tiny flowers. Charlie ran his fingers over it, frowning, then when he realized what it was, swatted Innes on the arm.

"Quit laughing at me, asshole."

"It's very pretty," Innes said, rubbing his injury. "I like it."

Charlie grumbled again, but he was smiling as he buried his face into the fluffy hotel pillow. He was asleep within a minute.

Innes wasn't far behind, but the last thing he thought before he followed was that Charlie looked quite peaceful when he slept. Calm and happy, like an emaciated blond cherub. It was cute.

Too bad it would never last.

# Chapter Eight

Innes's coffee landed on his desk with a *clack* of ceramic meeting wood hard. A couple of drops spilled over the sides of the mug.

He sighed. Charlie probably didn't hear it over the percussive noises of himself stomping around, going about his regular morning tasks with brutal professionalism. Half an hour ago, when they'd both come into the office from their own homes after bolting silently from the hotel before the sun had risen, he'd informed Innes of that day's appointments in a clipped tone without the usual teasing or insincere comforting.

Now, the old date on the calendar stand had been ripped off, the relevant forms stacked aggressively in the in-tray, and the messages Innes had to follow up on himself smacked onto the desk beside his coffee, and Charlie had yet to look at Innes a single time.

Innes dug his fingers into the skin above his eyebrows. He'd been expecting a bit of awkwardness, but he hadn't prepared for it to be this bad.

Charlie was angry. From the stiff set of his shoulders and the way he was avoiding Innes's eyes, it was hard to tell, but Innes thought he was mad at himself more than Innes.

"Charlie," he said, after a couple of stray pens on his desk were stabbed into their holder with alarming vigor. "Can we talk about this?"

"No," Charlie said flatly.

"Why not? This is obviously bothering you."

"It's not bothering me; I'm working." He thumped a case file a paralegal had dropped off for him on the desk and whipped around, heading for the door.

Innes stood up, raising his voice. "Then could you look me in the eye while you're working?"

Charlie froze with his hand on the door, then slowly swiveled around to face him, his gaze still stuck to the floor. Soon, with visible effort, Charlie raised his eyes until he was staring back with the same mutinous expression Innes had grown used to, silently expressing his displeasure with every tight muscle.

"Maybe it was a mistake," Innes said softly. There was no need for him to clarify what *it* was. Charlie didn't say anything, but it was obvious in the grim set of his lips that he agreed. Innes smiled. "But it sure was fun, right?"

Charlie raised an eyebrow, staying stubbornly silent, but Innes spotted a hint of a lift in the corner of his mouth.

"You can't deny that you had a good time," Innes continued. "I don't know how long it's been for you, but personally, I was experiencing an unparalleled dry spell. That was a hell of a way to break it."

"Glad to hear I could scratch that itch for you," Charlie snapped, his reluctant amusement gone.

Innes winced internally. Of course, he had to go and offend Charlie at a time like this.

"It wasn't just good because I hadn't had it in a while," he said, leaning on his desk so he didn't go over and crowd him. "It was amazing. Full stop."

Charlie's frown cleared, slowly replaced by a sly, self-satisfied smile. "It was pretty good, wasn't it?"

"And while I am aware there's a possibility that it was a terrible idea and we'll both regret it," he went on, encouraged by Charlie's change in mood, "there's also a chance that it wasn't."

Charlie squinted at him, crossing his arms over his chest. "How do you figure?"

When they'd both woken up that morning, it had been with the realization that it was a regular Wednesday. A workday. They'd tossed on their rumbled clothing and managed not to interact much at all, barring a clumsy exchange over who was going to press the down button on the elevator.

Innes hadn't had to think about much of anything until he'd been under the hot spray of his showerhead at home. Then, his head clearing and the familiar muscle ache of vigorous sex making itself known, he started wondering, not about how he was going to fix the situation he'd caused, but how he was going to make sure it happened again.

"We're adults," he said, stepping out from behind his desk over to the wall of books and trinkets, pacing alongside it. "We enjoyed ourselves. Who says we can't continue to enjoy ourselves?"

Charlie made a squawking noise of disbelief. "Common sense!"

"Why, though?" He stopped pacing. "Would it really change our dynamic so much? Do you flirt with all your bosses?"

Charlie swelled with indignation and drew a huge breath, temper lighting his eyes.

"That wasn't an insult," Innes said quickly, before Charlie could get a word in. "I flirted with you first. The problem was that you didn't immediately shut it down like I thought you would. I'm glad you didn't, don't get me wrong, but I wasn't expecting it, and I let it happen even though I knew it could go badly."

"You didn't *let* it happen," Charlie mumbled, then he straightened his shoulders. "I was there too."

Innes nodded. "Okay. We're in agreement. We flirted with each other, even though we work together. Then we followed the natural progression of that flirting and had sex. So, what do we do about it?"

"Why do I feel like you've got an idea?"

"Well, there's your chosen method: ignoring it until hopefully it goes away, and trying to forget that we've had our hands on each other's junk when you're handing me papers and things."

Charlie dropped his head into his hands. "God, you are such a child."

"Or we talk about it like adults," Innes continued as if he hadn't heard. "Make a few jokes about it over the next few weeks, never let it happen again, and the tension disappears."

"You think that's likely?"

"No idea." He tilted his head, considering. "It's possible, I suppose."

"What's your third option?" Charlie demanded. "I assume you have one."

"Instead of trying to forget it, we do it again." He put his hands in his pockets, laying down what he wanted in an even tone, honest and direct, without tricks or persuasion. "We scratch each other's itch for a while longer. No strings, just amazing, remarkably athletic sex."

"I hope you're the athlete in this situation," Charlie drawled, glancing down at his own slight frame.

"Naturally. You ever had sex with someone who could hold you up against the wall the whole time?"

Charlie seemed intrigued. "Can you?"

"I could when I was twenty-five," he admitted with a grin. "No promises."

Charlie laughed, then bit his lip in a stunningly attractive way.

Innes crossed his arms, marveling at the change in Charlie from a few minutes ago. "I have to say, you're taking this suggestion a lot better than I thought you would."

Charlie flicked his eyes up at him, his head still bent, a more serious cast to his expression. "I'm not lying to myself. It was good. I want to do it again. But I'm also aware of how complicated it could get. There's a reason why people advise against this. I've already told you that I'm not interested in the kind of relationship where money changes hands—"

"I wasn't going to offer you one."

"What if we want to stop?"

Innes lifted a shoulder casually. "We stop. Simple as that. I've never had a problem with dissolving a mutually beneficial sexual relationship."

He blinked when Charlie blew an impressively loud raspberry.

"That's a lie," Charlie accused, brandishing a finger at Innes. "Marie told me how long you sulked after the last guy."

"I did not sulk." Innes grimaced at the evidence in his voice of how bitter he still was over the whole thing. It wasn't even that he had any particular attachment to Elliott. He just hadn't liked giving up a toy he was still playing with.

Charlie looked at him like a mother would at a child denying a theft of the cookie jar. "So, if I ask your nephew about the last time, he'll corroborate?"

"All right, the only reason I was a *little bit*—" he ignored Charlie's disbelieving scoff, "—annoyed last time is because we still had months of good sex left. Every other relationship I've ever been in, we both had the same expiration date."

Innes fell silent, letting Charlie digest and turn over the information, weighing the pros and cons that Innes had already evaluated to death since the moment he'd started thinking of Charlie as more than a talented administrative assistant. Which was, when he thought about it, about two weeks before he'd even *started* as Innes's assistant. It was inevitable, really, that they would end up this way.

"I don't want to be that guy who fucks their boss for special treatment," Charlie said eventually.

"I don't want to be that boss who takes advantage of their employees. Let's not be either of those people." He waved away Charlie's urge to protest. "That's not high on my list of worries, either. If you were a low-level lawyer trying to advance up the ranks before you were ready or able, it might be an issue. You're not. You work for me, no one else. So, there's that problem solved."

"There's still an imbalance, though. You're my employer and you could fire me."

"I think the HR department would have something to say about that. You could sue, and you'd win, probably, especially if you pointed out that this entire conversation could be labeled sexual harassment, without the proper context. If you went public, my reputation would be in shreds, and if you settled privately, you'd walk away a richer man. That's a lot of power for you to hold, I think. Maybe it isn't equal, but since both of us are aware of that, and have acknowledged it, is there that much of an issue?"

Charlie stared, tense, frowning, but undeniably curious for a handful of ticks of Innes's office clock, then after a few clenches of his fists at his sides, he nodded. "Okay. I'm not going to be under your desk from nine to five, but if it happens, it happens. Provided the timing is right."

"Excellent," Innes said, fighting against the sense of triumph that made him want to fist pump the air. Instead, he closed the distance between them, intent on clearing up the final issue that had been plaguing him.

"I want you to understand, Charlie," he warned. "What I'm offering you isn't a relationship."

"Good," Charlie said, smirking at him as if he knew all about the speech Innes had loosely prepared in case this conversation had a successful outcome. "I don't want one. All I want right now is good sex I don't have to go out and search for. Clean, uncomplicated."

"Fine," Innes said, irked, but unsure about what.

"Fine."

It dawned suddenly on Innes how close they were standing. Close enough to touch, if they wanted. Charlie seemed to realize the same thing, his lips parting just a little bit as his eyes strayed to Innes's mouth.

Innes had been coasting on the good vibrations from last night all morning, but if Charlie was searching for a repeat right away . . .

The phone on Charlie's desk rang, shattering the thick press of tension Innes had been enjoying so much. Instantly, Charlie turned around and hurried away to answer it without a single regretful backward glance.

Still mourning the lost moment, Innes followed, leaning against his doorframe as Charlie sat down and switched into professional mode.

"Office of Innes Kent." He raised a questioning eyebrow at Innes. "Oh, Mr. Baker, hello," he said, significantly.

Innes nearly fell over with the force of his negative reaction. There was a mood he had to be in to deal with dear old Mr. Baker, and he was decidedly *not* in it. Charlie nodded, correctly interpreting his frantic head shake.

"He's busy right now, can you call back at— No, I'm sorry, he's tied up." Charlie's gaze flicked over to him, a twinkle appearing in his blue eyes. "No, you may not. Why? Because Marie doesn't work here anymore. You're welcome to try to call her at her new job, but that's in Oregon and I don't have the number."

Innes snickered as Charlie leaned back and made a face at him, pushing his chair into a lazy spin, making *blah blah blah* motions with his hand.

"Which attitude is that, sir? I do have a lot of them." There was a pause, during which Innes could hear Mr. Baker's voice over the line as Charlie held the phone away from his ear. "I don't have a supervisor, I answer to Mr. Kent only, and as I said earlier, he's busy, so you can talk to me or you can—" Charlie sighed and put the phone back in its cradle. "Call back later and pretend you weren't a gigantic butthole."

"Do they really do that?" Innes asked, unsure why he was interested.

"Call after lunch and suddenly act sweet as pie? Yup, especially if they didn't leave their name. As if I can't recognize their voice or their number on caller ID." Charlie tsked, the scornful *idiots* implied by his tone.

"You're a very intense person, you know that?" Innes said.

Charlie grinned, tipping his chair back and lifting his stubborn chin in a defiant, flirting smirk. "I've been told. Problem?"

Innes pushed off the doorjamb. "None whatsoever. Keep doing what you're doing."

He shut his office door on Charlie's widening grin, shaking off the stirrings of his libido. There would be time for that when he didn't have work to do. He was sure he wouldn't have to wait long.

Charlie let himself into the office quietly, so he didn't disturb Innes's phone call. He listened with half an ear while he cleaned up the cups and pitcher of water on the coffee table leftover from Innes's previous appointment.

"Everything's all set," Innes was saying. "I'm leaving after work a week from Friday and spending the night so that I won't be completely wiped for our big day out."

Innes sounded happy. A little less biting than usual in all his interactions. A lot of it had to do with the trip he was taking to see his daughter—and boy, was Charlie dying to ask about that whole situation—but Charlie was vain enough to think that the mutual orgasms they'd enjoyed two days ago had helped.

It had certainly helped Charlie. He'd actually sung in the shower when he got ready that morning—until his neighbor had pounded on the thin wall—enjoying the remainder of the high that he hadn't been able to appreciate when he'd been panicking over how he was going to face his boss again. After yesterday's conversation, though, promising more satisfaction where that had come from? He'd be singing for days.

He was finding it hard to regret anything that had happened. Even while he'd been kissing Innes that first time, rocked by how much he'd missed the give and take of tasting another person, he'd been well aware of how stupid it was. He just . . . decided not to care, for once. It was a liberating feeling, one he'd cursed himself for the morning after, but had made peace with after Innes's convincing argument in favor of letting it happen more often.

The man was an excellent debater. He wasn't a lawyer for nothing.

Tossing away the empty paper cups, Charlie heard Innes say, "No, don't worry, I'll pick you up. I'm renting a car, so I might as well put it to use." He lifted his chin in acknowledgment at Charlie as he passed. "Well, naturally it's a cool one. What, did you think I would roll up to your dorm in a mom van? Have a little faith. What's the point in having a wealthy father with a guilty conscience if you can't take advantage of it?"

Charlie choked on his own tongue trying to keep from laughing, and he wasn't the only one with that reaction. Innes had to hold the phone away from his ear to avoid the peals of hysteric giggling on the other end of the line.

"I'm glad you found that amusing. Shall we say ten o'clock next Saturday? I'll be outside the main entrance. You'll know me because I'll be driving the only Porsche in that godforsaken student wasteland. Have a good day. And Mimi?" Innes sat up, his fingers tapping an erratic pattern on the desk as he frowned down at his travel itinerary. "Feel free to call me between now and then. I'd love to hear from you."

Charlie didn't comment on the way Innes stared into space for half a minute after he hung up the phone, dragging a finger across the glass screen until he came back to himself.

"Tell me if I'm wrong," Innes said, snapping out of whatever reflective state he was in. "But it seems like I've got a free hour."

"Well, you don't have anything planned other than that case file you wanted me to remind you to read when you had time."

Innes sighed, pulling the offending file out of his desk. "That's right. God, if only you weren't so good at this job, I could have put that hour to good use."

Charlie stilled, the half-empty pitcher of water he was carrying sloshing almost to the rim at the sudden stop. He turned to look at Innes, whose eyes were twinkling in a familiar way.

Yesterday, they'd both agreed they wanted to have sex again, but it wasn't like they'd set a date in the calendar. There had been a moment when Charlie had thought it would happen right away, but then it passed, and they hadn't gotten it back yet.

"Good use, huh?" Charlie said, plunking the pitcher back down on the coffee table. "Well, it probably won't take you an hour to read one little case file, right? You got any suggestions about how you might use the rest of that time?"

Gracefully, Innes pushed his chair out from behind his desk. Then he flipped his hand over on the armrest and beckoned Charlie over with lazy fingers.

The little angel of responsibility—not to mention the Ghosts of Charlie Past who used to clean offices like these—wondered if it was a bad idea to encourage Innes. But neither of them stood up to the strength of how much Charlie *did* want to encourage him, nor could they come up with reasons Charlie didn't have a counterargument prepared for.

The office wasn't public, it was Innes's private workplace. They both knew exactly what Innes's schedule was. Charlie had already set out his *Be right back* sign. As long as they didn't yell the building down, they were fine.

Charlie took in the devilish smile on Innes's handsome face and the inviting space he'd made between his thighs and decided he wasn't going to be dumb enough to say no to an offer like that.

He shrugged off his suit jacket as he made his way over, laying it neatly on one of the guest chairs.

"Planning on staying a while?" Innes asked, but the eagerness in his face made his cool teasing less effective.

"It's my favorite. I don't want to risk it."

"Smart."

Charlie was about to make a comment along the lines of *duh*, but in the next second, he'd moved within reach of Innes, who took full advantage by pulling Charlie off-balance. He had to brace his knee on Innes's thigh, but before he could start to worry that he was too heavy, Innes was capturing his mouth in a deep, painstakingly thorough kiss.

The kind of hookups Charlie had been having hadn't involved a lot of kissing. He hadn't realized he'd missed it until Innes showed a fondness for making out like teenagers. Innes's lips were hot and confident, and his tongue . . .

Charlie would have been embarrassed by the disappointed sound that came out of him when Innes pulled away, but he was too busy chasing his mouth to get it back.

"More," he demanded, then he took what he wanted, holding Innes's face as he got his fill.

Innes was the one to break away again, pushing him up and off. Charlie was dazed, and it took him a while to realize that Innes was clearing a space on his desk.

"What—"

"Sit," Innes said—commanded, really.

Charlie was willing to let Innes take the lead on this one—to a point—so he got comfortable on the desk, which was so tall that his feet didn't quite hit the floor.

Instead of standing up and crowding Charlie, Innes rolled his chair over, running his hands up Charlie's clothed thighs in a single firm, even stroke with the bite of nails pressed in just enough to leave marks that would fade immediately.

Charlie drew in a quick breath as those hands brushed against his fly, his own hand shooting out to grab Innes's shoulder. Innes paused, then looked right into Charlie's eyes as he reached for Charlie's zipper.

"Is it my lucky day?" Charlie said, noting how much his voice already shook with anticipation.

Innes didn't stop pulling down the zipper for even a second. "I'm in a generous mood, so yes."

Charlie let his head fall back as Innes made quick work of his button, then his boxers, pulling out Charlie's cock and giving it a few strokes that were far from gentle. One of his feet banged into a drawer as Innes's smooth-skinned, manicured thumb brushed the bundle of nerves at the tip, coaxing him to full hardness.

"You want a condom?"

Charlie blinked, meeting Innes's eyes with effort and struggling to answer Innes's question.

"No," he decided. "You're forgetting, I file all your medical records. I know how many tests you've passed."

"God, this was such a good idea," Innes said passionately, then his head ducked and his mouth was on Charlie's cock.

Innes's tongue was as talented at this as it was at kissing. He used it to taunt, to play, to drive Charlie wild by giving just enough to make his stomach muscles twitch from the pleasure, but not enough to keep him from spreading his legs as wide as they could go, begging for more.

When Innes finally took as much of Charlie in as he could, Charlie's head dropped back again, and his arms trembled where they supported him on the desk. He moaned at every pull and drag of Innes's mouth and stifled a cry at a particularly hard suck and a flutter.

It put him more off-balance, but Charlie couldn't stop himself from putting a hand on Innes's neck, not pushing or directing, just playing with the soft, product-free brown hair at his nape and clutching at the hard-working tendons.

He had to bite his lip to keep the noises in when Innes picked up the pace, throwing everything he could at Charlie until he couldn't give more than a stream of choked-off curses as a warning that he was finished.

He slumped onto the desk after, breathing hard and staring, dazed, at the ceiling. He was dimly aware of the sound of Innes spitting into the trash can, which made him snort with laughter.

Poor Innes. How very *undignified* for him.

He struggled upright at the same time as Innes spoke, amusement coloring his voice. "I'll probably need my desk if I'm going to get to work."

Charlie shook his head, then fell bonelessly to his knees, yanking Innes's chair closer to him by the armrests. "You've got five minutes," he said, going for the button on Innes's pants.

"You think you can keep me running on time?" Innes asked innocently.

Charlie glared up at him, his lethargy burning away in the face of a challenge. "Try me."

# Chapter Nine

Innes heard the door open, but he didn't look over or even open his eyes. He knew it was Charlie from the distinct pattern of vibrations against his back through the floor.

He took a deep breath, wincing at the adjustment of his spine beneath his lungs. "Don't say anything," he gritted out as Charlie continued his progress across the room.

"Wasn't going to."

He scoffed. "Of course you were."

"Nope. My pointed silence would've been a way better judgment of your current situation, but you've ruined it now."

Innes silently grumbled until Charlie's feet came into view and he saw Charlie toe off his shoes. That persuaded him to give up any childish grudges and roll gratefully onto his stomach.

He groaned into the carpet when Charlie stepped gingerly onto his upper back. Charlie was short, but even he wasn't small enough that he could put his whole weight on Innes. Leaning against the desk made sure Innes could still breathe as he carefully moved his feet to the trouble spots.

Air travel was the *worst*, even in first class. At least he could be grateful that he'd done himself in on the ride back from San Francisco and not the other way around. It would have been a shame if he'd had to spend Saturday in bed with a heat pack.

He wouldn't have traded the weekend for being pain-free now. His big day out with Mimi had gone better than he could have imagined.

They'd done the tourist thing at Alcatraz, which they had found darkly amusing. They'd eaten amazing fish, and he'd bought her a bottle of top-shelf booze to take back to her dorm with the promise that she wouldn't do anything he wouldn't.

After that, he'd told her he had a surprise and, sucking up his pride and good taste in music, walked them both into a jazz bar. They'd lasted five minutes before she'd confessed that she actually hated jazz and the only reason she'd posted about it was because the prof for her music history elective was known to stalk students on social media and shamelessly favor the ones who listened to his pretentious music.

That had led to a discussion about how exactly Innes knew what Mimi posted about on Twitter, which had gone surprisingly well. Instead of being creeped out that her father was keeping tabs on her, she'd gone quiet for a while, then asked him how long he'd been a follower. They'd discussed the finer points of an article about the US penitentiary system she'd linked to over a month before while they made their way back to Stanford, leaving the jazz bar in the dust.

They hadn't fought a single time.

That wasn't to say they hadn't had their share of awkward pauses where neither of them knew what to say, and she'd been cold to him for nearly half an hour after she'd had to inform him of a shellfish allergy she'd had most of her life. But it was good. He'd learned a little about her, shown her that he did, in fact, care about her.

He'd also found out that she was distancing herself from her mother almost completely. He'd sort of gathered that from the way she'd re-introduced herself to the Kent side in the past year and from how willing she was to talk to him, but it was a relief to have it confirmed. It'd taken them years, but he was starting to think that perhaps he could be a part of her life in a way that Theresa had prevented.

It made a few aches and pains in his lumbar region worth it.

Something popped, and Innes let out a long, grateful sigh. That would give him a few hours of relief. Charlie sat down on the floor next to him to get his shoes on again.

"You're getting worse," Charlie said, undoing the knots in his laces. "Would you please consider going to a doctor? If I actually hurt you doing this, I'll kill you. Then you'll really need to go to a doctor."

"I'll consider it," Innes said, grunting as he rolled over and sat up. "No promises."

Charlie finished tying a neat bow on his last shoe and looked over at him, shaking his head but smiling indulgently. When he leaned in, Innes tilted his head up to receive his kiss, slipping a little bit of tongue in, just to keep Charlie on his toes. Charlie nipped him on the lip in retaliation, then stood and went about whatever it was he did on Monday mornings.

Innes watched him go, admiring what his pants did for the backs of his legs. He wasn't sure what it was about the backs of Charlie's legs that had him so fascinated, but it might have had something to do with how Innes hadn't really taken the time to look at that particular area that first time, the only time they'd managed to actually get naked.

They'd both enjoyed a week of quick mutual orgasms, after work or during Charlie's lunch break after Charlie had put his foot down about sex during working hours.

*"We'll never get anything done,"* Charlie had griped while doing up his belt and attempting to look professional.

*"No, but I'd be doing you instead, which is much more fun,"* he'd replied, which earned him a swat on the ass.

It was a struggle, but they managed to keep it professional, barring the occasional lapse, like the kiss they'd just shared. He'd quickly gotten used to getting off regularly again, which had led to some interesting texting on Sunday night when he'd been laid up with a bad back, bored and horny.

Charlie sexted with perfect punctuation, which Innes found incredibly hot for some reason. The single comma Charlie had missed during a critical moment had done more for him than anything either of them had sent up to that point.

"Are you going to sit there all day? Because you have a few appointments lined up that will be a little difficult to do from the floor."

"I'm going, I'm going." He hefted himself up, stretching carefully to test his range of motion. Not bad. "I get no sympathy, do I?"

"Not until your doctor prescribes it," Charlie said breezily as he opened the door to the hallway. "You won't be able to do anything upright if it keeps getting worse."

Innes rolled his eyes. "I'll still be able to pound you into—"

"Hello, Ms. Waterford," Charlie said loudly. "Mr. Kent will be ready for you in a few minutes."

Innes mimed zipping his mouth closed at Charlie's icy glare.

*Yeah,* he thought when Charlie slammed the door on him. *We keep it professional.*

"It's open," Innes called from the bathroom of his apartment on Friday.

He heard the sound of Charlie entering and gave his hair one last pass with the comb before going out to greet him.

"What did I say before I left today?" Charlie said, brandishing a garment bag.

"You said, 'Don't forget your jacket.'" He grabbed the bag, unzipping it and taking out his black dinner jacket, fresh from the dry cleaners. "I know. I'm the worst, you're the most amazing assistant ever, and I don't deserve you."

"Damn right. You're lucky I didn't have anything to do tonight."

Charlie stepped into the middle of the living room, looking around with unabashed surprise.

"What?" Innes asked, slipping on the jacket and adjusting the cuffs.

"It's so different."

Innes looked too, taking in the room he came home to every day. "From the office? Yes, I suppose so." It was still expensively appointed with the finest of everything that money could buy but in a clean, minimalist way. Nothing gaudy or tacky about it, just functional and modern. "The office is for show," he explained. "The most important clients are more likely to be impressed by ermine than chrome."

"Huh."

Charlie walked over to the fireplace, running his finger along the mantel to a dish filled with fancifully colored rocks Innes had let his decorator pick out.

"Would you like a drink?" Innes offered.

Charlie's hand fell away from the bowl. "Hmm? Oh, no. Thanks. I'm not much of a drinker. Never had the money to acquire a taste for it. The only time I ever drank in high school was more about quantity than quality."

"Maybe I'll have to teach you." Innes walked over to join Charlie at the fireplace. "A good glass of wine is a wonderful thing when you appreciate it properly."

He let his eyes rake up and down Charlie's body, taking in the casual clothes he never got to see. His T-shirt was soft enough that he could see the outline of Charlie's nipples if he looked hard enough, and his faded jeans were ripped above his left knee.

"Innes."

He glanced up, surprised at how distracted he'd been by the minuscule strip of thigh peeking out. "Yes?"

"You have a party to go to."

Innes hummed noncommittally.

Since the hotel, they hadn't exactly been choosy . . . it'd been easy enough to get off together on the desk, in the washroom, in the car right after they were done for the day, scurrying with straight faces past the reception desk like children hiding candy in their mouths. But none of those places were conducive to what kids these days liked to call "real sex."

"I should probably go," Charlie said, at the same time as he inched closer to Innes, running a finger down the lapel of his jacket. "The Kidney Disease Foundation would miss you."

Innes captured Charlie's hand, keeping it pressed to his chest. "Or you could stay. I could skip this one, write them a check in the morning to apologize. Aiden's making an appearance. I'm not needed."

Charlie scowled playfully, using his free hand to poke a sharp finger between Innes's shirt buttons. "Innes Kent. Did you forget your suit on purpose so that I would come over and you could have your wicked way with me?"

"No," he answered immediately, then he relented. "Not on purpose, at least. Perhaps my subconscious was doing me a favor, because that sounds like a plan I could approve of."

"Well," Charlie said, hooking his finger under the button placket of Innes's shirt and tugging him closer. "As long as no one's going to come after me for an organ donation, I'm—"

He broke off with a whoop as Innes grabbed him around the thighs and lifted him up, carting him toward the bedroom at top speed.

"Innes, your back—"

"It's fine, don't ruin the moment."

"I will destroy you if you get a spasm before I come—careful!" Charlie bounced as he hit the mattress, his hands shooting out to break his fall.

"Don't worry," Innes said, popping Charlie's button and tugging off his pants. "I can still make you come even if I'm on the floor writhing in pain. Somehow."

"But then I'd have to do all the work," he whined.

"Such a hardship."

Charlie sat up to take off his own shirt and boxers. Innes took his cue to get undressed but didn't toss his clothes to the floor as Charlie had. He'd only just gotten this suit back from the cleaners; he wasn't going to wrinkle it now.

He turned back to the bed from hanging them neatly in the closet, fully expecting Charlie to be waiting eagerly to get the show on the road only to find that Charlie wasn't even looking in his direction. He was on his stomach, rubbing his arms and legs over Innes's bed sheets after having kicked off all the covers.

Innes coughed pointedly. "Am I keeping you?"

Charlie flipped onto his back, still wriggling like he was making a sheet snow angel, his expression blissful and not even a little bit embarrassed about it.

"They're so *soooft*," he moaned, doing a little shimmy.

"I know."

With what looked like considerable effort, Charlie sat up, but he didn't stop moving his hands over the expanse of sheets. "Don't you feel like you're in a hotel all the time with sheets like this?"

Innes put a hand to his chest, sniffing in outrage. "Frankly, I'm insulted that you'd think I paid as little as a hotel would spend on sheets, even nice ones. These are far more expensive than that."

"I believe it." With one last pass of his hands, Charlie pushed up on his knees and made grabby hands toward Innes. "We doing this, or what?"

Innes thought about arguing that he wasn't the one holding things up. Instead, he climbed onto the bed, wrapping his arms around Charlie as they kissed, thrilled that this time he didn't have to worry their lips would get red and bruised.

He glided his hands down Charlie's body like Charlie's had swept over his sheets. Charlie's rib cage expand when Innes attached his mouth to Charlie's neck, then the lower back arch as he sucked hard, leaving a mark. When he reached Charlie's ass, his hand was guided to Charlie's hole, where he—

He lifted his head from Charlie's neck. "Why, you clever brat."

Charlie's red lips stretched in a grin. "I knew you didn't want to go to that party. Whether you were aware of it or not, you wanted me over here for one reason only. Might as well be prepared for it."

He pressed a finger into Charlie's wet and loosened hole, making Charlie squirm and hum. "Have I ever told you how sexy I find your ability to think ahead?"

"Mmm, read me more of my résumé," he said, his warm breath huffing against Innes's chest.

"As if you wouldn't love it if I said your use of logic makes me hard. Or that the way you work under pressure—" He surged his finger into Charlie, grazing his prostate and earning a guttural moan. "—gets me going. Or that the way you schedule orgasms into a private calendar I can't see makes me want to mess up your plans."

"How do you know about that calendar?" Charlie gasped out.

"I didn't know for sure until just now. But I *knew it*."

Charlie's laugh cut off with a strangled noise as Innes flexed his hand again. Charlie grabbed his shoulders, digging in with straining fingers against the jolt of pleasure that flashed across Charlie's face.

Innes hummed. "No more talking," he said, then grabbed Charlie by the waist, flipping onto his back and pulling Charlie on top of him by the waist.

Charlie didn't put up a fight, but quipped, "So, I'm doing the work this time anyway?"

Innes shushed him. "That's talking."

Rolling his eyes, Charlie took Innes's offered bottle of lube and condom and used them on him. By the time Charlie sank down onto his cock with businesslike deftness, Innes was nearly tearing his own expensive sheets with his tight grip.

Neither of them moved until the shiver of blistering hot fulfillment went through them both. Then, with slow, rhythmic rocks of his hips, Charlie broke the stasis.

"Oh, god—" Charlie said after a particularly well-aimed thrust, but he cut himself off, looking down at Innes like he was going to be scolded.

"I meant no *talking,* not *that,*" Innes said, mourning the loss of Charlie's rhythm. "We're finally alone. You can make all the noise you want, darling."

Charlie wrinkled his nose. "Darling? What— Ah!"

Innes had slapped him lightly on the thigh. "Shush."

"Make up your damn mind!"

"It is made up. No talking. Just reacting."

Charlie glared like he wanted to argue but Innes bucked his hips up, jerking him forward, and he used the energy that rocked him to re-establish their rolling, pitching motion.

Charlie was gorgeous like this, Innes thought with the jellylike substance his brain had turned into. He was a pillar of dark pink and blushing white above Innes, all tight lines and constantly moving limbs. The longer Innes watched, the longer they rocked together, the more he wanted it to end so he could chase away the wrinkled frown in Charlie's forehead and the flush that would drain from his cheeks when he was resting.

Innes reached out for Charlie's cock, stroking it hard and fast like he'd learned Charlie loved, groaning at the way Charlie tightened around him. Within a minute, Charlie had lost his rhythm, his hips twitching between Innes's grip and his cock.

Charlie's regular stream of rapid-fire nonsense announced his arrival at the end. "God, that's it, it's there, right there, f—"

Innes stroked him through it, fascinated by the slack-jawed, blissed-out expression on Charlie's face, then started to pull out.

"No, it's fine," Charlie blurted, pressing down with tired thighs so Innes wouldn't move. "Stay. Just finish."

He didn't have to be told twice. With little help from a limp, exhausted Charlie, who twitched at every movement as if he was in pain, Innes worked himself closer to the end.

They both groaned when Innes finally came, and they traded lazy, damp kisses while they recovered. Charlie slid more than moved to the side, curling up with his head on Innes's shoulder and their legs languidly intertwined.

Time passed in a fog of sweaty satiation that Innes found himself enjoying quite a bit, despite Charlie's apparent need to cuddle up. He was bony, but he knew where to put his elbows so he didn't bruise any sensitive areas.

"Am I allowed to talk now?" Charlie drawled when he'd recovered enough for his fidgety fingers to start drumming on Innes's sternum.

"That depends on what you want to talk about."

Charlie slithered down and propped his pointy chin on Innes's chest so that he could stare up at Innes's face without as much difficulty. Innes didn't look back. That wasn't a good angle for anyone.

"You were happier this week," Charlie said plainly.

Innes considered how he might deny it or blame it on some unpleasant aspect of his personality, but in the end, Charlie was right. He was happier.

"Yes," he said simply.

Charlie's fingers stilled on his chest. "What changed? I know it wasn't me, it was just these past few days."

"Mimi," he answered immediately, fighting a smile that felt more genuine than he normally was. "She called me. *Twice* in one week."

"That's great," Charlie said, but Innes could tell he didn't really get why it was such a big deal, and why should he? Innes didn't tell him anything he didn't have to know, and the fact that Mimi never talked to him unless she absolutely had to was something he'd always kept to himself.

"Do you want to talk about it?" Charlie asked.

Innes peered down into his open, earnest face. "Don't look at me like that."

"Like what? I'm not doing anything."

He grimaced. "That thing you do where you make me talk about personal stuff."

"I repeat, I'm not doing anything. I only asked if you wanted me to listen. I would if you wanted me to, but I'm not forcing you—"

"All right, all right, I'll talk, quit interrogating me." Innes smirked at Charlie's irritated huff, then got serious as he wondered where to begin.

"We're not that close." He winced. "That's an understatement. I don't really know her because I didn't raise her."

"Why?" Charlie asked gently.

"Mimi was an accident. I was seventeen, uninterested in women but pretending desperately that I was. There was this party, full of older kids I didn't know, and Theresa was there, the only person I recognized from school. I was drunk. She was not."

Charlie shifted, propping himself up on an elbow. Innes didn't face him, didn't even stop, because it felt so good to *talk*, for once, about something he barely let himself think about.

"I've never been sure whether or not she got pregnant on purpose. I'd like to think she wouldn't have done that, but it wasn't a secret that my family was wealthy. She said she didn't, but she said many things."

"Shit," Charlie said, and Innes had to grin, despite how tense this whole conversation was making him.

He nodded. "Her parents wanted us to get married. Said it was the right thing to do. My mother disagreed, said it would ruin both our lives. That was one of the only times I've ever agreed with her, and I was grateful. She convinced them to see her side of things, and so I remained a bachelor. But Mimi wasn't so easy a problem to fix. I wanted to give her up. Neither of us were ready for children, but Theresa insisted."

He closed his eyes against the memory of the panic that had plagued him for that first year. He remembered Theresa's pregnancy, that he knew nothing about. The first months of Mimi's life, standing around feeling useless while Theresa and her parents took care of everything, then judged him for not knowing how to change a diaper.

"I tried. Honestly, I did. For a clueless, recently uncloseted teenage boy, I think I did okay for a while. My brother and his wife helped, and I fit her into my life between school and rebelling against my parents as hard as I could, but by the time I'd graduated, Theresa was finished co-parenting. By the time Mimi was eight, I was out of her life almost completely. It was better for her. Whenever I tried to see her, Theresa would—"

He broke off, the words kept in for so long drying up when the memories got even harder to face. He sighed. It'd been a good run. He couldn't expect to purge everything when it went against his normal rule of nondisclosure.

"You okay?" Charlie asked.

"Yes," he said shortly. "But I'm done talking about this."

Charlie nodded and started tapping his restless fingers on Innes's chest again. "Okay. Can I say one thing?"

"If you must."

"I'm glad you're trying to be a part of her life again. I can tell you're conflicted about it."

Innes frowned. "What do you mean?"

"If you were really sure about wanting to get to know her, you'd be spending way more time at Stanford, being too generous with gifts and money, calling her every day instead of waiting for her to call you. Generally being a pain in the ass until she gets used to it. But you're hesitating."

Innes shifted, the sheets suddenly feeling less comfortable. "Is that your one thing? You've said it, we can move on now."

"No, that wasn't my one thing, you distracted me," Charlie snapped, then he softened his tone. Or softened it as much as he was able, being him. "I wanted to say that whatever your reason is for not letting her into your life completely, you're wrong. I've spent most of my life without a father, even a crappy one, and it sucks."

"Agree to disagree, then." Charlie obviously felt strongly about the issue, and Innes was grateful that he was willing to let it go. "I had at least one big impact on Mimi," he said, hoping to distract them both from more serious topics. "Her name. I don't think she knows, but I was the first one who called her that, and it stuck."

"Oh," Charlie said, obviously surprised. "It's . . . a bit—"

"If you say it's a stripper name, I swear to God I will kick your ass, because she is my daughter, estranged or not."

"Nope, wasn't going to. It just doesn't seem like your style."

Innes shrugged, jostling Charlie's head a bit. "Theresa told me her full name was a family name, but I never met or heard of any great-grandma Miriam, so it might have been another lie. I'm just happy the

Kents don't subscribe to that way of thinking, or my name would have been Arnold the third or something equally as heinous."

Charlie made a disgruntled noise. "Boy, do I get that. On all my paperwork, I'm Charles Junior. I got my father's name, but I've got fuck all else from the bastard."

Innes looked down, intrigued by Charlie's vehemence. For someone who was so in favor of fatherhood, he had quite a bit of anger stored up. But wasn't that Charlie all over?

"I like Charlie," Innes said, bringing up a hand to comb through Charlie's blond hair before he was even aware of it. "It suits you."

"Thanks. It's way better than my middle name." Charlie went quiet, pressing up into Innes's fingers, but Innes was not satisfied.

"Are you really going to leave me hanging like that?" He shook his head at Charlie's confused look. "What's your middle name? I'm dying to know."

Charlie snorted. "No way am I telling you."

"Jeffery?"

"No."

"Seymour?"

"No!" Charlie yelled, loud enough that Innes had to shrink away, but he wasn't about to leave it there.

He thought for a second, giving Charlie enough time to think he'd given up. "Thor?"

"What? No, of course not. I'm not telling you," Charlie insisted.

"It's Thor, isn't it? You're lying to me."

With great effort, sliding on the soft sheets beneath them, Charlie got up on his hands and knees and glared down. "Innes Beauregard Kent, if you don't shut up, I will post your birth certificate on Facebook."

"Spoilsport." Spitefully, Innes knocked Charlie's elbows so that he was suddenly off-balance, but it backfired immediately when Charlie fell forward and his sharp chin dug into Innes's chest, wringing an *oof* of pain from both of them.

Charlie started laughing first, but Innes followed, helplessly pulled in by the infectious sound until they both had wet eyes and sore stomach muscles.

It was then, giggling in bed like children before Charlie got tired of being sticky with the remnants of sex, that Innes started to feel . . . worried.

It wasn't an emotion he was familiar with. Stress, sure. He'd been dealing with that since college. But worry over an outcome he wasn't sure he could influence was as foreign to him as the freedom he'd felt when he'd spewed his story about Mimi.

This was worry, though, and it was caused by another feeling that had snuck up on him.

There was softness in the way he felt for Charlie. He wanted to know what Charlie's face looked like in the morning when he wasn't quite awake. Bring Charlie food at exactly the right time so that he'd be the hero of the day. Cuddle him.

He was already cuddling him.

That made the worry a little more urgent.

Worry over what, though? That he was going to go mush-brained like Aiden? Unlikely. He just had to watch himself, and the weird soft-and-fuzzy feelings would go away on their own when his relationship with Charlie came to its natural conclusion.

They'd be fine. Right?

"So, if your bed's this fancy," Charlie said, pulling away and scooting off the mattress. "What's your bathroom like?"

"Prepped with rose petals and champagne, darling." The quip—a little too sincere for Innes's liking—slipped out before he could filter it, but Charlie saved him before he could cover it up.

"It better not be. I'm not into that romantic shit."

"Mud bath and a beer?" Innes suggested.

"I would drown you in it."

And with that shockingly believable threat, Charlie strode off into the—thankfully mud-free—bathroom, his exclamations over the size of the tub floating out behind him.

Maybe Charlie's romantic inclinations would help keep Innes's in check.

# Chapter Ten

Charlie woke to a warm tickle between his shoulder blades. It took a few bewildered blinks for him to realize that it was Innes's stubble, the prickling morning length of it dragging down his bony spine, which Innes seemed to like, for some reason.

Charlie wasn't under any illusions as to what he looked like. He was short, skinny and skeletal, but he got the job done, and Innes didn't seem to mind, if the erection pressing up against the back of his thigh was any clue.

"All right, then," Charlie said around a yawn. "Go on."

"Such enthusiasm," Innes said in his ear, low and morning-rough.

"Give me a reason to be enthusiastic, then," Charlie challenged, stretching his arms and arching his lower body against Innes, half on purpose, half just because it felt good to take up space in the huge bed.

He didn't resist when Innes encouraged him to turn over, and he lifted his legs willingly when Innes picked them up, draping them over his arms so that he could kneel between Charlie's thighs.

He sighed in Innes's grip, choosing not to fight against the tide of drowsiness, even while Innes pushed his finger inside him where he was still a little loose and wet from last night. He let it happen with a sleepy acceptance, barely hissing when Innes added more lube and more fingers. He only really woke up when Innes was seated inside him, full and hot, bringing him closer to complete, energized awareness with every thrust.

He'd gotten used to how comfortable the sheets were overnight. His own bed would be hard to take, so he turned his face into the pillows while he could, enjoying the smooth, cool fabric against his cheek and the smell of Innes, of them together. Clean sweat, laundry, and expensive cologne.

It was with that scent in his nose that he coasted to climax. Not violently like he had the night before, but easily. Effortlessly.

Innes curled up behind him when he was finished, damp skin sticking in unspeakable places. His warm breath tickled Charlie's ear as he hummed happily.

"I have a very expensive coffee machine," he purred into Charlie's neck, once their breathing had evened out.

"Do you, now?" Charlie reached back blindly, grabbing a handful of firm thigh to try to ground himself in the waking world. "I'm too sleepy to tease you about overcompensation."

"And I would hope that by now, you know I have nothing to compensate for."

"That too."

Innes pressed a wet, sucking kiss to the peach fuzz at Charlie's nape. "Let me make you a drink."

"Yes. Something as black as your soul, please."

"Coming right up."

After Innes rocked the bed while leaving it, and left him alone, Charlie woke up a little more. Stumbled to the bathroom to try to feel human again. When he came out, there was a robe on the bed—fluffy, white, and impersonal, like a hotel—and a pair of folded black boxers.

Innes had obviously left them there, but there wasn't a note or a clue about why. Charlie had expected to be rushed out the door with a *See you Monday*. He would've been fine with that. Instead, there was a soft white housecoat and underwear that felt too expensive and would barely fit.

And he found he didn't mind that either.

Charlie had thought that Innes was more of a social creature than he let on. He could complain about idiots all he wanted, but he wouldn't have kept on doing the in-person charity events for the Kent Foundation if he didn't enjoy them at least a little bit.

Even a slow Saturday morning would be better with an audience, and Charlie was happy to give him one.

When he shuffled into the kitchen—hitching up the waistband of the boxers as he went—Innes turned around with a mug full of black goodness, the steam rising from it the same color as the thin T-shirt Innes was wearing. He set it down on the marble counter as Charlie reached it.

"Did you time that perfectly so you could look cool?"

Innes threw a smirk over his shoulder as he went back to the shiny coffee machine—which was, as Charlie had suspected, pretty girthy—to pour a second cup of a creamier-colored coffee. "Did it work?"

"Eh, so-so." *Yes*, but Charlie would take that to his grave. He sipped instead of telling the truth. "Oh my god. Can I wake up here every day?"

He hadn't meant to say that, but Innes just smiled again and leaned a hip against the edge of the counter and handed over his cup.

"Try mine," he said, then waited with a passive face while Charlie took a sip, then shook his head.

"Too sweet for me, but I can see how you'd like it. Tastes like . . . cake?"

"Caramel. Or at least, that's what the package says. Honestly, I've only had this thing for a few weekends, and I never have time during the week, not when I have to cook dinner too."

Charlie paused with his leg hitched halfway onto the stool next to the counter, then hurried to sit down. "You cook?"

"Very well."

"Huh. Wouldn't have expected that." He never made his own lunch, like Charlie did, but him packing lunch was harder to picture than Innes at this same counter, adding red wine to some pretentious beef dish that took thirty-six hours to make.

"I taught myself." A different sort of pride from usual shone through Innes's morning bleariness. A quieter kind of confidence. "Takeout and pasta with canned sauce gets boring after a while. I like it. It feels almost like a creative outlet. A nicer one than writing closing statements that the jury is only half listening to."

"Interesting. I never thought about it that way. When I cook, it's about necessity. I'm the master at making one meal last for three, but it's not particularly artistic. I eat a lot of potatoes and rice."

"You poor deprived thing. Stay over again and I'll make you eggs Benedict." His eyes flicked to the clock on the stove and he winced. "I'd make it for you today, except—"

Charlie snapped, remembering before Innes could tell him. "You've got that thing."

"Brunch," he sneered, but there wasn't much heat behind it. "A hellish meal, honestly. Strange timing, and it throws my rhythm all off. This one won't be too bad, though, otherwise I'd eat before I got there. I've been to one before, and the organizers aren't obnoxious. Just boring."

Charlie gulped his coffee down and barely managed not to lick his teeth to catch every precious drop. "I'd take boring over obnoxious any day."

"Liar." The kitchen light made Innes's eyes twinkle. Or maybe that was the mischief in his expression. "You took me, didn't you?"

"Fair. No regrets, though." At least not yet.

Their mouths were both coffee-flavored when Innes leaned in to kiss him, unhurried. Innes's unshaved stubble bit into his skin.

"Glad to hear it," Innes said, then his mug paused on the way to his mouth. "You don't . . ."

"What?" Charlie hoped Innes wasn't about to suggest he skip this event too, because that wouldn't fly.

"Well, events like these have been a lot more boring recently."

More boring? Why would they . . .

Oh.

That guy, the one Marie told him about. Evan? Elliott. He used to go with Innes to things like this, either before or after they fucked. The ghost of their relationship lived on in Charlie's calendar at work, in re-occurring events that had a note to check the availability of Innes's usual date.

Thank god they never scheduled sex in the same calendar. That would be too weird. The whole thing was a little weird to contemplate, honestly. He didn't judge Innes for being the type of person who would pay another man for sex and companionship. (Neither did he judge the man who was paid.) But it was easy to forget that Innes had once been—*was still?*—the kind of person who could be happy with something so cut and dry.

What he and Innes had was different. Not that much, and not really better, but still different. Charlie gave up everything that the other guy had, only for free.

Well, not everything.

"Have they?" Charlie asked, trying not to predict where this was going, since he'd probably be wrong.

"Interminably. Even in a city as big as this one, a lot of the same people support the same charities as the foundation. If any of them had something interesting to say, they've already said it."

"Sucks," Charlie said, his voice echoing broadly into his half-empty cup. If Innes was getting at what he thought, he certainly wasn't going to help him out.

"Do you want to come with me?"

Boom. There it was.

The warning he'd had didn't make him any less surprised to be invited . . . or less shocked that he actually wanted to go.

This morning—and the night before—had been fun. Actually fun, not just gratifying or exciting in a sexy way. He hadn't had such a good time in months, maybe years. It was like . . . a really nice date that was supposed to end with lunch but turned into a movie, then a night together, then the morning after, and kept on going.

Or, at least, that was what he assumed it felt like. He'd never had a date like that.

"Sure," he said. "Why not? Free food."

"And good company, I hope."

Charlie darted in to press a smiling kiss on a stubbly cheek. "You got me there. You sure it's not a problem for them?"

"It's buffet-style, so they won't care. Even if it wasn't, they know my name."

There was a kind of loose-jointed delight in how Innes moved as he drained his cup and put it in the sink, puttering around the kitchen with ease and smiling with less triumph in his eyes than Charlie would've expected.

"I have to shower," Innes said, scratching the mess of his product-riddled hair.

"Cool. Oh, I'll need clothes?" He might've been able to slip on some of Innes's boxers in a pinch, but their suit sizes couldn't have been more different.

"We can stop by your place on the way, if you want?"

The thought sent a bolt of panic to his stomach at the idea of two different worlds melding, but it was the only logical thing to do. "Sounds good."

"Okay."

"Good."

The pause that came after wasn't awkward, so much as full. They both had things they could be doing, and things they were looking forward to doing. Innes was visibly buzzing, and Charlie was feeding off it but unsure on this unfamiliar territory.

So he did the one thing he was sure about.

Getting off the stool was a smooth process and coming around the breakfast bar took seconds, more hesitancy disappearing with every step.

The other kisses from this morning were surface ones. Fun, like the whole morning had been fun, but nothing more than that. This one was more. Innes's hands snuck underneath Charlie's robe, grip tightening on his lower back as they kissed, until his nails bit in and Charlie had to pull away to gasp.

"I'm rescheduling your manicure appointment sooner," he breathed, his heart pounding.

Innes's eyebrows quirked. "Go ahead. I'll still find a way to leave a mark." He dipped his head and nudged aside the bunched fabric around Charlie's neck to suck a brief promise there. A threat. One Charlie hoped he'd make good on.

"Shower," Charlie said, nudging Innes away and shivering as the robe settled against his skin, colder now.

"I'm going, I'm going. Boss me around in my own home." But he was smiling as he said it, happily going off to shower alone. It was tempting to join him, but they'd never get anything done, and Innes's reputation among his peers depended on him getting to the brunch on time.

While Charlie waited, he sat on Innes's plush white couch, pulling an unbelievably soft throw into his lap. Somewhere, music had started playing, probably set on some kind of timer. It was nice. Low-key, turning the place into more of a home than a hotel room.

He'd charged his phone fully before coming here last night, so the shit battery was only half-gone. He woke it up and wasted some on taking a pixelated picture of his bare feet poking out from the blanket.

He sent it to Joy, along with the message, *How come nobody ever told me how awesome weekends are?*

Weekends with Innes, at least.

Innes's fancy car pulled up to the curb, and Charlie tried his hardest not to care about the shabby apartment building that towered over them.

"I'll be a couple minutes," he said, throwing off his seat belt.

"Take your time, I can entertain myself." Innes had already fished out a paperback from the center console, the one he was valiantly plowing through during lunch breaks on Mimi's recommendation.

Charlie was pretty sure the book wasn't really Innes's style, but he wasn't going to try to convince him to give it up, not when Innes's mouth had that mulish set that only appeared when he was talking to his family.

"Do you mind if I make some food for my ma?"

Innes looked up from thumbing the pages of the book. "Sure, just don't go crazy and make a four-course meal. We're plenty early, but only if we don't waste time."

"No, no, just something quick. I just didn't leave anything out for her last night, and I worry. She might forget to eat until, like, noon if I don't remind her."

"Oh?" Innes's finger had stilled, and while his face didn't show any particular feeling, there was a particular blankness there that raised Charlie's hackles far too easily.

"Yeah? What of it?"

Brows raised, Innes's pleasant expression turned a little amused. "Nothing at all."

"Good."

"Sure." To his credit, Innes managed to leave it be for two whole seconds while Charlie fumbled with the door handle. "Do you make all her meals?"

The defensiveness that often got Charlie in trouble reared its head. "She's an adult, she can do it herself, she just . . . doesn't. Sometimes. But it's not a big deal."

"I never said it was. Hell, I'm not certain my nephew actually could feed himself, and he's almost thirty. Good thing he has the money to get someone else to do it." Innes's smirk faded, and he looked down at the book in his hands. "And it's a good thing your mother has you."

That was . . . a surprising amount of sincerity for this early in the day. "Yeah."

"Now get out. If you make me late, you're fired."

Charlie snorted. "As if I'd be the one making you late."

"Smart-ass."

Despite Innes's threat, Charlie didn't rush on his way out of the car and up to the apartment. They had some time, and he was enjoying the morning too much to rush around and get nervous.

"Ma!" The door slammed behind him, and he wondered, too late, if she'd still be sleeping.

Thankfully, she was up and bustling around the kitchen, a cup of tea sloshing in her hand as she swiped at the counter with a rag between a couple of dishes Charlie hadn't done before he'd left the night before.

"Morning!" Her voice was as cheerful as he felt, their moods finally matching. "Did you have a good time?"

"Sure did." *Sleeping over at a friend's place* was the excuse he'd given her, which was kind of the truth. A lot more than sleeping, and a lot perpendicular to friends, but essentially the truth, so he didn't feel too bad about fudging.

"Breakfast?" Whether that was an offer or a request wasn't totally clear, but Charlie already had a plan.

"Not for me today," he said, getting out a knife and a banana that had to be used up today or tossed out. "I'm heading out for a little bit. Is that okay?"

"Of course, baby!" She hugged him from behind, her small stature meaning she had to stretch on her toes to kiss his messy hair. "You should have fun."

"I think I will." Stretching awkwardly, he gave her a peck on a flowery-scented cheek. "Hand me a bowl?"

Charlie made cereal-but-fancy, with his ma protesting the whole time that she didn't need it. He didn't care, because he wanted her to be as chipper as he was.

"I think you're two minutes away from singing out loud," she said, while he combed his hair at the kitchen table, unwilling to give up a little bit of morning quality time.

"Maybe."

"What kind of friend is this?"

The comb tugged a little too hard at the sly note in her pretty voice.

"Um." How the hell was he supposed to answer, when he didn't want her to know but couldn't lie? "Not Joy?"

"I figured that." She reached over and patted his knee, perfect unchipped nail polish vivid pink against his jeans. "Is it serious?"

This at least, he could tell the truth about and not worry about it being complicated. "No. We're just friends, honestly. But it's nice to have a new friend."

She nodded absently, the idea as foreign to her as it was to him. Then, out of nowhere, she asked, "Do you remember Mrs. Watkins?"

"Oh, god. Yeah. I wonder how she's doing."

It was the kind of question he expected from his ma, who loved flights of fanciful nostalgia, but this look back at the past he didn't mind.

He'd had a love-hate relationship with Mrs. Watkins, the home economics department head at his high school. She'd taught him everything he knew of garment construction that he couldn't learn from the internet, but they'd bickered over the restrictions of her assignments and the time she thought he should be spending on improving until the moment he'd graduated.

Ma brushed her spoon on the milky bottom of the bowl and looked out their kitchen window. "I always thought that if you were the same age, you would've been friends. You needed someone to push you, and Joy is too kind."

He probably wouldn't have pursued the hobby at all without Mrs. Watkins. He was old and wise enough to admit that he only cared about it at first because she told him he was average and could do better.

She'd been livid when she found out he wasn't going to go to college for it, or even try to get a job in the industry. He'd reacted badly to her disappointment, railing at her instead of at the unfairness of the world that made it impossible for him to do exactly what they both wanted.

He'd never gone back for a visit. He didn't even think about her anymore, unless he was slacking on making a seam perfectly straight, and snatches of her voice told him he'd only have to do it again if he didn't do it right the first time.

Since then, he hadn't really done anything right the first time. Everything else had been a series of mistakes or the better of two bad options.

Except this job, maybe. But then he had to go and make the mistake of Innes. And, of course, he was very well aware that every day they continued to do this was a mistake. He just stopped caring about crooked seams.

"Yeah, maybe," he answered, blinking away the recent past. "What about you? Any new friends? Mr. Flores, maybe?"

"No," she cooed, but she was blushing a little.

Charlie grinned, happy to see her bashful and thrilled, even if he knew the relationship wouldn't go anywhere. It didn't have to if it brought her a moment's pleasure and confidence.

His phone buzzed. It was a junk email from Jo-Ann's Fabric, not Innes hurrying him along, but it reminded him they were on a timeline.

"I gotta run." He darted in to kiss her cheek again, then disappeared into his room, feeling like a teenager getting ready for prom, complete with an open closet and indecision.

He looked over the clothes that lived at the back, out of the way, the few that were made to fit him, but never seemed to fit. Not when he lived the life he did, in and out of uniform, then in business casual for Innes.

In the end, he picked a shirt that hovered on the edge of being called a blouse. A bit of airy looseness in the sleeves, a tight floral pattern, a couple lines of peekaboo lace across the shoulders and collar bone. Nothing too crazy. It was brunch, after all, not fashion week.

After tugging on some pants that were just tight enough for decency, he kissed his ma on the cheek and let himself out. He thundered down the outside stairs, nervous excitement shaking his hands at the wrists. When he got in the car, Innes wasn't giving off an air of impatience, but he was frowning at his phone, which he turned for Charlie to see.

"Do you know what this is? Mimi sent it to me."

Peering at the screen, he took in the string of almost incomprehensible words, and an edited picture of Karl Marx?

"It's a meme," he said, less confident than he would ever let on. "You know what that is, Grandpa?"

Innes scoffed, already typing out a response. "Of course I know what a meme is. My generation invented them. I just don't know this one. They cycle through so fast these days, I can't keep up."

"Honestly, me neither. Nineteen-year-olds are objectively the funniest people on the planet, and you and I are powerless in their presence. She could eviscerate us both with a well-timed *Drag Race* quote, and we'd probably thank her for the third-degree burns."

"She is funny." Pride warmed Innes's voice. "Smart as hell."

"Wonder where she got that from?"

Charlie had expected Innes to preen, but he closed off instead. It was hard to tell what he was feeling, or if Innes even knew himself, but the moment was over quickly when he pocketed his phone and looked up for the first time.

His eyes widened a fraction. "Wow. You look great."

"I clean up nice, huh?"

"Just about as nicely as you dirty up."

Instead of taking the bait, he shared his own pride, his baby. "I made this."

"Wow," Innes said again, taking a bit of the silky fabric between his thumb and finger. "It's weirdly very you. Not that you look out of place in work clothes, but this is nice too. Different."

"Thanks." For caring? For pretending to? For not laughing outright? It didn't matter. His gratitude remained. "I'm hungry."

"Can't have that." Innes turned on the car and put it in gear. "Better step up my game, or I'll start thinking you're only using me for my body." Charlie laughed and rubbed his stomach as they pulled away from the curb.

Sometimes Innes thought Mimi looked more like Aiden than she did him.

It wasn't fair, honestly. They had similar features, the same coloring, almost. It shouldn't have mattered, but in moments like this, when Aiden was frowning, and his eyes were a little tired, like hers usually were, they looked like they could've been siblings instead of cousins.

Not like resemblance meant anything anyway. Innes was the spitting image of his father, and it'd never changed a thing.

"You look like shit," Innes said under his breath as he approached Aiden, who'd been hanging out near the edge of the outdoor venue. Most people hadn't gone into the tent yet, since food was still being set up.

Aiden sent a red-rimmed glare his way, his normally upright—or uptight, more accurately—posture slumped and stiff with the discomfort of an obvious hangover.

"Fuck you," Aiden grumbled at Innes, then he turned to Charlie with an accusing pointer finger. "And fuck you."

Charlie jerked back, already drawn up in outrage. "What did I do?"

"I know you had something to do with this." Aiden took a deep swig from the flute in his hand, which probably contained orange juice liberally spiked with champagne. "I was alone last night at the Kidney Disease thing, so I had to bear the brunt of talking to the organizer all night long. He is relentless. I got drunk just to survive. I hate drinking."

"Hey, it's not my fault you didn't bring a plus-one to save you."

"Elliott had an essay due," Aiden grumbled, but it was accompanied by the soft, sickening smile of the young and in love. Unmistakable and nauseating.

If Innes had been a little more on his guard, and a little less giddy that there would be someone worth talking to at this shindig, he would've been able to predict what a bad idea it was to bring up Elliott to Aiden when Charlie was around.

As it was, he didn't even have the presence of mind not to look to Charlie for a reaction.

Charlie showed everything on his face, all the time, and this morning was no exception. Innes watched the rapid-fire sequence of emotions as they played out. Confusion, then recognition, and a brief pause where they were almost off the hook. But then, inevitably, suspicion.

"Wait," Charlie said, not accusing just yet. Curious, for sure, and probably waiting to be proven wrong. "Elliott?"

Aiden looked even more uncomfortable, his blood-shot eyes sliding to Innes. "Have you said . . ."

"No," Innes answered.

"Do you want to do the honors?"

"Not at all. But we probably should."

Aiden grimaced. "How are you so calm about this?"

Now, that was easy to explain, with a shrug he knew would annoy Aiden. "Charlie knows all of my other deep dark secrets as a product of his job."

The look he slid to the mystified Charlie spoke volumes of his disbelief. "All of them?"

"Enough that shame is a bygone concept."

Through with being ignored, Charlie cut in, his hand hovering over Innes's arm before it went back down to his side. "Uh, do I need to know something important?"

"It's not that serious," Innes said, taking pity on poor, fragile Aiden, who looked like he would keel over from a stiff breeze. Lightweight. "I used to pay Elliott for his services. Aiden's dating him now."

The moment it was out of his lips, an unfamiliar tension pinched at the back of Innes's neck. He couldn't take it back now, and despite what he'd said to rile Aiden up, he was a little worried about what Charlie would think. Not about the way Elliott had decided to move on. That wasn't on him. But the reminder that Innes had been the kind of person to pay someone over a decade his junior to sleep with him—that he still was that person—wasn't something he wanted Charlie to remember.

But Charlie's face didn't crinkle in disgust like the worst-case scenario. It just went a little round everywhere as he thought it over. "Oh. Weird."

"You got that right. I like it better when I never have to think about it." Innes looked over as Aiden grimaced again, his gaze fixed on the slightly wilted grass under their feet. "Why are you here anyway? And why were you invited last night? We never used to run into each other."

Aiden cleared his throat, obviously wishing he was anywhere else, talking to anyone else, but he was nothing if not honest. "Mom thinks we're fighting or something."

"Ah." Good old well-meaning, nosy Catherine. His favorite sister-in-law, but that wasn't saying much. "So, what, she's hoping the generous spirit will bring us closer together?"

"Maybe." From across the lawn, one of the organizers announced that brunch was ready inside the tent. Aiden wilted and headed in the direction of more bracing mimosas and fatty breakfast foods. "Thank god."

Innes trailed after, but not before making searching eye contact with an uncustomarily quiet Charlie, who seemed to wake up from a daze and follow along, deliciously upright and poised in his fanciful outfit.

He looked good. Confident. Anyone observing them would think he'd come to events like this countless times. Only Innes knew enough to look at his hands, which wiggled at the ends of his wrists every couple of steps, like he could shake the tension right out of them and, with it, any nerves.

It was tempting to put a hand on him, maybe where the smooth fabric of his shirt pooled nicely in the small of his straight back, but that wasn't what Charlie was here for. While Elliott had been paid to be arm candy, Charlie was paid for something very different, and Innes wouldn't put him at a disadvantage by embarrassing him in front of anyone who could be a client in the future.

"Seating's not assigned," he said, putting his hand in his pocket instead of on silk-covered skin. "Preference?"

"Away from the buffet line," Charlie said, decisively. "The walk will be good for us, and I don't want to hear anyone complain about how this obscene amount of food is ruining their diet."

Innes secured them a quarter of a table in the farthest corner, where a clear plastic window fluttered back and forth in the slack tent wall, spilling light onto white tablecloth.

He introduced himself loudly to the rest of the table, then made way for Charlie to do the same.

"My new personal assistant," he clarified when Charlie had finished. "A miracle worker, honestly. Breakfast is the least I can treat him to."

There. Let the few people who overheard him spread around that Charlie wasn't that kind of date. His professional distance would do the rest, even if he couldn't truthfully say he wasn't giving Charlie a very special bonus after hours.

The food was as good as he'd promised, thankfully. He would've hated to be made into a liar. Charlie might have looked a little panicked at the platter of smoked salmon, but he'd added it to his plate on Innes's advice and enjoyed it along with the kinds of things he was more used to.

"What kind of food do you cook?" Charlie asked, while he picked apart layers of croissant with his knife.

"Good food." At Charlie's look, he went on. "Nothing too complicated, or things that take days. Simple, but impressive to look at. I'm not a baker."

Charlie had already started nodding. "Same. Too much math and stuff to go wrong. But I love a slow cooker."

"Ew."

"What's wrong with slow cookers??" It was loud enough that the woman next to Charlie glanced over, but her attention didn't linger.

Shrugging, Innes regretfully forked a sausage he should never have put on his plate onto Charlie's, instead. "Nothing, if you're okay with everything being drowned to death and also way too dry at the same time."

Charlie stabbed the sausage and stuck out his chin. "You just don't have my skills."

"I concede. And I don't want to learn." He wiped his hands, pushing his plate away in the hope that he wouldn't be tempted to finish the remains of breakfast. He didn't need it, even if he did want it. "I know as much as I need to keep myself from starving or living off catered meals like someone I know."

At Charlie's questioning brow, he jerked his head in the direction of Aiden, who looked a little less like death warmed over, but glazed as the person next to him talked with a mouthful of fruit salad. He just had all the bad luck at these events.

"You should rescue him," Charlie murmured, leaning in a little too close to be good for his own reputation. "Give him a break, at least for a couple minutes."

"Probably. Not right away, though."

"You're mean." Charlie knocked the edges of their fists together on the table, but his smile was wicked and approving.

"Demonstrably. But he's an adult; my obligation to take care of him ceased when I was no longer paid to babysit."

There was a particular hum Charlie used to punctuate his sentences that never meant anything good for Innes. Innes would never admit he was scared of it, but he was man enough to admit that unease slithered down his spine and he felt the urge to open his mouth whenever he heard it.

"So did your obligation expire for Mimi?" Charlie asked, deftly stepping over conversational landmines. "And, yet, you keep reading that book."

The tablecloth had a thick, rigid seam at the edge that dug into Innes's fingers as he fidgeted with it. "I don't think that's the same, is it?"

"No, it isn't," Charlie allowed. "But why do you think it's different?"

He could've just not answered. Anytime Charlie did this, his therapist routine, Innes could've just ignored it. It was tough to figure out whether he always fell for it due to Charlie's skill or Innes's own narcissism.

"I'm her father. Her blood. It seems callous to give up completely, especially now that she's an adult and can hold an intelligent conversation."

"But you are callous. And does blood really have anything to do with it? My father— Actually, wait." Charlie's fork clattered against his plate as he shut down, like he hadn't been the one to start this. "Let's not go there. I don't want to talk about that."

"You think I do?"

"Yes, actually. I think you're a little desperate to talk about your bullshit, otherwise you wouldn't have let me know in the first place."

*Was* he that desperate? Searching for approval from someone whose opinion he valued, maybe? He wouldn't get it from any of his own blood, that was for sure. He wasn't looking forward to the conversations he'd be having once they found out he was trying to reconnect while the getting was good. (While Theresa was in the dog house.)

"Not now," Innes said, too aware of everyone around them for much soul searching. "It's not the time."

"Okay." Without a fuss, Charlie turned those searching blue eyes away. "So, when's the earliest I can go back for seconds without outing myself as a total rube?"

It was hard not to touch Charlie when he leaned a little too close to scooch his chair out, and again when he came back to the table. Staying hands-off wasn't something Innes was used to, especially since before he'd forced himself to be more touchy with Elliott than his default. It was easier to piss people off that way, and he'd wanted to get his money's worth. Now that he was getting what he wanted for free, it was harder.

But he was mature enough to keep his hands to himself, even when Charlie's leg pressed against him as he finished his second, smaller plate, eyes sparkling like he knew exactly what he was doing.

When the waitstaff picked up the pace of their bustling, taking the remaining plates as the food portion of the morning wound down, Charlie perked up, the steel coming back to his spine.

"I love your dress," he said to the woman next to him, almost accusing in his forward tone. The woman had been sitting far enough away and was engaged enough in her conversation that she seemed startled to be addressed, but answered with a polite smile.

"Thank you."

"Where did you get it?"

If she'd been surprised before, she was floored now. Her visible shock didn't prevent her from answering the almost-impertinent question. "Givenchy."

Charlie nodded. "Oh, right. Their spring line is fantastic. Have you seen it? The colors are all in your palette."

The woman's mascara-ringed eyes blinked, but she was already smiling, and then they were off. The spirited conversation seemed to take away all of Charlie's remaining nerves, his hands relaxing on the tablecloth as they talked.

Was this how Elliott had felt? He could always hold his end of the conversation, but what was the point when most of the people they met weren't interested in chatting with Innes's arm candy. Innes felt just as redundant now, his opinion neither requested nor valuable in any way.

A bit of a nice change, honestly. Charlie could handle himself and his conversational partner, and Innes could relax and check his phone.

Nothing new, nothing interesting, except Twitter, which still overwhelmed him a little. Like pressing his nose against a window at a feast of hilarious and timely commentary, but being baffled by the door-locking mechanism.

He could check on Mimi, though, who seemed to understand it all.

"You always look like that."

Innes glanced up, his thumb switching the Off button on his phone automatically. Charlie was smiling at him with something close to fondness, and the woman was back to talking with her husband. "Pardon?"

"When you check on her." Charlie tapped on the oil-smeared screen of Innes's sleeping phone, his smile reflected imperfectly in the dark surface. "You look like my ma when she gets out the photo albums. She loves them, the nostalgia of my baby pictures is better than any TV show. She gets this happy-sad face, just like yours."

Nostalgia. That sounded right. So much of what he remembered of Mimi was from her early years, back when he was trying to make an impact, before he'd let himself surrender the uphill battle.

He didn't have many baby photos of his daughter. A couple from the hospital the day she was born. His parents might have stashed a few away from that one Christmas where she'd been allowed to see them for a couple of hours in the afternoon. But the bulk of his nostalgia had to come from seeing Mimi's adult face or her thoughts translated into pixels on his phone for everyone with an internet connection to see.

He'd take it, but it wasn't exactly his first choice. The new memories they were tentatively creating didn't make up for over a decade of missing ones.

"You okay?" Charlie asked.

"Of course." His voice was rusty from not speaking for so long, but he pushed through. "I'll be back."

The restrooms were thankfully located just inside the building, a few yards away from where the waitstaff streamed in and out of the kitchen, clearing the wreckage. Innes let his brain go blank, trying to recapture the excitement he'd lost.

He was fine. Charlie was here, keeping him on his toes, and when Innes came back to the table, he'd be over this strange introspective funk.

Except when he did make it back to his seat, Charlie wasn't there. Actually, a lot of people weren't in their seats, milling around instead, taking advantage of the brief time between the end of food being served and the beginning of gushing acknowledgments and lengthy speeches.

It took him a while to pick Charlie out because he'd ended up all the way at the other end of the tent. With Aiden.

Already headed in their direction, Innes's pace picked up, then he purposely slowed down.

What was he afraid of? That Charlie would hear something that was worse than what he already knew? Or was he more afraid that Charlie would spill something that Aiden was never supposed to know.

And since when did Charlie know the deep, dark secrets his family weren't aware of?

Since about day one, actually.

Charlie's confident voice reached him from a couple of feet away.

". . . can't understand him, that's not my problem."

Neither of them noticed him coming, too absorbed in their conversation and in keeping their body language carefully nonconfrontational to notice, but Innes didn't miss the way Aiden's hand was tight on his glass of water, or the way Charlie's smile had crystallized on his expressive lips.

But as Innes watched, some of the tension went out of Aiden's shoulders, and his voice was surprisingly soft as he responded. "Oh, I get it. You're like him."

Charlie frowned. "What do you mean?"

"Just . . . the way you try not to care. But you do."

And that was quite enough of that. Sliding in to Charlie's side, he put a friendly—but not *too* friendly—hand on his shoulder.

"Excuse me, Nephew, I'm going to steal my assistant."

They were gone, heading back to their table before he could say a thing.

"Having a good time?" Innes asked, trying to put Aiden's words out of his head completely.

"Yeah, actually. Made a new friend." As if on cue, the woman from their table smiled in Charlie's direction as they took their place against the tent wall to wait. "We're gonna keep in touch."

"Oh?"

"Antonia's on Instagram."

"Great." Another platform he hadn't even touched. "How terribly do you think it would go over if I asked Mimi for help learning how to navigate that site? Wait, app? Is it an app?"

"Oh my god, you're not even forty, how are you so bad at this?"

"It never came up until now. I had better things—"

"I don't know if she'd necessarily enjoy it," Charlie broke in, his lip quirking up. "But I know that's a super dad thing to do."

Innes rolled his eyes and pretended to grumble, but his pocket held the weight of his phone that didn't seem so heavy anymore.

He'd messed up, he realized. It'd been a mistake to invite Charlie, not because he wasn't good company, but because he was. There was no way Innes wouldn't be spoiled, now. The next time he came to an event like this, he'd have to copy Aiden's strategy. Hugging the wall with a drink in his hand, without a hope that someone else would somehow know exactly what to say.

The next time Innes's car pulled up along the side street of Charlie's address, the morning was gone, but the afternoon wasn't in full swing. Brunch was like that. Silly, really, such an in-between meal.

In the full light of day, Charlie's apartment building seemed even shabbier, and it was . . . a little hard to look at.

They were quite different, weren't they? Their lives, the places they called home. The standards they were used to. Innes was doing his part to improve Charlie's standard, but how was that supposed to make him feel, from an ethical standpoint? He should have felt guilty, shouldn't he? He was taking advantage of someone in a difficult situation.

But there were facts—rich boss, poor worker, plus sex equaled a worrying imbalance—and then there was Charlie, who turned to Innes with a smile that felt more powerful than all of Innes's money and connections.

"Thanks," Charlie said. "For the ride, and for inviting me."

"My pleasure, truly." He couldn't remember the last time he'd enjoyed a function more. "Anytime you— Mmpf!"

Charlie had yanked him forward by the collar of his dress shirt, his lips landing on Innes's with passion that felt inappropriate for a sunny afternoon in public. Not that Innes was complaining.

His eagerness pressed Charlie against the window, the driver's seat armrest digging into his hip as he stretched as far as the seat belt would allow, sinking his tongue into Charlie's maple-flavored mouth.

"Ow," Charlie mumbled after their teeth clumsily clicked together, but he didn't stop, and neither did Innes, because it was still good, even if it wasn't perfect. Good, and tempting enough that Innes wanted to put the car back in gear and drive them straight to his apartment, but it wouldn't be the smart thing—the responsible thing. And anyway, Charlie had different plans.

Charlie broke it off, turning his face to the side, so Innes's mouth wet his check. Smiling, flushed and shiny, he purred, "See you Monday." He whipped off his seat belt, jumped out of the car, and hurried up the sidewalk, out of Innes's reach.

Innes had to lean back and breathe for a bit before he could trust himself to be on the road.

This guy would be the death of him, faster than any rich, cholesterol-filled sausage.

# Chapter Eleven

A piece of limp cabbage roll fell into Charlie's plastic lunch container as he got distracted by his phone.

"Oh my god." He pushed his lunch away, as if holding his phone in two hands would make reality sink in a little faster.

"Yes, I'm here," Innes said, coming around the corner from the reception area. "I wouldn't think it would be such a surprise by now."

Charlie ignored him completely, reading the message on his phone for a second and third time. "I just got a commission."

To his credit, Innes pretended to be interested, leaning over Charlie's shoulder to peer into the phone screen. He did a pretty awesome job too, even letting the summer-weight suit jacket slung over his arm get wrinkled. From the quick glance Charlie took at his face, Innes seemed fully engaged, even though he probably didn't know what he was seeing or what Charlie was talking about.

"From Antonia," Charlie explained, rewarding Innes for good behavior, like he was a dog instead of a grown-ass adult who leaned heavily into self-absorption. "She was at the brunch weekend before last?"

"Ah, yes. I remember. Givenchy."

"Yeah!" That was more than Charlie had expected from him, so maybe he should start raising his standards for Innes's ability to care about what happened to other people in his life? Or maybe just about Charlie, since Aiden had been trying to get an appointment all week and Innes kept begging Charlie to say he was busy.

Not that Charlie needed much convincing to keep Aiden away. The casual way he'd written Innes off in conversation with a virtual stranger didn't make Charlie his biggest fan.

"How's that work?" Innes asked, still leaning over in Charlie's space, but looking at his face instead of the phone screen.

"She wants me to design a blouse. Something simple." He already had an idea of how he'd construct it, inspired by her vague recollections of a shirt she'd owned in the mid-nineties.

He'd been thinking about it all day. The design would have to be like nothing he'd done before, since he usually made clothes for himself and Joy, and Antonia's body type was completely different. Distraction was inevitable when he kept thinking about how he'd cut the sleeves to flatter her shoulders, or what length would be best or—

Innes's hand came down on Charlie's shoulder. Not a brisk pat, but tame enough that anyone coming around the corner wouldn't question it, but it was warm and gratifying. "That's great. Don't let her steal your attention away yet, though, all right?"

He phone *thunk*ed to the desk, a little clumsy in his shy surprise. "It's only one shirt; I'm not going anywhere."

"Ah, but Antonia has money, and you can make a hundred shirts. She also has friends."

"She does." The idea set a tumbling excitement going in his stomach, but he tried not to feed it, just in case it never came to anything more than this. Grinning up at Innes, he joked, "Don't worry. I won't forget you when I'm rich and famous because of Antonia's book club."

"Good. Because I'm not done with you."

Innes's voice had changed, still pleasant, still smooth, but deeper. Raspier. It was the first warning Charlie got before Innes leaned down. The second warning came when Innes stopped right before he got too close to deny the intimacy to hypothetical passersby.

Tilting his head, Charlie made room for him, wordlessly inviting him to press his lips to Charlie's neck. As soon as he made contact, Charlie's heart started to pound, even as goose bumps spread out from the point Innes's hot skin brushed light as an eyelash falling to a cheek.

Anyone could come around the corner and see them. They'd make all sorts of assumptions that would largely be true and would mean trouble for both of them.

But it was thrilling. And over too soon.

Straightening, Innes adjusted his jacket over his arm so it wouldn't fall and sent Charlie a twinkling smirk. "Well, this calls for a celebration, I think. Come over tonight, I'll make it special."

Charlie's lips parted in surprise. He'd never come over midweek, even though he'd spent nearly all of the last two weekends at Innes's, eating delicious food between rounds of even more delicious sex.

"Sure," he found himself saying, anticipation building on the excitement the kiss—and the commission—had already caused. "And thanks, by the way."

Innes paused in the action of turning back to his office, his head cocking with curiosity. "For what?"

"If I hadn't been at the brunch, I never would have met Antonia."

"Oh, don't do that."

The exaggerated eye roll and bored tone he was treated to made Charlie bristle. "What?"

"Try to downplay your own accomplishments. It's not cute. Getting a job out of a few moments of conversation takes more than just luck."

For a few seconds, he was speechless. It was nice to think that he actually *did* do it on his own, that if he hadn't met Antonia, something would've come his way from the time he was spending on Instagram, now that he had energy to spare and completed projects to post.

"I guess so," he allowed, grabbing his fork and tapping it on the bottom of his lunch container for something to do with his hands. Then he grinned. "I must have an innate talent for getting rich people to fall for my charms in under ten minutes."

"I changed my mind," Innes said, wheeling around and heading for his office. "Go get famous now, I'm done with your sass."

Charlie laughed and finished his lunch, his fingers already itching for scissors and drafting chalk.

When a phone went off from Innes's side of the bed, Charlie thought it was the alarm to get them up and get ready for work. He probably would've rolled over and ignored it, leaving Innes to press snooze, holding off Monday morning a little longer.

But then the phone kept ringing, and Innes answered it with a gruff "Hello?"

Charlie stayed in bed but caught a glimpse of Innes's naked back as he got up, grabbed a robe, and headed for the door.

"Hey, Mimi. Yeah, I'm awake." Innes glanced back and caught him staring, then winked as he let himself out. Charlie listened to one half of his conversation as he went down the hall. "Gimme a sec, I'll go into the other room. No, I am not going to tell you why, because you don't actually want to know. Hey, you're the one who brought it up."

Charlie's back-up alarm went off a few minutes later, so he heaved himself out of the warm, comfortable bed and into Innes's ridiculous shower. It'd taken him a few mornings to get the hang of all the different buttons, but he pretty much had it under control now. He scrubbed away the remainder of their lazy Saturday-turned-Sunday, preparing for the Monday grind.

He'd meant to do a lot more with his weekend, he remembered regretfully. He was going to cook, clean, and sew for two days straight, but he'd only just threaded a needle on Saturday when Innes had called him, and he hadn't needed much convincing to come over. After that, the only thing he'd cooked had been a dusty box of instant mac and cheese he'd found in a cupboard, and that had mostly been to tease Innes and his snobbish foodie ways.

They'd also spent their free forty-eight hours getting decidedly dirty.

Charlie grinned to himself in the fancy shower, then shut it off as the last of Innes's smelly, expensive body wash went down the drain. They'd woken up with plenty of time to get to work, but if he dawdled too long, he'd lose the head start he'd budgeted to beat the traffic.

Next weekend, he'd stay home. Even putting aside his chore schedule, he missed Ma, and the kind of easy companionship they gave each other, with her chattering away about whatever caught her attention that day, him listening with his eyes closed or fixed on a seam he was finishing, just happy to hear her so happy.

He'd do that. Soon. For one day at least, if he could peel himself off Innes's bed for long enough to think coherently.

Innes was finished with his phone call when Charlie came out of the bedroom fully dressed in clothes he'd left there last week that had been mysteriously cleaned for him. That reminded him of the sweatpants he had to return to the back of the drawer. Innes obviously wouldn't miss them because they were closer to Charlie's size than his, but it was certainly helpful to have something to change into while he was waiting for the next round or heading home in the morning when he didn't have work.

(If he also got a perverse sort of satisfaction from stealing clothes from whoever had come before him along with Innes himself, then he wasn't admitting it to anyone.)

"Give me ten minutes," Innes said as he passed.

"No rush," Charlie answered, knowing Innes always took longer getting dressed than he thought he would.

Charlie made himself toast and coffee while he waited, wincing at the grainy, dense bread Innes insisted was superior to Wonder.

"Freak," Charlie muttered into his coffee. At least that was good. Charlie could never afford beans like these.

He didn't have the time to make them lunch, but he did put some more coffee into a gigantic thermos for the road, so he'd at least save Innes some money at Starbucks.

He paused in the middle of screwing on the lid, wondering when he'd learned where Innes kept his travel containers and Tupperware. He couldn't remember exactly, just that it had made its way into his brain, along with a bunch of other little details, like how Innes kept a jar of extra-smooth, saturated fat–filled peanut butter in the back of the cupboard for when he couldn't stomach the gritty natural stuff. Or that Innes had a shelf full of books that he'd read and hadn't really liked, but refused to give away because what if he wanted to read it again? Or that Innes DVR'd poker games.

Charlie finished tightening the lid while he wondered if those were normal things to know about a fuck buddy. But then, that wasn't all Innes was to him. Charlie had learned private things about his employer before they'd ever had sex, as a part of his job. So maybe he was getting a little weird about it because he hadn't had a friends-with-benefits relationship before, much less a we-work-together-but-there's-also-benefits relationship. Maybe the fact that he'd slept over four nights out of the last seven was normal. Either way, he was putting himself firmly in the *not thinking about it* camp.

"Two more minutes," Innes yelled from the bedroom ten minutes later.

Charlie rounded it up to five and stuffed a few muffins into a plastic bag.

Four minutes later, he nearly dropped the thermos to the floor when the front door opened and in walked a woman, about his mother's age, who turned on him with a fierce glare, saying something in a crunchy-sounding language.

"Uh," Charlie said. "Hello?"

The woman looked him up and down with sharp, clear eyes. She didn't appear to like what she saw, because her mouth twisted and she shook her head at him before walking farther into the apartment.

Charlie almost gave in to the insane urge to apologize before he realized that a perfect stranger had let herself into Innes's home and was . . . rifling through the hall closet?

"Ah, Svetlana!"

Innes had finally come out of the bedroom and was approaching the woman with wide-open arms and a white smile. Svetlana smiled back at him, her wrinkles folding like an accordion into her cheeks and beside her eyes, changing her face so much that Charlie would have thought she was two different people if he hadn't seen the transformation.

Charlie stood awkwardly as they had a short conversation in Svetlana's broken English that ended in a short stand-off between them as Innes held out a crisp twenty dollar bill and returned her terrifying glare until she accepted it, along with a peck on the cheek that made her blush like a schoolgirl.

In the car a few minutes later, Charlie looked questioningly over at Innes in the driver's seat.

Innes shrugged and said, "Rule number one of bachelorhood. Always be nice to your cleaning lady because she knows where you sleep."

Charlie snorted. "That's rule number one, is it? Not that underwear is a one-use only product? Or that instant ramen doesn't count as a square meal?"

"It is too early in the morning for that kind of talk."

Any time before 8:30 a.m. was too early for almost any kind of talk for Innes, except for conversations with Mimi—and Svetlana, apparently. Charlie didn't mind. He didn't get a chance to just sit next to someone quietly very often. Ma always wanted to fill the silence with her cheerful commentary, and he and Joy were always too eager to catch up on every little detail they'd missed in each other's lives.

During the drive to work, he thought about Svetlana and her reaction to him.

She'd treated him like one of Innes's booty calls, he realized. Like Marie had told him, Innes had a type. Dear Svetlana had probably cleaned around other confused people in Innes's bed or his kitchen, and from the look she'd given Charlie, she didn't approve, despite her apparent fondness for Innes.

But Charlie was different from the others. Charlie wasn't in the habit of judging anybody's choices, but he wasn't getting paid to be there like the last guy. He knew he wasn't any more important to Innes than they were, but what they had was an agreement, not a transaction.

Wasn't it?

His mind immediately went to the reference Innes had promised him. The connections he had all over the city that Charlie was planning on using when he was ready to leave Innes's employment.

That was not the same thing, he assured himself. He was getting paid and later rewarded for doing his job well, which he would be doing whether he'd slept with Innes or not.

He put it out of his mind for the rest of the drive. First, he people-watched, looking for outfits that caught his eyes and imagining how he'd change them, until the staring made his eyes cross. Next, he studied Innes's calendar for the week, tilting the screen of his phone toward the passenger window so that Innes wouldn't see it and get annoyed that he was working before 8:50. He didn't want to have to play "keep away" again, not when they were on a busy street.

When they pulled into Innes's space in the parking garage, Charlie leaned over the console and gave Innes a quick kiss on the cheek. "See you in there. Soon, right?"

"In good time" was Innes's lazy response. He was smiling, even as his eyes flicked to the garage beyond his windshield.

Charlie shook his head. "Any chance you'll be upstairs sooner than 8:57?"

"Slim to none. But don't worry, I'll make up the time somewhere."

The actual words weren't that evocatively suggestive, but Innes still made them sound like the dirtiest proposition. Rolling his eyes, Charlie headed upstairs alone.

Charlie frowned at his fuzzy reflection in the elevator on the way up. When had mornings like this become so routine? He still slept a lot of nights at home with his mother, but in the short time he and Innes had been sleeping together, they'd spent a considerable amount of it . . . sleeping. In Innes's bed, in his home, then going to work together because it made more sense than Charlie going back to his place.

It was easy. A set of actions that could become a habit. But to him—admittedly inexperienced with what they were doing—it seemed like the way they fit together was more than an agreement and definitely more than a transaction.

It seemed like a relationship.

Charlie jammed the button to turn on his computer and scolded himself for worrying about nothing. Every interaction he had with any person was a relationship of some kind; it didn't have to be a *relationship*. That wasn't who they were, or what they wanted.

Not that Charlie was against it, as a concept. He wasn't a romantic, but he liked the idea of a life partner; yet that was all it was: an idea. He'd never had time for the reality. The arrangement he had with Innes was simple. Low-key. And that was fine.

The morning passed in a whirl of phone calls, emails, and details, and Charlie didn't have time to think about their changing dynamic. He was too busy racing around trying to keep things on time and in control to wonder if people normally kissed their casual sex partners on the cheek before heading to work.

"Innes, shouldn't I be sending a bill to Ms. Waterford?" he asked as Innes passed his desk on the way out to lunch with a client.

Innes stopped, squinting as he remembered the details, then he shook his head. "No. That one's pro bono."

"Oh." He started to make a note on his screen, but his fingers stilled almost involuntarily. "Really?"

"Yes." Innes shrugged off his suit jacket, folding it over his arm in anticipation of the early June heat. "It makes sense for the firm. The case is going to get some media coverage when it goes to trial. Not a lot, but enough that if we tell the press we're taking care of her fees, it'll give people a good impression and perhaps drive some traffic to the website from people who can afford us, like Ms. Waterford can't."

"Ah." Charlie let his fingers tap on the keyboard without pressing them, watching them tremble in their spaces. "Untarnishing your blackened soul with a little charity work. That's nice."

Innes looked skyward, but Charlie could tell he was a little more annoyed than his average teasing exasperation. "I'm not made of stone," he said, waspishly.

"I know."

Innes looked over at him, his face curiously blank, without even his default smugness.

"You're not noble," Charlie continued, staring back and hoping that his expression was a mirror of Innes's. "I believe that you're doing it for the reason you say. But you're not as cold as you like to think."

Innes looked at him for the length of three rings of the main lobby's phone, then he hummed, switched his jacket to his other arm, and said shortly, "See you after lunch."

"Don't get the cheese plate, we'll both regret it later," Charlie said, already turning back to his screen and finishing the sentence he'd been writing.

"I'm not lactose intolerant. How many times do I have to tell you?" Innes snapped as he left.

"I'll believe it when you stop getting stomach aches after eating lactose," Charlie yelled after him, then he slumped over, leaning his face on his hand and scowling.

He might have shot himself in the foot. He wouldn't be surprised a tiny little bit if Innes ordered a milkshake just to spite him, and damn the consequences.

"So, what's up with you today?" Joy asked him, putting down her knife and fork.

"Fa? Er." Charlie had his mouth full. He swallowed his bite of salad before he tried again. "What do you mean?"

"You're jittery," she told him, then she placed a palm overtop of his fingers, which he hadn't realized were beating out a hollow rhythm on her kitchen table. "More than usual."

"I'm fine, everything's good, I'm great," he said, rapid-fire.

She took another small bite, looking down at her plate as if it held all the answers, waiting until Charlie inevitably cracked.

"I did something," he blurted, pushing his plate away. It hit the salt shaker and knocked it over, so Charlie righted it, spilling more salt in the process. "I'm still doing it."

He told her about Innes. About the hotel, and the morning after, and how convincing Innes was, how easily Charlie let himself be convinced.

"And now we have sex all the time, and it's so great, I can't even tell you," he finished, running out of steam.

Joy folded her hands in her lap, processing. "Wow. That's quite a development. When did you say this happened?"

He looked down at his finger, drawing thin lines in the spilled salt. "About a month ago."

Charlie could tell she was surprised from the way she unbraked and turned her chair toward him, abandoning all pretense that she would go back to her dinner.

"Why didn't you tell me before?" she asked, reaching out for his hand again, stilling it and bringing it to rest on her delicate knee.

"It's not because I thought you would judge me." Her fingers felt solid and familiar around his. "You went with me to the hospital to get a dildo out of my ass when I was nineteen. I don't ever worry about you thinking less of me after that."

"Damn right." The armrest made a dull plunk under her finger. "I am the best, most understanding friend ever. So why the delay? You're obviously stressed out about it, and I imagine you could have used a friendly ear, which I could have given you any of the four times in the last month that we've talked to each other on the phone."

"I didn't want to worry you," he admitted.

"Why? Is there something I need to be worried about?"

"No, not at all." The hand she wasn't holding twisted at his side, tugging mercilessly at the seam of his pants. "It's just a thing that's happening. It probably wasn't a good idea to start it, but we did, and I have to deal with whatever comes of it."

"It's worse than that," Joy said slowly, peering at him like he was a magic eye puzzle. "You're falling for him, aren't you?"

He drew in a deep breath, and instead of letting it out immediately in an exasperated sigh or a firm denial, he let his chest clench with the lack of fresh oxygen until he couldn't stand it, and stood up, grabbing both his nearly empty plate and hers and taking them to the dishwasher on a burst of speed.

"Don't call it that," he said. "It's so cheesy, and it's not . . . not—"

"Accurate?"

His fork made a cringe-inducing scraping noise as he pushed the rest of his salad into the garbage. "Not really. I'm not in love with him. I'm just . . ." He put the plate down on the counter and stared at the shoes Innes had forced him to buy when his old ones started falling apart. "I'm starting to look at him in a romantic way when I really shouldn't. I *should* just appreciate him in a sexual way, which I do, don't get me wrong."

"Naturally. You did show me a picture, so I get the appeal."

His face started to warm as he recalled all the ways Innes's buttoned-up professional photo on the firm's website didn't do him justice. "Right. He's hot and we have chemistry. He already told me he's not the boyfriend type, and when he said it, I agreed with him. I thought, 'No way in hell would I want to date this guy.'"

"But you like him," Joy said. It wasn't a question.

"Yeah." He waited for a surge of disagreement from his own conscience, but it never came. The memory of the word in his mouth felt right. "I kind of do. Not sure why. All we ever do is argue. Well, that's not true. Maybe it used to be, but now we're past that. He actually talks to me, now, and more often lately, I like what I hear."

Joy didn't say anything while he finished loading their plates into the dishwasher. It was only when he sat down again that she said, "There's nothing wrong with liking him. There's nothing wrong with sleeping with him, either, in theory. Although, in practice, you might feel a little differently later on. But I'm glad for you. You still look stressed out, but you also seem lighter than you were, and I don't think it's just because you're having sex regularly again." They shared a moment of sly smiles. "But don't forget to protect yourself, okay? You're way more likely to get hurt than he is."

He looked at Joy, her familiar, patient, affectionate expression. She was wearing a dress he'd made for her years ago, tangible evidence that she was his biggest fan and his dearest confidante.

"Thanks," he said, through a lump lodged in his throat. He coughed, waving at everything left on the table. "And for dinner too."

"Any time. I kind of thought I'd be seeing more of you now that you don't work every night, but I guess now I know why you've still been a ghost."

He winced. "I'm sorry. I feel like I keep saying that, and it still takes me forever to come see you."

"Don't worry. It must be nice to have a love life again, even one like this."

"Speaking of which, how's UPS Taylor?"

"Back in the shorts again for the summer, thank god. I was missing those cute little knees."

Joy updated him on her work crush, then made him laugh with a few stories from the office, allowing him to avoid the topic of Innes for the rest of his visit. Charlie made sure to listen well, happy to let her life get the spotlight instead of his drama, for once.

He was listening so well, he nearly forgot to speak when she turned another question on him.

"So, what are you working on right now?"

For a second, he only blinked. "Working . . . on?"

"Designing," she said, significantly, like she was talking to a three-year-old. "You know. Your life's work."

"Oh! Yeah. Um."

He'd already sent a preliminary sketch for Antonia's commission, and was waiting for her final approval before he started. Other than that . . . technically, he was working on a shirt. For once, it was for himself, to wear to work when he was feeling bold. Not too bold, though—he wasn't going to go crazy or give Innes too much ammunition for teasing.

But, in reality, the answer to her question was . . . nothing. It'd taken until just this moment to realize that he hadn't touched his project bin in three—no, four days, between his weekends at Innes's, and some creative sexting a couple of nights before that.

"You know," he said, trying to summon the enthusiasm he knew was buried under his shock. "Just some odds and ends."

Four days.

And he'd meant to be so productive this past weekend.

He couldn't blame it all on Innes. The way he used to consider working on a design, then automatically discount it because he was too tired was probably engrained by now.

It was a little satisfying, though, to nurture a tiny spark of resentment at Innes. It wasn't as if Charlie would invite Innes back to the apartment he shared with Ma, but he was the only one of them who had to give up precious time if they wanted to extend their hookups all night. It was inherently unequal, as long as they were on Innes's turf.

"So secretive," Joy said, wiggling her brows at him, oblivious to his swirling thoughts. "Must be something big."

"Not really. Just getting back into the swing of things." He would. Starting tomorrow, or maybe even tonight, he'd put more effort into making time, like he'd always planned to if he didn't have to work so much.

"I'm glad." Joy laid a hand on Charlie's, squeezing gentle. "It's what you're meant to be doing."

"Thanks." Charlie smiled back, preoccupied by the thought that he wasn't known for doing the things he was meant to.

Ma was sleeping when he let himself in later, which he was thankful for. He felt guilty for even thinking it, but this week was her wedding anniversary with his father, so she was thinking of him more than usual. That, of course, meant that she'd been talking about him every damn day, forcing Charlie to do the same, biting his tongue the whole time.

What he was holding back burned his throat, but he couldn't say it. There was no reason for her to know, except cruelty, and he hoped he wasn't a cruel person.

He just missed feeling like he had someone on his wavelength. Someone who got him completely, by virtue of being there for every significant moment of his life, cheering him on while he defended her to his last breath. With the memory of his dad around, they were farther apart than he liked.

He did some dishes; the routine chore was soothing after a long day spent thinking deep thoughts and arguing with himself. He could barely remember the way he'd woken up slowly, surfacing by degrees under the familiarity of Innes's hands.

Though he tried to creep quietly through the dark living room, his mother woke up, and he watched fondly as she patted her hair, which was nearly perfect even though she'd probably been asleep for hours.

She smiled when she saw him. "Where've you been, honey?"

"With Joy." He turned on the lamp in the corner so they could see each other without squinting, then went through the regular Monday mail.

"Oh. How is she?"

"Fine. You can go back to sleep if you want, I'm just going—"

"Don't you think maybe you should take her out on a date one day?" She fussed with the blanket on her lap, folding and refolding it. "You get along so well. I think you'd make a great couple."

He put the short pile of bills he'd already paid and coupons he'd never use back onto the side table by the door with smacking force. "Maybe we would if I liked girls, but I don't. Just because I like Joy doesn't mean I want to date her."

She waved her hand in his direction. "I know, I know. It's just so difficult out there for people like you."

He fixed his gaze on an old stain on the carpet he couldn't remember not being there. "That doesn't mean I can change it. I wouldn't, even if I could."

"That's good, honey. I'm glad." She sounded so serious, so . . . lucid, that Charlie looked over, almost expecting her to be a different person, but she was still his ma sitting in her chair.

He took over folding her blanket into a neater square. "Did you eat?"

"No. I meant to cook something for the both of us. It's been so long since I did. I used to cook all the time for you and your father. He used to love my cooking, said I could have been a professional. I took care of him. He was useless at washing his own socks, you know—"

"I know." He laid the blanket back in her lap and headed for his door. "Good night, Ma."

Was it the fact that he had more time to spend at home that made him chafe a bit more at her stifling commitment to the memory of his father? Maybe. Or, potentially, he was just a terrible person.

Perhaps it wouldn't have felt like a net closing tighter around his limbs if he could share his own burdens. It'd been a long time since he told her everything, preferring to keep as many worries off her plate as possible, but having someone to talk to would have been nice. He had Joy, but there was only so much complaining he felt he could do to her before he felt like an ass, and even then, there was nothing like telling your family about your struggles. It was different.

"Charlie?" Out of the corner of his eye, he saw her reach out for him, but he didn't stop and neither did she. "I'm sorry, I know I ramble. But do you remember how you and your father used to love my macaroni?"

"Yes. I do. But I make my own macaroni, now, so I don't know why it matters," he snapped, gripping his doorknob with white knuckles, his stomach instantly tight and sick with guilt. "I'm tired, Ma. I'll see you in the morning."

He shut his door softly, guiding its progress the entire way, then stepping lightly over to his bed and sitting down. He was tense. His fingers ached from how hard he was holding them in close to his palms, biting marks into the callused skin.

In the morning, he would apologize by making her favorite breakfast, and on the weekend, he'd take her to the beach to watch the people go by and reminisce about when they used to play together in the water as a family, no matter how much it hurt.

But tonight, after a day of evaluating him and Innes, flip-flopping his opinion over and over, he couldn't handle listening to her talk about his father, because the worst thing he could imagine would be to end up in a relationship like hers.

A relationship where she gave and gave and his father never gave a single thing other than a meagre pay check from a job he hated but was too lazy to quit. And then when he was gone, she had nothing to show for all of that love she put in except a world of grief and an eight-year-old son who had to learn how to survive without a father or another parent who could function in the world.

Did Charlie do that? Give too much? Relationships weren't something he had much practice with, and in any case, he and Innes weren't in a relationship. At least, not a romantic one.

They never would be, because they weren't the type who settled down, especially not with each other.

If Charlie ever found a guy he could say *forever* to, he'd know what not to do. He'd know that he needed to have an equal partnership, with neither one of them doing more work than the other, either at home or in the relationship. He'd need to like his partner as a friend, not just a lover. He'd need to be able to fully be himself at all times, no holding back.

He wouldn't find that with Innes. He knew it, but that didn't stop him from wondering what it would be like if he could try.

# Chapter Twelve

The world still turned when Innes couldn't sleep.

It was highly unfair, actually, that crime still happened and court dates still had to be upheld when Innes had been up half the night, tossing, turning, and wasting time on his phone until he'd broken down, hugging a pillow.

Another injustice in his life was the speed with which his body had become accustomed to having someone to grab on to.

The question still remained, however: What was he going to do about it?

No more sleepovers. Obviously. This sleep deprivation could not continue.

No more Charlie? That seemed extreme. He wasn't there yet, but he needed boundaries. Now to figure out what those boundaries would be since Charlie had his fingers in every part of Innes's life.

Promises to do better didn't help him this afternoon, though, as he trudged back to the office from his parking spot, tired and irritated beyond belief.

It wasn't even just his lack of sleep. *Nooo*, of course not. Catherine— good-hearted, well-meaning, persistent Catherine—had to pick today to call him again, to harangue him. Not about the dedication he was missing for once, but about a new, exciting topic not broached for the past few years.

Mimi.

"If you're not going to see this through, it would be better if you didn't get her hopes up," Catherine had told him, her sympathetic voice barely loud enough for him to hear in the crowded lobby of the courthouse.

Innes's hand had tightened dangerously on his phone. "When have I ever bailed on any of you? I've seen through every commitment I ever made to the foundation, to the practice, and to all of you."

"No, you don't break promises, because you habitually don't make them in the first place. Don't forget, Innes. I've known you since you were eight years old. You're a runner. You run away from promises, instead. We—Mimi's family—finally have a chance to know her. I don't want to lose her because she got her heart broken again. You're like a brother to me, Innes, and I love you, but—"

"Save it. I've heard enough lip service from this family to last a lifetime."

The conversation had ended there, but he hadn't stopped having it over and over in his head. With a few rounds of practice, he'd been able to confidently tell the imaginary Catherine that of course he would see it through. He wasn't some scared teenager, terrified of hurting the one person who was supposed to love him automatically.

He'd been so preoccupied that he'd nearly made a fool of himself in front of his client, not to mention the judge and the opposition. He'd recovered, of course, because he was a professional, but it was still annoying.

Just inside the lobby of his building, Innes took himself to a less-trafficked area and drew in a few steadying breaths to pull himself together. He didn't close his eyes. That would've been too much for such a public setting, but he let his vision blur and go double as he sucked in air deep into his belly and tried to expel all the unnecessary tension on the way out.

The two people that approached him not a minute later merged into one as he blinked in surprise.

"Hey, Innes," said Elliott, his former contracted lover and his nephew's current boyfriend.

"Hello." The formality was stifling, but he honestly had no idea how else he was supposed to interact. "What brings you to my neck of the woods?"

"Aiden had to pick up some stuff from his office."

"Ah." Of course, the great Kent exodus. "So. How're things?"

"Oh, you know." Elliott's smile spread slowly across his wide mouth, big and bright. "Incredible."

A pinch of jealousy lodged itself somewhere around Innes's sternum at the sight of that smile. He'd never made Elliott look like that. He'd never wanted to, but it still felt like a failing on his part.

"I'm glad. You deserve it."

Elliott's eyebrows shot up and his smile dimmed suspiciously. "Thanks." The awkwardness became extra apparent in the short silence that followed, which Elliott thankfully filled. "Aiden said you've finally lined up a replacement for me."

Innes snorted at the idea that Charlie could be anyone's replacement. He was way too unique for that. "No, actually. Aiden's sources are wrong."

"You mean, you aren't sleeping with your new assistant on your lunch breaks and after work?"

That was . . . alarmingly specific. Annoyingly so, if not for him, then for Charlie. He frowned, trying not to tsk. "Does everyone know?"

"Probably not. Aiden is just observant, and he knows you better than you think he does."

"So he thinks."

"What's the scoop, then?" Elliott prodded with a cheeky grin. "Is he getting a bigger holiday bonus for services rendered?"

"Elliott, are we friends?"

Blinking, Elliott seemed to consider the question for longer than Innes would've thought.

"We're not strangers," he eventually decided.

"Let me rephrase. Are you under the impression that I owe you any information about my sexual partners?"

Elliott shrugged. "It's not like you didn't crow it from the rooftops, before. Your past few arrangements were fifty percent sex and fifty percent arm candy. I should know."

"Is it conceited to call yourself arm candy?"

"Why would you bother to keep this one a secret?" A spark of what looked to be genuine curiosity had kindled in Elliott's eyes.

For a second, Innes couldn't think of a reason. Not one that benefited him, at least. And what did Charlie care, really? He didn't answer to anyone else in the office, and he'd be leaving them all in his dust in a few years anyway.

Why hadn't Innes flaunted him the way he had the others, pushing it into the faces of his parents' memories that lined those hallowed halls?

"Maybe I'm a changed man," Innes said, pasting a disingenuous smirk on his face for show.

"Changed how?" Elliott's tone was pure disbelief.

"Maybe I'm having an office romance, and my perky assistant is falling head over heels for me." He sent a silent apology to Charlie for *perky*.

Elliott snorted. "I don't think there's much danger of that, not with the way you are."

The pain was unexpected, to say the least.

It didn't hurt badly. A sting, comparable to a paper cut, or an ungraceful fall onto a soft surface.

No, it didn't hurt very much, but he still didn't want to think about why it hurt at all. He didn't want to think about the time and effort he was putting into trying to make Mimi love him. About the way he'd battled for his parents' affections and lost the war.

And Charlie. Innes definitely didn't want to think about Charlie, who was so easy to love. For other people, though. Who had time for that crap? Not Innes.

"Naturally," Innes said, with a smile that felt like a slash where his mouth should be.

It hadn't looked as normal as he hoped, it turned out, because Elliott's eyes went a bit wide. "I—I didn't mean that," he stammered.

Of course he hadn't. Elliott was sharp sometimes, but he wasn't mean-spirited. He'd said something like that a hundred times before, and Innes had never thought anything of it, just dished it right back. It was why he and Elliott weren't together anymore, probably. Elliott was a lot nicer and less hardened than he thought he was.

"Oh, come on," Innes said, pulling a grimace and purposefully relaxing his posture. "You know I'm a heartless bastard."

"Right." Relief washed over Elliott's face, then he had to go and dig his own hole a little deeper. "You have to admit, you're not really the type for love. Loving or being loved. It's just not who you are."

He said it with the kind of conviction Innes wished witnesses on the stand would use. Like it was indisputable fact. He wouldn't be expecting Innes to take any kind of offense, because the Innes Elliott had known wouldn't have.

"Obviously. You and Aiden can keep all that." Let them have their premarital bliss. He didn't need it. "Anyway, I should go. Perky assistants to bend over my desk and such."

With an immature, grossed-out face, Elliott waved him off. "See you around, sleaze."

The familiar nickname slid off Innes's back as he left, not powerful enough to make a dent after everything else he'd had hurled at him that day.

The elevator doors shut Elliott out, leaving Innes with the realization he should have had yesterday, when his sleep—and his life, apparently—had been ruined.

If Innes wasn't the loving kind, if it was so ludicrous that he should love someone and be loved in return, then why the hell was he so close to falling in love with Charlie?

He'd messed up. Charlie was supposed to be simple, but this was way past the cutting-back-on-sleepovers stage. He had feelings beyond lust and the opposite of dislike, and he needed to cut them off.

Innes sat up from a deep, spine-crunching slouch when the door opened, admitting Charlie, who held the second office phone in his hand.

"Yes?" Innes was sure he came off as short in his attempt not to sound happy to see him.

"Phone for you. Personal," Charlie said, extending the handset so Innes could see the display.

*Danny Great Cocksucker*, it read. The name Innes himself had entered over two years ago into his phone after a night of self-explanatory fun and a few months of meaningless, regular sex, crudely and mercilessly shoved in the faces of other philanthropists at parties.

The red hold light blinked away as Innes looked at Charlie, whose face was as blank as he could make it, which meant that Innes could read it like a book. There was annoyance there, certainly, but more than that, embarrassment. Discomfort and dark disappointment.

Innes felt nothing as he took the phone, nodding at Charlie to dismiss him.

"Hey, there, Danny," he said when the hold light was off. "How have you been?"

He only half listened to Danny's summary of the last two years of his life. He watched Charlie snag the water pitcher and head unhurriedly for his desk, his posture perfect, shoulders down and back, looking for all the world as if he were unaffected, but Innes knew better.

"So, I'm in town, hot stuff, and I wondered if you wanted to get a drink?"

"Hmm?" Innes tuned back in to the conversation. "A drink, huh?"

Charlie stopped so quickly the water pitcher sloshed, spilling a few drops, and Innes knew he had his full attention.

It was the perfect moment. With a single date, Innes would be able to remind Charlie where they stood. It would probably put an end to their fling, but at least doing it in this way would make Charlie mad instead of sad.

Perfect. Except, he didn't want to do that. The thought of actually going out with Danny while Charlie stayed home cursing his name made his stomach clench.

"Sorry, Danny, I'm going to have to say no."

Charlie's hand tightened on the outer doorknob. Innes wished he could see his face, but he turned his chair around instead as panic set in.

"That's a shame." Danny was audibly pouting. Well, he'd messed that up. The opportunity for a direct hit was over, so he scrambled to at least deliver a glancing blow.

"Busy times, you understand, but check back with me in a few months if you're still in the city."

From outside, he heard the water pitcher slam down with enough force to break it if it had been glass.

Given a firm no, Danny didn't have much else to say to him. After he hung up, Innes felt the insane urge to chuck the phone across the room to relieve some stress but figured Charlie wouldn't like that much, and despite his misgivings, he didn't actually want to make Charlie's life more difficult.

To that end, he got up from his desk to take the phone back out to him but was stopped at the door by Charlie coming in, nearly running him over. When they'd both gotten their footing back, half in and out of the doorway, they said nothing, their eye contact prolonged and as taut as the silence.

Charlie broke it. "Finished?"

"Yes." He held out the phone, which Charlie took with steady fingers.

"Should I add anything to the calendar?"

"No." He stood back and huffed in disbelief as Charlie pushed past him into the room at large. "I'm not a complete bastard. I would never make you schedule sex with another person."

"Why not?" Charlie didn't look at him, straightening the group of chairs in the corner instead, moving them insignificant distances as he spoke. "I know what this is. I'm not your boyfriend. You never told me we're exclusive—"

"Well, I implied it pretty strongly when we stopped using a condom—"

"And I'd rather know about it, so I can stop trusting you." He froze, just as the breath in Innes's lungs did, then started moving again, across the room to the desk, which he cleared of the minuscule clutter. "Trusting that you can fuck me unprotected, I mean. Although, it was probably stupid for me to do that in the first place."

Innes could no longer stand being so far from him, so he went to his side. No easy feat, because Charlie kept moving, never planting his feet as he moved around the desk.

"No, it wasn't," Innes said. "I'm not running around putting my dick in everybody I see. You know that very well."

"Why would I care, though?" Charlie's voice was higher than normal. He abandoned the desk and looked to the pristine wall of shelves for something, anything to do, and Innes followed behind. "What the fuck does it even matter? Why are we arguing?"

"I don't know!" Innes grabbed him by the shoulder and turned Charlie to face him. "Would you stop running away from me?"

Charlie swiped Innes's hand away with a forearm, his face venomous, any attempt at neutrality forgotten. "I'm not running, I'm busy."

He tried to turn away again, but Innes stopped him, crowding him with hands at his sides. "Well, quit being busy and—"

He couldn't say how it became a struggle, but they grappled for a short time, Charlie's skinny, fast arms holding back little strength, his body twisting until Innes pinned him against the shelf. His goal had been immobilization, but once he achieved it, he had no idea what purpose it served, except to have Charlie there, listening to him, looking him in the eye while they fought about something they both agreed should be nothing.

Their eyes locked again. Innes felt some of the anger that had brought them here drain out of him. Not all, but enough that he was suddenly ashamed to have used his physical advantage to get Charlie against a literal wall. That shame was compounded by the fact that this position, so similar to the ones they'd been in before, after the lights in the building were out and they were alone, sent a shiver of awareness to his groin.

He gritted his teeth at the same time as he took a small step back, aiming to put as much distance between them as possible, but Charlie pulled him in, smashing his mouth to Innes's, hard and demanding.

The kiss softened by degrees, but it didn't get any less insistent, Charlie's lips and tongue taking everything they could get until their breath ran out and tiny sips of air in the midst of crashing together couldn't hold them over and they parted.

In Charlie's eyes was an answering warmth to the one Innes felt, and he knew for sure that he wasn't the only one affected by the way the space between them had disappeared. Charlie was still angry, but it was a destructive anger now, not gloriously righteous or quietly cold. He wanted to make a bad choice and hurt somebody and damned if Innes didn't want the same thing.

Charlie started the second kiss too, pulling Innes back in by his neck and holding him too tightly, fighting for a kiss they were both in favor of until the shock of Charlie's teeth nipping his lip made Innes pull away with a hiss.

He took only the time to check to make sure he wasn't bleeding— he wasn't, the ache was too dull and far away already for it to be that damaging—before he manhandled Charlie to face the wall on a surge of adrenaline. He unbuckled Charlie's belt quickly, distantly aware of how it clunked against the shelf—the shelf Charlie was mashed against by Innes's body.

He fished Charlie's cock out of his pants, giving it a single rough stroke that made Charlie's body jerk. Charlie was fully hard already, which eased a tightness in Innes's chest that he hadn't known he had. It meant that he wasn't seeing things he wanted to see. He wasn't imagining that Charlie was interested in taking out his frustrations in this way.

"Yes," Charlie rasped, pushing his hips back into the burden of Innes's arousal.

Innes pulled at Charlie's collar with both hands, baring his neck to the air even though he couldn't see it, then he raked his hands down the front of Charlie's shirt, forcing a hiss out of him as his fingernails dragged over the cloth-covered nipples. He bent his head to suck a biting mark on the side of Charlie's neck as he reached his waist, pushing down his loose, unbelted pants and boxers.

With Charlie's pants around his thighs, Innes had access to Charlie's prominent hip bones, which he dragged his nails over next, with less pressure than before, just to feel Charlie squirm against him. Then, with sure, dry hands, he pressed up into the space between Charlie's ass cheeks. Teasing, like he meant to keep going, snaking fingers into—

Charlie's hand flew back, landing on his wrist by luck more than accuracy. "Don't," he snapped.

Innes nodded against Charlie's neck, withdrawing and returning to Charlie's neglected, burning hot cock, his hand moving in uneven pulls, missing the smooth glide of lube or even enough pre-come to be helpful. He wasn't interested in anything that would hurt more than a sting of remembered strain.

"I could stop," Innes asked. He had to be sure, but he couldn't keep from adding a biting, "I'm not keeping you, am I?"

"No," Charlie gritted out, his hips bucking into Innes's brutal grip.

"No what?" He had to be *sure*.

"Don't stop."

At first, he did the exact opposite of what Charlie had asked. He stepped over to his desk on unsteady legs, yanking a tube of moisturizer from a drawer where it had lived, nearly forgotten and inching toward its expiry date for over a year. It didn't matter to him that it had seen better days or that the fragrance was a bit strong for him. It wasn't going to do any damage to Charlie, and that was all he cared about.

He spread a generous dollop on the scorching skin of Charlie's upper thighs, licking his lips at Charlie's broken cry at the cold shock, because it had sounded like Charlie always did when Innes entered him.

This time, fucking another warm, accommodating place would have to do.

He stroked Charlie with the same rhythm as he thrust himself between Charlie's thighs, mouthing the side of his neck and his twitching shoulders. Their breathing was loud and inelegant as Innes punched sighs and breathy moans out of them both.

As they approached the dizzying height of shallow, forcefully attained pleasure, it got harder to be so vicious in every move. Even when fucking him for real, Innes had never felt so much like he was using Charlie as a body. A hole.

His fingers had begun loosening to pull away when Charlie went rigid in his arms. His come splattered on the shelf, and his hand reached blindly for Innes, who caught it without thinking, the instinct to connect still strong.

*How dare he*, Innes thought, rational thought long gone out the window. What right did he have to barge into Innes's life and mess it all up with his sincerity and make Innes care about him? How dare he be so perfectly flawed in the ways that matched up with Innes's deep personal failings?

His orgasm felt empty and cold despite the sweat that had wetted the places they were still joined in the aftermath. There was no long, languid recovery where the buzz of re-entry to life charged them both.

Innes stepped back first, giving Charlie room to breathe, but he didn't go far. He did up his pants blindly, watching Charlie panting against the wall instead, pale and damply shining against the dark, matte wood of the shelf.

The scrape of Charlie's belt buckle and the sound of clothing being put to rights broke the spell that had stolen Innes's voice.

He cleared his throat. "You okay?"

Charlie exhaled shakily and stumbled away from the wall, avoiding Innes's gaze and question. Innes saw him wipe his hand savagely on his pants.

"I'm leaving," Charlie said, his tone absolutely blank, which did more to tell Innes how raw he was than a voice choked up with emotion.

Innes looked at his watch. It was just past four o'clock. Panic spiked in him as he watched Charlie head for the door, demonstrating his honest intent to leave early, something he'd never done before without apologies and an emergency to cite as the reason.

"See you tomorrow," he blurted at Charlie's back.

A pause, during which Innes listened to the blood pump in his ears, his pulse rising again even though it had begun to level out.

"Yeah," Charlie told the carpeted floor.

Relief. An icy wave of it, even though he was getting exactly what he'd wanted. "Good."

Then Charlie was gone, closing the door with a gentle snick and padding down the hallway out of earshot. Innes collapsed into his chair, his only movement an anxious tipping forward and back with his shoe, making him feel nauseated and light-headed.

Or maybe that was the sickening dread and the weighty, anxious feeling that he'd ruined the best thing that had ever happened to him.

"I wish your father could see you."

Charlie tensed at his ma's wistful tone, then hummed noncommittally. He'd been in a sort of comatose state for hours, sleepwalking through his chores and ending up on the couch in the living room, staring blankly at his phone while he batted away all the little worries that plagued him like flies.

Ma's quiet voice had jerked him out of the fugue he'd taken comfort in, bringing them all back.

Today had been a mistake. He'd known it was even while he said yes, eagerly accepting the bad decision, like he had all along, since the moment he'd first kissed Innes. Something had changed. Innes had changed, his newfound coolness letting Charlie know that he'd noticed how different their interactions had become, just as Charlie had.

The personal—the way he'd miss their banter, the way they'd fit, and the way Innes relaxed into closeness—he could put aside for the practical. He was worried about his job. Innes had assured him that nothing they did together would affect him enough to take it out on Charlie, but what if he'd been lying? What if he kicked Charlie to the curb without a recommendation and without the help he'd promised to get Charlie a job that would lead to his dream career?

Or had that always been a pipe dream?

Charlie wanted to trust that Innes wouldn't jerk him around like that, but it was hard to do when he knew how far Innes backed away from intimacy and giving a shit about people other than himself.

"He'd be so proud," Ma said into the awkward silence as Charlie turned his worries over in his head.

"You think so?" Charlie said on autopilot, then he clamped his mouth shut. His leg started bouncing up and down on the floor as he looked at the ceiling and wondered why he'd encouraged her. After nearly a week of this, he was running out of ways to change the subject to one he had the patience for.

"Oh, yes." Her lips curved in a painted-pink line. "Imagine. Wouldn't he be so happy to hear that you're working in a doctor's office?"

"A lawyer's office, Ma."

A caustic, whip-smart lawyer who drove him crazy and excited him, and made him want to break down all the walls Innes had built around his vulnerable parts because what he'd seen as he chipped it away made Charlie ache for him.

"Oh, is it? Goodness." She brought her hands up to her cheeks and widened her eyes like an actress in a horror movie about to be knifed. "I'm so silly sometimes. I should've remembered."

"It's fine, Ma." He reached across the space between the couch and the chair and patted her knee like he had all the other times he'd reminded her what it was he did to bring money in. "Don't worry about it."

She folded her hands back up in her lap. "In any case, he'd be so happy if he were here."

"You sound pretty sure of that," he said, purposefully wiggling his fingers so that they didn't close into fists. He didn't want her to see and to think that their conversation was the only reason he was tense.

She nodded firmly, her heavy clip-on earrings swinging. "I am. Absolutely. I can see his face. You have his smile, you know, so it's easier for me to remember. If he was here, he would—"

"Well, he isn't, though, is he?" Charlie said, with more volume than he'd meant and more than what the small room could handle. His voice bounced off the low ceiling, and he pushed up from the sagging couch to escape it. "Sorry. I can't talk about this right now, Ma. I'm going to bed."

"I don't want you to forget him," his mother said, her voice quivering like her eyes were welling up with tears fit for a Kodak moment.

He didn't look, giving her his back instead as he stood, unseeing, in front of the cluttered side table.

"Why not?" His fingers clenched painfully into his palms. "I've always thought it'd be the best thing for us both. I've never managed it, but that doesn't mean I haven't tried."

"Charlie!" The chair creaked behind him, but he could tell that she hadn't gotten up. "You owe your father some respect."

He turned around, his stress and the repetition of an ancient argument they'd almost had a hundred times burning away all his control and sympathy. "No. I don't. He was your husband. I don't care what you think of him after all this time, but I sure as hell don't respect him."

His mother shrank in on herself, her hands hovering next to her ears the way they always did when she didn't want to listen or do anything but hide. "Stop that," she said. "Whatever differences you might have, he still helped to make you the man you are today."

Charlie felt as though a physical shockwave had pushed him onto his heels. His face started prickling and a ringing grew louder in his ears. "In what universe did he make me who I am? Besides the obvious, what hand did he have in creating me?"

She opened her trembling mouth, but he surged forward, jabbing a hand at his chest. "I got me where I am, Ma. *Me*. I had no one else's help."

His mother didn't say anything. She bowed her head to her lap, hurt written plainly all over her face.

"But it doesn't matter," he hissed, "because the money I make now doesn't change the fact that he left. He *left us*."

"Charlie, you know he had to go," she said, softly. Reasonably, in a way she wasn't often.

A mirthless huff of laughter forced its way from his lungs. "No, he didn't. He should have taken care of us."

"He did. The money—"

"What money? He hasn't sent us a dime since I was fourteen. Why do you think I worked so hard, Ma? Even in high school, I worked so that you wouldn't have to, when it was so difficult for you to keep a job. I wouldn't have had to scrape by with straight Cs if I'd had some help. If he'd stuck around to do what fathers are supposed to do."

Her lip trembled as she searched desperately for something to excuse the damned man. "If he could have stayed, he would have, but he wasn't a family man. I knew that, but I thought that I could change him, so I—"

His foot lashed out in an explosive shove to the end of the couch. "That's bullshit, Ma!"

"Don't you swear at me, Charles!"

"Don't call me that," he snapped. "He could have stayed if he wanted to, but he didn't, so he left, and all I've got is his name and his mess. I never wanted either."

She sniffed, the sparkling tears finally spilling over. "He loved you, I know he did," she insisted. "This wasn't his life, but—"

"Stop it," he barked. The blanketed feeling of helplessness disappeared as his avalanching rage cleared to crystal-clear livid fury. "Do you know where dear old Chuck is, Ma? Did you ever even try to look?"

She hiccupped a single aborted protest, then fell silent. He let her struggle a few long moments, a crack forming in his need to hurt someone else with what he knew for a change, but it wasn't a big enough fissure to stop him.

"I wouldn't—" she stumbled.

His throat burned around his scoff. "No. You wouldn't. But I would, so I did. He wasn't even hard to find. He lives in Ohio. He works at a factory, cheers for the Patriots, and goes home every night to his girlfriend and their two kids."

He'd always wondered if she'd known. He'd kept his aching, shriveling silence on the assumption that she didn't, but it was good, in a way, to have her stunned silence now confirm that he was right in thinking she'd been none the wiser.

"I found all of that out with a quick google search," he said, his voice hoarse as if he'd been the one holding back sobs. "And now I can't forget it. I wish I'd never done it."

He walked on stiff, tired legs to the couch and sank down on it. Tears still streamed down her face, but he looked away from them.

"It was never that he wasn't a family man," he said to the worn-down carpet. "He just didn't want *this* family. And I can't let that go." His voice broke, and he let his head fall into his hands. "I keep myself awake at night wondering if I did something wrong. I was only eight. How awful must I have been that he could just walk away? Then I started to wonder if it wasn't me. If it was you who made him leave."

His mother squeaked next to him, a grieving, wet sound. He shook his head, then buried his fingers in his hair, squeezing tightly.

"But you were the perfect wife at home, keeping the house spotless and the laundry done, with dinner on the table at five every day. So it couldn't have been you, and that means that it must have been me. I've thought about it so much, Ma. Every day, it seems like. What did I do? What was it about me that made him turn tail and run without even saying goodbye?"

His eyes burned. He'd stopped crying over his father—even alone—when he was twelve and the only kid in his class who'd learned how to sign his own permission slips.

"I've got sisters," he rasped. "Eight and ten years old. He takes them fishing on weekends. They're cute. It's obvious that he loves them, so I know he's capable of it. He just couldn't love me."

"He did," his mother choked out.

He twitched his shoulder in a chilly shrug. "Not enough. Whatever love he might have had for us couldn't keep him here. Sending a few hundred bucks of child support every month for a few years isn't love. If he'd loved us, he would've taken care of us. I had to do it instead. Don't you remember?"

She reached out a hand to him, but he was frozen. "Charlie, your father—"

"Enough excuses, Ma!" He fired his limbs to push himself to his feet, using the height to tower over her in a way he never did. "Don't you think fifteen years of lying to yourself is enough?"

For a split second, the sorrow in her eyes flashed to fear, and it drained away his anger better than anything else ever could have. He sank to his knees in front of hers, clasping his hands on his thighs so she wouldn't think he'd use them to hurt her. She could never think that, he thought, panicking, his spine curving and his head spinning from the rush of fevered blood going cold and clotted.

"Did he know?" he whispered into her knees. He didn't want to ask it. If he could have held it in any longer, he would have, but this was the closest they'd ever come to answering the question that had tortured him more than anything else.

Her shaky breath ruffled the hair on the top of his head. "Know what?"

"Don't pretend, Ma."

"About . . ." Her throat clicked as she swallowed. "About how you are?"

At another time or place, he would have laughed at her practiced ability to talk around it. To leave out the words that the dictionary defined him as.

He lifted his hands from their frozen state, knuckling his fingers deep in his eye sockets. "Did he see something in me at eight years old that disgusted him? I didn't even know myself, not then. I'll never know how he would have reacted to me bringing a guy home."

Or sleeping in a man's bed, looking forward to a lazy morning neither of them had verbally agreed to but that just felt right.

Her hands landed heavily on his shoulders, shaking them with as much feeble force as she could. "You don't know he would've reacted badly. I've always left the door open for him. He could still try to reach out if you don't want to."

"I hope he never does," he murmured, numb now that the storm was over. "But I also hope that someday he comes out of nowhere and tells me he had a reason all along. That he loves me and didn't want to go. But I know that will never happen."

"Oh, Charlie," she breathed, then her fingers were on his neck, and his face was pressed into her knee, the first scalding tears seeping into the blanket over her lap. Her fingers combed through his hair as she made soft shushing noises until the pressure passed.

When he could talk again, he'd apologize. Maybe tell her what was going on with him and Innes, sharing his fear and doomed happiness the way he used to share everything with her. (When had that stopped? When had he become so separate from her orbit?) He'd tell her that it wasn't her fault and that he wouldn't have yelled at her if he hadn't already been wound so tightly.

When he could move again, and after he slept like the dead for a night, he'd go to work and end things with Innes. They could go back to how things were before they slept together like idiots. He could take a step back and be an employee, not a lover or a friend. Innes obviously wanted that too, despite how much fun they'd both had while it was good.

His mother's hand stroked his hair as his knees started to ache. Nothing would be the same, but he and his mother could pretend it was. Go back to the two of them against the world. Like always.

# Chapter Thirteen

I f there was a valid argument Innes could mount with all his experience in arguing, he would personally ensure mornings were illegal.

He lounged in one of the guest chairs, choosing its spindly arms and straight back so that there wasn't so much leather pressing against his skin. His head pounded dully, his irritation making the corners of his mouth tighten and his teeth clench.

*Early* was the worst word in the English language, the worst concept he'd ever been forced to grasp, and yet here he was, at the office, collapsed in an uncomfortable chair, *early*. He'd been there for half an hour, and the clock on the wall told him while it ticked closer to nine that it still wasn't a reasonable time to be at his place of work.

He felt hungover, though he hadn't had a drop to drink. He was exhausted after tossing and turning all night *again*, alone and undistracted so there was nothing to keep him from replaying every detail of the day before. Sorting through the memories certainly didn't help him relax, so it was an endless cycle of nitpicking everything and getting himself too stressed to even close his eyes.

*This wasn't supposed to happen*, he thought. He hadn't lost a wink of sleep over someone he'd slept with since Theresa.

And didn't that turn out *so well*.

His stewing was interrupted by the sound of the door swinging open behind him. He glanced at the clock to see if he'd lost more time than he'd thought by feeling sorry for himself, but he frowned.

"It's 8:35," he said, with a playful lightness he didn't feel. "If you know what's good for you, you'll march your ass out of here and get a coffee. It's too early for anything important."

"Um," a familiar female voice uttered.

Innes bolted up from the chair, smoothing his tie down his chest, like that would make him look fresh as a daisy instead of like he'd spend the night in his car in the parking lot. (He might as well have, for the amount of time he'd spent dwelling on what had happened inside the building.)

"Mimi," he blurted. "What are you doing here?"

She shrugged, looking around the richly appointed office instead of at him. "I've never visited you here. I'm on summer break from school and I thought I'd change that."

Innes stared at her. She was wearing jeans and a comfortable sweater—which, at second glance, might have been the one that Charlie had bought her—and looked almost as rumpled as he did with her hair thrown up into a messy ponytail and her face free of makeup.

"Well, come in, sit down," he said belatedly, realizing he'd been staring at her for longer than was socially acceptable. "Did you just get into town?"

He nudged the second guest chair with his foot, and she sat in it, sprawling out with a huge yawn.

"Yeah. My flight was so early I can almost convince myself that it was actually late. I took a cab here."

He shifted to reach for his wallet. "Here, let me give you some cash—"

"It's fine," she said, shaking her head and sitting on her hands so she couldn't take the hundred dollar bill he'd produced. "I actually wanted to talk to you."

"Okay. Not that I'm not glad to see you, but we do talk a lot these days."

"Yeah, but on the phone. It's not really the same."

He felt a twinge of disappointment, with a touch of annoyance on its heels. He wished she would have told him that all the long, friendly phone calls they'd shared in the past month didn't really count.

He shoved that aside and asked, "What's up?"

She fiddled with a rip in the knee of her jeans. "I've left this really late, but I'm still figuring out what I want to do for the summer quarter. Most of my friends have internships, but I didn't even try for one. I don't want to burn out, you know?"

"That's probably a good idea. You're young, you've got plenty of time." Not to mention an opportunity for shameless nepotism if everything else fell through.

She smiled at him, and a bit of tension left her shoulders. He wondered if he was the first person she'd told about her plans and if all the reactions she'd had were as favorable.

"Yeah, that's what I thought. But I have to figure out what I'm going to do until September. I don't mind living in the Bay Area for a while, but it's expensive to get a place, even if I found a roommate. And honestly, I think I'd get lonely by myself."

He hummed, neutral and uncommunicative, but on the inside, he was starting to feel the prickle of anxiety at the back of his neck.

She continued, pulling fiercely at the threads of denim now, "I'd ask Mom if I could stay with her, but—" Her lips thinned and her eyes went a little moist, but also steely. "—I'm not ready to let her try to be in my life again."

The air left Innes's lungs in a rush. So it had finally happened. Mimi had let slip more and more of her troubles with her mother, and he'd been waiting for the shoe to drop, but if Mimi wasn't letting Theresa in, that meant that at some point she'd been kicked out completely.

"I'm staying with Aunt Catherine until the end of the weekend," Mimi said, ignoring Innes's silence, "but after that, I wondered—" She paused, her throat clicking as she swallowed. "Aunt Catherine said you have a guest room in your place. I thought maybe I could stay with you."

There was static in his ears. As Innes coughed his unwillingness to speak out of the way, the noise seemed to swell, then grow more high-pitched with his rising panic.

"Ah," he said, after a deep breath through his nose. "Well."

"I'm a good roommate," Mimi said, clutching her knees with both hands, leaving the torn scrap of fabric mercifully alone. "Or at least that's what my friends at school think. I keep my room clean."

"I—" he tried.

"I don't play loud music," she went on, not giving him a chance to say anything either way, which Innes knew was a sign that she knew the way it was headed. "I can't cook for shit, though, but you said you know how to do that. You could teach me."

"I would love to," Innes cut in, leaning forward and putting his hands over hers. Looking down at them, he realized it might have been the first time he'd touched her since she was . . . maybe ten years old, the last time he'd hugged her before she went back to her mother after their yearly birthday lunch. Then, she'd shrugged him off, staring mutinously at the ground after suffering five long seconds of standing stock-still with her arms at her sides.

"I would love to teach you how to cook, Mimi," he repeated. "But I'm not sure this is the best way to do it."

She didn't say anything. Staring at him with wide eyes like she'd done when she was ten, and he hadn't been able to come up with a single thing to talk about in the dining room at Cheesecake Factory.

He wanted to close his eyes and mourn. *It was going so well*, he thought. Now it was all going to be ruined because Innes couldn't—

He *couldn't*.

"I'm sure you're a wonderful roommate," he said, feeling like his smile would break his face. "But I know I'm not. I've been a bachelor for too long, I'm afraid; I've picked up some terrible habits."

"I don't care," she said, her lips thin from displeasure once more. "You couldn't be worse than the freshmen I have to share a building with. You could just ignore me. It would be fine—"

"Mimi," he interrupted, squeezing her hands to make her stop. "I don't think it would work. I'm sorry."

He wanted to shoot the clock on the wall. Take it out back and empty a clip of a gun he didn't own into its smirking, *ticking* face.

"Why not?" Mimi said.

"What?"

"I don't care if you say no." Her gaze slid away from his as she said it. Clearly, she did care. "But why? Is there a reason why you won't even consider it? Give me *one*."

The only sound he could produce was the rasp of his own breathing. She was waiting for him to say something, anything to make it all better, but what could he possibly tell her?

In truth, he had multiple reasons, none of which could ever pass his lips. How could he tell her it was because he was still figuring out how to keep someone else at arm's length, for his own self-preservation? How did he explain that having her there was a risk he didn't have good enough odds on to take?

How did he tell his only daughter, who'd only just started to trust him, that he was afraid that if she spent more time with him, she'd realize why she'd stopped loving him in the first place?

"I'm sorry," he said again, as soft as he could get away with without not saying it at all. "I really am."

He saw her eyes shutter the moment he said it. As she pulled her hands out of his grasp, he saw all his fragile hope disintegrating even as his mouth opened to do damage control he knew was worse than useless.

"How about this, though. I'll help you get a place. We'll find a sublet, I'll foot the bill so you can have a great summer."

She stood up, backing up awkwardly into the arm of her chair in her effort to put space between them. "It's fine," she said, tightly, looking at the floor.

He stood up with her, the static coming back as he grasped for ways he could fix this. "No, really, I don't mind."

"I know you don't," she said, her eyes snapping furiously to his, no longer glued to the floor in dejection. "You never mind throwing money at the problem until it goes away."

"Mimi," he said, reaching out for her, but she backed up, holding up a guarding hand. She shook her head. The wetness gathering in her eyes trembled but didn't fall.

"I'm just another problem to you," she said, her voice dead flat. She turned away from him, heading for the door.

"That isn't true." He followed, close enough that his hand could hover over her shoulder as she left him behind. "Mimi, please, would you listen to me?"

She knocked his hand away as her other hand closed over the knob. "No. I'm done listening."

His stomach twisted as he let her go, his whole being screaming to do something other than watch, but there was nothing he could do. When she reached the end of the hallway, he took a single involuntary step forward, an aborted move to try one last time, then she was gone.

But not before she nearly tripped over Charlie turning the corner on his way to his desk.

The vital, vibrating energy of Charlie was too much for Innes in that captured moment in time, so he backed away from the door, meandering sightlessly to the wall of shelves. A terrible choice, really. If he was trying to avoid thinking in his numb, detached state, he shouldn't have gone back to the place he and Charlie had had their reckoning a day earlier.

"Innes," he heard Charlie say. "Who was that?"

"That was—" he stumbled, the words in his mouth drying up over the past tense. "Mimi."

He could feel the physical force of Charlie's surprise. He didn't need to look to see the gears turning in his head.

He didn't care to do anything but let his eyes go out of focus on the spine of a book until Charlie demanded, "What did you do?"

A spike of cold, sharp fury pierced through his blur of bitter composure. He pinned Charlie with a look that made him take a step back.

"What is that supposed to mean?" Innes said, ice dripping from every syllable.

Charlie pursed his lips, his jaw working under his skin. "She was upset. What happened?"

"No, you asked what I did. Because, of course, it's got to be me who fucked up. Right?" He used his consonants as weapons, hurling the sharp sounds across the room. "Because I'm so fucking awful."

"That isn't what I meant."

Innes huffed an imitation of a laugh. "Yes, it was. And for your information, what I *did* was send her packing. She's done with me now because apparently refusing to let her live with me means I'm selfish and I don't want to even have a daughter. Happy now?"

"She—" Charlie blinked and went completely still. "She wants to live with you?"

Fresh grief hit him like a shockwave after a bomb dropping. *Wanted* would be a more accurate word choice, but his throat closed up too tightly to do more than nod.

He knew his relationship with Mimi would be irreparable if he didn't run after her and give her some plausible reason why he'd refused. He knew it in the way he could know the screen of a phone was smashed to pieces, even if it was still facedown on the concrete. He couldn't tell the future, but he *knew*.

"Why did you say no?" Charlie said, his incredulity becoming clearer with every word. "That's— It's what you've wanted all this time. To see her more, to be her father, and now you kick her out? You give up? What the hell, Innes?"

"You have no idea what you're talking about," Innes gritted, his teeth hurting from the pressure in his jaw.

The longer he looked at Charlie, who was nearly shimmering with pent-up displeasure, the more he wanted him gone. Out of his life so Innes could pack away what it felt like to care and forget how to do it.

"You think you know me?" Innes spat, triumph flaring as Charlie stepped back again from the venom in his tone. "You think you know my life because you clean my office and guard my door like a good dog? You don't know the first thing about me."

Charlie said nothing, his shock melting into an anger that turned his eyes incandescent but was nevertheless a fraction of the bonfire that raged inside of Innes. Every word burned like acid as it spewed out, hurting him as much as it hurt Charlie.

"I don't need a kid messing up my life, and I don't need you, either, trying to tell me how to live. You're nothing. Just a convenient lay and a condescending chump who gets off on being superior."

Charlie's voice was a gravel pit in miniature. "Look who's talking."

Charlie's feeble attempt at the kind of damage Innes was doing elicited the first positive emotion Innes had felt in what seemed like hours. *Yes,* said the part of him that would regret everything tomorrow. *Fight back. Tear out a chunk of me to keep as a souvenir of this low point.*

"At least I know it," Innes said, already exhausted. "At least I don't pretend that I'm better than you or anyone else. I don't snake my way into people's beds and try to make them play out some domestic fantasy to fill a void because Daddy didn't love me."

The silence could have drawn blood. Innes felt speared on it. Smeared across its edge even though he'd been the one to inflict the hurt. That was it, he realized. He'd found the breaking point that would put an end to everything they were or could ever be.

"You finished?" Charlie asked. His arms were crossed over his chest, but Innes could see his knuckles turning white in the crook of his elbows.

"Am I? Why don't you decide? You seem to want to control every other part of my life lately."

Charlie's mirthless laugh sounded as empty as Innes felt. "All right. Fine."

He turned on his heel and marched out of Innes's office, straight-backed. Tall in pride, if not in height. Against his will, Innes was drawn to the door Charlie left open behind him. Weighed down by hollow satisfaction, he watched as Charlie gathered his things from the desk.

A few pens. A mug. A paper tray, the contents turned out onto the desk in disarray. A few pictures taped behind the computer monitor where Innes had never noticed them before. It took only a couple of minutes for all traces of him to be removed completely.

There was no dramatic pronouncement. No famous last words. Only the echo of Charlie's footsteps and the certainty that he wouldn't come back.

When Innes was sure Charlie had left the floor, the building, and his life, he shut the world out behind the door. *Mission accomplished*, he thought. No more attachments. No more itch of an encroaching significant other leaving a toothbrush in his bathroom. No more assistant, which was annoying, but fixable.

Back to the status quo. This was the way all his relationships ended, no matter how shallow they were. Charlie and Mimi had both found out that he was as much of a bastard as he told people he was.

It was better that way, he told himself, staring unseeing at his shelf of expensive things. He'd be happier.

Had he ever been happy?

With a snap of his arm and the last fume of anger before he shut down completely, he grabbed the nearest thing—a round amber paperweight—and threw it at the door, where it landed with a sound as loud as a gunshot that ended a life.

# Chapter Fourteen

**C**harlie flipped the end of his tie over, tugging it through the loop to create the knot, the cool silk slipping through his fingers with confidence. He pulled it snugly to his throat, lifting his chin to practice how he would attempt to alpha male a few businesses into at least taking his résumé, even if it got tossed in the shredder as soon as he left.

He knew it was a long shot. Most places these days smiled politely and refused if someone tried to give them a hard copy. He'd probably do as well to hand them a sheet of construction paper with the words *I'm a good human, please give me money* written on it in glitter pen.

But he'd already exhausted his options in this week's online postings. He'd spent all of Sunday in a blanket cocoon sending emails and submitting documents to any job he was remotely qualified for. Now, it was Monday. No more blanket cocoons, no more self-pity. Time to work, so he could find himself *work*.

He'd needed the break, he could admit to himself. He'd been exhausted emotionally, smarting from the insults Innes had hurled at him with stunning accuracy, and in desperate need of a few days to feel sad and sorry for himself, filling sketchbooks with designs of dark and visceral colors because it felt good, even if they might never see the light of day.

It had felt like much more than a lost job and a dissolving of a mutually beneficial sex-friends arrangement. It felt like a breakup. He didn't have much experience with those, but he felt like doing all the things people on TV did. He'd slept long but unrestful hours, running away from thinking by shutting off his brain with unconsciousness. He'd eaten all his favorite things, hoping comfort food would ease the ache in his chest on the way to his stomach. He hadn't cried. He was too angry for that—at himself and Innes.

But he'd breathed brokenly into Joy's shoulder for an evening because in a real, tangible way, it *was* the end of a relationship. Not a good one, but Charlie had been happy in those few weeks. He'd enjoyed the sensation of getting to know someone in a base, primal way, learning what Innes liked in bed, then somehow stumbling into genuine affection, and learning what Innes was like when he stopped defending his emotions with quite so many long, sharp spikes.

The worst part was, he knew exactly what had happened, and it wasn't just an argument where Innes said some hurtful things. It had been an excuse. Innes had been hurt, had probably felt as raw as Charlie had about the last time they'd hooked up.

But Innes's inability to process normal human emotion didn't make his reaction right or okay. He'd been cruel when he didn't have to be. Charlie wasn't about to try to tame a savage beast who had no interest in being domesticated. He'd rather walk away with more good memories than bad.

He mourned the loss of Innes's promise, though not as much as the loss of his good company. Maybe if he could have stuck it out, ignored how childish Innes had become in his pain, he could have walked out of there with the means to make his dream a reality. But he wasn't that kind of person, and in the end, a good reference wasn't worth all that bullshit.

It just made the search for a new job that much harder.

But this time around, as he picked places to beg for a chance, he was letting himself be a little choosier. He had a more impressive line on his résumé, now, and a bigger portfolio of things he'd been working on in the last few weeks. Most importantly, he had a nest egg he'd clawed together for emergencies like this.

Maybe applying for internships and fashion-adjacent jobs wouldn't get him anywhere, but he had to try. If not now, when would he? This felt like his last chance. A Hail Mary, and he wasn't going to waste it.

"Charlie?"

He gave his tie a last tug and picked up his suit jacket on his way to the kitchen. "Yes, Ma?"

"Oh, there you are."

She was spooning something from a pan onto two plates at their tiny kitchen table. "What's this?" Charlie asked as she placed a few slices of toast on the plates next.

"I made you breakfast. You better eat it before it gets cold."

He obediently sat down, picking up a fork but not digging into the simple, delicious-looking scrambled eggs. "Ma—" he started.

"Don't start with me," she said, brandishing her eggy spatula at him. "It's the least I could do."

When she sat down next to him to eat, he grabbed her hand, squeezing it, then bringing it to his lips to kiss.

While he'd been wrapped in a blanket on the couch, his mother had been the one to make dinner and keep the apartment from becoming a total wreck.

They hadn't talked about their fight, beyond Charlie trying to apologize and Ma going so far as to cover his mouth so he couldn't speak. She'd held him instead, wrapping him in a hug so strong that he'd forgotten how fragile he'd always thought she was.

"Love you, Ma," he said now.

She smiled and poked him in the arm with the clean end of her fork until he started eating, swallowing past the bundle of nerves in his throat that was slowly tightening at the thought of having to beg and lie his way to the manager of at least two dozen businesses today.

Breakfast was quiet. He wasn't in a particularly talkative mood, still getting back to normal after an eventful few days. Well, weeks, really. The entire two months he'd worked for Innes had been a roller coaster.

*God*, he thought. *Was it really only two months?* He felt fundamentally changed, and not only because he now knew how spreadsheets worked.

He washed their dishes when he was finished, carefully not leaning too close to the sink so he wouldn't have to change his shirt. While Ma dried their plates, he told her all the places he was going to go and explained why he wasn't holding out much hope that any of it would pan out. She smiled and nodded, and Charlie was pretty sure she mostly understood, even though she wasn't too familiar with online application processes.

When he returned from his bedroom after fetching the folder full of résumés he'd resented paying for at the local library, she told him quietly, but with a fragile confidence, "I think I'll go and see if Mr. Flores down the hall would like to get that cup of coffee with me."

He barely kept his mouth from falling open in shock. "Yeah," he said, a beat too late. "Sounds like a great idea."

The past was the past. Charlie had always tried to believe that, even while his mother clung on to it. But maybe this was her way of telling Charlie that she was loosening her grip on it.

It was a start, at least.

"And maybe you'd better—"

She cut herself off, staring down at her finger as it nudged the butter dish on the table.

"What, Ma?" Charlie prompted carefully.

"Do you think it would help if I spoke to a doctor?"

Her words were small and uncertain, but they filled Charlie's chest with a kind of hopeful joy he hadn't felt in a long time.

It could help. He thought back to all the research he'd done into adult ADHD. The inattentive kind, that came with time blindness and executive dysfunction, not hyperactivity. But maybe it wasn't that. Maybe it was something else, or that *and* something else, but a doctor would know, or at the very least help Ma to manage better than she had been.

"I don't know," he said, trying not to show his relief. "It wouldn't hurt."

"You're right." Her chin lifted, and the worry that tensed her lips melted away. "Can you make me an appointment?"

"Of course, Ma." He kissed her cheek. "Anything you want."

He hugged her before he left, tightly, with his face buried in her perfume-scented shoulder. They'd be okay. Charlie would find a new job, even if it didn't line up with his dream career. And he'd make sure it was a better one than he'd had at the restaurant, because he knew his own worth now. He'd get insurance, and get Ma to a doctor. Ma would still be Ma, but she'd try to expand her world to include the present. He'd be fine.

If he felt a twinge of disappointment that he wouldn't have a fascinating man with a wicked sense of humor and a guarded heart to share his troubles and successes with, then that was his business.

Innes had been staring blankly at the screen of his phone for five minutes when his office door opened. He looked up, and his stomach did an odd shimmy of both disappointment and shocked happiness.

Mimi stood in his doorway, a resigned frown on her face.

"I can't believe you actually came," Innes said, as he dropped his phone to the desk with a clatter.

He'd called her an hour before and had been unsurprised when the call had gone straight to voice mail. He'd tried to keep his tone even and unemotional, but as soon as he'd hung up the phone, he started worrying he sounded like a robot.

This caring gig was bullshit, but he couldn't stop. Not when it was Mimi at risk.

She shrugged and said nothing, her lips pursing mutinously.

He took a deep breath that quaked a bit in his chest on the exhale. "Can we talk?"

She nodded but didn't look any happier.

"Hit that light for me, would you?" he said, pointing to the switch on the wall by the door.

When Innes had gotten to work that morning, none of the lights had been on. After having been shut down for the weekend, no one had yet come down the hall, and everyone knew better than to enter his office without permission.

The reminder of his solitary existence didn't sting any more or less than the countless others. He'd been running into all sorts of tiny hitches in his normal routine that made him stumble and pause and remember.

Thankfully, he'd been busy. Suddenly having to do the work of two people meant that he could spend long hours here in his office, writing his own emails and answering every call that came through, no matter how inane.

The hours after work—the few that remained after he spent far longer working than he usually did—were harder. The weekend, when he'd run out of time-sensitive things to do or projects that needed a next step taken, had been the hardest. But he'd gotten through with the help of a bottle of very nice whiskey.

Innes wasn't in the habit of doing things he wasn't naturally good at. Everything he'd become an expert in or attained a level of quality at, he'd already had a good head start.

He was discovering that he wasn't good at moving on.

Mimi settled herself in the same chair she'd used the last—and only—time she'd been in his office. Innes hesitated to join her in the other one, not eager to put himself back in the position he'd been then with all the cascading feelings that came along with it. If he sat down there, would the panic come back? The desire to lash out?

But he also wanted to be close to her for this conversation. Some things just couldn't be discussed over a desk. He sat in the other chair, then pulled it closer, alongside hers, so that they both faced forward. It was different enough that he wasn't bothered by it, and this way, if Mimi wanted to keep looking at the wall the whole time, then she could.

"I'm glad you're here," he began.

"You're lucky Aunt Catherine is so good at getting people to do things they don't want to do," she said, staring straight ahead with a cold, catlike intensity.

"I am."

He'd have to get Charlie to send her a fruit basket or something, he thought, then backtracked. No, not Charlie.

He'd been resetting his equilibrium again and again since the moment Charlie had left. Remembering anew each time he wanted to text Charlie an observation he'd enjoy, or when he needed distracting from a problem, or when he got into bed and his sheets were cold.

On Saturday night, he'd gone to a club, trying to reset once and for all, and had sat in the parking lot until the neon light of the sign had given him a headache. At home, he'd opened the door to his guest room, leaning in and taking in the dusty odor of disuse.

Regret was not a feeling he was familiar with. Everything he did, he did with purpose and absolute assurance that what he'd done was right.

He felt regret now.

"When you were born," he said, looking up at the blank ceiling, remembering, "I wasn't allowed in the delivery room. Theresa didn't want me there, and frankly, I didn't want to be with her." He winced and thought about trying to soften the dig at Theresa with a lie, but it wouldn't do him any good. "The first time I saw you was when one of your aunts—Georgia, I think, it's a bit of a blur—marched into your mother's hospital room and demanded to see you. She brought you out into the hall to see me."

He looked down at his hands, the same ones that had been clenched in his lap for almost twenty-four hours as he'd sat on an uncomfortable bench, waiting for any news he could get.

"Theresa's parents were furious. The nurses were hovering around, all worried that this crazy shouting woman would do something, but all she did was bring you to me. Georgia held you out for me to take, and you were so small." He swallowed past his dry throat, refusing to look over when he saw Mimi's attention turn to him out of the corner of his eye. "She said, 'Take your daughter,' and I was so scared of you that I couldn't do it. I refused to touch you because you looked so fragile, and I was sure I'd mess it up. I looked and looked, and everyone around me got angrier, and you started to cry, and I still couldn't do it."

"What happened then?" Mimi asked. Her voice was tight, but Innes couldn't tell if it was from anger or . . . something else.

"Georgia took you back, I went home and I didn't see you again for a week. I ran away from you when you were less than a day old." Finally, he swung his gaze in her direction, meeting her bright, pain-filled eyes. "I've been running ever since. Every time I would get close to you, I've gotten scared. What if I mess it up?"

She scoffed, looking away again. "Yeah. What if."

Innes had to laugh, even if it wasn't funny. She was smart enough to know that his hypotheticals had ended up hurting them both, even if he was only understanding that now. "I know it's not an excuse, but I want you to understand that it's never been about you. You're perfect, and that's one of the reasons why I've kept you at arm's length." His lungs squeezed out a breath that was almost another laugh. "I'm so imperfect, Mimi; you don't even want to know."

"So is everyone," she said, fiercely, pushing her chair back, but staying seated, shrinking away from him even as she glared. "I never wanted you to be perfect, I just wanted you there."

"I know. And I wanted to be there. I love you, but—"

"If you loved me so much, why did you leave me with her?"

Innes inhaled in the quiet after Mimi's question was flung sharply into the conversation. He'd never meant to discuss this with her. He hadn't acknowledged it, but he'd intended to take this conversation with him to the grave if Mimi didn't bring it up first. He'd thought that it was unlikely she ever would, but after getting to know her over the past month, he realized that had been a very stupid assumption.

"It was the best thing for you," he told her simply.

"Why?" Mimi demanded.

*No turning back*, he thought. *No more running*.

"Theresa would come down so hard on you whenever I would take you for a weekend. Interrogating you. You'd call me crying, asking to come back, but that would make it worse. Theresa would never change, so I decided it was better if I left you alone."

"No, it wasn't," she said, shaking her head almost imperceptibly, but once she started, she couldn't stop until it looked like she was trembling in her denial. "She's my mom, and I loved her, but she's—" She flinched, then tossed her head dismissively. "She's not a good person."

"I know."

"No, you don't." Her fisted hands came down on the arms of her chair with twin thumps. "You weren't there, so you couldn't possibly understand how much she fucked me up. I didn't realize how bad it was until I was away from her. It was better after Jerry moved in, but—"

She curled in on herself, pulling on the hem of her T-shirt like a lifeline. The curtain of her hair fell over her face, so Innes could only hear the wry, insincere smile in her voice.

"I can't stand it when people whisper. Did you know that? Well, no, of course, you wouldn't. But whenever she would get really mad, she would whisper everything, like that would make what she said any better than if she'd yelled it. My roommate thinks I'm crazy because every time she's quiet for more than ten minutes, I start thinking she's angry with me, and I have to ask if I did something wrong so I can fix it before it gets worse."

A jolt of shock made Innes grip the arms of his chair. "She never—"

"No, she never hit me." Mimi's head snapped up, her eyes sparking with quiet fury. "Sometimes I think it would have been better if she did because then I would have known she wasn't a good mother way earlier. Try explaining to a child that their mom isn't supposed to hold their hand so tightly in church that it hurts. Or that normal moms didn't rip up the pictures you drew them because you colored outside the lines, or convince you for years that you were stupid because you got a B minus in math two report cards in a row. Little things. Stupid things."

Innes's heart pounded. Mimi had painted a picture of a childhood he'd given up a lot for her to not experience. A sick part of him wanted to laugh at how the hues she used were similar to the ones that comprised his own young years. Hers were etched in wide swathes of cruelty disguised as love. His were more delicate, an impressionistic portrait of care devoid of love.

What a goddamn mess they both were.

"I—I never knew it was that bad," he stuttered. "Theresa was always intense, but I thought that was because she hated me."

"She did. She said so many awful things about you, about all of you. I thought you were terrible people for so long. It was easy for me to believe because if you weren't awful, why would you leave me with her when she wasn't good at being a mom?"

"Because I wasn't any good at being a father, either."

Mimi burst up from her chair, putting distance between them as her voice rose in volume. "Were you worse than her? Would you have lied about her and poisoned me against her?"

"No, never." Regardless of his feelings about Theresa, a child didn't need to hear that.

"Would you have been obsessed with me wearing dresses and makeup and pretty hair all the time because you wanted a perfect little copy of yourself?"

"No."

"Would you have scrubbed my hands raw every time I came home from seeing my other parent—" Her voice cracked, the tears brimming over at last. "—screaming at me because you were all nasty, sick people?"

"No, but that's why I had to go away!" Tripping over the leg of the chair, he closed the space between them, pulling her in, quickly so that she couldn't think to back away. He held her so tightly he could feel the bones of her shoulders under his arms.

"She couldn't just let you be with me for a few hours each week. She always had to punish you if you showed even the slightest bit of love for me or the rest of your family. It was horrible. We all . . . we decided that it was better if we stayed away from you. You'd be happier, and Theresa would stop using you as a pawn to make me suffer."

"Why didn't you take me away?" Mimi whispered into his shoulder.

He felt his arms begin to tighten, already used to the sensation of holding Mimi, even though it had been so many years. For this explanation, however, his need to look her in the eyes won over his desire to never let go. He eased her away far enough that he could see her face, his hands still gripping her shoulders to give them both an anchor.

"You have to understand," he said, wincing at how patronizing he sounded. "This was almost twenty years ago. I was a single man. Gay, so likely to stay that way, as far as the courts were concerned. Still in school, no job to speak of, and only my parents' generosity to count on until I had an income besides my trust fund. There was a good chance that if I tried to get sole custody, I'd get turned down, since Theresa's parents could have hired lawyers."

The fact that her eyes were wet didn't make their disbelieving look any less harsh.

"There was also a chance we'd win," he allowed. "And that terrified me more than the alternative. The only reason I let myself get to know you at all was because I thought I couldn't mess you up if I only had you for short bursts. The thought of being the one responsible for your well-being was more frightening than losing you completely. I was seriously convinced that I would taint you." His throat jerked with tightening regret. "This way, at least there would be a chance you would be happy."

Mimi sniffed inelegantly, already packing away the spate of tears. "Well, I wasn't."

Innes's short sigh burned his throat. "I'm getting that now. We thought . . . I thought I had done the right thing. All I did was make you feel as unloved as I felt all my life. I can't tell you how much I regret that."

She nodded jerkily. In the depths of her eyes—dark brown, like his—he saw an understanding, an acceptance of the choices he'd made and why he'd made them. It wasn't quite forgiveness—they'd have a while to go before they reached that, if she allowed him to reach it— but she understood.

She cleared her throat, but her voice was still a little raspy when she asked, "Why won't you let me stay with you?"

"I was scared. What happens if I start to love you like I did when you were little? At any time, you could decide that you hate me again and go back to your mother, and I've lost you again. It felt safer to keep you at arm's-length. But all that did was lose me both you and—"

He stopped and shut his jaw with a *click*. That was quite enough sharing and caring about his romantic life, he decided. There was only so much an emotionally constipated idiot like him could manage.

But Mimi wasn't about to be brushed off. "Me and who?"

"It doesn't matter."

"I think it does. You seem pretty broken up about it."

He frowned. "What makes you think that? Can't I be broken up about this touching father-daughter moment we're having?"

"You could. But it's more than that. Otherwise, you would have cracked years ago and taken me away from her." She shrugged, but her eyes were sparkling with wry teasing, a welcome change from the previous tears. "You're a big-shot lawyer now. You could have rescued me."

"I didn't know you needed rescuing so badly."

"I know that now. And I get why you didn't. I'm still mad at you, though, so I'm also a little bit selfishly glad that someone broke up with you if that means you'll stop being an idiot and start being a dad."

Despite the serious topic and the panic that still clenched in his chest, he smiled and shook his head. "You sound like him," he said.

She seemed to suddenly realize that they'd been standing with Innes's hands on her shoulders for a long time. She stepped back and tilted her head, fixing him with a penetrating look. "So. You're gay, huh?"

He blinked. "You didn't know?"

"Not for sure, until you said it just now. I kind of figured it out from some things the family said, but Mom never confirmed it or anything."

"Really?" Great, there was another bombshell he didn't even know he'd dropped on her until it'd already gone off. "I didn't keep it a secret. Far from it. I would have thought Theresa . . ."

"No." Her expression tensed, eyebrows drawing down, but it cleared almost right away as her eyes widened. "I think she might have been embarrassed. Maybe she thought she turned you gay."

He snorted. "No. I was gay long before she came around. Just completely in denial about it."

"Makes sense."

"I could take this opportunity to make a comment about Theresa being terrible enough to actually make that happen, but such misogyny is beneath me."

"Okay." She crossed her arms, raising her eyebrows, clearly waiting for a follow-up. Clever girl.

"She is a colossal bitch, though," he couldn't resist adding. "Irrespective of her gender."

Mimi's laugh seemed like it was surprised out of her, sweeping away the last of the tension. "This is a weird way to make me feel better."

"Is it working?"

"Yeah."

He was suddenly exhausted. It was barely nine o'clock on a Monday morning, and he already felt like he needed a weekend from the effort of a conversation long put-off and the sheer magnitude of the work he had in front of him still to do.

"I don't know how to be a dad," he said honestly. "I'm terrified I'll screw it up."

"Well, you couldn't possibly do any worse than you have up until this point. Is that comforting?"

"Surprisingly, yes." In a deliberately casual motion, he patted her on the shoulder. "Great. We are amazing at consoling each other."

"We sure as shit are." She didn't look at him funny or acknowledge the motion, which Innes counted as a win.

"Now that I'm trying to parent you, do I have to scold you for swearing?"

"God, no. It's ingrained now, there's nothing you can do."

"Thank fuck."

She laughed again, a high, free peal that made her face scrunch up with genuine humor. It was infectious and made Innes's lips twitch into an unpracticed smile, and it made him want to never recover if that meant he could make her laugh.

"Mimi," he said insistently, even though he hated to ruin the carefree moment. "Would you come and live with me in my huge apartment's opulent spare bedroom? It's got a walk-in closet and its own bathroom. I'll even cook for you sometimes. And teach you how to be a wine snob—"

"You had me at my own bathroom," she interrupted. "I am so tired of the dorms. People are slobs."

"I agree. That's why I live alone, so don't screw it up for me," he said, pointing at her with his version of a stern look.

"Understood."

Shaking out his hand, he exhaled a hard breath. "All right. Wow, that felt pretty good."

The round of applause she gave him was slow and bitingly sarcastic. "Excellent first attempt at parenting."

"Well, it wasn't the *first* attempt. I did try at the beginning. I taught you how to blow spit bubbles when you were three. Your mother hated it."

"Nice."

For the first time since she'd walked in and they'd started this wonderful disaster of a conversation, they ran out of things to say, but it wasn't uncomfortable or tense. It felt like the beginning of something. He'd only just begun to make up for his mistakes, including the ones he'd made recently, but she would give him room to try.

She took a deep breath and let it out with a shake of her head and shoulders, like a dog getting rid of the vestiges of sleep.

"I'm going to go," she said firmly. "Aunt Catherine will want to know what happened, and I guess I'd better pack up all my things so I can move into your place."

"Haaaah." The noise came out of him without his intention, and he cleared his throat to try to cover it. "Good. Cool, yes, that's good. Your things. Excellent."

She rolled her eyes, heading for the door. "Please don't kill yourself pretending you're completely fine with this. I know it'll be an adjustment, and I appreciate you trying."

"Adjustment. Yes." He swallowed hard around the nerves that flared up every time he thought about someone sitting in his favorite chair in his living room. "I'll text you later with the details," he called after her as she went down the hall, leaving his door wide open.

"Good, because I have no idea where you live," she shouted back, flashing an impish smile just before she turned the corner.

As if he hadn't already had as many touching family reunions as he could handle for the day, Aiden stopped by his office as Innes was packing it in, which wouldn't have been an odd occurrence if Aiden hadn't finished up his final case the week before.

"Yes, come in, come in," Innes said anyway, at Aiden's knock and hesitant greeting from beyond the door.

"Hey, just checking, am I in a parallel universe?" Aiden said, poking his head into the room. "Or did I walk into my uncle's office without having to get past a guard dog?"

"Your eyes do not deceive you." Innes shut down his computer with a firm tap of the button. Perhaps firmer than was really necessary. "I am between assistants right now, not that it's any of your business."

"Oh." Aiden shoved his hands into his pockets and leaned against the wall next to the doorjamb, looking particularly casual in his normie clothes. "Are you . . . okay?"

Innes chose to misunderstand him, slapping a stack of papers into an orderly pile with a threatening, pleasant expression pointed in

Aiden's direction. "It's happened before and it will probably happen again soon. Nothing I can't handle."

Aiden held up his hands in surrender, straightening up from the wall. "Fine. Just don't poach anyone from downstairs for your replacement. I only recently got Joan and Rosario to start referring to me by my name instead of 'Catherine's son.' Though I suppose they'll go back to calling me whatever they want, now."

"Could be worse. The only reason they stopped calling you 'Cutie Pie' is because Catherine had a word with them."

Aiden groaned, covering his face with a wide palm. "God, I did not need that reminder. I wasn't going to say anything, but just for that, I'm going to tell them that you gave your blessing to their nickname for you."

"Jesus, not—"

"Stud Muffin Senior."

"Good lord."

Aiden tapped a finger on his chin thoughtfully. "Begs the question, though. Who is Stud Muffin Junior? Goddamn it, I bet it's me."

"That's it, you are not getting a Christmas card this year," Innes declared, sweeping a couple of pens into a drawer and slamming it shut.

"Have you ever sent a Christmas card in your life?"

Innes straightened, frowning as he cast his memory back. "I honestly don't know. There's a chance a particularly festive assistant might have done it on my behalf."

"Doubtful. They'd be too afraid you'd go full Grinch on them."

"Bah, humbug." There was a short pause, during which Aiden shifted on his feet, not quite looking at Innes. "Any particular reason you're inflicting your presence on me?"

"Mom," Aiden admitted with a wince. "I was in the area, and she wanted me to see if Mimi had come by. You're still in one piece, so can I assume you worked it out?"

"We did, actually." The truth felt remarkably good. It wasn't only a tentative peace they'd reached, but a new bridge over deep and troubled waters.

Aiden nodded. "I'll call Mom off, then. Oh, one more thing." Aiden disappeared back through the door, raising his voice so Innes could hear him with growing curiosity. "This arrived downstairs. The delivery person asked for Charlie, and I told them I'd bring it up, but evidently, there's no Charlie to deliver it to."

Aiden backed up through the door, dragging a large object covered with a translucent plastic bag on wheels. It didn't take Innes long to realize what it was, and what Charlie had done.

"Enjoy it, I guess," Aiden said, tugging the plastic off the leather executive chair with a small flourish. "It looks nice."

"Yeah," Innes said, absently, making the same observation to himself.

The leather was a rich chocolate brown, a shade or two lighter than his current chair, but still a good match for the rest of the furniture. It was padded heavily in the lumbar region, and the seat was deep and wide, but the look of it still managed to be classic and sumptuous, with its dark bronzed metal legs.

It probably had cost him a pretty penny without him having realized it, but the longer he looked, the more he loved it, and the surer he was that it would have to be dragged out from under his cold, dead ass. Not a particularly nice image, but he couldn't help that he felt strongly about office furniture, and right now, he felt *strongly* that he wanted his old one out immediately.

"Innes."

"Hmm?" He looked up from the sturdy, dark stitching of the seat at Aiden, suddenly remembering his presence. "Thanks for the delivery. You want a tip or something?"

"Don't worry about it," Aiden said wryly. "I just wanted to say that I'm sorry."

Innes raised an eyebrow at him, daring him to elaborate.

"About Charlie. He was good for you, and I'm sorry it didn't work out."

The bitter regret that had been rising from the deep place Innes had tried to bury it swelled, and Innes's first instinct was to lash out with a sharp knife to where he knew Aiden would feel it the most.

Instead, he said, "Me too."

Today had been a day of honesty, after all. If he couldn't reveal a little bit of his self-inflicted heartache to his closest family member— besides his daughter, a revelation that cheered him up a bit—then who could he reveal himself to?

If Aiden was surprised by his candidness, he did a good job of hiding it. He gave Innes a final nod and let himself out, helpfully taking the plastic bag from the chair with him.

Innes took care of the rest of the packaging, ripping off a tag or a piece of tape here and there, tossing the extended warranty pamphlet on his desk with a shake of his head and a long-suffering glance skyward. *Of course,* he thought. Charlie *was* the one who'd ordered it.

When there was nothing but the scent of new leather to indicate that it had come directly from the store, Innes shuffled the old chair out of the way and sat down in the new one, perfectly aware that his daily allowable quota of moping was quickly running out. He settled in, leaning back and letting his memory flick between all the times he'd sat at this desk in a chair far inferior to this one and seen Charlie flitting about the room in a whirlwind of efficiency or sitting in the guest chair, radiating fierce, stubborn pride.

"Damn it," Innes said to the empty room.

The chair was perfect. The high back supported his spine in a way that made it sigh in relief, easing a low-level pain he hadn't been aware he was feeling. Even if the chair hadn't looked right at home in his gaudy, terrible office that he somehow loved, he would have had to keep it anyway, just because it was the most comfortable thing he'd ever sat in.

All those times Charlie had told him to do something about his back, he'd been aggressively showing him how much he mattered, when Innes hadn't thought he was the type to matter to anyone.

"Damn it," Innes said again. He'd fucked up so bad. First with Mimi, then with Charlie.

He was already on the road to fixing his mistakes with Mimi. He'd be damned if he wouldn't at least try with Charlie.

There wasn't a shoe available on earth that could make schlepping around LA neighborhoods without a car comfortable. No insoles, no socks, no heel padding could make Charlie feel like he was walking on a cloud. Or, at least, none that he could afford.

Charlie trudged up the stairs to the apartment, wincing with every step. He was ninety percent certain he had a blister the size of a quarter on the ball of his foot, but he hadn't dared look, too worried he'd knock himself out from the smell.

"Ugh," he groaned, already sick of job hunting, and he'd barely even started.

He pushed open the heavy fire door and stumbled out into the hallway, already picturing the bliss he'd feel when he sat down on the couch. He blamed his distraction for the fact that he didn't notice the person standing outside his door until he was less than five feet away.

Innes was peering at the number nailed to the front, his hand raised in a loose fist right in front of it, poised to knock.

"Innes." Charlie was stuck firmly to the ground, all his aches and pains forgotten in his shock.

Innes turned around, surprise obvious in his jerky body language, but it was quickly covered up by a return to his customary posture of untouchable sophistication.

"Hello," he replied with an easy smile that faded slightly when Charlie just stared at him, his tired brain sandblasted with shock. "You're a sight for sore eyes."

Charlie glanced down at himself, shaken out of his stupor by a flood of embarrassment. He was wearing one of the suits he'd bought himself with Innes's money, an outfit he knew he pulled off, but he was sweaty, red from the sun, and rumpled beyond saving. He wished he could come off as cool and unaffected as Innes did, but it wasn't in his power, or even in his nature to be anything but completely honest in word, action, and unfortunate blushing complexion.

"How did you know where I live?" Charlie blurted.

All traces of a smile dropped off Innes's face. He shifted on his feet, making the cheap flooring under his expensive shoes creak. "You're not the only one who has access to the personnel files at work." he said, raising his chin, defiantly unashamed of his breach of employer-employee privacy.

Charlie would have been mad, but he was pretty sure he'd do the same thing if the situation was important enough. The problem was, he had no idea what Innes wanted, so he was stuck between outrage and guilty understanding.

Neither of those feelings were important, however.

"I think you should leave," he said.

With a confidence he didn't feel, he marched toward his door, pulling out his keys quickly in the hope that he could get inside without having to have a real conversation. Innes backed up out of his way and didn't stop him physically, but he stopped anyway when Innes spoke.

"Would you talk to me? Please."

Charlie's key was in the door. All it would take was a twist of his hand, and he could be gone, out of Innes's reach. That would be the easy route, but of course, that wasn't what Charlie did.

"Why?" Charlie demanded. "What possible reason would you have for wanting to speak to me? We both got everything we needed out of the time we had. Now it's over because you don't need me. Or anyone. So—"

"But I do," Innes said, crowding Charlie against the door in a single step, then backing off again, holding his hands up and deliberately relaxing into a defensive posture that was nevertheless beseeching. "I do need . . . someone."

*You*, he didn't say, but Charlie heard it anyway and immediately stopped himself. But once thought, the idea wouldn't go away, and Charlie was caught.

In the quiet hallway, the moment stretched out, letting Charlie look his fill at the man he'd seen nearly every day for almost two months. He'd known he'd missed Innes's company in the short time they'd been apart, but he hadn't realized just how much his eyes had missed the sight of him.

Innes seemed tired. The tightness around his mouth and the day's worth of stubble on his normally clean-shaven face made him seem older, as did the sprinkle of a few new gray hairs that Charlie could have sworn he wasn't imagining.

Paradoxically, the longer Charlie stared, the more he missed him because, despite the annoying jump of his heart and the pictures of their accidental intimacy coming back, he couldn't let himself believe that Innes had really come here to tell him he needed him.

"I never realized how apart I was from everyone else," Innes said, his soft voice echoing tinnily around the close hallway. "I have this huge family. They all live within two hours of me, some of them closer, and I don't know them. I don't even care about most of them because I never thought they cared about me. I still don't know if they do. But I forgot—" He paused, looking down at the floor to give a rueful laugh. "If I ever knew, I forgot what it was like to have someone close to me. Someone who cared if I worked hard, or slept well, or drank enough water. Or ate too much cheese and felt awful later. Or who even cared if I was alive at all."

The glint in Innes's eyes when he raised them to Charlie's was one Charlie had seen before, when Innes was entirely focused on a problem, teasing it out in his mind with no regard for anything else in the room until it was completely finished.

"You cared," he said, low, rough, and amazed. "You cared so much that you battered your way through thirty-six years of feeling unlovable just by being stubborn enough not to go away. And I still don't understand how you got under my skin, but suddenly you were everywhere, in my bed, in my goddamn mind, at the corner of my eye all the time, and I *didn't mind*." He shook his head, appearing utterly baffled at the idea. "I wanted you there. And it scared me."

The anger Charlie had thought he'd spent the last few days getting out of his system came back in full force.

"So you being terrified of actually giving a shit about another living person means I should forget everything you said?"

"No, that's not what I'm asking," Innes rushed to explain, jamming a hand through his hair, which was always so perfect, but now looked as scattered as the rest of him. "I didn't come here to monologue at you until you forget what an asshole I was."

"Then why did you come?" Charlie pressed, unwilling to let him off the hook even for a second, not when he was the one who'd started this. "I'm not desperate enough to come crawling back to you because you flatter me a little. We had what we had, then you ruined it."

"I know. That's why I'm here. Because I ruined it, and I wanted to ask if you could think about letting me try to fix it."

Fisting his hands by his sides, Charlie wrestled with the relief that washed over him. He'd never expected a Hollywood romance. He'd seen too much heartbreak for that. But he'd never let go of the silly what-ifs, and they'd only gotten harder to ignore when he'd seen how perfectly two people's lives could mesh without them even knowing they were fitting together.

"How?" Charlie croaked.

Innes opened his mouth, but nothing immediately came out. It was like he hadn't expected to get this far, so he hadn't properly prepared this part of his speech. Bad planning on his part. Charlie had never been able to convince himself not to listen to everything Innes said.

"I'm not a changed man," Innes admitted. "Not entirely. Nobody changes overnight, but I've had a few nights since you left where I tried to sleep and replayed everything I said to you and imagined how it could have been different if I'd been smarter or less terrified. What I'm trying to say is that I haven't changed, but I've learned what the worst possible outcome of pushing you away is, and it's worse than anything that could happen if I let you in."

Innes took a step closer, staring down at Charlie with an openness he'd only ever showed during sex, when emotions were simmered to double strength.

"Maybe we discover we're both too headstrong to work," Innes said. "Or you end up hating how easily I can pick and choose who to empathize with."

It was a distinct possibility. Charlie had never been with anyone who made him crazy the way Innes did. But then again, no one had ever made him laugh like Innes had, or make him feel like the darker parts of himself were okay, and as loveable as the righteous parts.

Loveable.

What was love, except the acceptance of the other person's flaws?

"I leave sewing pins everywhere," Charlie's voice came tumbling out. "It's a problem. You'd probably hate that."

His face flamed immediately with embarrassment that he'd jumped straight to the living-together part of a relationship that didn't exist yet, but Innes only smiled, relief making the crinkles beside his eyes appear warmer, more natural if not less deep.

"Yeah." Innes took another step, bringing them so close they were almost touching. "Charlie. Do you think you could start to forgive me?"

"I could if I let myself," Charlie answered immediately. "I think I'm already half there. You're not as hard to read as you think. Your fear was written all over you. Between me and your daughter suddenly giving a shit about your well-being, you were cornered. But you still said terrible things."

Innes winced, but he didn't move away or back down. "I know. And I'm sorry."

"How do I know you won't go back to being closed off and commitment-phobic?"

"You are not making this easy for me, are you?" Innes said, but he grinned.

"No, because you don't deserve it," Charlie said, glaring to counteract his urge to give in to his own grin. "And it's a legitimate concern."

Innes tilted his head, his smile turning rueful. "I miss you. I wake up every morning alone and suddenly I'm lonely when I never was before. And I keep cursing your name for showing me what I was missing, but I wouldn't take it back. No matter how terrible feelings are, no one could convince me to give them up, because then I wouldn't know how happy it makes me to see you wake up in the morning. That's how I know that this is different. That *I'm* different."

All the times that Charlie had looked up at Innes like this, close enough to touch—or sometimes already touching—had all been leading here, Charlie realized. From the first time Innes had crowded him, drawn in as Charlie had been drawn, they'd been pushing each other out of a comfort zone neither of them had truly been comfortable in.

"My dad left," Charlie blurted, not taking his eyes off Innes.

Innes didn't need to wince. The understanding in his eyes was enough. "I'm sorry."

"Yeah. What you said about my . . . issues—"

"That was completely uncalled for. I should never have said it."

Charlie made sure his eyes were unyielding. "No, you shouldn't have. But as much as it is absolutely killing me to say this." After taking in a deep, choked breath, Charlie said, haltingly, "You might not have been . . . completely off base."

Innes wisely didn't say anything. He didn't even nod or try to disagree, he just kept his steady, open gaze on Charlie's, until Charlie was ready to explain what that meant for them.

"It fucked me up," he admitted. "If I had the money, I'd probably get help for it, but I don't, so I have to make do with my own observations. I tend to overcompensate for one caring parent by caring about other people."

"No, really?" Innes said, because at the end of the day, he was still Innes. If he was anyone else, Charlie wouldn't still be standing there.

"I can't do that with you," Charlie said. "I can't."

Innes's chin tilted up stubbornly. "I won't let you, then."

"But it isn't your job to make sure I don't." So, why was he even bringing it up? Because it was important, that was why. "I need to work on myself too. That's all I'm saying."

"I hear you. Works in progress, both of us. We can agree not to expect perfection."

"Exactly." That was if Charlie took the leap. He was talking like he'd already decided, but had he? Under Innes's intense gaze, he could barely think of the answer.

Charlie turned away from him, staring at the key sticking out of the doorknob instead, to try to clear his head.

Innes couldn't be called a good man. He had flaws, and most of his virtues were the type that didn't benefit anyone but himself. He'd probably hurt Charlie again, if not any time soon, then someday, with words that weren't careless, and that were more painful for the fact that they were well thought out. He was far from perfect, and their relationship would be a hell of a lot of trouble.

Charlie turned his key in the lock and gave the door a firm push, swinging it inward as wide as it could go. He turned around and looked at Innes, finally letting himself smile.

"Okay," he said, breathlessly.

Innes's eyes widened, fiercely bright with delight. "Yeah?"

"You make a good argument, Mr. Hotshot Lawyer," Charlie drawled.

"Oh, please, I'd never insist on my full title. Best Boyfriend Ever will do."

Charlie rolled his eyes, and so he didn't see Innes swooping down to kiss him hard. He fell back against the doorframe and melted into it with a hum of longing for the contact he was already getting.

When they broke apart, Charlie shook his head to clear it for an important topic.

"If we do this, there's no one else," he warned. "You can't decide that now your heart has grown three sizes that you're going to go out and fall in love with everybody. Tell me if you want someone else."

Innes shook his head. "Not a problem. I've been surprisingly monogamous for a heartless bastard uninterested in romantic attachment. I don't think I'll have any trouble falling in love with only you. You're the only person I've ever wanted to get close to."

Charlie's insides gave a glad wiggle, but he made a show of scoffing. "Of course. I got pretty good at taking care of you, didn't I? No surprise that I swept you off your feet. You better not make me regret it."

Innes leaned down, brushed his lips over Charlie's, and whispered, "Never."

Innes kissed him again, and Charlie poured any tenderness he'd kept inside into returning it, uncaring that anyone could walk past and see them. It was only the sound of his mother inside the apartment that made Charlie pull away, but he didn't go far.

He kept Innes in place by holding the back of his neck and panted into the few inches between their mouths.

"I'm not going to work for you again," he said when he could summon a brain cell again.

"No," Innes agreed. "I'll miss your efficiency, but I'll survive. However, I am going to fulfill my end of the bargain. You'll get your foot in the door, like I promised, then we'll be even. Any pestering you do will be of your own volition."

His heart swelled with gratitude and relief. "Thank you."

"Don't thank me, it's the least I could do. The last time you had to look for a new profession, you got a vain, selfish, but devilishly charming lawyer attached to you. If I let you find your own job, who knows what kind of trouble you could get yourself in?"

Charlie's laugh echoed down the hallway until it was smothered willingly by the first of many breathtaking, unguarded kisses.

# Epilogue

*Six Months Later*

"Innes!"

"Mmm?" Innes looked up from his phone, noted that it was Charlie who'd burst into his office in a barely contained blur of excitement, and went back to the screen, frowning at it as he scrolled through an emailed copy of his rental agreement.

"Hi," Charlie said when he'd plunked himself on top of Innes's desk, happily seating himself between Innes's knees. "I'm done!"

"Oh? That's great." He paused in his scrolling. "Did you know that my apartment building allows cats but not dogs?"

"What? No, I didn't. Did you hear me?" When Innes failed to respond, Charlie plucked the phone out of his hand, breaking the spell of hyper-focus he'd been under, and took Innes's face in his hands.

"Huh?" Innes said, intelligently. Blinking his tired eyes, he pulled his face out of Charlie's grasp. "Sorry, I was miles away."

"I did it," Charlie told him, bouncing a little bit on his perch in excitement. "It's finished and it turned out great."

Innes squeezed Charlie's thighs. "That's wonderful, darling. Can I see, or is it not for public consumption yet?"

Charlie pulled out his own phone and flicked through the photos he'd taken from every angle. Innes had seen bits of the project before, but the finished project—a modern take on a medieval knight's costume—was more than he could have imagined. Charlie had been working on the commission for months, ever since the designs he worked on in the evenings after his internship had blown up on social media. If this was the kind of thing that resulted from a few concept art sketches made public, Innes was more than convinced that the tablet he'd bought Charlie for his birthday was worth every penny. Mimi had assured him it would be, but Innes was the type to believe things when he saw them.

He only wished he could see it a little clearer.

He tugged Charlie's arm—and the phone—a little farther away, squinting to make out the finer details. His eyes hadn't been so tired since his days of beating Aiden's ass at Nintendo on family holidays.

"Do you need glasses?" Charlie asked him point-blank, once he gave up on making out the decorative stitching on the button panel.

"Don't worry. Mimi's already on my case about it. Between the two of you, I'll have bifocals perched on my nose within a week."

"Good, you've already accepted the inevitable. I wouldn't be so pouty about it, though. Studious is a good look on you."

This time, it was Innes's turn to put the phone out of reach. He pulled at Charlie's arms, and Charlie slid into his lap with no resistance. "Interesting," Innes said. "Do you have any papers that need grading? Because I could be convinced to put on a sweater vest."

Charlie gave a theatrical shiver. "Mmm, wool blend. Just the material I want to have rubbing on my naked body."

"Can you quit ruining my fantasy with your sartorial knowledge?" Innes directed at the ceiling.

"Can't help it, sorry. I might have some suede patches that would do in a pinch."

"Do let me know if that pinch"—he snaked his hand down and tweaked a handful of Charlie's ass—"ever arrives."

Charlie yelped and bit his earlobe in retaliation, then kissed him, slow and deep until they had to make a choice to either stop or find somewhere more private to continue. Since they had somewhere to be, the decision to stop was made mutually but reluctantly.

Tonight, Charlie was going with his mother to a therapy session. It wasn't a big deal, Charlie kept saying, just a way for her case worker to get a better picture of their dynamic and to involve Charlie as much as he wanted to be involved in her progress—which was, predictably, quite a lot. They'd be fine, but it wouldn't do for them to get distracted.

Charlie tended to do that to him. Distracting him, motivating him, tiring him out ...

"You're not old," Charlie told him as they both calmed down, stroking down the front of his shirt.

"Did I say I was?"

"No. But you get a particular wrinkle here when you're worried about a new gray hair or something. And you shouldn't get all bothered about it." He leaned forward and kissed the small gathering of wrinkles at the corner of Innes's eyes. "You're only getting better with age."

"Thanks." Innes tightened his hand on Charlie's hip, then brushed his other thumb across Charlie's dark eyebrow, then his cheekbone, then his lips, and ended with a kiss in the same place.

"Are you guys leaving, or do I have to brace myself for more cuteness?"

Marie came bustling in, emptying the water pitcher and dropping the last stack of papers in Innes's tray for tomorrow.

"Stop it, woman, or you can get on the first flight back to Oregon," Innes said, with no heat and even less effectiveness.

"Don't you joke about that, or my husband will personally come in here to beat some sense into you. He was even more unhappy than I was in that place, and he would rather die than give up the title of stay-at-home dad."

"I don't know how he does it," Charlie said. "I think I'd go crazy."

Innes would never purposefully piss off Marie's husband, since he was the main reason why Innes had gotten Marie back after a string of mediocre assistants. They were all better off this way.

"It's not for everyone, that's for sure," Marie said, gazing up at the ceiling like she was sending a private prayer of thanks to whichever deity had blessed her with a husband who preferred his wife to do the breadwinning. "Anyway, are you leaving, or should I leave the light on?"

"We're going, don't worry," Innes assured her as she headed for the door, then Innes gave his arms to Charlie to support himself as he climbed off his lap.

"You ready?" Charlie asked, tugging down his shirt where Innes had had a hand under it earlier. "I have to pick up Ma's pills on the way if I want her to have them before her shift tomorrow."

Innes stood up and followed Charlie out into the hall. "I'm definitely ready. I think if I caused you to be even a minute tardy, Joy would eviscerate me."

Craning his head around, Charlie asked, "What does Joy have to do with tonight?"

"As if you aren't going to tell her every detail."

Snorting, Charlie started walking again. "I think 'evisceration' is a bit of an exaggeration, but I don't want to test the theory."

"Comforting. At least your mother loves me." Innes pouted as they neared the elevator.

"My mother likes everyone. Joy will lighten up once she realizes you're in for the long, long haul." Charlie led the way onto the elevator, jamming the Close Door button out of habit.

"What would convince her, do you think?"

"I don't know, maybe I'll ask—"

Charlie looked up from hitting the Ground Floor button and saw the key that Innes had fished from his pocket and was holding in front of him. Neither of them said anything for the entire duration of the door closing and the elevator starting to ding as it zoomed down.

"Move in with me?" Innes asked, holding out the key for Charlie to take.

It wasn't a suggestion that came out of the blue. They'd been talking about it for a couple of months, both of them eager for Charlie to stop shuttling back and forth between the two apartments when he was most of the way moved in to Innes's. The main reason why they hadn't bitten the bullet yet was Charlie's mother. After Charlie had been the one paying the rent for so long, it had been a hard transition for his mother to enter the workforce again, one that she was fully on board with, but it had taken some time.

Now, with Charlie's mother enjoying her new job as a caller for a local charity, and the lease coming up on their two-bedroom, it made sense for her to try living alone.

"You sure?" Charlie asked, taking the key and holding it tightly in both hands, his smile blinding despite the question.

"Absolutely," Innes told him, pulling him in by the waist just to feel his warmth and his body against him, solid and familiar. "Never been more positive. I think we've earned a little time to ourselves."

Later, sitting next to each other on Innes's living room couch, Charlie was distracted from the sketch he'd been trying to make. The concept drawings for his new boss's brainstorming meeting weren't due for another few weeks, but he liked to be on top of it, and it helped that he liked what he was doing.

Was the pay spectacular? No, but it got the job done, and getting into the industry through an up-and-coming private label was priceless, especially given the amount of time he had to work on his own projects.

Tonight, though, it was hard to focus. It didn't help that he knew they'd be heading to bed a little early, so they weren't tired for brunch tomorrow with Aiden and Elliott. It didn't really matter if they got enough sleep, though, since Innes would make a show of complaining, then be the first one ready to get in the car. No, the book didn't hold his interest when he had the key Innes had given him to stare at as he sorted through his emotions.

He was excited, sure. A bit trepidatious too. He'd lived with only his mother for so long in one place that even though they'd been tentatively planning this, and Charlie spent most nights here anyway, it felt huge.

"It won't be too crowded?" Charlie blurted, even though he knew the answer. He just had to be sure. "When I'm living here, I mean."

Innes looked up from his phone, still squinting a little until his eyes seemed to adjust to the change in focus. "Only in summer, but you and Mimi will work it out," he said, matter-of-factly with admirable pragmatism. "As long as I don't have to get involved in squabbles over the TV remote."

"As if I'd be the one picking fights about the sacred Monday night *Antiques Roadshow* viewing party."

"I'm a simple man, Charlie, with so few pleasures left to me in my old age."

Charlie snorted, but it was mostly rote because the joke was an old one and well-worn. Innes wasn't old, and neither was he as simple as he claimed.

He'd let Charlie in enough that his depths were as known to Charlie as his own.

The key was almost burning hot in his hand. He knew he should go and put it somewhere safe, but he focused on the warm metal digging into his palm, not quite hard enough to hurt.

Having it felt somehow more special and more life-changing than a marriage proposal would've been, a concept that he'd entertained. *Forever* no longer felt so far-fetched after all these months.

They'd get there, eventually. Innes could have bought a ring, composed some pretty words, and Charlie would've been happy, sure, but not as happy as this gesture made him. A plain little bit of brass made his heart leap more than promises of for better or for worse, because this was just as important to Innes, and just as big a step.

"Hey," Charlie said, shoving Innes's phone away and climbing into his lap, taking up space like he had in all the other areas of Innes's life.

"I Innm!"

"I love you, you know that?"

Charlie felt and saw the stiffening of surprise in Innes's face and body, even after all this time and the repetitions of the words, but it faded quickly into a smirk. "Of course I know." But then the cheeky smile softened into something warmer. "I love you too. Punk. Don't rob me blind in the middle of the night, okay?"

Charlie scoffed in the back of his throat. "You'd let me walk out of here with your life savings."

"Got me there. I'd probably even help you cart out the TV."

"Not with your bad back, Grandpa."

Innes tipped his head back onto the couch, laughing to the ceiling, but then grew serious once again. Not too serious, though. There was always a hint of mirth in those eyes.

"I'd carry anything you wanted," Innes said. "As long as I got to keep you at the end."

"Good, because it's too late to get rid of me."

"I know."

Charlie leaned in for a kiss, a warm weight still resting in his palm. The key to their future.

Dear Reader,

Thank you for reading Chloe B. Young's *Worth Trying*!

We know your time is precious and you have many, many entertainment options, so it means a lot that you've chosen to spend your time reading. We really hope you enjoyed it.

We'd be honored if you'd consider posting a review—good or bad—on sites like **Amazon, Barnes & Noble, Kobo, Goodreads, Twitter, Facebook, Tumblr,** and your blog or website. We'd also be honored if you told your friends and family about this book. Word of mouth is a book's lifeblood!

For more information on upcoming releases, author interviews, blog tours, contests, giveaways, and more, please sign up for our weekly, spam-free newsletter and visit us around the web:

**Newsletter**: riptidepublishing.com/newsletter
**Twitter**: twitter.com/RiptideBooks
**Facebook**: facebook.com/RiptidePublishing
**Goodreads**: tinyurl.com/RiptideOnGoodreads
**Tumblr**: riptidepublishing.tumblr.com

Thank you so much for Reading the Rainbow!

RiptidePublishing.com

RIPTIDE
PUBLISHING

# Also by
# Chloe B. Young

*Without Precedent series*
Worth It

# About the
# Author

Writing is just one of the many ways Chloe gets her storytelling fix. In her other life, she sings and acts to fulfill the urge, and is never far from a stage.

When not writing, she cooks with too much garlic, sharpens her eyeliner to a deadly point, and tries to accept that she's turning into one of those people who only wears one color. (Pink.)

Website: chloebyoung.com

Tumblr/Twitter/Instagram/Facebook: @cbyauthor